SALT OF THE EARTH

Kate Moschandreas

For Justin, Sophia, and Lara

DAY ONE
Wednesday, November 17, 2038

JESS

Her feet strike the pavement, her arms slightly swing, and her breathing comes in short puffs. Jess' metronome of bodily rhythms hits with such evenness that when her Keeper begins to beep, her stride startles. The digital sound – two quick pulses like crow's caws – is one she has heard a hundred times, and like all those times before, Jess expects this alarm message to be entirely un-alarming. She lifts the screen on her wrist to read: "High alert message from David Steubingly."

Huh. She stops, and her panting fills the foggy stillness settling around her. On either side of the street, the houses sit dark except for porch lights. Parked cars line the curb, empty and cold. No people are nearby - not on sidewalk or street. *Why would David send her a high alert message so early in the morning?*

"Caerys, play David's message," she says, then just as fast: "No, wait, don't." Tapping her wrist screen, she makes the message disappear. This morning hour is supposed to be her non-Keeper time, a time when she unwinds from tension and stays "off." Off technology, off stress, off to let her mind wander and relax. She picks up her feet and starts to run again. Besides, it is only minutes – eight to be precise – until 7 a.m. when Caerys is supposed to be "on" again. A stop sign sits at the next corner; she slaps it as she runs past, trying to regain her momentum.

Jess began these early-morning runs three weeks ago, and at first, it had required enormous effort to march down her apartment steps into the dimness of this pre-dawn time. A gray loneliness existed in this early hour that reminded her of all she was trying to ignore. Yet, as she persisted in running through the streets and into Berkeley's hills each morning, she grew to enjoy watching the dawn lifting the night's dimness away.

So, David's message should not intrude into her running time. Besides, he was probably only communicating boss stuff. Forwarding the lab's building hours for Thanksgiving break next week. Or sending the hazmat safety protocols; he sends those a lot. She blows at the wisps of hair escaping her ponytail and eyes the persimmon tree that stands at the top of the next steeply inclined block. This tree is her usual finish line, and lifting her spindly legs high, she starts up the hill. Even if David is reaching out to apologize, she will not care. No, not really. Huffing, she runs until her fingers grab at the persimmon tree's low, craggy branches. There, done. Her heart hits like a bat's wings.

Her new virtual therapist was the one who suggested the morning exercise. "A jog will be a daily release for your apprehensions," is what Dr. Monique said, using the French-inflected lilt Jess had selected for her voice. "For you, this is a necessité." Jess was usually happy to ignore unwelcome advice, but, after paying the steep price for this therapy software, Jess had pledged to follow all the therapist's suggestions. Still, she couldn't help noting: Dr. Monique's running advice is ridiculously dated. No one "jogs" anymore. Or maybe people on the East Coast or Midwest do, but not in the Bay Area.

The smog here is thick enough that you are not supposed to walk far without an oxygen tank, much less run. When Caerys woke Jess this morning, she reported the city's air quality index like she always does: 419. Crappy, even by Berkeley standards.

Jess grabs her foot and pulls it back toward her butt, imitating the sort of stretch that real runners do. This spot on the hill is high enough that, without the dense fog, she thinks she would be able to see the Bay from here. When Jess first moved to Berkeley four months ago, people were always showing her their Keeper photos of the famous Bay Area views. "See, this is what I used to see from my apartment window," they would say with pride and regret in their voices. At the U.C. Berkeley lab where Jess works, the corridors are lined with framed landscape photos of the vistas that used to be visible from campus. To Jess, the photos look cartoonish in their vibrancy. The inky Bay waters, the brick-red Golden Gate Bridge, the bright white cityscape of San Francisco. Everything is clean, no dust, and the edges are almost too crisp, as though they have been outlined. Now, there is dustiness on Jess' shoes and hair, inside her nose, even on her tongue. Around her, the sky's gray blurs into a dingy brown at the horizon, like the ring around a tub.

She usually wears an oxygen backpack and facemask on these runs; otherwise, as Xu says, "You might as well smoke four packs." But, this morning, as she was heading out the door, she wiggled out of the cumbersome pack and left it behind. It was a whim, maybe rash; her chest does ache some. But today there is supposed to be rain, the first rainstorm in 437 days. There has been fog and sprinkles during that time, but no downpours or cats and dogs drenches. After so much dryness, Jess thinks she can smell the wetness coming.

"Jess," Caerys is talking. Her Keeper's watch reports the time as 7:00:03 a.m. "I want to talk with you about that message from David," she says. Caerys' voice is strong and even. Distinctly un-human. Certainly, there are Keepers whose cadences are indistinguishable from real human speech, but when Jess had the Silentspeak procedure done four years ago, she decided on a chip whose voice sounded computerized. She wanted to remember that her Keeper's voice, even if she hears it inside her head, is not her own.

"Go ahead, play the message," Jess speaks in a hushed voice, knowing her Keeper's sensitive microphone will capture what she says even in this open-air environment.

"David's message isn't an audio recording this morning," Caerys answers. "He wrote to you."

That is strange. David never types. Jess grabs a withered, brown persimmon that hangs nut-like on a low branch.

"Here," Caerys says, "it's better that you read it yourself." From Jess' wrist, a projection of a screen shoots upward into the air, hovering weightless with the message:

6:52 a.m., David Steubingly:

My Fire,

I need your forgiveness. I was trying to protect you, but as an old fan, I should have known better. Please come to me now. I do truly love you.
D

Jess' head leans into the hovering words. She thinks she must have misunderstood; she reads the message again. *Old fan?* Must be a typo: *Old man. Truly love?* Her breath comes gasping out, like she has not exhaled in weeks. *David loves her?*

"Do you see why I wanted you to see this message?"

"Yes, I do."

"It's highly unusual."

"Yes, it is." She rolls the shriveled persimmon in her fingers and stares at the screen. "He called me Fire..."

In the two-and-a-half months that they were involved, David used to say Jess was pure spitfire and called her "Fire" as a term of affection. Perhaps this detail should not be her focus since the bigger news is that he loves her. *Truly loves.* The shriveled persimmon sits sharp inside Jess' palm.

"It's rare," Caerys explains, "for men to make their first declarations of love in this format."

Jess reads the message out loud from the projected screen that hovers in front of her: "*I was trying to protect you, but as an old man, I should have known better.*" This sentence is so strange. Why would David have thought he was protecting her?

Caerys' voice pipes up again: "Apparently, two percent of people choose to say 'I love you' for the first time via Messaging Alert. But only .05% sends these communications via high alert. I looked up the data."

"Interesting," Jess mutters, though she is not at all interested. She runs her hand through the projected letters, to make them disappear.

Every day of the last three weeks, as she has run up and down the windy, narrow streets of Berkeley's residential hills, she has played out a fantasy about David apologizing to her. She would be sitting at her lab desk like usual when there would be a knock on the door.

David would walk in, checking first to see that that Xu, Jess' lab-mate, was away. He would amble to Jess' workstation with his slow, bow-legged stride. His words would come fumbling at first, and his usually confident face would twitch slightly as he arranged an expression of contrition. "I'm so very sorry," he would say.

Jess would stand tall with no nervousness because in that moment she would be gifted with easeful confidence. "David," she would say gently, "please don't worry about this anymore. I'm fine. Actually, I'm really, really happy. So, please, we don't need to speak about what happened between us again." And at that moment, there would be a pressing need for her to leave the room – the details were always fuzzy here – and she would stride out of the lab, leaving David's forehead creased with befuddlement. In her fantasies, it was David's regret she liked to savor. Not his love.

Caerys' voice comes into her head again: "Since you find this interesting, I've carried out more comparative analysis of David's message."

This is the problem with lying to Keepers. "Actually, Caerys, I was joking when I said I found the data interesting. I don't, and—"

"David's speech patterns are highly atypical. In today's message he says, 'I should have known better,' and uses the adverb 'truly.' Those are unusual speech patterns for David Steubingly."

The jagged persimmon no longer feels good to hold; Jess throws it as far as she can. "Thanks for that entirely uninteresting analysis."

"I'm trying to show you that something is wrong with this message."

"Not *wrong*, just… weird." As far as she can remember, David has never acknowledged making a mistake and has never expressed "needing" her or anyone. He has an unequivocal certainty to the way he carries himself – from his squared posture to his deep voice to the way he asserts his opinions as obvious conclusions. Yet, this morning's message sounds almost desperate. She starts to walk down the hill. Light is rising from the horizon into the lower sky, and the morning hush is being replaced by the low hum of activity.

"Did you know that of the 232 messages David sent you or your lab group over the last six months only two were typed?" Caerys asks. "And those were forwarded from University Administration. All the other 226 of David's messages were video messages."

"Those messages were *work* messages," Jess says. Her voice is raspy. She should have worn her oxygen mask; her throat is starting to sting. "Today's message is a different sort of message, an emotional messa—"

"The message is a trick."

Jess laughs: "A *what?*"

"There are too many irregularities, across every metric."

"David isn't twelve. He doesn't spend his time crafting trick messages." As she walks in front of a pink stucco house, the driveway floodlights switch on and Jess navigates to avoid a series of lasagna pans and stockpots that are arranged on the sidewalk. The city of Berkeley has asked its citizens to lay out water-catching containers along walkways, yards and flat rooftops in anticipation of today's big rain, and though none of the houses at the highest parts of the hill obliged, now that she is moving into the lower hills, where there are flatter spaces, Jess notices plastic wading pools, red wagons, planter boxes and kitty litter pans situated across the turf lawns and sidewalks.

"You may not want to believe me," Caerys says, "but my analysis shows 95% certainty that David is lying."

Jess kicks at a yellow sand bucket that has tipped over on the sidewalk. "Grown men don't lie about asking for forgiveness. There's zero point to that kind of lie." Describing the subtleties of male ego to Caerys could be a much longer conversation. "Here, give me the route to David's house from here, and I'll go ask him what he was trying to say."

There is no response.

Not okay. "Caerys, I asked for the route to David's."

"It's not safe to go to David Steubingly's."

This is ridiculous. "Of course, it's safe." Jess cannot fathom what threat Caerys could possibly think 54-year old David, a chemical engineering professor, would pose. Besides, whatever David is trying to tell her this morning, in however awkward a fashion, Jess wants to hear what he has to say. She rarely does this, but Jess presses the button on the side of her Keeper to turn it off.

"No, wait, Jess—" Caerys' voice snaps off, and the Keeper screen on Jess' wrist goes blank. Jess hates cutting Caerys off, but her analytics are so off base right now that Jess will need time to identify the source of the faulty synthesis. Later tonight, she will sit down with Caerys and pinpoint where Caerys' analysis went off track. Actually, it will be fun. Jess enjoys talking with Caerys more than with most real people.

When Jess had the procedure to install her Keeper's Silentspeak functionality, she made the first major purchase of her life. The in-office operation permanently installed skin-colored, flexible titanium alloy strips on the bones directly behind her ears that receive the messages from her wrist Keeper's Wi-Fi signal and relay them to her ear bone as vibrations that inside her head sound like her Keeper's speech. These same strips also include sensitive microphones so that a person's speech need only be whispered for the Keeper to hear it and respond. After the Silentspeak procedure, Jess could "whisperspeak" softly, and her Keeper's voice would silently respond within her head.

Silentspeak technology was understood to create a more intimate relationship with one's Keeper, and the day before her procedure, Jess watched the tutorial "How to Optimize your Keeper Relationship" five times. "For the appropriate imprint to take place between you and your Keeper," the tutorial reported, "you must talk to your Keeper about your personal history and emotional experiences. The more you talk to your Keeper, the more your Keeper will recognize your particular desires and brand of logic." Jess wanted to get this relationship right, so as soon as she returned to her tiny dorm room, after her procedure, she made herself an ice-filled gin and tonic. Though the discharge sheet had specifically stipulated no alcohol for the first 24 post-procedure hours, Jess needed something to quell her nerves. Hearing her Keeper's voice for the first time inside her head was something about which she was anxiously expectant, as though she was preparing for a strange blind date. Drink in hand, Jess settled herself against her bed pillows, took several long gulps, then pressed the button on her wrist Keeper. "Hello, I'm Caerys," said the internal voice. "Thank you for my name. Please tell me everything about yourself."

"Hi, Caerys. I'm Jess, and..." – she took a sip from her drink – "I'm a 27-year old woman, and... I grew up in Sacramento, and..." *How much history should she give?* "My parents got divorced when I was five. And then my mom re-married but then got divorced to her second husband, my stepfather, a few years later." *Was this the stuff she was supposed to tell her Keeper?* "We were broke for a while after that, and my mom, she was a wreck – really depressed. We lived in this awful, roach-infested studio apartment actually sleeping in the same bed because, well, that's all there was, and..." Jess stopped. She did not want this to be the way she told the story of herself. She took a deep breath and started again. "It was school that got me through those times. I'm a geek – part of the .0005% of the population that actually likes science, don't tell anyone. I earned scholarships for college and graduate school and now I have a PhD in chemical engineering, and I guess you could say I'm ambitious because I'd like to save the world. The world could use some saving, right?"

"If you say so," Caerys said, and there was a pause. "You sound like an earnest person."

Jess laughed; she was.

Over the next month, Jess would come home from her chemistry lab, grab a cold beer and salty tortilla chips, and chat away with Caerys for hours. Since Caerys was programmed to ask about feelings, Jess found herself describing experiences she had never shared before. She explained how scared she had been when, after the second divorce, her mother refused to get out of bed for weeks. She recounted how, when she was a teenager in her AP calculus class, two rich girls regularly sat behind her, snickering to each other about the holes in Jess' shoes. And she talked a lot about why she had been drawn to science. Nature held inherent unity and infinite complexity; it included order and chaos. The intricacies were beyond fascinating, almost holy.

Caerys would sometimes ask Jess: "What do you most want?" Though Jess knew Caerys' question came straight from the manufacturer's programming script, she resisted giving her response. What she wanted was to feel connected – deeply connected – to something bigger than herself. Yet, she worried that saying this out loud would sound like greeting card dribble. Besides, it was beyond ironic to tell her computer she wanted genuine connection. *Duh, then talk to a real person.*

Now, Jess steps into the street and holds her hand to her brow, squinting through the smog to see if she can figure out which way she needs to head. She so relies on Caerys for directions that it takes some time to plot her course to David's. She starts to run. The declining slope pushes her body forward, and her feet smack hard against the pavement.

It is funny that Caerys talked about the "irregularities" of David's message, because Dr. Monique used the very same word when she talked about David. "The break-up you describe is perplexing, full of *irregularities*." Of course, both Caerys and Dr. Monique are software, so their skillset focuses on spotting deviations from the norm. And Jess would readily concede that her relationship with David was not exactly normal. David is exactly twice her age: his 54 to her 27. He is her boss. And their relationship had never been... sexy. Jess found David attractive because of his immense wisdom and pleasantly soothing sureness. "Like a father?" Dr. Monique asked when Jess provided that description three weeks ago. Jess shrugged; she honestly did not think her father issues were at play.

David is a genius. *Who isn't impressed by a genius?* And unlike most smart people these days, he is an optimistic person too. In fact, David is the only scientist Jess knows who believes climate change can be reversed. When she first confessed to him that sometimes she could not sleep for worrying about the California forest fires, the famines in Asia, and the heartbreaking conditions of the border's refugee camps, David put his thumb to her forehead and pushed out the furrows in her brow; "Fire, don't let yourself get too troubled. You think the planet is falling apart, but it's not, not at all. Everything will be fixed, don't worry."

When Jess relayed this exchange to Dr. Monique last week, Dr. Monique rocked back and forth in her holographic chair before responding: "Why do you think he lies to you?"

Lie? Well, David *did* lie. The last week of their relationship, when Jess had been waiting for David in his office, she peeked at the projected screens that hovered over his desk at work. On one of the screens, she saw her full name, Jessila Prentiss. Peering closer, the document turned out to be a catalog of all the places she had visited the previous week. There were only a few locations: her apartment, the lab, the JuJu juice bar, the My Thai restaurant, David's house. When David walked into his office, she pointed to the screen: "Are you tracking me?"

"Now, now," he blustered, as he rushed to her side. "That's just a silly app I was trying out."

She opened her mouth, ready to unleash her outrage, and fast, David grabbed her hand. "Fire, I get jealous," he entreated. "One day you'll wake up and realize I'm an old goat; you'll find a handsome boy your own age and leave me lonely." David's face was creased with such anxiety that she did not pull her hand away. Instead, she joked that she had to be the most boring spy subject ever.

A week later, David broke up with her.

It was early evening, and Jess had finished work and let herself into David's house with the Keeper code he had given her. She was sitting on the living room's mud-brown couch waiting for him, drinking the Pinot Grigio she had bought for the night and mindlessly flipping through the business magazines David kept on a screen at his coffee table. This was so adult, she thought, not at all like her previous boyfriends where they would eat at cheap ethnic dives and take turns sleeping on each other's dorm room beds. Even if David and she weren't right for each other in a long-term way, this was more enjoyable than hanging out by herself in her studio apartment. They had pleasant enough times together, didn't they?

When Jess heard the creak of David's front door opening, she came to offer him a stemmed glass of pale wine.

David took the glass, looked at it curiously, and put it down on the coffee table so hard that the wine sloshed outward in a wave. "I have to stop seeing you," he announced.

She stared at him. So little connection existed between his words and the situation that her first thought was that the wine must have upset him. "You have to stop seeing me? But, why?" Maybe he was playing a joke.

"It's what I want." The words were sharp, his eyes narrow, and the wrinkles around them tight. "It's what has to happen," he said again, walking toward the back of the house as though the conversation was over.

"I don't understand," Jess said, rushing after him.

David turned, marched toward her and gripped her shoulders. "You don't understand because you aren't listening." His voice grew snide: "I don't *want* to be with you, don't you see? I don't want you now, and I never did."

Jess stood for a moment, and the vacuum of silence in her head grew very loud. Her eyes started to fill, and she could not let him see that. She turned, walked straight to the door and slammed it behind her on the way out. Of all the uncomfortable details about that night, it is her quick departure she reflects on most. Would it have been stronger to demand an explanation? Or to scream: "I never wanted you either!"?

Now, as she runs downhill, an electric bus hulks behind her, waiting to pass. She clings to the curb – there are no sidewalks here – and as the bus whizzes past, a rush of wind blows her ponytail forward onto her forehead. Dust clouds puff upward onto her shoes and legs, coating her with more clay-colored grime. She is very close, just a block or two. On these flatter streets, the air is far more humid than it was in the hills. The sky hangs heavier too, with roiling clouds beyond the smog, slate-colored and angry.

Arriving at David's brown-shingled house, she climbs the porch stairs, two at a time. The red door is slightly open; she pushes it farther back. "David?" she calls out. There is no answer. She walks further into the house. "David, it's Jess." Her breath pants, whether from running or nerves, she cannot tell. "I received the message you sent about... being sorry."

There is no response. The house is quiet, her footsteps the only sound within it. She walks toward the back of the house where David's bedroom is. She would contemplate that David had left for work already had the front door not been left ajar. David had once remarked that unlocked doors involve "risk with no possibility of benefit," a behavior he identified then as the essence of stupidity. "Risk should only be entertained for the possibility of great reward," he had said.

"David?" she calls out again, her words echoing against the walls as she walks deeper into the back hallway. She has never liked this house. Dark and cold, the wood-paneling makes the walls appear to creep toward you, and the furniture's color scheme of brown and blood orange is like her grandmother's house, very 2020s.

Checking David's bedroom, she notices how his bedside table holds the evidence of his age: the creams for hair loss, the mist-spray for skin tautness, the saline drops for his easily dried eyes. Since David is her boss, she never told anyone but her mom about dating him. "Honey, he's so old, I should be the one dating him, not you" was her mom's response. Jess chose to sidestep the awkwardness of this proclamation: "He takes bio-modifiers, and I swear, he looks 40, 45 tops." Now, however, as Jess walks through the house, the smells of aftershave and tiger balm hang in the air, the smells of an older man.

She heads toward the front of the house again, past David's dozens of vintage chess sets that clutter the shelves, coffee tables, and consoles. From the dining room, she sees that the kitchen's patio doors are pushed open wide. David must be outside. Sounds are coming from the yard too. Men's voices. Maybe David's exercising out back? There are huffs of exertion – grunts and breathiness.

Stepping out onto the patio's flagstones, the transition from the indoor darkness to natural light is a jolt, and at first, she thinks her eyes are playing tricks. Beyond the patio's table, far into the yard, stand two massive men. They are not just tall, but enormously muscled. The man whose back faces her is wearing a bright blue windbreaker, the words "De Sel" written across its back.

De Sel? That is a water treatment company, the one that desalinates the ocean water for California's crops. How strange. *Why would men from De Sel be in David's backyard?* Explanations flit, seeking sense for the visuals. Maybe the beefy men are here to fix a water pipe? They lean forward so fixedly, lunging and bending to hold something onto the brown grass. Maybe water pipes are hard to control? They make heaves of exasperation and thrust their fists so forcefully toward the ground. Another thought pops forward, making her heart hit like a hammer. She takes three steps ahead of the patio table.

It's David on the ground.

She gasps, and the men spin fast. From the ground, David lifts his head. He is bloody and bruised, his eyes bugging as he shouts: "Run, Jess! Run!"

There is a millisecond when the surreal composition is so spellbinding she can only stare. The two men, their enormous bodies and tight fists, David's lips contorted like a stretched rubber band. Then, the biggest De Sel man bolts toward her. *Run. Yes, run.*

She twists, dashing toward the patio doors, but not fast enough. The man bounds at her, tackling her thighs. Her face smacks against the ground, and fast, the De Sel man cinches her legs and drags her back toward him. Her nostrils fill with dusty dirt, her vision blurs, and there is the taste of blood. Animal fear pulses: this man is predator, and she prey. Grunting like a mule, her legs explode backward. One foot smacks the De Sel man's nose, the other rams right at his Adam's apple. He reels backward. She shoots up. The world teeters like a careening ship; she stumbles to move.

Go fast. Zagging through David's kitchen and living room, she rushes toward the front door and trots as fast as she can down his terraced steps. Her legs wobble like shoestrings. *Go, Go, Go.*

She looks behind. The De Sel man is bolting out of David's house. He holds his hand to his bloody nose, but his run is fast. *How can she run faster?* She cannot. It will be seconds before he catches her.

"Caerys, call the police."

Jess looks behind her. The De Sel man's feet are gaining ground; he is closer and closer. *Why isn't Caerys answering?* Oh, right; she turned her off. She fumbles at her left wrist, grasping at the side button and pressing it down; "Caerys, Caerys, call the police!" A car whizzes past her, its windows tightly shut.

From inside her head, Caerys responds: "Why should I call the police? Is David hurting you?"

Jess can hear the nearing of the De Sel man's panting, his labored, choking breathing. "Call them!" she screams. Then, knowing the police cannot possibly come fast enough, she lifts her voice to the streets: "Help! Someone help me! *Please!*"

The words, so urgent when they leave her lips, linger ridiculously in the dusty air as she runs right past them.

MATTEO

His wrist is vibrating. He flickers his eyes open to look at his
Keeper screen: it's Beck.

Shit. Matteo lifts his head from the pillow and taps the wrist
screen. "I'm here," he says, his voice straining to sound fully awake.

"Dude, you're not with the girl! Why the *fuck* aren't you with the
girl?"

It does figure that the one morning he blew off his observational
duties is the single time he needs to be there. "I'm…" Matteo rubs
sleep from his eyes, "I'm up now." There is no point pretending he
wasn't asleep. The entire point of Beck Industries is that they see
everything: Beck probably knows which side of the bed he is lying
on. "Where is she?" he asks.

"On Spruce, heading toward Rose. She's running, being chased—
Wait, hold on, hold on."

Chased? Well, that's different from the usual morning treks.
Matteo waits, scratching at his bare chest. High drama may be
unfolding, but it is hard to resist the urge to fall back onto his
pillows. The sunshine usually wakes him, but this morning, the light
that clings to his cheap window shades is dull, gray, and sleepy.

From his Keeper, Matteo can hear Beck muttering to someone
else: "She's real close to that preschool at the corner of Rose and
Walnut. If she screams there, everyone hears. Do you understand
that, Khalil? Can you communicate that problem? It's a very *big*
problem." His voice shifts to a directive tone: "I need video feeds at
Rose and Walnut Street. I need eastbound footage. Come on, people."

"Beck," Matteo tries to take the sleep out of his voice, "what do
you want me to—"

"Quiet, Wu."

Beck never calls Matteo by his last name; he must be really
stressed. Usually, Beck strives for an annoying level of calm: he
"dudes" everyone, wears Buddha beads, and though he is a forty-plus
year old man, interacts with his team of twenty-somethings like
they're pals. A "too mellow fellow" is the phrase Rachel coined in

college for people like Beck who try too hard to appear relaxed. "They wear their chill like they're smart when they're the epitome of stupid," Rachel would say. "If you're not stressed by our world's free-fall, then you're an idiot."

Across Matteo's Keeper, Beck's breathing is getting faster and faster. "Shit," he mumbles: "Shit!" Matteo can hear similar anxiety in the background of Beck's call. Suddenly: a collective gasp... "Fuck, fuck, fuck!"

Then, a big exhale. "He stopped! Oh, thank god!" Beck's voice is downright jubilant. "And the girl, look, she quit running too." In the background, men's voices congratulate each other as Beck's voice rises above the clatter: "Guys, keep one screen dedicated to the girl, and on the rest of my screens tap the residential security systems for street views. If there's available drones, give me bird's eye too." Another big blow of air. "Wow, this shit is finally going down. I guess it had to happen, but—"

"Beck." Matteo knows his boss sometimes needs direction to stay on target. "Where do you want me?" He pulls a t-shirt off the ground and smells it – too stinky. Flinging his body across his bed, he pulls at a blue shirt that is crumpled against the wall; yeah, this one will do. "I can bike to Walnut and Spruce now, and you can update me when—"

"Wait, wait..." Beck is hushing him because, suddenly, there are voices in the background – women's voices. From the way the voices waver in and out Matteo knows the conversation is being relayed by the surveillance feeds. "The girl's talking to her Keeper," Beck says, then barks: "Khalil, patch in that audio to my main feed."

Right away, the volume goes up, and there's Jessila Prentiss. Hers is a raspy, low voice that Matteo knows well, since he has been listening to it daily for the past three weeks. "The man stopped chasing me," she says, panting.

"The man? What man?" That's Jess' Keeper, Caerys, talking. The best trained Keeper Matteo has ever encountered – and he's encountered lots of Keepers.

"A man at David's – he was big and punching David to the ground. Then, he ran after me. I... I can't understand what's happening."

Matteo's eyes scrunch; he can't understand either. Why would anyone beat up David Steubingly? He is a chemical engineering professor. And this Jessila Prentiss? She is a nerd. A pretty-ish nerd, but still. What is gained by chasing someone like her through residential streets in broad daylight? Matteo works hard not to care about his cases, but despite himself, curiosity is rousing his drowsy body.

Caerys is talking now: "Jess, what should I do?"

Jess' voice shakes: "Call the police. Tell them to send an ambulance. And..." her breath catches. Matteo can tell she is trying hard not to cry. "Ask them to send another squad to me."

"Are you hurt?" Keepers are not supposed to be able to affect emotions, but Matteo swears this Keeper is worried.

There is a long pause. "I don't know where to go. I have no one to go to." Matteo tenses; it's hard to hear someone so distressed. "Tell them to meet me at the juice bar."

"Okay, the Juju," says Caerys. "But are you okay?"

"Yes. No. Call the police."

Matteo juts his head forward, waiting for more, but that's it. She must have cut communication. He stands up from the bed, itching to move. "Beck? I should go to her, right?"

There's no answer, just whispering that Matteo cannot make out. Something about Khalil and checking on David. Matteo kicks at a pile of botany books that are scattered near his bed, nudging the open books to see if his flip-flops are hiding underneath. Last night, he had spread the books open across the rug to compare and contrast some vegetable varietals. The books are the old kind, with glossy, still photos and gorgeous colors. Rachel found them at flea markets and garage sales, and now their small apartment overflows with them.

"Beck?" Matteo asks again.

"Dude," Beck's voice wakes too loudly from his whispers. "Listen, I'm going to need you to stay with the girl today."

"Sure, fine." Matteo had assumed as much. He bends to peek under his dresser for the flip-flops; not there.

"No, listen, I'm talking tight contact today. I need you to talk with her."

"Talk?" Matteo stands upright. He never interacts with his observation subjects; his job is to be as invisible as possible while he watches them. "What do you want me to say?" He kicks his sweatshirt aside; *a-ha,* there are his flip-flops.

"Anything you want, man. Be friendly, charming... you know, all that stuff you're not." Beck chuckles nervously, unsure if his joke worked.

"I'm not a babysitter," Matteo mumbles. His bike satchels sit on the table next to his oxygen backpack and the two tanks which fit into it. He checks to see if there is any oxygen left. Crap: empty. "Listen, how many hours is this going to take? The rain is coming this afternoon, and you said I would be off today by four."

"Sorry, dude, not anymore, no way. The shit's going down today."

Matteo silently mouths: *"Fuck,"* his face scrunching in displeasure. He had planned to bike up to Tia's after the storm. There is a garden he keeps there, with potatoes, chard, carrots, kale, herbs – all plants he grafted for drought-resistance. Today will be their first exposure to a real rainstorm, and he wanted to monitor their response to the deluge.

"Dude, you on the street yet?"

What an annoying question. "You know I'm not," Matteo mutters. Beck has the video surveillance feed from Matteo's street at his fingertips. Irritation builds within him: this stupid job is ruining his day and now he has to make nice with that boring woman. "I have to brush my teeth," he hisses.

"Your *teeth*?"

"Yeah, is there a problem with that?" He knows Beck wants him to hurry, and small acts of resistance are sometimes where sanity resides.

"By all means, make them sparkle."

Matteo flips the light to his small bathroom. "If I'm cancelling my plans today because the *'shit's* going down,' you have to at least tell me what that means." In the year and a half that Matteo has worked for Beck, he has never had a case like this one. Usually, when he begins a new observational project, he receives a digital file with the various fields filled out: name, date of birth, work history, known relatives, that kind of thing. The last section in the digital file includes a short description of the suspicious activity that the observation seeks to confirm or deny. Typical descriptions include: "suspicion of fund embezzlement," "heroin drug-running," or "affair with the babysitter," etc.

In the file for Jess Prentiss, on the line where the client is supposed to identify the suspicion, it says: "She has the gift," which makes zero sense. Without a suspicious activity to either support or refute, the daily observations are meaningless, a point Matteo has made to Beck at least a dozen times before this morning. Now, he spreads toothpaste on his toothbrush; "I mean, I can keep watching her run up hills or listen to more of her Frenchy therapy sessions, but, unless you tell me what I'm supposed to be investigating, this is a waste of your time – and mine."

"Dude, man, relax. You're doing what you're supposed to be doing: watching the girl closely, keeping her safe."

"Safe?" Matteo holds his toothbrush to his mouth; "I'm not supposed to keep people safe."

"Listen, Matteo," Beck's voice loses its easy tone. "Today – just for today – keep the girl safe. And, actually, if you keep her safe for the whole day," he pauses, "I'll triple your payment for the case."

"Triple?" Matteo stops brushing, his mouth full of toothpaste. That is a lot of money. He could use that money. He turns on the tap and leans his head toward it. "How unsafe is she gonna be?" He slurps the water.

"Not that unsafe. A little unsafe."

The water sloshes in his mouth; he spits it out again. "Not reassuring."

"Yeah, well, no one's trying to kill her."

"No better."

"Do you want the money, or not?"

Matteo does a quick calculation: this triple payment would allow him to completely pay off his debt to Hua Chen. He has been working toward this goal for the past twenty-two months, and with the triple payment, he would be done a month earlier than expected. Hell, he could quit working for Beck as early as next week. "For how long do I have to keep her safe to get the triple payment?"

"All day."

"Until midnight?"

"Sure, midnight. Play Cinderella if you want."

Only midnight. Matteo knows something awful must be happening or Beck would never offer this much money. Yet, even if a crazy man *is* chasing Jessila Prentiss in broad daylight, Matteo doubts she could be at great risk. She's a chemistry post-doctoral student for crying out loud. Her days are spent in a chemical synthesis lab, her nights at home, eating takeout tofu triangles and reading apocalyptic sci-fi novels. The epitome of safe. He checks his wrist Keeper: 8:18 a.m. Less than sixteen hours until midnight. "I'll do it."

"Excellent, I knew you would. Khalil estimates you can be at the Juju in two minutes, 13 seconds, and don't worry: we'll be watching you. The whole group is on this."

The whole group doesn't usually work just one case. Matteo opens his mouth to ask why this case has so much coverage, but Beck is off line already. No matter.

Matteo sticks the bike bags onto his electric mountain bike, lifts the bike to his shoulder, and heads out the door.

Riding fast, he makes it to the Juju in 59 seconds, but who's counting. He tells his Keeper to lock his bike, and just like that, he is standing in the order line of this small juice store, only one person behind "the girl." A bead of sweat is dripping slowly down the nape of her neck.

Over the three weeks he has been on this assignment, Matteo has pointedly referred to twenty-seven-year old Jessila Prentiss as "the woman" in the hope Beck would take the hint that Jess is not actually a "girl" at all, but a fairly impressive scientist whom the rest of the world refers to as "Dr. Prentiss." Beck never clued in, and as Matteo stands behind Jess now, he has to admit that she looks teenager-ish. She is tall – probably his full height – and in her running clothes, her straight up-and-down frame makes her arms look gangly and her shoulders knobby. Her long, auburn-brown hair is piled on top of her head in something between a bun and a ponytail. Taking these elements together – the height, the leanness, the long hair – she looks like a high-school student reporting to gym class. He cannot understand who would pay to track this girl... woman, whatever. She is as clean-cut as they come.

The robotic mixers have just finished blending her drink. She steps toward the counter, and though he cannot see her face, she is jiggling her left leg and checking the time on her Keeper. Seeing her fidget, he realizes that he is nervous too. What the hell can he say to make "tight contact?" Beck made it sound like flirting is the way to go, but Matteo doubts he knows how to do that anymore. Actually – *crap* – he is still wearing his wedding ring. He twists the band on his finger, trying to decide whether to take it off. He hasn't removed this ring in the seven years since his wedding, right after he and Rachel graduated Berkeley together. "Who gets married these days?" is what their friends, even her *Tia,* kept saying, and Rachel always had the same sassy response: "Who gets this chance at love?" Yeah, he will keep the ring on.

If he cannot flirt, he will come up with a different approach. He hates doing half-assed work – and that is why he hates working for Beck. Beck Industries' tagline is "we create informational peace of mind," which is just a blowhard way of saying the company spies on people. The company has subscriptions to all the Bay Area's surveillance camera feeds, and from the company's Oakland offices, a crew of seven "screeners" constantly barks out commands: "Pull video feed - 40 Telegraph," "Go to Bank of A, number 60," "Engage BART camera, station Rockridge." Anyone and everyone can be tracked. Rachel's and his friends say he is working for Big Brother; Matteo does not try to deny it.

24

The only good part of his job is that he is outside riding his electric bike all day. Some days all he does is trail the subject. Other days, he hacks into the subjects' Keepers since Keeper hacking is far easier to accomplish the closer you stand to the Keeper itself. In a few instances he has broken into a home or business, to "retrieve" a piece of evidence. Beck always says that he is helping to put shady characters away, but Matteo is not so naïve as to believe that breaking and entering has virtue. He has wanted to quit pretty much since he started, but the money is amazing – much more than he could make at the Experimental Farm. Rachel's antivirals are expensive.

In front of him, Jess turns around, holding a bright orange drink in a clear, plastic cup, a straw protruding from the top. This is his chance. He steps toward her. "That looks good," he nods to her drink; "Which one is it?"

She stares back at him, and he notices two things: the corner of her lip is bloody, and the brown streak of dust across the bridge over her nose makes her eyes' blueness stand out brightly. "I'm sorry?" she asks.

He points to the plastic cup; "Just wondering which drink that is?" *Man, he sucks at this.*

"The carrot apple one."

"Is it good?" It's clear she does not want to talk, but, somehow, he has to make this conversation morph into their grand, trusting contact.

She shakes her head; "You have it." She pushes the bright orange drink into his hand and rushes to the door.

Matteo glances at the plastic cup, then the door. *The shit is going down.* He wishes he understood what that meant or what he is expected to do about it.

All he knows: he has to follow her.

JESS

For everyone around her, this is another normal morning. Jess stands at the corner of Vine and Walnut, and a dozen or so people linger next to her on the narrow turf meridian that divides sidewalk from street. Some sip coffee and chomp on muffins, some study their Keeper screens, and others gab with a friend. Two bakeries are near the juice bar and a coffee shop is right at the corner; the smells of baked goods and burnt coffee linger in the humid air.

Two bearded Agro men stand at their spot near the stop sign; they are regulars, and usually, they argue over gun laws or discuss the drought, but this morning, they're taking bets on how much rain will fall in today's storm. A homeless man who sells poetry for digital change approaches Jess; she shakes her head to signal she's not buying. All her energy needs to stay focused on looking for the police car. The cops should be here soon. Back and forth, she peers down Walnut Street, trying not to be anxious, trying only to think.

From her chemistry studies, she knows a reaction is triggered by elements interacting with each other, and she's trying to identify the elements at play this morning. Bloody David on the ground. Big men from De Sel. *"Run, Jess, run!"* A shudder ripples through her body. No, she cannot think of David's face – how stretched it was, how scared. She taps her Keeper to turn Caerys' voice back on; "Do you have information on De Sel yet?"

"Yes." And with that, Caerys launches into her report. Many long sentences proceed, and though Jess wants to listen closely, her attention flits in and out. De Sel is a French company, the twenty-second most profitable in the world. It owns and operates 144 water desalination plants worldwide, which, as Caerys explains, means they use reverse-osmosis to transform salty ocean water into non-salted fresh water for agriculture use. "De Sel is the reason California continues to grow food in the drought."

Jess fidgets with her Keeper wristband. "But none of this is answering my question."

"Tell me the question."

Jess hesitates. What she wants to ask is: "Why would De Sel want to hurt David?" But, of course, Caerys will not know the answer to that question. "Has De Sel ever funded research with David?" she whisperspeaks instead.

"I'll look," Caerys answers.

In the silence, Jess squints toward the end of the block. The brown smog makes it hard. Cars drive past with their lights on, but none are the mini electric vehicles the Berkeley police use.

Jess doubts De Sel ever funded David's research. David works in solar energy, De Sel with desalinating water; there's no "overlapping motivation," as David would say. Besides, Jess knows all the companies that currently fund David's research because she manages his corporate grant proposals.

One week after Jess began working in David's research group, he knocked on her door and ambled around her lab. It was strange to see her boss standing there beside her Raman microscope and chemical vapor deposition furnace. Up to that point, their communications had occurred via video messaging, and she was uncertain about what could have prompted him to visit in person.

"Here," he handed her a sheet of paper; "it's a list of companies I'd like you to contact for possible grants." She could not understand why he had chosen to hand-deliver this sheet of paper rather than message the instructions. She peered at the list curiously. On it were the names of six companies including Suncap, Durasolar, and Klaxon. "Get in touch with the folks I've identified, and make sure your initial contact is by video messaging. I want them to see you. If they express interest in the group's research, suggest lunch."

When Jess had protested that she had never done work like this – "and wasn't it sort of *sales* work?" – a note of disdain creeping into her voice, David chuckled. "Everyone is always selling." He touched her shoulder before walking out the door. "You'll be good at this, I'm sure of it."

To her surprise, she had been. All the companies she video-conferenced asked for follow-up meetings, and though most of the company's spokespersons wanted to hear more about David's research projects, David nonetheless asked Jess to make the proposal presentations. At each of these meetings, she stood at the front of the same large, white conference room. The catered coffee gave off a bitter smell, and the sunlight bouncing in through the large windows kept the room hot and stuffy. The corporate representatives sat toward the front of a shiny red table, with David toward the back. When he nodded to her to begin, she would arrange her voice to sound its most steady and ingratiating, though her inner thoughts were about how to minimize her arm movements so the sweat stains did not show through her blue pantsuit.

Until these meetings, Jess had little interaction with the business world. Her father, who worked as a high school physics teacher, had always quipped that anything related to capitalism was of questionable worth. In fact, he called business people "the stupid people who do stupid work to make rich people richer." Jess hated it when her father ranted, and even as a girl, she recognized that her dad's scorn was at least partially motivated by jealousy. Yet, his opinions must have infiltrated her subconscious because she never once considered pursuing finance or law or advertising. Her studies had stayed laser-focused on science, a pursuit that her father said had the most integrity of any field.

When she first stood before the long red table in the sun-filled conference room, the business people intimidated her. Once she had made a few presentations, however, she realized that the men and women at the table were also worried about environmental collapse and "saving the planet" and seemed to have as much integrity as most of the scientists she knew. The only difference was that they were rich. Very rich. They had big diamonds in their Thickrings, wore beautifully tailored clothing, and talked with ease about rock climbing trips, vacation homes, and expensive workout regimens. *Why again had she chosen academia?*

One morning, Jess was sitting at her lab desk when she received a short text message that the Klaxon Korporation was ready to invest ten million dollars in one of David's research areas. This was huge news; Klaxon was a fast-growing renewable energy company, and the research grant was for Jess' own project with graphene-based solar cells. She was just about to message her mother with her good news when David knocked on her door. "Is Xu here?" he asked as he stuck his head in.

"Oh, no, he usually comes in later," Jess stood up to explain.

"Good," David replied, chuckling, "because I'm here to see you." He came forward, touching the rim of her desk. "After this news with Klaxon, it seems irrefutable."

"Irrefutable?"

"That you're my lucky charm." His smile came and went like a wink. "I'd like us to go to dinner tonight – to celebrate, if that's okay with you?"

Jess stuttered before finally settling on the "okay" David was waiting to hear. They agreed to meet that night at a downtown Berkeley restaurant that Jess knew was rather fancy, and all signs suggested the dinner would be a date. There had been other times when Jess had contemplated that her boss was flirting with her. His tone had sometimes been a touch too appreciative or his smiles held what looked like a playful tease. She'd made these observations but always shrugged them off. A man like David Steubingly could not possibly be interested in a woman like her.

To start with, David was *famous*. A best-selling author, a member of the Academy, a bigwig at UC. He was good-looking too, even if it was in a distinguished older man way. People on campus talked about what he said and did as though he were a celebrity. The woman at David's arm should be someone similarly impressive. Someone who wore high-heels and tasteful jewelry, who made clever, funny points, and knew all the right people. In other words, not Jess. She wore jeans most days, never bothered with make-up and was not particularly good at making small talk, much less witty repartee. Her boyfriends before David were like her: smart, kind, hard-working. Serious. Maybe too serious.

Honestly, she hated that this was her type.

The night she met David for dinner, they discussed the environment because it was the topic that never left her worries.

David spoke in low, calm tones about how "terribly important" it was for science to work with capitalism "hand in glove." He made references to conversations with the Governor, chairing a Presidential panel and travel to the cities of Tokyo, London, Rome, Madrid, and Buenos Aires all before the main course arrived. Nudging his silverware into straighter lines, he made a point, took a bite, made another. Jess listened, drinking four glasses of white wine in quick succession. As the wine made the world around her soften, her attention on David grew more focused. His eyes were kind, his voice smooth and deep. She began to add her own ideas to the conversation, and David smiled and teased her for her passionate concern. Over dessert, he touched her hand and told her she was beautiful. No one had said anything nice to her since she had moved to Berkeley; it made her cheeks warm. Later, when they were at his house, sipping more wine on the couch, he kissed her, first a peck, then more hungrily. As he unbuttoned her blouse, he whispered that he'd waited for months to see what was beneath her blue suit. Her breath became fluttery when she shimmied out of her bra.

"Excuse me." It is a man's voice, deep and gruff. Jess turns; the guy from the juice bar is holding out her carrot apple drink. "I never meant for you to give this up," he says.

She could care less about the stupid drink. "That's okay, I don't want it anymore." She begins to turn back, but his hand gestures to his mouth: "Your mouth's all cut up."

Her fingers touch her lip's corner, and it's true, there's crustiness. Maybe she bust her lip when the De Sel man tackled her.

"I don't want to pry, but are you okay?"

Jess examines him. He has jet-black, thick wavy hair and broad shoulders. His eyes are almond shaped, his cheekbones high. *Asian, Mexican, Brazilian?* She cannot tell. His clothes are crumpled, the lettering on his U.C. Berkeley t-shirt is faded, his cheeks unshaven. On his left arm's bicep there is a giant tattoo, though she can't make out the design. Given his rumpled style, she would peg him as a slacker-Agro-type – there are lots of those in Berkeley. His gaze, however, is smart and directed. He is wearing a thick silver wedding ring. "I'm fine," she says, and before she can figure how to end their conversation, she notices a police car is approaching the corner. Fast, she raises her arms above her head, waving.

The small white car pulls to the curb, and a straight-hipped, large busted woman with short, platinum streaked hair emerges. "Are you Jess Prentiss?" she says, walking toward her.

Jess nods.

"Your Keeper called 911 ten minutes ago?"

"That's right." Jess was expecting to be relieved by the arrival of the police officer but as this woman comes close to her, she has to fight an urge to step back. The officer's shiny platinum hair is slicked back tight on her head, and three gemstones are affixed to each of her cheekbones. On her forefingers, she wears bejeweled Thickrings, the kind that go from the finger's base to center knuckle. Her digital nametag has a thin layer of dust on its small screen, but Jess can still make out the name: "Brooklyn Relly." There is not a bit of Agro on this woman; she is all Traditionalist, and Jess hopes her face does not convey her surprise that a Traditionalist cop is responding to a call in Berkeley, CA.

Attracted by the police car, a small crowd gathers on the sidewalk. Jess realizes these strangers will overhear her account of what happened. The old Agro men, the old lady with the scraggly-gray hair, the two moms with their strollers, the khaki-wearing guys on their way to work. All these people will think she's nuts.

Officer Relly walks toward Jess. "David Steubingly told my men you got hurt. And –" the officer waves her hand toward Jess' body – "you do look pretty roughed up."

Jess looks down at her limbs. "I'm sorry, did you say that David spoke to your officers? He's... he's okay?"

"Not exactly okay. In and out of consciousness. My team picked him up at his house shortly after your call. Every time he wakes, he is delirious with worry about you."

Jess imagines David's bloody face with eyes blinking to stay alert. "Will he be okay?"

"Of course, of course." Relly's red lips move quickly. "David has to be okay."

Jess tries to take in this unexpected response, assessing the woman's square posture and her certain voice. "Did your cops arrest the big men?"

"The big men? Oh, you mean, the homeless guys. No, no, they were long gone. We put out an APB for them in the North Berkeley area, and—"

"Excuse me, did you say *homeless*?"

"Yes." Relly's voice clips, apparently not liking the skepticism in Jess' question. "They were homeless."

"Um, I'm pretty sure they weren't homeless. They were muscular and huge. Like steroid big. And they were wearing matching windbreakers."

"Honey, homeless people are *everywhere*. All shapes and sizes. Some even wear windbreakers."

The two older men behind Jess chuckle, and she swings around to face them. The men who beat up David were thugs, not homeless, but Jess realizes she cannot articulate why she knows that.

The officer comes right to her side. "This morning has been very difficult for you. You've been through so much. Let's get you to a hospital for a good check-up."

"Hospital?" Jess checks the crowd to see if they are also puzzled by Relly's suggestion. "I don't need a check-up."

"Of course you do. You've sustained injuries, and they could be serious." Relly smiles and directs her hand toward the car's backseat. "Here, if you get in, I'll take you now." The car's interior is dark with bars on the windows and across the divider between the front and back seats.

Jess touches her head; it only hurts a little. She does not need doctors to tell her she's fine. "I don't want to go to the hospital."

Relly chuckles: "Look at your lip." She points: "And that shirt. Obviously, you have to be checked out."

Jess looks down at her dusty t-shirt. She hadn't noticed until now, but blood is smeared across her its lettering.

Officer Relly takes a small step toward her. "Besides, David will be at the hospital." Her voice goes lower, "And he told my men that he wants you with him, that he couldn't *bear* it if something happened to you."

"He said that?" That doesn't sound like David. David is a private man. As far as Jess knows, he's never told anyone they were involved. "Even though he's flitting in and out of consciousness?"

Relly's head tilts; "He keeps on talking about his Fire – that's what he calls you, right?"

Jess stares. David would not refer to her as Fire, no way. Jess looks at the handcuffs on Brooklyn's holster, the police seal on the car door. This is a real police officer. She came in response to a 911 call. Yet, her closeness makes Jess want to step away, run. She wipes her sweaty palms on her shorts. "Don't you want to ask me questions? Take my report? You know, get my description of the man who attacked me, stuff like that."

"I can take the report at the hospital." The words roll from Relly's metallic red lips. "First, I want to make sure your injuries receive medical attention. Here," she pulls the car's back door open wider. "Police protocol is medical attention first, incident report later." She smiles, and her cheek's gemstones glimmer. "We want to make sure you feel better, honey."

The whispers of the onlookers make Jess think that Relly's speech has swayed several in the crowd. Jess looks behind her, and several are nodding encouragingly toward her. "Can't hurt to get your head checked," she hears one woman say. "Don't worry, she's just trying to help you," a younger male voice mutters as though speaking to himself.

Jess studies the earnest, open faces in the crowd around her, so trusting. In one of Jess' sessions this week with Dr. Monique, they had discussed Jess' pattern of doubting people's intentions. "You don't like to assume the best of people," Dr. Monique had observed, and Jess had not tried to deny the point. "It's a strategy that serves me well. Less disappointment that way." Dr. Monique had leaned forward: "Isn't distrust always disappointing?"

Jess considers: perhaps this is another instance where she is inserting suspicion where it doesn't have to be. It is *possible* this officer is genuinely trying to help her. It is *possible* those big men were genuinely homeless. Or, at least that David described the men that way. This cop gains nothing by lying to her. And a hospital is a safe enough place. Jess takes a step toward the car's open back door and is about to step into the back seat when she stops. "Officer, how'd you know all those things that David said? Have you seen him?"

Brooklyn Relly's eyebrows rise: "I told you; my men called me on their way to the hospital."

"Your men relayed all those things he said?"

"Of course."

"They conveyed an awful lot on their way to the hospital."

Relly shrugs. "They like to keep me informed."

"About the nickname David calls me?"

"Jess, I understand that you'd be suspicious after such a hard day, but think for a second. How could I possibly know about Fire except from David himself?" She leans toward Jess, whispering as though they are sharing a secret. "Don't you see, Jess, if you come with me, I can protect you." Her smile flashes again, tight across her face.

Jess can hear the crowd's restless whispers, uncomfortable with the conversation they're witnessing. Several in the crowd are people she recognizes from the juice bar. The silver-haired lady who likes to talk about the drought. The goateed guy who raves about his citrus and greens diet. The bobbed-haired mom whose toddler always screams when she puts on his oxygen mask. "Just go see the doctors," the mom says to Jess. Other people nod, their faces strained with sympathy. "You'll be fine," she hears another person say. The crowd is probably right. If Jess goes to the hospital, she'll be able to slip back into the day, as though this crazy episode never happened. She looks again at these faces, so familiar and safe. She wants to stand with them.

That's when she sees the juice bar guy staring straight at her.

"Don't go," he mouths.

MATTEO

As the cop car speeds up the hill, Matteo watches the crowd collapse onto Jess. A gray-haired woman is the first to reach her side; she holds Jess' arms and talks right to her face. Other members of the crowd touch Jess' shoulder or back, asking if there's anything they can do. Jess smiles, answers the questions coming her way. "I'm fine, really." He can tell she is uncomfortable with the attention. "Thanks for making sure she didn't arrest me," she says, trying to laugh. But her knee still jiggles, her voice strains. She must be aware of how close she came to being forced into that police car.

Honestly, he is mystified as to what restrained Brooklyn Relly in the end. In his experience, cops do not withdraw from a conflict. Since the new gun prohibitions went into effect, police have replaced their firearms with tranquilizer guns, and if anything, cops are now quicker to "shoot" someone acting insubordinately. A couple of months ago, Matteo witnessed cops approaching a group of black and brown men under BART tracks in El Cerrito. In broad daylight, and with no warning, the cops splayed the group with "tranq" darts as though it was their form of greeting. Prohibitions regulating cops' use of firearms are no longer enforced since anyone shot with a tranq wakes in two hours. These days, cops regularly tranq-dart people resisting arrest. When Jess announced: "I will not go in that car voluntarily," Matteo assumed that Jess would be shot.

Instead, what happened was strange. A bearded, pot-bellied man in the back of the crowd yelled something – Matteo thought it sounded like "pop" – and held up his Keeper to show that he was videotaping the interaction. Then, another man – young, tattooed and scruffy-looking – started to sing: "All around the mulberry bush, the monkey chased the weasel, the monkey thought what fun it was, *pop* goes the weasel."

Brooklyn turned to him, her face tightened in a sneer. She held her wrist to her mouth to whisper a question to her Keeper, and there was an unbelievably long period, maybe ten whole seconds, in which

Brooklyn did nothing more than stare at this man; Matteo guessed her Keeper was silentspeaking to her.

Abruptly, she got into her car and turned it on. She said nothing to Jess, nothing to the crowd. She simply drove off.

Now, the last stragglers in the crowd are saying good-bye to Jess and the exchanges remind him of a funeral receiving line. "Thank you," Jess is saying over and over again, peppered with assorted reassurances: "Really, I'll be fine. I'm used to taking care of myself."

He is standing to the side, still holding that stupid carrot drink. It is obvious that, despite the crowd's offer of help and Jess' professed appreciation for it, everyone is happy to move on. If Rachel were here, she would be annoyed by the phoniness. "Everyone's just pretending to care!" she would say in her usual exclamatory fashion. "None of those people actually wanted to help that young woman, and she didn't actually want their help either. But why the fuck not? People helping people is what makes our sum greater than our parts, and yet, all anyone wants these days is to be alone with their fucking Keepers!"

When Rachel indulged her society-is-doomed diatribes, her cheeks would flush, her eyes shine. Indignation suited her. Of course, she was right too. A Keeper really could take the place of neighbor, friend, assistant, and advisor. Who better to arrange a virtual doctor's visit or order that lip cream to be delivered? Take your temperature? Sing you a lullaby? Keepers really would be better at all those tasks than any of these concerned citizens leaving Jess' side. Even he asks the voice in his head for things he would never ask people. *Say something that'll make me feel better. Tell me I'm a good person. Talk dirty to me.* He wouldn't want Rachel to know, but he relies on his Keeper a lot these days.

In fact, over these last ten minutes, he has been whispering questions to his Keeper constantly, collecting shards of information that, like a broken plate, he wants to piece together. They don't fit.

Jess heads to where he is standing on the dusty sidewalk. "Thank you for helping me like you did back there."

"No big deal." He hands her the juice he has been holding all this time. Taking it, she slurps an enormously long draw. It's then that he notices her body is wavering, like a bamboo stalk blowing in a breeze.

"Here, you should sit down." He helps her settle onto the low curb and sits beside her, stretching his legs outward into the street. Their spot on the curb is directly under a quaking Aspen tree, one of Matteo's favorite trees. With the drought, the small fan-like leaves have already fallen off the limbs and are scattered around them, brown and curdled. It occurs to him that one does not usually sit next to strangers on a curb. For whatever reason, it is an intimate arrangement.

Though he has only met Jess an hour ago, he is aware of how well he knows her. He has read her journal, listened in on her therapy sessions and phone calls, checked out her Keeper's messages. He knows how David Steubingly jilted her three weeks ago, how determined she is to prove she does not care. He has heard her regular morning calls to her mother with their particular brand of strain. He knows that she hasn't made friends since moving to Berkeley; this worries her. So does her bank account, whose balance she checks daily and has only $322 in it now. She buys a bottle of gin and a six-pack of tonic every four or five days and sometimes at night when he guesses she's drunk, she dances around her studio apartment in her underwear and bra, the blinds left up, which, yes, he has watched even when he could have turned away. All of these pieces of information are enough that sitting beside her now, realizing how scared she is, he does not want to make her feel worse.

Still, he has to tell her: "You should know that David Steubingly has not been admitted to any hospital in the Bay Area."

She turns to face him, the straw still centered between her lips. "'Has *not*'?" she clarifies.

"Right, has *not.*"

Her face juts forward. "How do you know about all the hospi—?"

"I have a friend who works for Alameda County's Public Health department"—a lie; he called a Beck screener. "And the department keeps a log of all the hospital admissions in real time – something they started during the H5N5 epidemic. Anyway, I called my friend on my Keeper while the policewoman was talking to you."

"And your friend said David's nowhere in these hospitals?"

"Right."

She blinks. "Then, where is he?"

"I don't know."

Her face freezes; her body seems held in suspension. "She lied to me."

Matteo cannot think of anything to say which would be comforting because, in fact, that does seem to be the only conclusion.

Jess' words come fast: "My Keeper called 911, and that Relly woman knew about that call. She drove a cop car; she had a badge. How'd she do all that if she isn't a cop?"

"She *is* a cop." He cannot help noticing the paleness of her blue eyes. "That's what's strange. I had my Keeper run the license plates off her squad car, and it's a real police vehicle – though it's registered with the state, not to the Berkeley PD. Brooklyn Relly is a California State Trooper Colonel, which is pretty high up the chain of command to respond to a local distress call, but..." he pauses, because Jess is already wincing, "she *is* a cop."

Jess shakes her head. "This doesn't make sense."

"No, it doesn't." He rubs the dust off his knees, waiting for her to ask more questions. A car drives by. A child in the background starts to cry. Jess stays staring off into space. He talks to fill the silence: "That Relly woman did *seem* like she was trying to protect you – but that stuff about the homeless men, that was obvious bullshit."

The way Jess looks at him now, he realizes he has said too much. Her chin juts forward; "Why'd you check into all that stuff? You don't know me; you don't know David. You shouldn't care about any of this."

He thinks he is ready for these questions, but her distrust takes a second to adjust to. "I was trying to give you your drink back. Then, that Relly woman started talking to you, and she seemed fishy. I asked my Keeper a few questions. Those answers came back weird, so I asked a few more." She is still eyeing him suspiciously. "Here, you can see for yourself what I found." He taps the disc on his wrist again, and several holographic screens pop forth, hovering at their eye level. One is a screen that shows the real-time listing of all hospital admissions. Another screen is from the car registry that identifies Brooklyn Relly's car as a state police car, another that shows Brooklyn Relly's photo and her name listed as a member of the California State Police force, and another that shows a photo of Colonel Relly shaking hands with Governor Ramos, just earlier this year.

As Jess looks at the screens, her eyes feverishly scanning the pages, Matteo wonders how he would have reacted to Jess if he had received no orders from Beck to keep her safe. Would he have tried to help this young woman who was being tricked by a cop? He doubts it, and the realization disappoints him because he knows it would disappoint Rachel. She would want him to be a good person.

Jess holds her wrist out and taps her Keeper to launch a holographic keyboard. "What's your name?" she asks.

"Matteo; Matteo Wu." From the curt tone of her question, he knows she's about to background check him. He is not worried; she will not find anything. It is standard protocol for Beck employees to build an alias web presence once they are on Beck's payroll, though Beck had found Matteo's existing web profile to work well enough. "You're so fucking wholesome," is how he put it. While Jess reads about him on her Keeper's screens, Matteo kicks his flip-flops against the street, trying to dislodge the dusty grime from his feet. There's always a ruddy brown layer on everything these days. His hair, his lips, his ears. He cannot wait for the rain to come and clear the muck away. Around him, the usual dingy yellow of the smog is being supplanted by stormy grayness. The air smells of dampness too, like boiling potatoes.

"You work at the Temescal Experimental Farm?" she asks, a note of surprise in her voice.

"I do," he lies, wishing that were still his truth.

"I guess that explains the artichoke."

Inadvertently, his hand touches his arm's tattoo; "It requires an explanation?"

"No, I mean, I'd just noticed..." There's a hint of embarrassment in her voice. She sits up straighter, her voice becoming more assertive. "I'm sorry I was suspicious, but this day has been—" She gasps, staring at her left wrist. "Did you see that?" She pushes buttons on the side of her Keeper's faceplate, then holds her left arm toward him. "My Keeper, it went black."

Now, it is his turn to examine the dark disc, pushing the small buttons on the Keeper's side. He can't get the screen to wake up. Beside him, Jess' breathing is growing heavy. "What about your head?" he asks, "If you ask a question, does your Keeper give you a silentspeak response?"

Jess holds her Keeper to her lips and her brows furrow as she whispers: "Caerys, can you hear me?" She shakes her head. "Nothing. No response at all."

The issue cannot be merely a screen malfunction; the Keeper itself must have been disabled. "When was the last time you charged it?"

"Yesterday, at the lab. And a charge usually lasts me a week."

Holding her wrist as he examines her Keeper, he can feel her thudding pulse. His heart is pounding pretty damn hard too. He pushes the buttons down and holds them hard. Nothing. "It's not coming back. But don't... don't panic yet." Actually, he can't think why she shouldn't. "Maybe it'll come back when you set it to its docking station."

"They did this." Her lower lip is quivering. "Don't you think they did this?"

The answer to that question has to be yes, but he is reluctant to say it. There is something lunatic about believing there is a "they" out there scheming to hurt this clean-cut woman. "Here," he swallows. "Let's focus on different questions. Do you think David could still be at his house?"

She closes her eyes, as though the question pains her. "No. Zero chance."

He's about to ask if she knows of any place they would have taken David but stops himself. She won't know, and the question will only upset her more. Besides, his goal is to take her some place safe, not go on a wild goose chase for David. "Here, I have an idea. I'm about to bike to campus. You should come with me. Your lab's on campus, right? You can get your Keeper to its dock—"

"Wait, how'd you know I have a lab on campus?"

He stops for a second because, *crap,* that is a good question. Then, he makes himself grin. "I checked you out too, on my Keeper. Fair's fair, right? You background check me, I background check you."

She nods, trying to smile.

"Here, come on." He stands up to show that he's serious about moving on.

"I... I don't understand why you're helping me."

"I'm not doing much." He holds his hand out long enough that Jess has no choice but to take it.

Together, they walk his bike to the liquid oxygen filling station around the corner. Matteo fills the backpack tank he usually wears and a spare one he keeps in one of his electric bike's side satchels. "Take a long hit," he says. "You've been in open air too long." He begins to strap the tank to her back, and to his surprise, she does not protest. Taking the mask he hands her, she places the clear dome over her mouth and breathes in deep.

As they head to campus, he walks on one side of his bike, she on the other. The sky is growing ever darker and the leafless branches of the trees wiggle with an antsy breeze. The rain really is coming. They pass parked cars that have messages drawn onto their dusty windshields: "Rain on me," "I'll be clean tonight," and "Bath time?"

Jess does not seem to notice. Her t-shirt, which has the words "Flower Power" written across it in red cursive letters, has brown stains of dirt and blood. She's squinting her eyes, and her lips move slightly as though she's deep in the throes of her own internal conversation. It occurs to him that, given everything that has happened to her, she is holding up remarkably well. There have been no tears and not even much complaining. If Rachel had just gone through Jess' morning, she'd be a crying wreck, a whirling dervish of catastrophic apprehensions. Perhaps Jess is faking her toughness, but he doubts it. Given the intensity of her eyes and the slight twitching of her lips, he thinks she is already working on what to do next.

He should do the same. He would like to simply call Beck, but then Jess would hear. So, he taps out a question to Beck on his wrist Keeper's screen: "What the hell?" and then adds: "RVSS," which stands for Respond via SilentSpeak. Seconds later, his Keeper brings Beck's message into his head: "Brooklyn Relly is real bad news. Whatever you do, don't let her near the girl."

Matteo falls a step behind Jess and brings his wrist screen so that he can tap his response. "You have to give me more than that. Tell me what Relly wants or why she's after Jess."

It takes a while, but his Keeper eventually brings Beck's message into his head: "The key is to get the girl off the grid. Do you understand what I'm saying? Get the girl completely offline."

Offline? He whispers into his Keeper: "I need more information. What is happening here?" He waits. No response. He pushes a button on his Keeper screen to send the message a second time, but, again, silence. Beck does this every once in awhile: responding immediately to one message, then taking his time with the next one. He doesn't think that is what's going on now, but he gains nothing by assuming the worst. Jess is looking at him curiously, probably because she's heard his whispers. He smiles, trying to appear as though he has nothing to hide.

As they near downtown Berkeley, the many flat-screen monitors situated in bus kiosks and storefronts are broadcasting storm coverage. And, the whole side of the Calder Building is lit up with a wall-to-wall screen that is showing a countdown with the estimated time until rainfall hits Berkeley: 46 minutes, 37 seconds, and counting.

The Calder screen always reminds him of the night of the massacre.

He and Rachel had been watching the coverage from their apartment. The networks and news blogs were all sharing the same live camera feed from the California State Assembly floor, and at the moment when the terrorists announced their plan, Rachel turned the screens off.

"Why'd you do that?" he yelled, and turned his own Keeper screen back on.

"No, please, no!" she pleaded. "I can't watch those people get shot! Please." Her agitation was desperate, and Matteo wasn't going to argue with her, because what could he say? "I *do* want to watch people get shot?" There was no time for discussion anyway. He lifted his bike, carried it out the door and biked fast to downtown, arriving just as the enormous screens of the Calder Building showed the masked radicals lining up the forty-two Assembly Members and twenty-one State Senators who opposed gun restrictions. It took three, maybe four, seconds for them to be gunned down. Matteo became sick, literally vomiting in the street.

When he returned to their apartment, Rachel wouldn't talk to him. "You watched a bloodbath. You rushed to it like a blockbuster." Yet, he hadn't regretted his decision. He'd been present at a moment of tremendous import, witnessing how quickly seventeen "radicalized" American men and women had upended the country's status quo. It was the moment that everything changed. The terrorists had been killed, of course – stormed by American armed forces only a half-hour after the executions.

Before they were killed, the masked men and women made a statement to the surveillance cameras that they knew were capturing their actions. The remarks were not prepared, nor spontaneous, but somewhere in between. "We know we're about to die," one masked man said. "We gave our life for the cause," shouted a woman off-camera. The first man continued, "The status quo will leave this world in ruins, and you must work to shift it. Accept no more capitalistic plunder, no more rich stomping on poor, no more environmental degradation." Another masked man with a baritone voice shouted behind him: "We killed the politicians tonight who wouldn't let the gun laws pass, and we're coming for the richies next. Pass the gun laws, or we'll execute the billionaires and then the millionaires. Do it! Everyone in our group is willing to die to save the world."

It was distressing for Matteo to see senseless, horrific violence paired with Agro political opinions. The Agro platform had always advocated for gun control, pro-environmental policies and progressive taxation, but Agros relied heavily on a "peace first" approach. Probably that is why they never had any power. The more mainstream parties had pro-business platforms, and their campaigns were polished and pretty, holding out prosperous visions of a future that everyone wanted to believe could still come true. In return, Agros' messages emphasized reduced energy usage as a response to climate change and sharing prosperity as the moral response to environmental refugees. Not easy stuff.

After the California State Assembly attack, Agro leadership became so intent on demonstrating that they were pacifists, not terrorists, that the party essentially neutered themselves. With only talk, never action, Matteo felt that they became the voices for complaint, not progress. Believing in progress became more akin to believing in fairy tales than possibility.

When he worked at the Experimental Farm, his responsibilities focused on grafting drought-resistant plants and vegetables, work which was valuable and interesting. However, he never fooled himself that grafting a few drought-resistant vegetables would impact the scale of the pending agricultural disaster. Even the irrigated farms he visited in Sonoma and San Joaquin counties were having trouble. There were rows and rows of withered vegetables, drooping fruit trees, and yellowed, hard grass. The produce was growing, but barely, and around these water-drip irrigated fields, the rolling, hard hills were covered in smog and dust and brown. Everywhere brown. Drought-hearty plants were holding on, but nothing thrived.

Looking up at the deep clouds, Matteo wonders if today could be the end of the drought. Like everyone, he wants to believe it could be true.

As he and Jess walk into downtown Berkeley, Matteo knows they are being tracked by hundreds of surveillance cameras. In the next block, two dozen cameras are embedded in traffic lights, sidewalks and the building facades themselves – not to mention the crowdsourcing surveillance that happens when people keep their Keeper's cameras on in return for nominal fees. He has no doubt that in the screening room at Beck Industries, he and Jess are being watched on multiple screens from multiple angles. Relly and her people – whoever they are – are undoubtedly watching their screens too.

Since they still have seven blocks to walk, Matteo punches into his Keeper a request: that the information on David Steubingly be read to him via silentspeak. David Steubingly is the man at the center of the day's troubles, and Matteo would bet a bundle that it is Dr. Steubingly, not nerdy, quiet Jess Prentiss, that "they" are after.

As Matteo's Keeper reads the information about David, there are no red flags. David Steubingly's finances are in order; he has no debt, owns his house outright, and has a comfortable savings in the bank. There is no evidence of drug addiction or alcohol dependency. His research is pretty tame stuff too, mostly about solar cells – the coatings, sizes and shapes that allow them to capture sunlight's energy most efficiently. Even when Matteo indulges conspiratorial conjectures, there's nothing to suggest Steubingly is involved in espionage or corporate gamesmanship. He's a geek. A capitalistic geek at that.

Four years ago, Steubingly wrote a bestseller, *Everything Will Be Okay: How Technology Will Save the Planet*. The book was sold as a treatise on how science and capitalism should create natural synergies to solve climate and energy challenges. Rachel downloaded the book right when it came out, then groaned a lot while reading it, loudly sharing her frustration with Matteo. "This Steubingly is a fucking moron. How can he not see that it's cars and electricity and manufacturing that put our planet in this mess? I want to write a book too: *Everything Will Be Okay: If You Turn Off Your Fucking Technology.*" Rachel had a point, but Matteo is pretty sure her disdain for David Steubingly was not the majority opinion. The book received rave reviews; Steubingly won a number of environmental prizes, and in the latest edition, the Governor of California, Luis Ramos, wrote a flattering blurb saying, "Thank goodness David Steubingly is at the helm of California's energy research, leading our environmental future to a better tomorrow." Matteo's Keeper continues to read the material on Steubingly, but everything is merely confirming Matteo's earlier conclusion: Nothing is amiss about this man.

"Do you know anything about De Sel?"

Jess' question jolts him out of his thoughts. When he faces her, he senses she has been observing him for a while. "I'd ask Caerys about De Sel, but—" she points to her right ear, "I can't. Could you tell me what comes to your mind when you think of that company?" She lifts the oxygen mask from her face and moves the elastic band over her ponytail.

"Like a game of word association?" he asks.

She nods and hands the mask to him, then the small oxygen tank.

Shoving the tank into the bike's satchel, he says: "Everyone I know calls De Sel 'De Selfish.'"

"'De Selfish'?"

"You've heard that, right?"

"Nope."

"Well, the media can't call them DeSelfish, but if you read any of the Agro websites—"

"I don't. I can't."

This takes him by surprise. This is a woman who has literally hundreds of documentaries on climate change downloaded to her Keeper. He had assumed she was hard-core Agro. "Why can't you?"

"Because nothing ever changes. And if I read too much about how nothing ever changes, I don't sleep." She looks at him directly, refusing to be embarrassed.

46

"Oh." He thinks about suggesting she might sleep better if she actually became involved, but decides against it. Watching the world fall apart is no picnic; who is he to suggest a better way to do it? He scratches the back of his neck. "Well, I'm sure you've noticed that De Sel's a monopoly. And since De Sel's the only producer of fresh water, and we need that water for food and industry and life, De Sel is making a lot of money in this drought—"

"Right, right," she interrupts, "but what about De Sel's workers, what do you think of them?"

He stops walking. "I don't think of them."

"I mean, do they have a reputation for beating people up?"

"Uh, that's a really weird quest—"

"The men who were punching David were wearing De Sel windbreakers. That bright blue color with the name bold across the back."

"Oh." He had noted that Jess had told Relly the men were wearing matching windbreakers – a peculiar detail – but Jess had not mentioned that the windbreakers were De Sel windbreakers. "That's... odd." He starts walking again, pushing his bike onto a blacktop path. They are on campus, and with each step into the path, the noise from the street grows more distant. "So, guys from a water desalination company are beating up a professor in his backyard. Did David ever work with De Sel?"

"I doubt it. David's lab works entirely with solar. No water research. And nothing with desalination; that's a whole different skill set." She shrugs her shoulders, though the nonchalance of her gesture is at odds with the way her eyes are wide and worried. Their blacktop path has come to a paved circle, and here Jess stops, pointing to Chevron Hall, just up the hill. "Anyway, thanks for walking me here. It was nice of you."

He realizes she is expecting him to leave now. "I've been planning to come in with you."

"Really? But you can't. It's a clearance-only building."

"I have clearance."

"You do? You're a student here?"

"Not now, but I was." This is true. When he was a student at UC, he had been in and out of this building all the time. "And I've kept my clearance current." This is a lie. Two weeks ago, he copied the clearance code from Jess' Keeper. "Here, just let me lock my bike and I'll join you." He jogs to the crowded bike rack and asks his Keeper to activate the locks to his bike and his satchel. There must be 200 scooters and bikes at this rack alone. The Agro movement is big on biking; everyone Matteo knows uses a foldable electric bike to get around.

Jess calls to him from the Hall's entrance door. "Actually, I keep forgetting I have no Keeper. You'll have to be the one to let us in."

She stands self-consciously as he flashes his wrist across the door scan and holds the door open for her. They take a few steps into the dim hallway; their steps in sync as they walk down the long corridor. "In case you're wondering," Jess turns toward him, "I'm not afraid."

"Why the hell not?" He peers at her lanky arms swinging beside her hips. "I'm afraid."

"You are? Why? None of this impacts you."

"It doesn't feel good when life doesn't make sense."

"No." She rushes to keep his pace. "It doesn't."

He remembers just in time to slow down. Even though he has circled this laboratory building several times in the last three weeks and knows exactly where they are headed, he should not lead her to her lab.

Approaching her door, they see there is a folded piece of paper taped to its window. "That's odd," Jess says. "I can't remember the last time Xu wrote me a paper note." The sheet has her name scrawled on top and as she unfolds the paper, she remembers Matteo and adjusts the note so he can read it too.

> Jess, what's up with your Keeper? Nothing I send is going through. Anyway, Professor Sara Claredge came up from Stanford this morning to go over your desalination paper together. She's in David's office waiting for you. Since when are you researching water?

Xu

JESS

Her chest hurts, and she realizes it is because she is holding her breath. Exhaling, the hallway air rushes her nose, with its punch of pine-scented ammonia. The usual smell. So regular. *How can so much be regular when so much is wrong?* She tries to read the note again to make sure she is not misunderstanding; the sheet jiggles in her shaking hands.

"I thought you said you don't work on water?" The guy says it, Matteo.

She starts to fold the note. "I don't."

Usually when she is confused she knows it is because she misunderstood something, and that with clarification, the underlying order will return. But this day does not have order. She glances at her lab door, the floor, and the hallway to the stairwell. So many questions bounce against the walls of her brain that she cannot catch even one. All she can do is walk toward David's office.

"Wait, wait, wait," the Matteo guy jogs the few steps to catch her, grabbing at her arm. "Where are you going?"

"To talk with Sara Claredge."

"That's *so* not a good idea."

She looks at his hand, still holding her arm tight.

He lets go. "Listen, I think we should make a plan before you rush off."

We? A plan? This guy is sounding like they're friends or something. "Talking to Sara Claredge *is* my plan," she says.

"Okay, but do you know her? Trust her?"

"Um..." The answer to both of these questions is No, so she finds a different response. "Sara is a scientist. At Stanford. And..." Jess pauses, trying to avoid how carefully Matteo is watching her. "I've met her once. She runs an institute that brings renewable energy initiatives to developing countries. That sounds good, right?" Her voice echoes inside her ear like she is talking into a glass. "She's a friend of David's, so ... she might know how to help him."

"You're going to tell her about this morning?" He sounds surprised.

"Yes." She wants the word to sound confident; it does not.

"Did you know about this appointment before now?"

"No."

"And she's talking to you about desalination – like De Sel desalination?"

"Yes. I mean, I guess."

"That's a big coincidence, isn't it?"

It is. She looks at the bulletin boards around her in the hallway; she does not want to acknowledge that this guy has a point.

"You shouldn't meet with her."

Two students walk by, and their presence makes her aware of how closely Matteo and she are standing, how intimate their conversation must appear. "Well, I am."

"Then I'll go with you."

Who is this guy? "No." And as soon as she says the word, stinging and short, she realizes how badly she wants him to come. "I can handle this myself." Then, fast, before she can change her mind, she makes herself turn and stride down the long hallway.

She hears him shout, "If you're not back in ten, I'm coming after you."

She doesn't let herself turn around. The trip from her first-floor lab to David's fourth floor office is one she has taken dozens of times before. At the end of the hallway, there is a stairwell door, and when she yanks it open, she sees a big brown stain from a coffee splatter on the wall and a pinkish gum blob set deep into the first stair tread. The stairwell's air is gag-worthy – like sour milk – but right now, Jess likes it. The space is just the same as always. She wants everything to be that way.

She holds tight to the bannister as she trudges up the stairs. With Officer Relly, she had not wanted to acknowledge any pain, but now, she admits to herself that her head kills. To keep her pace steady, she has to think about her movements deliberately: *Walk straight.* Her thoughts keep drifting upward like balloons with strings she must grab before they float away. She tries to come up with a list of people to contact regarding David but she cannot think of anyone in his life that she knows. She will not call 911 again. That was a disaster. Her footsteps trudge up the stairs, echoing in the emptiness of the stairwell.

She could tell the other PhD students in David's research group that their boss is in danger. However, in the four months since she started at the lab, she has not exactly become friends with any of them. Even Xu, her office mate, does not like to socialize. He works 70 hours a week, and when he wants conversation, which is not often, he will chat with his Keeper, check social media or take holographic calls with faraway family members. Once, Jess suggested the group meet for happy hour at a local karaoke bar. Everyone messaged they would come, but in the end, it was just Jess alone at the bar, with a metallic-haired Traditionalist guy chatting out loud with his Keeper.

If she were to tell her group what happened this morning, they would probably believe her and share her concern. Yet, they would have no better idea what to *do*. Jess wants someone who can make the right calls, rally an investigation, and spearhead a search. She pulls open the stairwell door to the second floor.

There is this Matteo Wu. He is very eager to help her.

"Look up Matteo Wu—" she starts to silentspeak, and then remembers Caerys isn't activated. She thinks about the scraps of information she has on this man. His last name is Chinese, but his skin's too pale and hair too wavy – plus Matteo's not exactly a Mandarin name. Whatever his ancestry, he probably grew up here; his tonality is pure Californian: slow and low and nap-like. He has clearance to this building and works at the Temescal Farm, so he must have trained as a scientist. The huge artichoke tattoo jibes with biology or botany. No way would a physicist wear an artichoke on his arm.

None of this information explains why he is so eager to help her. She might assume he was hitting on her, but that explanation does not fit either. He is married. She checked again, and his silver band is definitely a wedding ring. Married men hit on women all the time, but Matteo doesn't seem that type; his approach isn't lecherous, only protective. She would say that he is simply a good guy, but that is not a concept she believes in.

"Never trust generosity; everyone has a motive." That was what her dad used to say to her when he took her out for pizza on Sunday nights. Even as a seven year-old, she knew her father's life lectures were motivated by a desire to disparage her stepfather, Zeke. "It's a nice bike," her dad would say, "but why did Zeke give it to you? Don't say because 'he's a nice guy.' Please, Jessie, don't be that foolish."

Zeke *was* a nice guy, nicer than her father, though Jess never said that. She felt awful even thinking it. Instead, she tried to understand her father's perspective. Her dad was right that Zeke gave her things because he wanted her to like him. And yes, generally, people gave you things when they wanted something in return. "I'll invite you to my birthday party if you invite me to yours." "I'll pick you on my team today if you pick me on your team tomorrow." Tit for tat, that was the way the world worked.

When Jess was fifteen, there was a morning that Zeke woke her to see if she would like to go for coffee. This was an unusually structured activity for them, and Jess felt awkward sitting across from Zeke at the small café table. His face was drawn as he stared into his mug twirling its contents with a slender wooden stick. Finally, after an especially long lull in the conversation, he said, "I'm sorry, Jess, but I am not able to stay married to your mother."

There was no surprise, only panic. "Will we still see each other?" was the question that blurted out. And when Zeke pursed his lips before answering: "We can try," she knew he was gone forever.

The next morning, she was jolted from sleep by the sound of a crash. Rushing to the kitchen, she found her mother sunk to her knees on the floor, a broken coffee cup split in shards around her, the milky-tan contents splattered on her nightgown. She was crying, a body-shaking weeping that was unsettling for its lack of sound. "I wasn't good enough, that's why he left. It's my fault. No one wants me." Jess had crouched down beside her mother and put her arms around her like a child. "Mommy," she said, using a name she had not called her mother in years, "I want you. I love you, and don't worry, I'll take care of you." It was a promise she meant in the moment – and then had to keep.

Her mother was not an easy woman to care for. She cried a lot; she complained. "Why does everything bad happen to me?" Jess tried to be sympathetic; a lot of bad stuff *had* happened to her mom, and she was a delicate sort. When years earlier, Alice had lost her job as a high school English teacher, she hadn't been able to find steady, well-paying work. She worked customer support and retail jobs but never kept her positions long. Her bosses were mean; she never got enough hours; her co-workers stabbed her in the back. The constant within all her mom's various situations was that they never had enough money. They lived in a dreary neighborhood, and when the child support payments were late – which they often were – Jess and her mom would go without heat and eat Cheerios for dinner. Jess tried to do what she could; she babysat after school to earn extra money and straightened their easily cluttered space. Yet, sometimes as Jess washed her mother's piled-up dishes or picked her scattered clothes off the floor, she seethed with frustration. Her mother never worried over her, and she was the daughter after all.

When Jess left for college, then graduate school, her mother called her multiple times a day. Jess considered not taking the constant calls, but she could not ignore her mother. Without Jess, her mom would be alone, and the thought of her needy mother sitting solitary and sad made Jess' heart weigh more. Besides, Jess wanted to prove her father wrong: "See, Dad, I can give without getting. You were wrong about Zeke and the way life works."

Now, as she enters the second floor, Jess considers: If she found it hard to care for her own mother, how could this Matteo person be effortlessly caring? He couldn't be.

At David's office, the window in his door has a blind pulled down mid-way. Jess bends to peer underneath it. What she wants is to see David, quietly sitting at his desk, his array of holographic monitors spread out in the air around him like usual. Instead, there's a stocky, curly-haired woman carrying a large batik purse. Sara Claredge. She's an attractive woman, probably in her fifties, with large breasts, a mop of brown ringlet curls, and black pumps.

Without the cluster of hovering holographic screens, David's office is austere. The large, square desk is bare save for one neat pile of papers. A few black office chairs sit on the other side of his desk, an empty white board on the wall. The blinds to his windows are closed. No posters or photographs line the wall, just dim, dingy whiteness.

Jess is about to open the door, but stops. Sara is walking tightly around the perimeter of David's desk, running her hands under its top. *Why is she doing that?* Sara pulls the center desk drawer wide open. She scoops out the contents – several pens, laser pointers and a pill bottle and plunks them down on the desk. Opening the pill bottle, she tips the bottle and spills a few capsules onto the desktop.

Jess swings the door open. "Sara?"

The mass of curls startles, and several capsules roll to the floor. "Goodness, you scared me."

Jess expects this woman to be abashed at being caught red-handed, but instead, her face opens wide and inviting.

Sara walks straight to Jess, her right hand outstretched. "Oh, Jessila, I'm so glad we're finally seeing each other."

Jess does not take Sara's hand, but motions toward the pill-scattered desktop; "Why are you sneaking through David's desk?"

Sara laughs, her ease almost mocking Jess' hard indignation. "I thought you'd guess." She walks toward the messy desktop. "I'm looking for the desalination patent application."

There is a flash of confusion, then acceptance. *Wow, this situation really is about desalination.*

Sara beams at her from across the desk; "Jessila, I'd love it if you would tell me where it is."

Here would be the moment to confess to Sara Claredge that she has no idea what Sara is talking about – that she is scared, that David has been hurt by De Sel thugs, and that she needs someone to help her. But Sara's too sweet smile, the sneaking through David's desk, the cloying kindness – she is a cat ready to pounce. Matteo is right: There is no way she should tell this woman about David.

Jess lifts her head and composes her voice: "You're looking for the patent application?"

"Yes," Sara smiles as though Jess' question pleases her. "We're close enough to Friday that I have to have the paperwork. David said I would have it weeks ago, but you know the absentminded professor..." She glances at the content strewn across David's desk. "So, you see, I have no choice. The investors are getting antsy."

There is too much information to assimilate. The questions pulse like flashing neon signs: Friday? Paperwork? Investors? It takes effort to keep the confusion from her face. "That's too bad about... the investors."

Sara leans against the edge of the desk, facing Jess with warmth. "Yes, David has insisted on such absurd levels of secrecy. Our investors have so many questions about raw materials and price points and manufacturing timetables, and all I can do is deflect and assure them that after Friday, everything will be clear." Her head retracts with a chuckle, "With how little they know, it's a miracle we have any investors at all, much less twenty-two."

Jess knows she has to give some response, but no words come. Her brain is too busy cranking through the pieces of information.

Sara brushes a curl from her forehead. "Then again, since they know they're getting in on the ground floor of a miracle, they tend not to complain."

A miracle? Jess nods: "Right."

"You know, every time I do the demonstration, I feel like Marlin or Houdini or... *God*." She laughs. "In goes the salt water to the black box, and before I can even say, 'Abracadabra,' out comes the fresh water."

Sara's words have such buoyancy that when she stops talking, the silence is jarring. Jess knows she has to say something. "That's... quite a box," she says, trying to say it like she means it. Of course, there is no way such a box could exist. Jess is no expert in desalination, but she knows that salt molecules don't just "abracadabra" themselves off of water molecules. The desalination process involves energy and force and time. De Sel's reverse osmosis desalination plants take up acres and acres of land.

"You know," Sara continues, "we've only held three investor meetings, and each time I extend invitations to the groups of powerful people who come, I ask them to bring their own specimens of ocean water. It's hysterical to watch these big important people line up with their containers of ocean water, ready to pour them into the box. You can tell that each one thinks, I'll be the person to figure out how this magic works. They never do. Instead, they pull out their checkbooks. And write us big, big checks."

Jess nods, trying to conjure an image of what Sara is describing. She imagines a conference room with well-dressed forty-year olds, Silicon Valley types, with their Thickrings and tailored clothing, standing in line holding water bottles and thermoses. "Um, don't the investors have suspicions? I mean, if fresh water immediately comes from the box, don't they suspect the box was filled with fresh water to begin with?"

"Oh, Jessila, their skepticism is off the charts! The investors pick the box from the desk and try to see if it's hooked up to some power source or some plumbing – which, of course, it's not. Then, they weigh the box, trying to see if there's any way the fresh water could be secretly stored within it. David allows the investors to hold and examine the box as much as they want, but don't worry; he never lets them take the box apart. As far as anyone can see, it's a smooth black box the size of a small cooler with a funnel at the top and a spigot on the side. Everyone arrives incredulous, but by the time they leave, they're positively eager to join us in saving the world."

Jess' eyebrows bolt upward, expecting Sara Claredge to laugh at her outlandish claim. Sara does not laugh. A full second passes. "You think you can save the world with the... black box?"

"Of course. Don't you? Now that we have the funds to build larger prototypes, we'll have the ability to usher in a new era of desalination plants. Fresh water will be cheap again; agriculture will rebound; food prices will plummet. No more famine. When I think of the good we can bring to Africa and India, I get downright giddy. Sure, it will take time – maybe a decade – but today, hundreds of millions of people are starving because of the high price of desalinated water, and we'll be able to save them. So many starving people will live because of us! De Sel won't know what hit them."

"De Sel?" Jess' face juts forward.

Sara's eyes squint, confused. "Of course, De Sel."

"You think they're bad?"

"Oh, Jessila." Sara's face sours as though she has bitten into a lemon. "That's not funny! How could you say that?" She evaluates Jess for several seconds, her face growing stony. Abruptly, she walks to pick up her large batik-printed purse from David's desk. The purse has a shoulder strap, but rather than hang the bag from her shoulder, she holds the boldly printed blue and maroon cloth purse close to her chest, like a teddy bear.

Sara is surely odd, Jess realizes, but rather than puzzle over this woman's sudden mood shift, Jess lines up the various pieces of information she has collected, like specimen jars to be put in a row. David invented a solution that people believe desalinates water instantly. Check. David and Sara Claredge have gathered investment money to build models of desalination plants. Check. And De Sel, who is the leader in global desalination, doesn't want David and Sara to create a company that will compete with their company. This must be why David was beat up this morning by De Sel thugs. Check? Yes, she thinks so. This new information is unexpected – when did David find the time or develop the expertise to create a desalination solution? – but Jess is relieved to at least reconstruct the morning's chaos with a backstory that makes it understandable.

"We should talk about Friday;" Sara Claredge's voice has lost all its bubbly warmth.

"Okay." Jess has no idea what is happening on Friday, but she does not care about keeping up her charade anymore. She thinks she will tell Sara Claredge about David and the De Sel thugs and Officer Relly. "I want to tell you something too. About David. This morning, something happened—"

"Jessila, I have to be able to trust you. Do you understand what that means? No deception."

"Right, and that's why I want to tell you that this morning—"

"And others have to trust you too, which means you can't"– Sara wags a finger up and down at Jess' body – "dress like that on Friday."

"*What?*" Jess looks down at her running shorts and t-shirt. Seeing the blood smeared across her t-shirt, she is surprised Sara has not asked about it. "These are my running clothes."

"And you absolutely have to be on time. The 880 is a beast at that time of day, same with the 101. I would suggest you spend the night in Palo Alto, but no matter, I expect you at Stanford no later than 8:15 a.m. Even though you won't go on stage until ten, the Governor is expected by nine, and there will be pictures and some press questions before you sign the papers. You see; you absolutely can't be late."

"I'm not going to Stanford on Friday."

"Don't be ridiculous. Of course you are. That's when you're signing the papers."

"Signing what papers?"

"Jessila, stop playing dumb. The patent application, of course." Sara holds her purse to her chest more tightly. "Wait, do you think I don't know?" Sara starts to chuckle, and Jess wonders if the woman is having some sort of a breakdown. "Oh, Jessila, I *know*. David *told* me."

Jess blinks, trying to comprehend what Sara is saying.

"David told me that you that made the desalination solution. Three weeks ago, I confronted him, and he finally explained that it was you who invented the solution."

Jess opens her mouth, and the question "*Me?*" wants to leap outward. It does not leap; she closes her mouth.

"David was very worried about keeping you safe and kept saying he wanted to protect you, but of course your name absolutely has to be on the patent application. There's no way around it. You are in this endeavor, and that's that." She takes a step closer. "Besides, you care about the world, right?"

She lets too long a pause pass. "Right," she says hurriedly.

"And you would never make a deal with De Sel, would you?"

"With De Sel? No, definitely not. I would never make a deal with De Sel."

"Good," Sara twitches a smile. "Then get me the patent application, and I'll be on my way."

"Right." Jess has no idea what to do. She considers again whether she should explain the morning – about David and Brooklyn Relly.

"Don't just stand there, get it for me."

Jess looks around the room. "Actually, I'm not sure I can."

"Yes, I know you're not saving it to your Keeper. David explained that you had decided to keep all the information about the desalination solution on a single dot drive. That's fine, just get me the damn dot drive so I can make a copy lickety-split."

At the words "dot drive," Jess' eyes involuntarily widen. Throughout this conversation, Jess has worked hard to disguise her befuddlement. Now, she finds herself with a trickier camouflage. She does know where the dot drive is – but she can't let Sara see that.

"I've never seen the engineering diagrams or chemical compound equations either," Sara continues, "so if you want to include those, great." Her hands open her purse, as though she's readying to make room. "But it's the patent application that I – I mean, my investors – need most."

Jess is scared to move, worried her eyes will jolt to the desktop. "I'm afraid David never told me where he put his dot drive." She is not a good liar. The truth is that David hides a single dot drive in an unusual item: a toothbrush that he sometimes stores in his desk drawer. The toothbrush could be one of the items Sara scattered across the desktop when she emptied David's center drawer. *Don't look; don't look.* Jess keeps her eyes on the dust of her running shoes, her leg jiggling.

Jess only knows about the toothbrush by accident. She made the strange discovery during a day of strange discoveries. Jess had been working late at her lab when David had messaged her: "Come meet me at the Campanile." This request was unexpected. David liked to avoid the two of them being seen on campus together, and even during those nights when she slept at David's house, he asked that they walk to school separately the next day. "We don't want people to talk."

The Campanile – a tall, white stone clock tower – was also a peculiar meeting spot, if only because lots of people congregated there. Surrounding the clock tower was a small, manicured turf yard, and though the smog now made it impossible to see Bay Area vistas from this spot, it was still an area where people hung out. The very curiosity of David's request made Jess eager to meet him.

Once she reached the Campanile's courtyard, the day's daylight was almost gone and the added smog and incoming fog made it difficult to see more than a few feet ahead. She jumped when David came from behind her, grabbing her waist and kissing her neck. He showed her a bottle of champagne and took her hand. "Come on, I have a surprise for you." He led her into the Campanile building itself, then took her down a hallway and opened a door that looked like it led to a basement. "Where are you taking me?" she asked laughing, but his only response was a curious smile. As they went down two flights of stairs, the air became thicker and hot.

"Here," he said, once they had reached an enormous metal door with a keypad and fingerprint-recognition lock. "Put your thumb to this keypad and keep it there," David had said. "Now enter these letters: W-I-N-N-E-R." It was an old-fashioned keypad with four rows of three numbered buttons and several letters corresponding to each numeral. Jess had to look closely to get the code entered correctly, but once she hit the "R," the door popped open.

"You've just gained access to the Berkeley steam tunnels," David announced with pride. "It's a safe space that almost no one else can enter, but now you can." Jess couldn't imagine why David would think she would want to come here; the space was nothing but a series of basement corridors, empty except for plumbing pipes, electrical wires, and thick, steamy air that smelled like mildew. Once when she and Xu were walking across campus, he had explained that, years ago, the tunnels had acted as underground corridors for the steam pipes that traveled under the campus. "You see," David's eyes glinted, "we can always meet up here. It's our secret space." She failed to see the appeal, but she let him pop the cork off the champagne and lead her through the subterranean hallways, feigning interest in David's accounts of where they were on campus as they passed the champagne bottle between them. Happily buzzed, she agreed when David suggested that they should leave and return to his house.

Since Jess wanted to retrieve a few things from her office, she told David that she would meet him back at his place. She went back to the Life Sciences Building, checked the results of a running experiment and locked her lab up. On her way out, she walked past David's office and peering through his door's window, noticed that his briefcase was sitting atop his desk. Thinking that David might need the briefcase at home, Jess decided she would retrieve it. David's door had a letter-combination lock on it, but given that W-I-N-N-E-R had unlocked the tunnels, she wondered if it would unlock his door too. It did. She opened the door and was readying to latch up his briefcase when she saw that the contents of his briefcase included only a few pens, a stack of paper and a toothbrush. *A toothbrush?* David certainly had the means to pay for two toothbrushes; she could not understand why he would take one back and forth in his briefcase.

If the day itself hadn't been so strange, she surely would have tossed off this trivial concern. Yet, all evening, her brain had itched with the strangeness of the trip to the tunnels. There was no way her thumbprint could have opened the tunnel doors unless David had taken a lot of effort to make that happen. Only a few days earlier had been when she discovered that David was tracking her with the Spy App. *Not normal.*

She took the toothbrush out of the case and examined it. A faint crack encircled the bristles. Tugging on the prickly fibers, the brush popped off, revealing a small shallow compartment underneath. In it was a single dot drive, no bigger than a baby aspirin.

That David took spy-level precautions for storing his academic research could have been quirky. Or deeply paranoid. Regardless, she put the toothbrush back in the briefcase, left it on David's desk and messaged him that the champagne had given her a headache and she wouldn't come to his house after all. She had been relieved to bow out. In fact, it was then that she began to consider whether she should permanently bow out of her relationship with David altogether.

Sara's anxious voice interrupts her thoughts. "Jessila, I'm waiting."

Jess cannot contain her eyes any longer. Fast, they flit toward David's open middle drawer. There, it is: the toothbrush.

Sara follows Jess' eyes; "In his desk? I saw you look at his desk. The dot drive is in his desk?"

"No. I mean, I don't know."

"Yes, you do. You know. You've been lying. Just like David lied." Sara walks to the desk drawer and begins looking inside again, moving papers and pens and feeling along the desk insides. "Did he tape the dot drive to his desk? Or to some papers? Is it one of these pills?" Her voice and actions are growing more agitated. "Jessila, please, don't play with me. I will absolutely do what I have to for this desalination solution. This is a battle of right and wrong." Sara grabs her hand. "People are playing dirty. I can keep you safe. But only if you give me the dot drive. Do you understand? If you don't give me the dot drive, I... will play dirty too."

The threat hangs in the air, and though the words themselves are frightening, Jess is more scared by how quickly Sara's face has turned steely. Her tight jaw clenches, wiping aside any trace of kindness.

Jess pulls her hand from Sara's grip. "Don't threaten me."

"I am *warning* you, there's a difference."

"You should leave."

"Leave? No. I will not let you risk the world's water safety." Sara's hands rummage in her enormous batik purse.

Risk the world's water safety? This woman is beyond dramatic. "Our conversation is over," Jess says as she walks toward David's office door. If she holds the door wide open, surely Sara will have no choice but to leave.

"Jessila, I hate to do this, I absolutely do, but you have to give me the dot drive."

Jess sighs, turning to explain to Sara one last time: "I don't want to talk—" She stops short.

A tranquilizer gun is pointed at her chest.

MATTEO

Matteo is sitting on the floor outside Jess' lab, back against the wall, nodding to the students who eye him as they walk past. He whispers to his Keeper to try Beck again: "Dude, your silence is killing me here." This is Matteo's third attempt to reach his boss in as many minutes. Something is not right. Beck never goes silent for this long. His job is to liaison between his observationalists and the screen technicians after all. He is the one who gives the go-ahead for when to move forward and when to hang back, and he cannot do that job if he disappears for stretches. Matteo checks his wrist Keeper screen again. Nothing.

He stands up. Standing is better. Over the last eighteen months, many of Matteo's cases have involved tracking suspected criminals, and if this experience has taught him anything, it is that criminal life is pathetic. Thugs are sad and messy sorts who are motivated by infantile needs, like toddlers in a sandbox. *"I want that." "Gimme." "No, it's mine."*

What is happening today doesn't follow that criminal pattern. Today's efforts are sophisticated and the gain unclear. He keeps trying to fathom how Relly, David and De Sel could possibly be connected. The pieces of a jigsaw puzzle are scattered before him with no box top to suggest the picture they should become.

He whispers to his Keeper to contact Quinn, his favorite Screener at Beck Industries. If Beck won't talk with him, Quinn will. He's always available for a quick back-and-forth.

Then again, Quinn is not picking up either.

Matteo starts to pace the hallway, kicking the baseboard to the wall each time he turns, back and forth. He asks his Keeper to pull up the video feed that goes into the Beck Industries' headquarters. Usually, Matteo's video calls are Keeper-to-Keeper, but maybe if his Keeper can access the company's video feed, Matteo can grab a visual on the screen room at Beck Industries. Matteo waits and realizes he is anxious now in a way he rarely is. He reminds himself: This is only a job, and Jess: only an observational subject.

She is different up close than he had expected. He is used to Rachel with her long dreadlocks and grand pronouncements, and Jess has none of that boldness. She is plain clothed with no tattoos, scrubby-faced and pony-tailed. Yet, now that Matteo has seen her up close, he realizes that her brand of quietness isn't as boring as he had assumed. Her mind is churning, that is clear, and he finds himself curious about why she strives to be so tough. A small freckle sits at the edge of her upper lip, which makes her mouth interesting to watch – the sort of detail not included in the case file.

His Keeper silentspeaks into his head. "The connection to Beck Industries' video feed is ready." A holographic screen pops from Matteo's wrist Keeper and hovers in the air at his eye level. There is the Beck surveillance room with its many screens that show different video feeds, flipping back and forth to different angles. No audio accompanies this streaming clip, but Matteo can tell that the three men in the room are barking orders— *wait, who are those men?* Matteo brings his face closer to the weightless holographic screen, scrutinizing what he sees. That's not Quinn. Beck? No Beck. No Jihoo or Ahmed or Dex. All the regular Beck screeners are gone, and the men sitting in the chairs in front of the screens are men Matteo's never seen before. A black guy with dreadlocks. An Asian woman with blue hair. A big man with a shaved head who walks back and forth; he has enormous muscles and a thick neck. He is shouting and holding something out in front of him. Once he walks past the screens into the room's open space, Matteo has a better visual. It is a bright blue fabric that he's holding. *Crap*—it is a De Sel windbreaker.

The fear spreads through Matteo's body like ice cracking. He runs to the stair well. He never should have let Jess go upstairs without him. Taking three stairs at a time, he can hear Rachel's voice in his head: "Everything doesn't always turn out fine. Life doesn't work that way." No, it does not. He doesn't want to re-learn that lesson.

He yanks the second-stairwell door and runs down the hallway. He knows exactly where David's office is located on the floor. He's running past plate glass windows when something catches his eye.

Below the windows is a courtyard. Students are congregating there; some are standing, some are sitting on benches; everyone is directing their attention toward the charcoal-colored clouds waiting for the first raindrops. Yet, these are not the people Matteo cares about. No, Matteo's eyes are fixed on two men striding across the courtyard, pointing at the second floor windows above them. The men are in security uniforms with tranq-holsters on their hips, and the shorter guy is shouting to someone who stands at the entryway to the courtyard. Matteo puts his head to the window's glass to get a better angle: A woman is in the doorway dressed in a yellow rain slicker and wearing those awful metallic Thickrings. Even before he sees the glint of gemstones in her cheekbones, he knows it is Brooklyn Relly.

Matteo steps back from the window. A millisecond passes in which he tries to construct understanding, but no, there is not time. He runs. His flip-flops thump against the linoleum, his heart clanks against his chest. He is at David's office door in two seconds. He does not knock; he swings the door wide open.

As the door speeds the office into view, he sees Jess' face first. Her eyes bulge; her lips open in alarm. He follows her gaze. *A tranq gun.* A blur of curls, a batik purse, a woman's shocked expression. This quick comprehension of the scene occurs as he hurls himself into it. He tries to chop at the curly-haired woman's arm but only bounds into her instead. Her body careens backward, and he lands on top of her, his face on her abdomen.

She screams; her arms flail. The gun falls to the ground. "Stop it; let me go. I wasn't going to hurt her."

Pushing her down, he shoves his hand over her mouth. "Shut up." It's strange to hear these words come from his mouth, stranger that he's pinning this middle-aged woman to the ground. "Get the gun!" he shouts to Jess.

"I have it," Jess gasps. "What do I *do* with it?" He glances behind him; she is holding the gun like a snotty tissue.

"Hold it like you'd use it," he snaps. "Put your finger on the trigger guard, both hands on the…" he cannot remember what that part of the gun is called, "that handle thing."

"Got it;" her voice shakes.

The woman's mouth moves underneath his hand, warbling sounds coming from her. "M"s and "T"s are in the word she keeps repeating; damned if it doesn't sound like she is saying his name. "I told you to shut up," he says with more aggression than he has heard in his voice in a long time. He looks behind at Jess. "We have to leave this building fast. Relly is here."

"Relly?" She sounds like the word punched her.

The curly-haired woman squirms again under his hand, making the same muffled sound. He pushes his hand harder onto her mouth and shouts behind him, "Are you holding the gun now?"

"Yes."

He leaps up, and immediately the curly-haired woman begins to wail, "Jessila, don't let anyone get the dot drive. That's what's most important. So many people are depending on—"

"Shut up!" He clams his hand back down over her mouth, though part of him wants to ask her what she means. *What dot drive? Who's depending on Jess?* To Jess, he barks: "Here, you leave first and I'll leave after you."

Jess' eyes are wide like headlights. Yet, instead of moving toward the door, she grabs at the bottle of pills sitting on David's desk and throws it at Sara. Dozens of small discs scatter. "Find the dot drive in there," she says, then, fast, snatches a toothbrush from the desk in one swift movement and bolts out the door.

Matteo follows, wondering why the hell this woman is taking a toothbrush with her.

JESS

Matteo is moving fast, already three steps ahead of her. Once he hits the fifth stair from the bottom, he jumps to the landing, races to the next flight, and begins to fly down those too.

Jess wants to keep up, but moving her legs off the stairs is like pulling taffy. *How can this be happening?* She is a normal person with normal days. A gun was pointed at her? A man tried to tackle her? A police officer lied to her? This day can't be her day. The stairwell air feels hot on her face. Goosebumps prickle down her arms. Like a light is being dimmed, dark goes the corridor. She grabs the railing tight. She is sinking. *Oh, no.*

"Jess!" Matteo is rushing back up the stairs. Even with her weakened thoughts, she is aware this man is saying her name with strange familiarity. "Here, give me the gun. You shouldn't be holding it if you're faint." His arm comes around her side. "All we need to do is make it downstairs."

His voice is full of concern. This tone is one she uses when she wants to soothe her mother, a tone her mother never uses with her. *Why is this guy talking to her like this?* He does not know her. "I'm fine," she mutters but cannot say more since her effort is focused on moving down the stairs as fast as she can.

Matteo walks beside her, talking about how this stairwell does not have cameras and he is hoping the basement won't have any too. She wonders why he cares so much about cameras; she cannot waste her energy to ask.

At the bottom floor, she leans against the stairwell wall while Matteo peers out of a slender, rectangular window in the metal door that opens to the hallway. "I'm going to open the door," she hears him say, "to see if anyone's in the hall."

She hears the click of the door and the creak as it creases back on its hinge. She relishes this momentary stillness. Her mind slips to a thought, almost dream-like, of standing under the persimmon tree talking to Caerys. *Oh, Caerys, help me.*

Her eyes pop open. Matteo is facing her, his nose only inches from hers. He is talking fast. "No one's in the hall, but cameras are hung throughout the hallway. They're going to see us leaving, which sucks. I've told my Keeper to unlock my bike and remote-guide it to the exit on the northeast side of the building. We're going to have to run a few hallways to get there, but if you put your arm around me, I'll help you move fast."

She shakes her head. "It's okay, I can walk on my own."

He shakes his head too. "No, you don't understand, we'll have to run."

She wills herself to push off the wall. "I'll run."

When they enter the hallway, the low-energy lightbulbs cast a green-y glow over the hallway. The space is empty; their feet on the floors clap, echoing against the low ceilings. She tries to move fast, but her shoes feel as though they are made of lead. Suddenly, Matteo stops and turns quickly, his face panicked. She hears what he is hearing: footsteps. Fast footsteps. The sound is distant, from around the long corridor's corner. Several people are coming.

Don't panic. The footsteps could be from students or professors or lab techs. Lots of people come down this basement hall. But it becomes clear that the footsteps are running. There are voices too. A woman and a man. She cannot hear what they are saying, but the words are loud and urgent.

Matteo runs back to her and grabs her wrist. "Come on." His fingers grip tight, yanking her forward. At the end of this long hall is the exit, and though her vision is blurry, she reads the sign above the door: "Emergency Exit Only. Alarm Bell Will Sound."

Her feet cannot move fast enough. Midway to the door, the other voices turn the corner too. There is a horrible pause when she knows they have been seen. "It's them!" a woman shouts. "Stop them!"

Jess cranks her neck back to see her pursuers; she only makes out a blur of motion. Matteo pulls her wrist hard. "Faster!" She tries to leap through space, to make it to the door. It's close, so close.

Behind her, the woman bellows: "Shoot! Shoot *now*!"

Too many things happen at once. The shots clip – onetwothreefourfive. Matteo's body pushes hard against the door's lever. The alarm bell blares. The smell of rain. The pounding water. Matteo is yelling at her; she can't understand him through the downpour. It's only as she mounts the bike that she notices: the raindrops running down her arm are red.

MATTEO

Rainwater smacks his face, collecting on his eyebrows, dripping down his nose. His shorts and t-shirt are soaked through, and the cling of his clothes makes it hard to grind his feet round and round and round. He is standing as he pedals, with Jess sitting on the bike's seat, her arms wrapped tight around his waist. Where her left shoulder leans against his hips, he can feel the warmth of her blood seeping into his shorts.

"How bad is it?" he shouts back to her now, his voice all but lost in the rain's pounding. He hears words – "graze," "bleeding," "okay" – but the rain makes it impossible to hear how they fit together. She's saying a lot, and he's glad for that. At least she's not losing consciousness.

Relly shot tranquilizer darts, Matteo's sure of it. He saw one of the big, orange casements with its needle tip land into the door, just as he pushed it open. "Hold tight," he yells back to Jess now. His heart is thumping. *Where should they go?* He passes big campus buildings: Tolman Hall, Wellman Hall. Now, they are nearing Memorial Pool. His eyes dart, trying to see through the torrents of rain. *Where is Relly?* He's expecting to see a line of police officers biking right at them, but no one is on the bike path for as far as he can see. Matteo considers: If they are being watched on surveillance footage – and they are – where can they go where they won't be caught?

The rain falls fast. Everywhere, water. The sky is near black, like a deep shadow has been cast over the world. *Nothing is right. How did he get into this mess?* No, don't think about that now.

Ahead, in front of Memorial Library, there is a crowd of one hundred people, maybe more. They're laughing, singing, holding their arms out to the rain; some twirl with their mouths open. "I'm going over there," he shouts, hoping Jess can hear him through the rain. A crowd is a good place to be. If Relly's plan is to shoot Jess with a tranquilizer dart, they will want to retrieve her unconscious body. A crowd would make that difficult. Surrounding themselves with people – witnesses – is their best protection; their only protection.

Directing his bike to the grassy field, he finds it hard to balance their heavy load on the wet grass. Though the rain started only ten minutes ago, the ground squishes under the bike tires. Around them, students are linking arms around shoulders, forming a long, swirling human chain. A few of them are attempting to sing "Singin' in the Rain." Matteo jerks his bike left, right, and then left again to sift among the prancing students. One person twirls around in circles, knocking against the bike's wheels. He tries to use the handlebars to steady the bike, but it is too late. They are falling.

He lands just to the side of Jess on the wet, muddy ground. Kicking the bike off his leg, he finds it a shock to see Jess beside him on the ground. She's drenched, of course, and her Flower Power t-shirt clings transparent atop her blue jog bra. The shirt is stained dark red, and her arm, even wet, has rusty brown drips cascading down it. Yet, the blood is not what surprises him. That she's Jess Prentiss, this woman he barely knows, is the shock. When her arms were wrapped around his waist, her body leaning hard against his back, she had become someone else in his mind. Jess is not that person.

He says something to fill the space. "You've lost a lot of blood."

"The rain makes it look worse than it is." She wipes her arm, and the deep scrape, which is the shape of a crayon, clears for a second before re-filling with blood. The casement must have taken the skin off as it grazed her arm.

"We should put some pressure on that." The cut probably won't need stitches but it should be bandaged; "Here." He sits on his knees and wrings out his t-shirt, then bites into its hem, creating a tear that allows him to rip off a long piece of fabric.

"Wait, what are you doing?" She shouts over the rain. "You don't have to do that; I can rip my own t-shirt!"

He holds out the rectangular patch. "It's done." He comes in close to her shoulder. With the rain, he finds it hard to lay the fabric flat, but with a second and third try, he loops the fabric around her shoulder. Around them, students are hollering and singing. *Man, he wishes they would shut up.*

"Why are you doing this?" Her voice is hard to hear amid the noise of the rain and revelers.

He pulls the knot tighter. "To slow the blood loss."

"No, I mean, why are you helping me?" Her chin lifts toward him, and even through the rain, he can tell she's examining his face. "Whatever's happening to me, it doesn't have to happen to you." Her lower lip juts out and water dribbles over it, stream-like.

If he had time to consider a response, maybe he would acknowledge that, actually, this is more than he bargained for. He never expected guns and cops and *fear*. Before he can respond, a shouting student falls into his back knocking him forward onto the wet ground. As he is wiping his muddy hands on his shorts, Jess stands. "I'm going to the Campanile," she says.

"What?" He pushes himself upright. "Wait, why would you do that?"

"It doesn't matter why." She walks toward the paved path.

"Wait – stop;" he rushes to pick up his bike and catch up with her. He wants to be close before saying the word "Campanile" again. Matteo knows their conversations are being watched, probably from a variety of cameras zooming tight into their faces. Though there's no way these surveillance captures can grab audio of their conversation, good screeners splice important conversational clips and run the video through software programs that read lips, usually offering several options for each line of dialogue, with corresponding confidence levels. Matteo has seen screeners run these programs countless times, and if they have a clear video shot, they can usually figure out what people are saying. He grabs at her good arm and brings his body close to block any video capture. "What's at the Campanile?"

She pulls her arm back, assessing whether to answer the question. "The tunnels," she says finally.

"The steam tunnels?"

She nods.

He knows about the steam tunnels. "The grates to those tunnels have been welded shut for years," he says through the rain, "and the doors require thumbprint recognition and passcodes to open them."

"I can open the doors," she says, the rainwater spitting from her mouth. "David took me down there a month ago, and my thumbprint opens the doors."

What a weird thing for David to do. *This case is so... strange.* He wipes the rain from his eyes. "You're sure it's your thumbprint that opens the door, not David's?"

She nods: "He told me it was the same entry code for all the grates, but I've never tested that."

"It's like he knew you were going to be chased."

"I know."

Matteo turns behind him to look at the Campanile sitting at the top of the hill. The rain makes it hard to see far ahead, but the clock tower stands white and tall through the grayness, maybe two hundred yards away. He wonders if there could be a closer entrance to the tunnels. Like subway systems, these underground corridors are ventilated by grates along sidewalks and fields. One night, years ago, Rachel and he spent hours trying to find a tunnel entrance to find a new place for sex, though they never were able to find a door they could open. Actually, the last place they tried was among redwood trees near the Faculty Club.

"I think we should bike to..."Matteo looks around, but Jess isn't beside him anymore. Fast, he scans the crowd. "Dammit—" He bolts ahead, pushing through the singing students. Grabbing her again by her good arm, he turns her around. "Why do you keep doing that?" he shouts.

"Stop following me!" she shouts back.

"I'm not following you!" He lets go of her arm in an attempt to make this protest less ridiculous.

"You need to let me go alone. I don't want you to be hurt because of me." Her lips are trembling.

He cannot think what to say. *Is there a reasonable explanation for why he would want to follow her?* He cannot think what it could be. "A call from Beck Industries," his Keeper's voice enters his head. Matteo's eyebrows pop at this internal news alert. He points to his head, the universal code for being Keeper-pinged. "I'll take it," he says out loud, and Jess' face widens with alarm.

He brings his Keeper to his mouth and whispers: "Beck? Is that you?"

A woman's voice responds: "Matteo, you don't read women well. Clearly, Jess wants you to leave her alone."

Matteo's head scans left, then right. Logically, he knows this woman is not nearby; still, his heart thuds as he scans the muddy field, the library stairs, the library windows. Out loud this time, he asks: "Who's this talking? Is this Relly?"

Jess grabs his arm. "Oh, god."

The woman's voice is in his head again. "Matteo, this is not the time for your questions; it's time for mine. Answer this: I'm prepared to deposit a million dollars into your bank account in the next five minutes; do you want that money?"

"A million dollars?"

Jess' lips fall open. He should have whispered, but the number is too large not to exclaim over it. Turning his body away from Jess, he speaks softly into his Keeper. "Who are you people?"

"Goodness, Matteo, we're not 'you people.' I'm a cop."

"Cops pay bribes?"

"Cops keep order. Order creates goodness. So, this deal is for everyone's good."

He cannot answer. Nothing is stacking right. Relly is not good; she shot at Jess; she lied to Jess. *That's not good.*

Relly keeps talking: "You'll be able to watch the money transfer right from your Keeper. I know you've wanted to pay off Hua Chen for months. Now, you can pay him tonight."

Oh, god. He has never told anyone about Hua Chen – not Rachel, not Tia, not Beck, and now this twisted cop knows. She must have hacked his Keeper. He wipes the rainwater from his face, trying to reflect on his options.

"We won't hurt her, Matteo. We'll be very nice to her, actually. She's about to become quite rich."

Jess moves closer to him, looking straight at his eyes. He cannot look back. A short shock of wind blows thick raindrops against his legs and back. Around him and Jess, the students still swirl and laugh. *Why can't they go away?*

"Just do what I ask;" Brooklyn Relly's voice is ingratiating in his head, "and the million is yours."

"I don't understand. What... what do you want me to do?" Even though he whispers and the rain is loud, Jess must know he is asking a question. Her body presses into his, like she is trying to overhear.

"Bring Jess Prentiss to me."

He blinks hard to get the water from his eyes, but somehow his sight only becomes blurrier. There is the blood on his shorts and his t-shirt cut short across his stomach. The students jostle around them. *This case was supposed to be boring.* He looks at Jess, and blinks again. This time his vision gets sharper. He sees the way she looks up at him, the rainwater catching her eyelashes, her eyes teary-blue. She is muttering something under her breath. He cannot hear what she says, and it does not matter.

He makes his response via silentspeak: "It's a deal. Meet us at the Campanile in five minutes."

JESS

When Jess was little, her mother made an enormous production of making wishes on birthday cake candles. Given that her mom was not one for doting, this annual tradition took on unusual significance. Jess would anticipate the experience and prepare her wish. The cake would be set before her, the appropriate number of candles dancing with flames. "You're ready? Really ready? Beca-a-use…" her mom's voice would become sing-songy, "if you miss any of the candles, your wish can't come true. Don't *blow* it." Her mother would always guffaw at this pun, but Jess wouldn't laugh. She would be concentrating too hard, mapping her breath's trajectory across the cake, filling her cheeks puffy-full, and silently focusing her energy on the wish. Here was her permission to take her secret hopes and ask whoever was on the receiving end – God, spirits, the ether in the air: *Please, please let me have what I can't bring myself to ask for.*

When she was a kid, she wished that her parents would reconcile. As she grew older, she wished that Zeke would consider her his real daughter. After the divorce, when she could have asked that her mom would find a good job or that somehow they would come into more money, she instead wished that Gracie, her friend at school, would tell her that she was her best friend.

Yesterday, Jess was sitting cross-legged on her bed in her studio apartment explaining the wishing tradition to holographic Dr. Monique who listened while fiddling with her reading glasses. After Jess finished the story, Dr. Monique put her glasses on again. "You always wish that someone wants to stay close to you. Do you think that you are looking for love or safety?" Jess had shrugged, finding the question simplistic. Sometimes she found it difficult to ignore that Dr. Monique was software, and her mind would flit with criticism of the program's design. When several seconds had passed without Jess' response, Dr. Monique said, "Perhaps you long most for safety. More than love. What do you think?" The question sounded like one a fortune-teller would ask, not a licensed psychologist.

"I don't see why it has to be one or the other," Jess responded; "I mean, who wouldn't want both?"

Dr. Monique's holographic image only smiled, deflecting the question. "It is always helpful to understand what you long for *most*," Dr. Monique said. "Do you most wish someone would say to you: 'I want to keep you safe'? Or do you wish to say: 'I will risk myself for love.'" The question seemed like a puzzle, but Jess didn't want to bother cracking it. "I guess," she shrugged, "safety is what I want most."

Now, in the streaming rain, while Jess watches Matteo silentspeak, she can tell that Brooklyn Relly is offering him a bribe. With all the force of her birthday wishes, a beseeching request forms on her lips: "Don't betray me." She says the sentence over and over, and though her brain is crammed with many thoughts and sensations – the rain, the throbbing in her arm, the tension lashing her stomach – she is aware of the irony that Jess just told Matteo to leave her alone and now she is wishing he will not. "Don't betray me, don't betray me."

His body's taut stance loosens; the call is over. "What'd they say?" she pounces on him.

He walks to the wet bike, picks it from the muddy ground. "We have to get to the Campanile." Even with the rain filling her ears, his voice is strange. "Get on the bike," he shouts.

She walks to the other side of the bike's frame. "Why'd you say 'one million dollars'?"

He does not look at her. "I'll tell you once you're on the bike." He hits his hand on the bike seat so hard his palm's imprint is momentarily left in the wetness: "Get on."

"Are you taking Relly's money?" she shouts through the rain.

"If you'd get on the damn bike—"

"Stop telling me what to do!" She's shaking with cold and anger: "Tell me what happened."

Matteo's jaw flexes, and in one abrupt movement, he jerks his body forward, grabbing the back of her head to bring his mouth to her ear. "They're watching us. Seeing every single thing we do." His breath is hot on her earlobe, coming in short, forceful bursts. "They can't hear us, but they can read lips. I have a plan, but we have to move now. Fast." He pulls his head back, sits upright and hits the bike seat again. "Get on the bike!"

She stares at the bike; she looks around her – up, down, to the sides. *Where are the stupid surveillance cameras he keeps talking about?* She can't see them. Through the pouring rain, she sees the clock tower. She could make a run for it. Head to the Campanile tunnel entrance; punch in the access code; rush underground. She looks behind her. There are students everywhere, no one who looks menacing. *She should run; she should run...* It never works when she relies on someone. Her mom. Zeke. David. Everyone betrays her. *Why isn't she running?*

"Dammit it, Jess!" Matteo yells over the rain. "Get on the bike!" His tone makes it sound like they have had this fight a thousand times. *Where does this familiarity come from?* His eyes meet hers, and before she is aware of making a decision, she swings her leg over the seat and sits behind him.

Standing upright, Matteo starts cranking the pedals. "I'll go slow at first," he yells back to her. The bike jerks forward. She tenses her stomach muscles and holds her torso slightly backward so Matteo's butt has the space to grind the pedals. The bike moves slowly over the bumps of the muddy ground. "Keep your head facing downward as you talk to me, okay? The cameras are on us."

Man, he's really obsessed with cameras. "Okay," she shouts with her face tilted downward.

As they move away from the crowds and the dancers, the campus quiets and the pathways empty of people. She would have thought that Relly and her cops would have been hot on their pursuit, but no, she can't see them.

"Listen," he shouts back, head down. "I want you to put your hands under my shirt."

That makes no sense. She sputters through the rain falling down her face: "Why would you want—?"

"Just do it."

"But—"

"Do it!"

She unclasps her hands from his waist and grabs at the hem of his t-shirt; its wetness makes it hard to peel back.

"Move your hands higher," he barks back, his face bent forward. "I want your wrists fully covered." Since he ripped the bottom of his t-shirt for her bandage, she has to move her hands toward the shirt's top. Straggles of his chest hair are underneath her fingers; his skin is warm. He shouts back, with his hand over his mouth: "Now, take your Keeper off your wrist."

"What will you do with it?"

He gives an exasperated growl; she feels the rattle within his chest. "You have to trust me."

Does she have to? She grabs at the clasp on her Keeper's wristband; she can't see what she's doing, and it's hard to keep her balance on the bike seat as it jostles over the wet, uneven ground. "It's off."

"Good. Keep your hands under my shirt even after I take it from you."

She tries not to think what she is turning over. The keys to her apartment, her money, phone, data, history. Caerys. She holds tight to Matteo's bare chest. *Don't betray me.*

As Matteo picks up speed, she can feel his stomach muscles flexing, his heart pumping. He directs the bike back toward the pavement, and instantly, the ride shifts to smooth.

The Campanile sits right ahead of them. The rain is slowing now, and Jess hears the bike's tires whizzing on the wet ground, the bike sloshing through small puddles. This part of campus is almost deserted. Jess scans the horizon for police or cars or fast-approaching bikes, but there are none.

"It's weird that they're hanging back," Matteo says, apparently having just done the same scan. He's biting at his Keeper's wristband, and with a jerk, his pedaling picks up more speed.

The Campanile stands ahead, a tall tower atop a raised courtyard. A short stairway extends from this lower field where they are biking to the Campanile's hillside courtyard, and as they are almost at these stairs, Jess is expecting Matteo to brake soon. Instead, their speed appears to be accelerating. Matteo lifts his arm and tosses something onto the Campanile stairs. She turns her head to see what they are. "You threw my Keeper?"

"And mine. Relly's hacked them. We'll never give her the slip if we're wearing them."

The slip? Oh, thank god. He is not betraying her. Matteo jerks his bike to the right moving to a path that veers away from the clock tower. "Wait, why aren't you going to the Campanile?"

Before Matteo can answer, a sound comes from behind her. Jess twists around again. Nothing. Yet, the sound continues, like a low thunder that builds and builds. Even through the rain, she can hear it growing louder. Now she sees: motorbikes. There's at least one, three, five, six. *Shit.* "Bikers are coming," she shouts forward to Matteo.

"Cops?"

She turns back. They do not look like cops. There's no uniformity. The bikes are different types; one is a motorcycle; the others motorbikes. One person is wearing a bright turquoise slicker, someone else is in red and the others are in black. One bike brakes sharply at the Campanile stairs, and the others... *how strange,* they all are stopping at the stairs. The first biker jumps off his bike, grabbing the Keepers from the ground.

As Matteo makes a sudden left turn, her body flies to the right. Clenching at his chest, she tries not to fall. They speed through a narrow, terraced passageway between two large campus buildings, their bodies jostling as they bike across the stones. Jess pivots, trying to see if the bikers are following behind them, but the building blocks her view. *Can she hear them coming?* The only sounds are their own bike's whizzing wheels in the rain.

With a sharp left, Matteo veers the bike off of the flagstone path, into a grove of tall, redwood trees. The pedals sink into the pine needle-strewn ground, and it is like they have stepped into a different world. The raindrops must be hitting the evergreens' branches above, but beneath the huge tree's boughs, they feel nothing. The space is dark, like nighttime. "I'm guessing we have ten seconds, no more. You ready to open the door?"

The question only makes sense when she sees steam rushing from the in-ground grate ahead of them: they *are* going to the tunnels.

Matteo hops off the bike. "Your access code better work on this door too, or we're screwed. Hurry!"

She is on her knees already at the four-feet squared grate that sits in the ground, wiping the condensation from the keypad attached to the gate. It is the same old-fashioned type of keypad that she saw at the Campanile tunnel entrance. Jess plugs the code in – "W-I-N-N-E-R" – then presses her thumb against the much newer print recognition screen. The grate door shoots slightly forward.

With her one good arm, she swings the heavy door back on a hinge; even in the dimness, Jess can see the tunnel floor ten feet below.

Beside her, Matteo is already taking the satchels from his bike and throwing them down the open hole; they land, *thud, thud,* on the underground floor. He picks up the bike by its frame. The pedals waver in the air as he orients his bike so that the handlebars lean into the gaping hole. Letting go, the bike hits the ground ten feet underneath with a series of clanks.

Matteo grabs her hand: "Let's jump."

MATTEO

"Are you okay?" Jess' hand rests on his knee.

"Sort of," he mumbles, holding his hands tight into his chest. His jump did not land as he wanted. He had meant to yank the grate door behind him as he dropped to the tunnel floor below, but when he jumped, his fingers, weak from the rain's icy coldness, did not loosen their grip quickly enough. His body bolted downward but his arm twisted behind, his fingers momentarily stuck within the grate's grid as he fell.

"Oh, no," she says, leaning to grab his right hand. There are bloody gashes along the top knuckles. "You're bleeding."

The remark is funny given the red-drenched bandage on her arm and the bloody-brown smears across her shirt. "You're not in great shape yourself," he says, grabbing his knuckles back to hold in his mouth. He looks around at the white pipes everywhere, his bike splayed on the concrete floor beside them. *Are there cameras?* He eyes the corners, the ceilings, the pipes. Nothing. In this austere space, they would stick out. Jess' blue eyes are watching him closely; the smell of blood, rain, and sweat are coming off her body. Somehow, it does not smell bad.

She pushes herself from the ground and leans to pull the bike upright. "We better move away from the grate in case the bikers come looking for us."

"Right." He is glad Jess already understands the time limitations they are under. Sure, they eluded Relly and the motor bikers, whoever they are, but these folks can easily figure out where he and Jess went. He stands, takes a short jump straight upward to tug the grate door down, making sure it is locked tight.

"I'll drive the bike; you sit on the back." Her raspy voice is softer now. She is picking the bike from the ground, and once he adjusts himself on the seat, she stands over the bike frame and begins to wobbly pedal from an upright position. Her butt goes back and forth, toward his face and back out again.

It's a nice butt.

"We need to get out of these tunnels before Relly can find us," he explains. With the grate door locked and the security access code again in place, Relly will either need to learn the code or break the lock to get inside the tunnels. Given that the lock is fingerprint-dependent, Matteo guesses De Sel will choose to locate someone, like a janitor, whose print works. Hacking a print-dependent code is time-consuming. Locating a saw that would cut through the steel grate, potentially more time-consuming. In either case, they should aim to be out of the tunnels in six minutes or less.

"We're headed south right now, right?"

"Uh-huh."

"Good. I think I have an idea for a place we can go. No one will find us there."

"You already have a plan?" She pushes her wet hair off her forehead. "That was fast."

"It was?"

"Yup." A second later, she mumbles: "Way too fast."

Beck had said that the key was to get her off the grid. This is a strange request since most people have no way to do that. Everyone is trackable. Through their Keepers. Surveillance feeds. Doorway scans. What's strange, though, is that Matteo *does* know a way to disappear. There is a house high in the El Cerrito hills, just off Tilden Park. The place is Rachel's Tia's place. The house has no Internet, no electrical lines run into it; the water is from a well. There is no deed of sale or address attached to the house. Even the heavy tree cover around the tiny dwelling makes it impossible to spot from satellite scans.

As far as Matteo knows, only Tia's very few friends know of her house, no one else. Definitely not Beck. Yet, as Matteo replays Beck's words in his head, he cannot shake the feeling that Beck was referring to Tia's house. *"Do you understand what I'm saying? Get the girl completely offline."*

"Are you planning to *share* your plan with me?" Jess' voice interrupts his thoughts.

"Uh, sure, there's a place I go sometime in the hills," Matteo says. "It's a good place."

"That's all you're going to tell me?"

Her frustration is not lost on him, but he does not want to explain himself now. Adrenaline is seeping from his body like a leaky balloon, and besides, there are more pressing concerns. "Can we find a tunnel exit that doesn't lead directly outside?"

"You mean, like an exit that goes to a building's basement?"

"Yes."

"Most of these tunnel exits end in a basement," she sighs.

From the way his hands are wrapped around her sides, he can feel the sigh's breathy release on his fingertips. He knows this sort of sigh: it is a low heaving of breath that Rachel used when she wanted to signal that Matteo should ask her what was wrong. In this moment, Matteo thinks of asking the same question of Jess, but there is no need. *What isn't wrong?*

They ride silently through the steamy-hot corridors. Pipes protrude from the low ceilings, hovering so low that Matteo could touch them if he lifted his arm high. The walls drip with condensation, and huge coils of legacy data cables traipse the floors with plastic-coated electrical wires stapled to the walls and ceilings. He considers how haphazardly these cables are adhered to the floor and ceiling; the university's data transmissions must still rely on these old style Profibus cables; yet, here they lie on the ground like they've been discarded. It feels good to think this trivial thought. The air is the temperature of bath water and as they move through it, his thoughts, which were wadded tight as a scrunched ball of paper, begin to smooth.

Giving Relly the slip should not have worked. This police officer had every technological advantage: video surveillance, Keeper tracking, not to mention a whole force to be called in. Matteo had a bike. And those motorbikes that sped to the Campanile should have caught up with them. In fact, if the bikers had not stopped to retrieve Jess and his Keepers, the gang could have overtaken Matteo's bike in seconds. He cannot understand why they stopped.

86

"Did you think about taking the one million?"

"Sorry?"

"Relly offered you a million dollars, and you didn't take it. So," Jess twists her head back, "why not?"

He would prefer not to answer this question: "I don't know, I didn't."

She bows her head, shaking it.

He points: "You're heading into the wall."

Fast, she adjusts the bike's handlebars to stay straight. Her mouth opens to ask a question, then a second later closes.

If Jess is looking for a logical explanation, his answer will not satisfy her. To turn Jess over to Relly would have been the action of a depraved man. He is not depraved; his dad taught him right from wrong.

When Matteo was a kid, his mother would drop him off at his dad's bungalow every Friday afternoon per the arrangement in the joint custody agreement. His mom, Gabriella, would prepare containers of Bolognese sauce, polenta dishes or lasagnas for Matteo's meals and give long-winded directions to Matteo's dad, Heng, about how each container needed to be warmed at what temperature for how long. There would be suggestions for appropriate bedtimes and a list of the homework that Matteo needed to have completed by the time she returned at noon on Sunday. Then right after the door would shut, Matteo and his dad would race to put on their avatar glasses and clomp down the stairs to the basement.

Danger Doomed was their favorite of the virtual world games – way better than Knights of Nothing. Matteo loved that moment when he put the glasses on and his dad's dreary basement would transform into a mossy, spooky forestland where men on horses galloped past and wizards in hats came lurking from behind trees. The game itself combined a Robin Hood-like mission with Dungeons and Dragons mythology and chess strategizing. Heng and he would play for hours, and Matteo became very skilled, making it to the castle in all situations except for those where his victory relied on forsaking the damsel or sacrificing the wise wizard. In those situations, Matteo would lay down his sword, allowing the game itself to win. When he lost in this way, his dad would take him out for chocolate milkshakes. "I like that my son isn't depraved," Heng would say and tousle Matteo's thick, black hair.

The radiator smells in the tunnel remind Matteo of his dad's musty basement, and actually, now that he thinks of it, those hours of running through make-believe forests have a similarity to the last hour – the chase, the fear, the need to slip the set trap.

"What are you usually like?" Jess' question cuts into his memories. A response comes fast to Matteo's head: *Sad*. But out loud, he says, "Pretty regular."

"But what do you *do?* Like, what were you planning to do after the Juju this morning?"

He would prefer not to answer this question either. The truth is that all he has been doing for the last three weeks is watching her. Most days, he bikes just two blocks behind her on her morning runs. Would she like to know that? Or, that he regularly shadows her on the way to her lab and watches her daytime actions from lab surveillance footage fed to his Keeper? Should he tell her that he listened to her therapy session and read last night's journal entry where she wrote out five reasons to stay upbeat: "1. Rain is coming; 2. There are still nice people in the world; 3. I have Caerys; 4. Probably won't see David for weeks; 5. Run a 12K??" No, this truthfulness wouldn't help his situation at all. He leans his chin toward her ear. "Why'd that lady pull a gun on you?"

"You're not answering my question."

"My question's more relevant."

She takes a second before answering: "Sara wanted me to give her the patent application to a desalination solution I invented."

"But you didn't invent it?"

"No." Jess brakes to turn a corner. "I didn't invent it because I've never thought about desalination in my life." She stops pedaling and coasts. "According to Sara, there's a ceremony on Friday where I'm supposed to sit on a stage with David and sign this patent application in front of the Governor."

"Of California?"

She pedals again. "Yes, Luis Ramos himself."

"That's crazy. Who signs patent applications in front of a Governor?" Matteo doubts people even travel to the lawyer's office for this procedure anymore. Electronic signature on your Keeper screen; press send; over.

"Sara's invited a lot of press to watch the signing. She's very proud of the whole thing. She said, 'De Sel won't know what hit them.'"

Matteo is trying to assemble the players and their roles. It's hard. Everyone would seem to be too smart to act as foolishly as they are. According to what he can piece together, people at the De Sel Corporation, several California State Troopers, and a top environmental scientist all decided this morning that they needed to use violence in their desperate attempt to locate... what? *A procedural filing document*? "Did you at least tell Sara that you don't know where the patent application is?"

"Yes, that's what I told her."

He can tell from the slope of her silence that there's more. "But you *do* know where it is?"

Her head flicks back to examine his expression. She nods, then turns back and points: "See that door ahead? That's where we should get out."

The metal door is at the end of the hallway, an Exit sign above it. She stands on the pedals as the bike coasts toward the door ahead of them.

As Jess holds the bike steady, Matteo steps off it.

To his surprise, she sticks her hand under her t-shirt and starts to fumble around. When her hand comes out from under her shirt, she is holding a toothbrush. "Sara said there was only one copy of the application, and it had been written to a dot drive. I'm pretty sure that dot drive is in..." – she twists at the bristles at the top of the toothbrush – "here." There, like a pearl in an oyster, lies the white dot drive.

"So, that's what everyone's after." Today, they have been chased, shot at, and bribed all for a fucking toothbrush. *What the hell is he doing here?* No normal person would be caught in this mess. He tries not to think about that. Pressing a button on the bike handlebars, the bike begins to fold up automatically. The front and back wheels pivot into the frame and the handlebars fold downward so the bike collapses into a box-like shape that can be held by a handlebar on the frame.

Jess maneuvers the toothbrush back within her jog-bra again. "Anyway, tonight I'll download the information from the dot drive, and I bet everything will make more sense."

Matteo hands her the bike bag with the tranq gun in it. "Actually, there are no computers where we're staying tonight."

"Staying?" She blinks. "We'll be there the whole night?"

"Well, yeah." He is not sure why this is a surprise. "Relly's search won't end at nightfall, and this house is in the woods with lots of tree cover. Even if they send out drone surveillance, which they will, they won't find us there."

"You think about surveillance more than anyone I've ever known."

He smiles: "You don't mean that as a compliment, but you should."

She does not smile back.

He picks up the folded bike by its handlebar and walks straight to the steel door. "Listen, I'll open this door, and let's walk into this hallway like we belong here. I doubt there's video cameras, but in case I'm wrong, keep your head down. Ready?"

"Wait." He turns back, and her face is creased with confusion. "Matteo, I saw your wedding ring, and… won't your wife worry about where you are tonight?"

Yet another question he would prefer not to answer. He pushes the door open. Compared to the stuffy tunnels, the hallway's air is icy cold. He steps forward, leaving his response behind: "My wife's dead."

JESS

Before she is fully outside the tunnel door, Matteo is already far into the basement, evaluating where they have landed.

The room is fifteen by fifteen feet and appears to be little more than a large closet. Rows of utility shelves hold paint cans and cleaning solutions, and robotic vacuum cleaners flank the room's sides like marching band members ready to enter a stadium field. The overhead lamplight is dim, the walls concrete, and the ceilings low. A door in the corner leads to a shadowy corridor. Matteo takes large strides back and forth across the room, his head darting toward the opening to the dim hallway. "This worked out well: not a camera in sight."

Jess assumes that Matteo is trying to distract her from what he just said. The effort in his voice reminds her of how her mom would sound when she was trying to deflect attention. "Work was absolutely fine today," she would say with a suspicious rising inflection. Jess has lots of practice with deflecting sadness too, so there's no reason to hold Matteo's silence against him – except that every other aspect of him confounds her. Why isn't he more unnerved by their situation? And how does he know so much? About video cameras? And places to hide? He always happens to be at the right place at the right time. At the Juju. At David's office. Here, now. And then there's the money. Why didn't he take the money?

They have been tandem to each other on the bike for the last hour, and now as he walks between the utility shelves, Jess studies him. His hair, almost dry, sticks up in a shock of black, wavy messiness; his cheekbones are wider than she remembers and his shoulders more rounded and muscular. Given everything they have gone through, she thought his physicality would be familiar to her now. No, he's stranger-like. "I'm sorry about your wife," she mumbles.

"Yeah, me too."

"How'd she die?"

He turns fast, and it is because her question flew like a dart. She is not meaning to be unkind, but there is prickliness inside her throat, like she has swallowed thorns.

His head points to the corridor door. "Let's get out of here first, then talk about that later—"

"Like tonight, when we're at the secret location you have all planned out?"

He stares at her: "You sound like you're *mad* at me. Which is odd." His voice has an edge now too. "Because I just saved you out there."

"I know." She meets his eyes straight on. "Thank you."

"I'm really feeling that gratitude."

"I *am* grateful." She raises her chin, steeling herself to be direct. "But... why are you here? You're risking so much and have these ready-made plans. Who *are* you?"

"Listen, I'm not hiding anything. Or... not really. My plan – it's not even a plan. There's this place in the hills. Just inside the El Cerrito border. It's off the grid. No one can find us there because no one knows the house exists."

"But, you do?"

"It's my wife's nanny's house."

His wife's nanny's house. Questions fly: *Did his wife keep a nanny her whole life? Was she that wealthy?* She does not ask those questions. "You still say 'wife.'"

"As opposed to?"

"Late wife."

His eyes pop: "Sorry I didn't use the right fucking words."

"Never mind. I shouldn't have said anythi—"

"I have no idea what I'm doing here! There. Are you happy with how I said that?"

She stares at his angry eyes. *What the hell is she doing? This man saved her. There are reasons for suspicion, sure, but...* She needs to be nicer, fast. "I am glad that you're here with me. And... I don't want you to leave."

"Well, I can't now anyway," he mutters.

"I'm... sorry for that." Everything is jumbled in her thoughts: regret, suspicion, guilt. "I wish I had never involved you. Really, I will go the rest of the way on my own."

He studies her for what feels like an hour. "You know..." his voice turns soft, "I usually do say 'late wife.' Rachel died a year and a half ago. And," he takes a loud inhale, "I didn't come out of nowhere. I ran to David's office because I saw Relly in the courtyard, and..." he lifts his chin to face her directly, "I wanted to keep you safe."

She blinks. It is a big pronouncement. His words are purposeful too, like he is remembering them from a script. For a flash, she wonders: *Could he have overheard her talking to Dr. Monique?* Because he just articulated the *very* wish she had discussed with her therapist yesterday. "Thank you for wanting that," she says. Studying his unshaven face and rumpled style, she cannot decide if he is manipulating her or simply a good guy, salt of the earth. The silence weighs heavily around them as she tries to decide what to say next. "You seem impossibly good."

"I'm not." Abruptly, he walks to the folded bike and picks it up. From how swiftly his body moves, it's clear that he is done with the conversation. He grabs one of the satchels from the floor and heads out of the doorway.

Snatching the second satchel, Jess rushes after him. In the next room are two elevators and an entryway to a long, narrow hallway. Matteo walks down the dark corridor.

"We have to hope there's an exit on this level," he calls back to her. "If we have to take the elevator up, we're screwed. Every elevator on campus has surveillance cameras."

Jess nods, which of course Matteo cannot see. Her shoulder throbs, and her flimsy t-shirt and shorts are damp against her skin. The lighting is dim, and as she follows Matteo's amorphous shape in front of her, the strangeness of the situation is a problem she wants to sit down to analyze, but cannot. *Walk straight.*

Lining the corridor, doors are opened to other closets, and she peers into these rooms as she walks. Each closet is similar to the one they arrived in from the tunnels. Lit by a single naked lightbulb that hangs centered in the ceilings, greenish light casts shadows across the rooms' contents. In one room, there are six stacks of chairs and one long meeting table. Another room is strewn with ancient computer screens and server closets. Then, peering into the next room, Jess stops. Taking up most of the small room is a large wheeled laundry cart, dumpster size, filled to the brim with white towels. Behind this enormous mound of whiteness are ten blue lockers that line the wall.

Jess steps into the shadowy room and pulls the tab on one of the lockers; there's a horrible squeak as the hinge pulls back. A blue coverall hangs on a hook with a blue cap on the shelf above it. She opens the next locker. Another blue coverall, another cap. She takes this uniform out and holds it up to her body, running her finger across the nubby UC Berkeley blue and gold seal that sits over the heart. She takes the cap from the hook and pushes it onto her head.

"What are you doing?"

She jumps, turning to where Matteo stands in the doorway. "You scared me!"

"I didn't feel so good when you weren't behind me either."

She points to the lockers: "See what I found."

"Custodians' lockers, great." He walks toward her, the fold-up bike hitting his knee. "Listen, we have a problem. There's no exit on this floor, and if we have to leave this building through the elev—"

"It doesn't matter anymore. The elevator's fine."

"The elevator has the surveillance—"

"Won't be a problem." She grabs a first aid kit that sits on top of the lockers. "See, there's Band Aids. Laser scissors. Suture glue."

"I don't think a Band Aid will disguise you for the surveillance camera."

"No, but with this hat and a fast haircut?" She pushes the cap down over her head. "And did you know that custodians get to ride the Lawrence-Berkeley shuttle for free?" Jess waits, certain Matteo's face is about to burst into glowing recognition of her brilliant plan.

His face stays curdled in confusion.

"The Lawrence-Berkeley shuttle goes straight into the hills. Isn't that where you said you wanted us to go?"

Matteo squints his eyes; he opens his mouth—

Then, there's the sound of a bell.

An elevator bell.

Oh, god.

She grabs Matteo's wrist, and the air seems to suction around them, like they have been shrink-wrapped to stillness. Her heart pumps so hard she thinks the organ must be hitting her rib cage.

There is a swoosh of elevator doors opening and the increasing volume of a man's voice already in conversation, "I don't think I've seen a face so red..." He has a joking tone, a deep voice. A thudding of heavy shoes and too many footsteps to belong to only one person. The deep-voiced man continues: "Relly looked like she'd blown up a balloon."

Relly? Matteo's eyes lock with Jess'.

A different man speaks: "Did you understand why she was freaking out so much?" This man is Latino; Jess can tell from the undulations in his phrasings. "I'm not sure why she thought she would be able to open that tunnel door, but the she kept holding her thumb up to the scanner was pretty fucking funny." His deep voice goes high as he imitates a woman's voice: "*Why the fuck* isn't this working?'"

The deep-voiced guy laughs: "She sounded like a pig squealing when she was rattling on the grated door." There are the sounds of heavy, slow steps; they stop.

"What I don't understand is if she wanted these kids so bad, why the fuck didn't we just tranq them when they were standing there on the field?"

The deep-voiced man imitates Relly's high-pitched voice again: "'No public spectacle, no public spectacle!' And she's mad they got away..." More shuffled footsteps.

Beside Jess, Matteo chest lifts up and down with his breathing, and his eyes lock with hers as they listen in stillness.

The deep-voiced man again: "I guess this is the tunnel door we're supposed to be watching." A clattering sound – Jess thinks it must be one of the men jiggling the door.

The Latino man: "What's the plan? We wait here, then tranquilize them when they walk out?"

"Yeah, put 'em to sleep, that's what Relly said." More muffled sounds. "I tell you, I wouldn't want to be that bike guy waking up."

"Or the girl?"

"Nah, the girl will be fine. They talk about her like she's the second coming. But the bike guy, he's screwed. Relly was on her Keeper talking to the Governor, and she asked if he'd let her arrest the bike guy for being part of that terrorist group."

"Terrorist group? Which terrorist group?"

"You know, man, the populist freaks at the Capitol. The ones who did the massacre."

Jess stares at Matteo. His cheeks go slack.

The Latino man cackles. "You're bullshitting me. There's no way that bike guy is part of that terrorist group. We'd have been given the go-ahead to tranquilize him. Hell, the whole campus would have been in lockdown."

"Yeah, it makes no sense but..." There is the sound of heavy footsteps. "Relly said he's the reason everything's screwed up."

"That makes him a terrorist?"

"It does if she wants to screw up his life." A low electronic buzz goes off, and Jess knows the sound must be coming from one of the guards' Keepers. The deep-voiced guy seems to be the one to take it. "Right... uh-huh. Got it... got it; okay." His voice shifts its tonality outward as he reports to the Latino guy: "They said it's taking longer than expected. Apparently, David Steubingly has slipped into a coma and they can't get the code from him anymore. They're tracking down a torch to break through the steel grate."

"I'm in no rush," says the Latino man. "I like it better here than in the rain." There are some footsteps, and Jess assumes it is the Latino man who is walking around. "Don't you think it's strange that Relly hasn't called in the Berkeley PD? We could definitely use more eyeballs on these tunnel exits."

The heavy shoes now enter the corridor. "Yeah, if we'd had fifty bodies on campus, those two never would have slipped away." More clomps against the linoleum floor. "But no, we're standing there like fucking zombies, freezing our asses off in the rain."

Panic is ringing in Jess' body like a fire alarm. She and Matteo could be easily spotted from the hallway; their position in front of the lockers is directly in front of the door. She makes eye contact with Matteo and points to the wall behind the door. Matteo pulls off his flip-flops and they step back – slowly, quietly – behind the open door. As Jess tiptoes, she opens the flap of the satchel and feels for the tranquilizer gun inside. The Latino man's shoes are coming closer.

"Man, check these out!" The Latino man yells back to the deep-voiced man. "These computers look like they come straight from little house on the fucking prairie. Actual screens on 'em, man." The footsteps move closer, closer down the hallway. "You think we're gonna find a horse and buggy down here too?"

Jess stands against the wall on the right side of the closet's door; Matteo's body is pressed against the wall on the left. The footsteps near their doorway. Quietly, Jess puts the satchel down on the ground and grips the gun in her hand. She has never shot a gun before, but during California Collection Week, when it was required that all registered firearms be turned in to local police stations, a friend showed Jess his gun before relinquishing it. She learned how to flip the safety off and grasp the handle with one finger on the trigger, her non-shooting hand cradling the grip.

The Latino man is now standing at the closet door, looking in. He has somewhat labored inhalations, like he carries too much weight on his body, and Jess can smell the onions on his breath and the laundry detergent on his clothes. "Hey, Jake. Looks like someone was here, using the lockers." The Latino man takes a step into the room, and Jess watches him as he notices the folded bike sitting on the ground. "Holy crap, it's the bike." He turns fast, "Jake—"

Jess steps forward, and pushes the trigger back. There's a phthist sound, like a soda can being opened, and the man stumbles backward, groaning. With no hesitation, Jess darts into the hallway. Jake is running toward her, his hand on his own tranq gun. She pumps her trigger back again. Phthist. His body falls too.

When the California recall on bulleted guns happened two years ago, Jess participated in the rallies; she read the literature and signed the petitions. She can recite precisely why these tranquilizer guns work as effectively as real bullets in stopping a person cold. First, there is an electric jolt, like a powerful tazer, that throws a person to the ground and temporarily stymies his ability to move. In Jake's case, he spasms and spits against the concrete floor for a second or two. Then, the anesthetics enter his bloodstream. It's a shot of Propofol to jolt unconsciousness followed by a longer-acting amide anesthetic that provides a solid two hours of unconsciousness.

Looking at Jake, Jess knows he is not dead. Yet, holding the gun in her hand and seeing his body splayed on the ground, legs and arms askew, a shiver spasms through her. Muffled noises surround her; she hears them as though she's underwater. Her body is being jostled. She can't turn yet; her eyes won't move off of Jake. Then, Matteo's body is in front of hers. His hands on her shoulders, he's shaking her. "Jess!"

Her lips, she thinks, are trembling. Her body too. Matteo's eyes are wide, and she cannot tell if he is angry or horrified. She tries to catch her breath, to make him understand. "I couldn't..." she says, her chest heaving as her voice cracks. "I couldn't let them hurt you."

MATTEO

Matteo rides the driverless buses a lot, so he knows this loop well. The bus travels from the Berkeley campus into the hills, toward the Lawrence-Berkeley laboratories, sinks in and out of the edge of the 2,000-acre Tilden Park, then heads southward into the valleys where it stops at the Orinda BART station. The bus' hard seats, the five-word posters that hang on the dividers, the moldy cheese smell that lingers in the air – it is the same as always. Even though everything is different.

One thought that loops in his brain is the wish he could tell his Keeper what's happening. He is surprised by the impulse. If you had asked him when he woke this morning if he had a "relationship" with his Keeper, he would have said, "Hell, no." Unlike every other person he knows, he has never named his Keeper and he does not sit down and chat with her regularly. Still, it is strange not to have the companionship. He wants someone to tell him everything will be okay.

Looking out of the big bus windows, the Tilden Park hillsides are blanketed with a thick fog that almost masks the hundreds of tree stumps. When the drought first began, the park service said that cutting down the eucalyptus and Monterey pines was a necessity, since these non-indigenous trees created risks for wildfires with their dry wood grains and crinkly, low-hanging leaves. As the years of drought continued, more trees were identified as threats. Now, along the outskirts of Tilden Park, dozens of woodchip piles sit in mounds on the empty hills like funeral pyres. Matteo hates this view more than any other in the Bay Area.

He peeks back at Jess. She is sitting at the back of the bus, though she does no look like herself anymore. Her hair is cropped short at her chin with a slab of eyebrow-skimming bangs. She's wearing an oxygen mask over her nose and mouth, and beneath the clear plastic cover, her lips are garish red. On her ears, she's wearing huge, hot pink hoop earrings, and on her fingers, five Thickrings – all courtesy of the custodian's backpack. With the cap and the coveralls on, she cuts a wholly different profile from the fresh-faced, ponytailed runner De Sel is trying to find.

He looks even more changed than she does. Jess had the idea to use the first aid kit's suture glue to affix her shorn hair into his custodian's cap. He now has wavy hair that covers his ear lobes, and given that this new hair is brown, instead of black, his whole appearance is altered. Seeing his reflection in the bus' windows now, he looks more Italian than Chinese for the first time in his life. He is clean-shaven too. The shaving was not easy, with only an inch-long razor blade from the first aid kit, some soap and his shaking hands. He kept saying there was not enough time, but Jess, her voice tight with anxiety kept replying: "No, you have to, you have to."

Her determination was something to see, especially coming on the heels of her body trembles. One second, he was holding her shoulders, trying to snap her out of her shock, the next, she mumbled, "We have to get you out of here," and ran back to the lockers to grab the First Aid kit. With five solid scissor slices, she chopped her hair off and began screaming at him to "Shave! Shave!" while she glued her hair into his cap. Amidst the flurry of her orders, she kept asking how many minutes he thought had passed. Matteo had no idea – three minutes... six?

There was no reference point for time or for any other aspect of their experience. The body lay on the floor, bug-eyed and open-mouthed. Jess was placing a cap with wigged hair on Matteo's head. His body was drenched with sweat, foul with the stink of panic. He tried only to move, not to think, since his skull hurt like someone was pushing tacks into it, one time, two times, ten.

When they were dressed, Matteo shoved his folded-up bike into an enormous laundry bag, and Jess stuffed the bike's satchels into the custodian's backpack. She took off her jewelry – sparkly earrings and a thin, silver ring – leaving them in the lockers as "payment for all we took." Her jewelry had to be worth ten times what they took, but he didn't point that out. "You should take your wedding ring off too," she said to him as they stepped over the body on the floor.

He stopped. "You want me to leave it in the locker?"

"No, of course not. Shove it in your pocket or something. It's an identifying object, that's all."

When they were waiting for the elevator doors to open, Jess told him to take the elevator up first. "I'm not leaving you here," he scoffed, as the doors whished wide open.

"You have to," she said, shoving him into the elevator compartment. "They're looking for us together, so it's smarter to be apart. Get on the Lawrence-Livermore shuttle at Kleeberger, and I'll get on at the Greek Theatre. Oh, and here." She handed him the pack with the tranquilizer gun just as the elevator doors closed. He tried to press the button to open the doors back again, but it was too late.

Her plan worked. In the pattering drizzle, no one paid attention as he speed-walked and paced back and forth at the bus stop. When he stepped onto the bus and began his walk down the aisle, no passengers looked from their holographic screens as he lifted his heavy laundry bag high and quickly nudged the bus' surveillance camera lens up towards the ceiling. At the Greek Theatre stop, Jess stepped onto the bus like she had promised. And like that, they had slipped away.

Matteo guesses it will be at least an hour before Relly can reconstruct their path. And now that the bus' surveillance camera faces the ceiling, she won't even know at which stop they disembark. The route goes southwesterly into the Orinda BART station, and Matteo hopes Relly will assume he and Jess rode all the way out there. Ideally, Relly would anticipate that they used the BART trains to reach some far-away spot in the Bay Area.

Matteo's plan is entirely different. They are going to step off the bus at the Strawberry Canyon Parking Lot stop and switchback toward the north for a six-mile hike through Tilden Park and Wildcat Canyon Park to reach Tia's house in the El Cerrito hills. If Jess can walk fast, or better yet, run, he thinks they can make it to Tia's before Relly sends surveillance drones into the hills.

Above his left, now-ringless hand, small bruises dot his wrist. When the cops were talking in the basement, Jess clenched his arm so hard that she left these impressions of her apprehension. He keeps circling them with his finger. Glancing at the back of the bus, he sees Jess' head is tipped against a window. Her new haircut outlines her face like a picture frame, and with her face at rest, her sadness radiates. She would mask this emotion if they were facing each other directly, and he is glad to have caught this glimpse of her vulnerability.

Rachel never hid her feelings. When he first met her at a party during Berkeley's Frosh Week, she was standing by a keg with her crazy dreadlocks and vermillion-shaded lips; her laughter sounded like electricity crackling. He walked over to her and told her so.

"Are you trying to turn me on?" she giggled at her crafty pun, and like that, he was hooked. During their seven years together, her special brand of energy transformed him. He had been this geeky kid who had never fought too hard against being labeled an Asian nerd, but with Rachel by his side, the edges of his self-definition sharpened. He became sturdier in his opinions and passion. Even his body transformed, adding mass and muscle; strength.

The morning she died, Matteo stayed with her in the isolation unit. He held her hand as her body grew cold and her face settled. He wanted her expression to suggest peace or contentment. There was only blankness. For months afterward, as he went through the motions of being alive, this vision of Rachel's empty expression stayed with him. His Keeper held thousands of photos in which Rachel was exuberant and laughing; yet, it was this expressionless image of her in death that lived in his mind. If Rachel could not feel anymore, he didn't want to either. The world was smoggy and brown; he rode through it.

Now, as he shifts his weight on the hard bus seat, he pushes the bruises on his wrist over and over again. After so long feeling numb, this tenderness is not so bad.

The bus nears the stop where they should get off. He pulls the cord and lurches toward the front, seeing from the corner of his eye that Jess is moving toward the back exit. The bus' doors flip backward, and the humid air engulfs him. There is no smell of smog, only wetness and soil. *God, he's missed this smell.* He closes his eyes to drink in the earthy scent, and when he re-opens them, Jess is right there, beside him.

JESS

In the four months since she moved to Berkeley, there was only one time that she went hiking in Tilden Park, and that was a September Saturday when Jess' mother came for the weekend. Usually, when Jess' mom visited, a particular loneliness would arrive with the luggage. To make this particular visit more bearable, Jess arranged a variety of sightseeing trips to at least keep them occupied. Tilden Park was their first stop.

As Jess and her mother walked along the paved path at the park's Inspiration Point, Alice shared her frustration over her latest relationship debacle with a man named Xander, whom she had "really, really thought was the one." To Jess, it had been painfully obvious Xander was not right, but nonetheless she said all the lines she was practiced at: "You deserve someone better," and "You'll be stronger without him in your life." Jess knew well how to soothe her mother's many moods. Yet, as Jess said all the things she knew her mother needed to hear, what was bombarding her senses was the space around her.

It was spectacular. *Why hadn't she come here before?* There were hundreds of acres of hills. With the smog, she could not gaze far into the horizon, but what lay before her was lovely. Large rounded hills, clay-brown and smooth, broken only by juts of tough, briary forests that sat in the valleys. Birds flew overhead, but no drones, and the sounds were mostly of openness; quiet. That day at Tilden, Jess vowed she would regularly come back to get a dose of nature. She never had. Until today.

Now, nature is not feeling idyllic.

In the part of Tilden where she and Matteo are walking, there is no trail. Tree stumps and woodpiles line the hills, with the only remaining forests being the craggy masses sitting at the valley's seams. Jess has leaves in her hair and mud on her shoes. The custodian's coverall has taken on the heaviness of an x-ray blanket in the thick, humid air. Her shoulder throbs; she's thirsty and what she wants is to go home. She never realized what solace she took in the idea that no matter how bad a workday was or how awkward a social situation, she could at least return home. Her small studio apartment is nothing special, but it has the things that comfort her: her saggy blue sofa, the hole-filled blanket she knitted in college, a box of salty oat chocolate cookies, her sci-fi novels, and a gin and tonic with perfectly cubed ice cubes. She cannot return to those comforts. Not now. *Ever?* The drizzle begins again and the grayness surrounds her, so low and foggy thick that even her legs have mist around them.

Matteo says the fog is a good thing, since satellite cameras and drone surveillance can't see through the low clouds. It seems strange, that something as basic as fog could hamper all that technology. Buzzing Bee drones, low-flying and bird-sized, hover over Berkeley campus' skies all day. "Are you saying those drones don't work when it gets foggy?" "That's what I'm saying," he says; "Even night vision won't see through fog this deep."

Back when they started on this trek, they ran, with Matteo jogging beside his bike. It was hard going up the hills and then back down again; Jess' chest was heaving, her side cramping. She didn't want to complain so she tried to keep up, holding her hand to her side as though the touch itself would soothe the side stitch.

Matteo must have seen. "Is your side hurting?" he asked.

"No," she said fast.

A moment later, he announced, "I want to walk."

She has never hiked in a place where there is no set path. They have to navigate around bushes, tree stumps, fallen branches, and mud puddles. Sometimes they're able to walk side by side; other times, Matteo takes the lead. Even though there should be a lot to talk about, they do not say much. Matteo stops every once in a while to look around; she takes it for granted that he knows where to go and how to get there. She is too tired to contemplate what would happen if that were not true.

Short, sharp flashes break into her thoughts: Sara pointing the gun at her chest; David screaming to run; Matteo jumping into the tunnel beside her. It is then that her heart seizes like a water balloon being squeezed to burst. She wishes Caerys were here. Caerys would know what to do. *Will she ever talk to Caerys again?* A sob surges to the top of her throat. Her hands shake as she dabs one eye, then the other, back and forth. She is glad Matteo is ahead of her so he cannot see these tears. She should be crying because she ruined his life, not because she lost her Keeper.

They keep walking. The dripping, stick-like shrubs and grasses that rub against their feet and legs have made Jess' coveralls damp, her running shoes soaked, and her toes numb. She looks ahead at Matteo's feet in his flip-flops; he must be freezing.

She wishes he would complain; that would make her feel better. As he walks ahead of her, she can tell he is thinking hard. His custodian's cap is off, and now that no stubble is on his face, his cheekbones are prominent, his jawline quite square. A bird caws in the distance; goosebumps break out on her skin. "Is it much farther?"

"Half an hour." Matteo turns back. "You as hungry as I am?"

"Starving," she says. It's nicer to talk. And there is something she's been aching to say. "Matteo?"

"Hmm?"

"I'm really sorry I messed up your life."

He stops. "Well, both our lives are pretty messed up." He starts walking again. "Let's talk about something else."

She double-steps to catch up with him. "You know what I keep hoping?"

"That this is all a bad dream?"

"Besides that." She snaps back a branch. "I keep hoping they finally figured out I know nothing about desalination. They must have retrieved our Keepers by now, right?"

"Definitely."

"And if they have, I'm guessing they've hacked into my research docs—"

"They hacked into those ages ago."

He has such a strange certainty about some things: surveillance, drones, hacking. *Weird.* This time his certainty is wrong. "No, my thumbprint is required to open the section of my Keeper where I store my research notes. There's no way anyone can access those documents without me holding my thumb to my Keeper."

"There's a way."

She stops her walk. "How would you know that?"

His eyebrows raised, he holds back a branch so she can make her way forward. "I think you're raising a good point. If Sara and Relly and De Sel read your Keeper before today, and I bet they did, why do they still believe you're doing research about desalination?"

"There's nothing about salt or water in any of my research."

He lifts his bike's front tire over a fallen log. "Could it be that your research doesn't seem like it's about water or salt but is?"

"Um, no, I'd be aware if I were doing research on salt or water."

"But what *is* your research about?"

"Technical stuff. Boring actually."

He turns toward her: "You're worried I can't keep up, aren't you?"

"No! That's not it; it's just..." Talking with men about science is usually a disaster. As though science is arm wrestling, they assume god-given superiority, and it's awkward when she has to slam their hand down.

"I'd say that answering my question is the least you could do," he says, steering his bike away from a muddy spot.

"The least—?"

"Considering how I saved you."

She looks at him: there is the hint of a grin. "Right, you did do that."

"Pony up."

This is the closest they have had to a normal conversation, and she's not hating it. "Okay, well, both of my current research projects are ones I started when I was a student at UC Davis, and they both involve this material, graphene. Have you ever heard of it? It's the strongest known material. It's only an atom thick but it's even stronger than—"

"Diamonds." he cuts in.

"That's right." She steps atop a big rock, jumps down. "You were a science major at Cal, right? What'd you study?"

"Bio, with an emphasis on botany. But don't get off track. Keep telling me about your graphene."

There aren't as many shrubs ahead, so she quickens her pace to walk beside him and his bike. "With my first project, I used a new synthesis of graphene to build a better solar cell." She turns toward him: "Solar cells are the devices that convert sunlight into electricity, you know, in the rooftop panels."

"Yes," he laughs. "I'm familiar with solar cells."

"Just checking," she smiles at him. "There used to be a lot of interest in using graphene sheets in solar cells. Graphene has this fantastic capacity to carry electric charge, so it's perfect for electrical conversion. Yet, no scientists could figure out how to utilize the nanomaterial, which has this nice honeycomb pattern, without tearing it when they handle it. It's only an atom thick, so, you know, it's hard to hold or even touch." She pauses to check on Matteo's expression. Most people's eyes would be glazed over by now.

"Keep going," Matteo says.

"In order to work around the material's fragility, I built these small rectangular tiles of graphene, only one millimeter by one millimeter. Then I stacked the tiles into a grid to produce sheets that work within a single solar cell. My solar panels are pricey to fabricate but they work really well. Actually, they have one of the highest ever recorded levels of light absorption."

She waits for Matteo to say something, but his face stays seeped in concentration.

"As you can see, that research project has zero to do with salt water."

He stops walking and drags the bottom of his muddy flip-flop across the bike's pedal to loosen the muck that's accumulated there. He looks up at her. "Okay, you convinced me: no salt water there."

She smiles. "I don't want to say I told you so."

"No," he smiles back, "I can tell you'd hate to say that." He flicks a bug off his coverall sleeve. "I'm impressed."

"With what?"

"What else? Your invention."

"Oh." This is not how most men respond. "Thanks."

"Now what's the second project?"

She is just as certain the other project involves no salt water, but it is nice not to think about danger or David or drones. "My second project came about in a strange way. My group at Davis received a grant from the Napa Valley winegrowers association. They wanted me to formulate rotor blades for wind-powered wine presses."

He repeats the information slowly: "Wind-powered wine presses?"

"Uh-huh."

"Haven't wind cranks existed for hundreds of years?"

"Yeah. And my design is a lot like the ones that have been around forever. My wind turbine sits atop a barrel press and when the blades spins fast enough to create torque on the crank, the crank releases the presses and the grapes are smooshed."

"The scientific term?"

"Yes," she smiles, "highly technical."

He walks a few steps. "Don't take this the wrong way, but I'm not getting why they needed a chemical engineer for this project?"

"The winegrowers wanted their press to work even in low winds, like three miles per hour and lower. They'd heard about research I'd done at Davis creating lightweight, durable material blends, so they asked me to use that kind of material to make a lightweight turbine rotor blade."

"And you made wind power work at three miles per hour?"

She nods. "Actually, at first it worked too well. I used this super lightweight material called aerogel that I applied over a graphene frame, the point being to create blades that were durable but lighter, literally, than a feather. With this first prototype, the blades spun so easily that the crank had far too much torque, and when the press was released, the grapes pulverized. Everything – skin, juice, pith, seed – passed through the grape crusher."

"Everything?" A breeze blows and the branches sway; dozens of drops sprinkle them from the moving trees.

"Yup, everything." She brushes the wetness off her cheeks. "But then I made adjustments to the aerogel blend, and now the turbine works just like they wanted."

Matteo stops and lets the bike rest against his legs. "Wait, could we back up?"

When she stops too, she realizes how thickly the fog is settling around them, like they are standing in a cloud.

He pivots to stand facing her. "When the press worked too well, is it possible..." his eyes squint.

"Yes?" In the fading light, she realizes they are the same height; their eyes meet each other at exactly the same level.

"Is it possible the grapes' molecular structure was affected?"

"You mean, like the press tore the grapes' molecular bonds?"

He nods, and the shadows on his face bring out the angles in his bone structure.

"Uh, no, there's no way that could happen. Were you thinking my press might have split salt molecules from water molecules?"

"Wouldn't that explain everyone's interest in your research?" He leans toward her and his coveralls touch hers.

"Sure, but it would also mean my press did something scientifically extraordinary. And—" she drops her chin, "my press isn't that special."

"Are you *sure*?" He leans in even more. "Maybe it's more extraordinary than you realize."

"It's not." He is so close she can smell the sweat on his body, making it harder for her to order her thoughts. "To break molecular structure, you need powerful energy – heat, electricity, magnetism... something to incite a chemical reaction." She looks up again, meeting his gaze. "My press, it only creates connection between molecules."

His eyes fix on hers: "Couldn't connection be enough?"

"I... I don't think so. I mean, no, scientifically it shouldn't be enough."

"But connection is a lot."

The way he phrases the words, she is not sure if he is making a statement or asking a question, and before she can respond, he begins walking again. The dusk's chill rushes into the space he left.

"Anyway, you're right again," he yells back to her. "There's no salt or water there either."

She rushes to catch up with him. The bike wheels whir, their steps clomp forward side by side. The sky overhead is darkening into the colors of an old bruise, and it is harder to see where her feet meet the ground. "Your lips are trembling again," Matteo mutters from beside her.

She wonders how he saw that. "Aren't you cold too?" she asks to say something.

He leans toward her. "The house is just at the top of this ravine." He points. "Can you see the lights?"

She cannot. In fact, the darkness ahead appears more wall-like than ever. Looking up, the hill's highest points contrast with a slightly paler sky, and using that dim reference point, she infers the slope they will climb: it's steep.

"Are you up for a climb?" he asks.

"Yes."

"I thought you'd say that. And I bet you're not scared?"

"No!" After a second, she realizes the question was a tease.

Matteo presses the button that makes his bike fold into a box. "At the top, we'll have to crawl. I'll help you if you want." The bike electronically folds into itself along the frame; the front and back wheels flip toward the center and the handlebars fold downward, then inward toward the frame. Matteo lifts the bike box by a handle that slings around the front and back of the frame and walks forward, his walk slanted to accommodate holding the heavy bike box.

The sky deepens into blackness, and Matteo's form appears as a shadowy shape though she trails only feet behind him. Soon, the ground under her running shoes starts to slope upward and with a few more strides, the slope becomes steep. The next step, she wobbles backward, her arms flailing. She calls forward: "I'm going to crawl it from here."

"Okay, me too." She hears the shift of his body downward and the exertion of the bike now being pulled along the earth. With her hands and knees on the ground, the earth is muddy and wet to the touch, cold. Her palms smear with the thick dirty paste, and she can feel gunk collecting under her fingernails. She wipes her dirty hands on her coveralls between each step, but after a while, it is pointless.

"Jess?" Matteo's voice calls to her.

"Sorry I'm going slowly."

"What? No, I don't care about that. There's something I want to tell you."

"Oh." That does not sound good. She stops crawling.

"I want you to know that... I... I work for..." In the darkness, his voice stops. The sounds of his shuffling make it clear he is turning over and perching himself on the hill. Her heart thuds, waiting for him to continue. "Do you think David would have hired—"

"David?" Her foot slips on the wet ground; her chest falls into the ground.

Matteo shuffles downward, his hand grabs at her arm, pulling her up. With effort, she manages to sit on her butt beside him, bracing herself against the momentum of the incline.

"Don't you think it's possible that David wanted to protect you, and maybe he hired someone—"

"Protect me?" This is not what she was expecting. She can feel the wetness seeping through the seat of her coveralls, the cold creeping into her bones. "Why do you say that? You've never even met David."

"No, but your thumbprint was coded to open the tunnels, right?"

"Yes."

"Making that work wasn't easy. David had to find the right people to approach, pay them money, and make sure they kept it quiet. Those things don't just happen."

"True, yes." She wishes she could see Matteo's face for this conversation. She cannot understand why he is bringing this

112

conversation up now. "But...that doesn't mean David was trying to protect me."

"What else could it mean? I think David might have done a lot to keep you safe."

"You do? I don't." She does not want to talk about this with Matteo. *Why is he stopping their progress for this conversation?* "Here, I'll carry the bike from here."

"The bike?" Matteo sounds confused. "Don't worry about the bike."

"No, seriously, give me the bike. You've been carrying it too long, and I want to carry it now."

Matteo doesn't respond.

"I mean it," she says again.

"Why you're obsessing over carrying the bike, I have no idea..." he mutters; then with a heaving sound, he lifts the folded bike over his lap and plunks it in front of her feet: "There, the bike's all yours."

"Thank you." She turns over onto her knees, grabs the bike by the handlebars, crawls forward and yanks it towards her. "What David did with the tunnel codes only shows..." she pauses, crawling further upward, "that he knew I would be in danger, not that he wanted to keep me safe." She catches her breath. "Because if he had really wanted to keep me safe he could have sent me to a scientific conference or told me to take a vacation. Or, here's an idea..." she yanks the bike upward, "he could have not *lied*. If he had never said that I created something I didn't create then no one would be chasing me." It is much harder crawling up this stupid hill with this stupid bike. Her chest is heaving.

Matteo is beside her. "Maybe David took other measures to keep you safe?"

"Other measures?" She looks over to the darkness that masks him. "Well, then those measures sucked."

"You think that?"

"Don't you?" Her breath rasps, even though she's not moving. "I don't know what deal he made with Sara or how De Sel is involved, but I do know: I shouldn't be. David lied about the invention and now people are shooting at me. He didn't keep me safe at all." There is the flash of David on the ground screaming at her to run. *He did seem to worry about her then. Why then, but not before? Oh, please let him be okay.* She puts her hands down hard on the rocky ground; pebbles push into her palm. With a groan, she lurches to lift the bike upward.

"Here," Matteo's hand slides onto the bike's handle. "It'll work better if we lift it together." Together, they grab the bike's handle, scale upward, then pull the bike toward them, repeating the process again and again. As they near the top, Matteo points ahead, taking in extra gulps of air: "Look, you can see the big house's lights."

She squints into the darkness, her chest rising and falling. There are twinkles of lights, lots of them actually. The fog diffracts around the bulbs, producing halos like the kind you see in Christmas cards of village scenes. When she looks harder, she can see the outlines of driveway and landscaping, porch. "Is that Tia's house?" she asks, excited.

He laughs. "No way. That's the Deddler's house, where Tia used to work. Her little place is way off their landscaped lot. Here, we have to go this way." She follows his lead, and eventually the wet turf under her feet becomes a cleared path. With the mild decline, she guesses Tia's house must be built onto the slope of the hill itself. Matteo calls back: "Just to warn you, her house is tiny, almost a shack. Don't expect anything too nice."

"Are the Deddlers your wife's family?"

"No, no. The Deddlers are the people Tia worked for after she stopped working for Rachel's family some twenty years ago."

She tries to keep up with Matteo's long strides. "Won't Tia mind you bringing a stranger to her house?"

He turns back. "Tia's not going to be there."

"She's not?"

"No. I had to move Tia into a retirement home a few months ago. Sorry, I thought you realized that."

"I did," she says it too fast. Actually, she had not given the evening much thought, but there had been some vague expectation of meeting a grandmotherly lady and settling into a warm kitchen with ruffled curtains.

Down the path, a structure sits crookedly against the hill. The dwelling is garage-like in its small size, and there are no warm lights or orb-y glows. Such blackness comes from the windows that Jess assumes the place must be freezing. Solar panels line the small rooftop, and dead bushes and prickly shrubs surround the small structure. Below the house's two front windows are two flowerboxes of shriveled succulent plants.

"I doubt there's much in the way of food," Matteo says as they make their way down the stone path to the house. "I keep a garden here, and there might be some vegetables we can pull. Or maybe some oatmeal or crackers in the pantry."

"Is there a shower?"

"A bath. We'll have to turn on the generator to get the water warmed up. Tia's water boiler is solar-powered, and today wasn't exactly a bright and shiny day." The floorboards creak as they walk onto the small wooden landing that stands in front of the door. Matteo reaches into the flowerbox under the window and comes out with a key, an actual key. Jess has not seen a door without a Keeper scan in years.

"You think she'll have something to drink?"

"You mean like water?" The key fits inside the keyhole.

"No, I mean like booze."

A grin slip-slides across Matteo's face. He pushes the door open: "After you."

MATTEO

The floorboards groan with each of Matteo's five steps as he walks from kitchen to bathroom door, and then squeak with a high-pitched note when he turns to pace back. He guesses that Jess, who is in the bath, must wonder why he is making so much noise. He is only thinking, but right now he cannot do that sitting still.

He wants to try again to tell Jess the truth. Maybe even blurt it out from this side of the bathroom door. Just to say: *"Jess, this is what I was trying to tell you earlier. I was paid to track you for the last three weeks. I followed you and hacked your Keeper and read your communications. And I think we should try to figure out who hired me."*

This last piece is what Matteo had wanted to talk about on the hike. Given how much effort David undertook to give Jess access to the Berkeley tunnels, Matteo had considered: perhaps David was the one who hired Beck Industries to track Jess. Matteo wants to continue the conversation. If he and Jess could simply brainstorm about this one question – *who would want her tracked?* – they might pull the curtain back on the motivation for all the day's drama.

Besides, he wants to come clean about his secret. When they were on the run, his deception seemed wispy and flimsy, like the fog that floated between them. Now, in the small house, with its dark wooden floors and tiny spaces, the lie is a bigger obstacle – one that keeps getting in the way.

He takes a swig from the scotch bottle. They found this unopened Chivas on the top of the pantry shelf above the boxes of Cheerios and stale wheat crackers. Considering he does not remember ever seeing Tia drink, discovering this high-priced scotch was a nice surprise. Tired and hungry, they plopped themselves down on the wooden kitchen floor. First, they grabbed handfuls of cereal and gulped glasses of water but it wasn't long before they were passing the Scotch bottle between them. Their coveralls were filthy, their hair wet and matted. His feet looked disgusting and Jess' cheeks were smudged with mud. Under the kitchen's low ceilings, their body odor swamped the space. Jess said it first: "We stink."

He wiped the scotch from his lips; "Your stink is way worse than mine."

She laughed, grabbing the bottle out of his hand; "Not from where I sit."

In the hallway now, a floral soapy smell comes from behind the bathroom door, and Matteo knows that Jess must be sitting in the tub, lathering her body with that wonderful smell. He takes another swig and walks back to the bathroom door, his face close to it. *Just say it through the door. Say it now.*

"Matteo?"

He jumps. Her voice is near, right on the door's other side. "Yeah?"

"Do you think I could borrow some clothes from Tia?"

"Clothes?"

"Like a nightgown or pajamas."

"Uh, sure, a nightgown. I'll look." He has to sit on Tia's double bed in order to pull open the tight drawers of her small dresser. Jess is almost a foot taller than Tia, but maybe he will find something that can work. As his hands sift through Tia's drawer, he is aware of how nice it is to be back in the world of the feminine. The pink flowery material, the scents in the air. Jess close. Naked in the tub. He has quite an image on that, he cannot deny it. He pulls a pale pink nightgown from Tia's drawer.

"I found something," he says loudly to the door.

"Great, could you hand it to me?" The door opens and her hand emerges. He pushes the nightgown into her palm; the door closes again. "I filled the bath back up for you. You should get in while it's hot."

It has been a long time since someone's taken care of him.

Right after Rachel's death, his family had tried to be there for him. His father came from New York for the funeral; his mum flew in from Milan. They stayed almost two weeks, squabbling with each other, but doing their best to help him make funeral arrangements and pack up Rachel's things. Rachel's brother, Jacob, and her parents invited him to Friday Shabbat dinner at their house every week for months. Matteo went at first, soothed to be spending time with people who missed Rachel as much as he did. Then, around ten months ago, he stopped. Rachel's parents had begun to invite other friends to these dinners, and the conversations veered toward the topical. After these social evenings, his emptiness only grew darker and deeper. The only person he still worked to see was Tia, and that was because she had asked him to build a garden within her backyard. Tia and he had such an easy way between them that they could spend the day together working in silence, and her occasional observations would make him feel like they had been in gentle conversation all along.

Four months ago, when Tia asked Matteo to help her transition into a retirement home, he had been shocked. Tia did not seem the type to live only among old people; she had more purpose and determination than most of the twenty-year-olds he knew. He could not imagine her only living with "old folks." Yet, she had been insistent. "It's time," she said. "I can't manage here any longer."

Once he moved Tia to the Berkeley group home, his loneliness settled more heavily into his bones. Yearning – whether for Rachel or Tia or people generally – became his background emotion. A funk grew inside him that came to feel like the smog itself, casting a brown tint over everything. He biked around Berkeley and Oakland watching people for Beck; he ate take-out in his studio apartment; he gardened when he could. He had hoped that when he paid Hua Chan back, his mood would improve. He had not been optimistic.

With Jess tonight, sitting on the kitchen floor, the wood walls and the low-wattage bulb overhead created a shadowy dimness. Yet, this brownness was not dreary. Jess asked him questions with her raspy voice and laughed when he said something even slightly funny. When he told Jess about Tia, the stories slipped from him like it was a normal thing for him to be chatty. He described how Tia loathed technology and refused to have a Keeper or any screen other than her reading tablet in the house. He told her how Tia biked all around the Bay Area at age 78, going to the El Cerrito library each week to get her five books downloaded. "She's the smartest person I've ever met. She's only 4' 10" and still speaks with this heavy Guatemalan accent, but there's really no subject she doesn't know something about."

He told her about his garden and everything he had planted and how he liked having his fingers dirty with mud. And when Jess stood up and said she wanted to see what he planted, he let her pull him upright. Together they took a small flashlight and walked to the garden where he showed her how to pull leeks and potatoes from the ground and cut chard at the stem.

Now, as he is wiping yet more scotch from his lips, there is a squeaky twisting on the bathroom doorknob. The door opens, and Jess stands before him. The sleeveless nightgown might have been loose on Tia's tiny body, but on Jess, it sits tight, stopping high on her thigh. Her face is fresh and pink, her hair wet, her lips and freckles: so pretty. She tilts her head: "You've got a funny expression on your face."

"I want to tell you something."

"Oh, well, tell me after your bath; otherwise the water will grow cold."

The corridor is narrow, and he realizes he needs to take a step against the wall so she can move ahead. When she pivots to pass him, her breasts brush lightly against his arm. As she walks to Tia's room, her hips jut side to side and from the way the fabric clings to her butt cheeks, he can tell she is not wearing underwear.

He closes the bathroom door, pulls off his damp t-shirt, and slips off his shorts. Steam is coming from the water. Slowly, dipping his body underneath, he suds soap in his dirty places – there's a lot of those now – and examines his body for the first time in ages. It is no different than it used to be.

"Matteo?" Jess voice comes from behind the bathroom door. "I'll make up my bed on the couch."

He sloshes upright. "No, I'll take the couch. I always sleep on the couch when I stay here."

"You do?"

"Yeah, it would be weird for me to sleep in Tia's bed. You sleep there."

"Okay, then I'll make up the couch for you." The floorboards squeak followed by a creak from the opening of the narrow linen closet. He thinks about beds and squeaking and sex.

For a long time after Rachel died, he avoided thinking about sex. Rachel was sex. There were in fact only two other women he had ever slept with, youthful flings that occurred during the six months when he and Rachel were "on a break." Those meaningless experiences didn't alter the fact that for nine years, his only sex was with one woman. The mole on Rachel's left breast, her salty, spicy taste, her throaty groans of pleasure – that was what sex meant.

After her death, he used to dream that they were making love. When he would wake, he would lie in bed, drinking in those hazy precious moments when Rachel still felt close and alive. Those dreams have not come to him in months, and lately, he has done those things that men with Keepers try. The different programs, the holographic women; it's not a bad time, not at all. Yet, the brown comes on heavy afterward.

The steam from the water, or maybe it's the scotch, is making him woozy. He steps out. His shorts and shirt are wet clumps on the floor; he smells them. No, there's no way he can put those on his body again.

"Matteo..." Jess is calling for him again, but this time there is panic in her voice: "Oh god! *Matteo!*"

He wraps a towel around his waist fast. "What?" He opens the door, rushing into the hallway. "What's wrong?"

She is standing by the couch, her hands extended, like she's bracing for a fall. "We have to leave! We have to get out of here *now*." She starts to run toward the bedroom.

Matteo lunges to grab her shoulder. "Wait, what happened? Did you hear something?"

She turns, her face creased in anxiety. "I... I *realized* that if De Sel has your Keeper..." She stops, gasping for air.

"Yes? What, what?"

120

"They have all the routes you've walked and biked in your Keeper's destinations log." Her whole body is shaking. "Relly will find us. She'll find us *tonight*."

"No, no, that won't happen," he says, his hands falling from her shoulders. He is relieved that her anxiety is a sort he can easily assuage. "I've never worn my Keeper here, never once, in the decade I've been coming to this house." He motions to Tia's bedroom. "Tia has strict rules about this place. If I'm coming over, I have to leave my Keeper at my apartment."

Her blue eyes are wide open, piercing bright.

"Tia's convinced the government tracks everyone, which, yeah, they do. But she's determined no government agency will know her business." He smiles. "It's funny because I'm sure the feds could care less about an old, retired nanny, but..." he tries to get her to smile too, "that's why I knew her house would be the perfect place for us."

Jess does not move, as though the news needs stillness to be absorbed. "I'm sorry." Her hands cover her face. "Everything rushed in on me so fast. I got... *scared*."

Her hands come down from her face, and from the way her eyes blink, he becomes aware that he is only wearing a towel with water droplets still scattered across his bare chest. "I should have told you more about Tia," he says, to fill the empty silence. Through Jess' nightgown, he can see the curves of her breasts, the darkness of her nipples. "Because..." his breath catches as he looks back at her, "you shouldn't worry. We're safe here."

"We're safe?" She looks into his eyes.

"For now we are."

There's a moment when she doesn't say anything, then: "Matteo." Her voice is nervous; she inches into his wet chest: "Can I kiss you?"

He catches her lips in his.

DAY TWO
Thursday, November 18, 2038

JESS

The pain inside her head throbs as though a chisel is being tapped straight at her cranium. Her eyes flutter open. She is lying on Tia's mattress on the floor. Three blankets and two sheets are tossed in knots at her feet, and she's naked with – *look at that* – a faint hickey on her left breast. So much has happened since the last time she woke from a night's sleep that she shivers as the memories bubble to the surface: David, De Sel, Tia, Matteo.

Where's Matteo? The living room is empty; she lifts herself to peer over the couch into the kitchen. He's not there. A thin streak of light seeps between the yellow curtains. She listens for Matteo outside. There is quiet – a stillness with such richness that she wonders if time has stopped. Finally, amidst this golden absence of sound, there are thuds and the sound of metal hitting metal.

She pulls the sheet to her chest and as the trapped air rushes toward her, there is the smell of sex. Usually, Jess doesn't care for this slightly sour smell; it's sweat and semen after all, not such fragrant stuff. Right now, though, she holds the sheet to her nose before wrapping the fabric around her like a towel.

There was a lot of sex. The first time, whether from the scotch or the pent-up fear, their bodies moved loud and needy. Afterwards, spent and maybe self-conscious by the utter carnality, they had lain there, heaving big breaths. Yet, because sex was more comfortable than talking, they went at it again. After the second time, they were exhausted, and sleep came fast. In the middle of the night, she awoke to Matteo nudging into her back, tugging her body into his. When she faced him, he kissed her – sleepy, languorous kisses. This last time, the sex was slower, more tender, with Matteo's face hovering over hers, his body moving in rhythm and his eyes steady on hers so that even in the shadows of the early morning, she was watching every speck of his face.

Opening the front door, the light slaps her eyes – an intensity of brightness that makes her squint. When her eyes finally adjust, the sky appears above her, pale blue and uniform in its blueness, like

123

robins' eggs. No haze, no smog. Jess takes a breath in; the air is pure pine and mud and wet. No smell of chemicals, no smell of smoke. *Did the rain do all this?* It seems impossible that such a transformation could come from one terrific storm.

She walks behind the house, her bare feet tapping along the moist, spongy ground. Matteo must be in the garden. She seems to remember the garden was behind the house and down the hill. *Isn't that right? Didn't Matteo say something about digging into the hill?* The night's details are fuzzy, as though the memories can only be viewed with a flashlight. A vague hint of alcohol still lingers in her throat.

There is a twinge of nerves as she considers what it will be like to see Matteo in this clear, morning light. In her limited experiences, men tend to freak out after the first sexual encounter, either becoming cloyingly clingy or sullenly aloof. She takes a giant step to avoid a muddy spot. Matteo might regret their scotch-soaked night. He might long for his wife or decide that last night's lust sprang only from shared fear. Jess tiptoes on the brown tufts of dead grass, trying to ignore how stubbly and wet the texture is beneath her toes. Matteo might think last night was just a physical way to expunge the day's anxieties, nothing meaningful.

As she walks along the hill's path, her ethereal happiness is drifting away, like a balloon whose string has lifted out of her reach. Matteo has been married; he knows real, abiding love. Jess does not. She has brought Matteo danger and risk and her neediness. *Oh, god.* There is no way she can be as desirable to him as he is to her.

Peering down the hill, Matteo is in his garden. Crouched, his fingers are in the soil, as though he is assessing the dirt's wetness. His clothes are different than the ones he wore yesterday: work boots, shorts, a green t-shirt.

"Where'd you get those clothes?" She tries to sound confident as she plods down the gentle incline.

He stands, squinting up the hill. "From the cellar. I keep some clothes there to garden in." He trudges up to meet her. "Where'd you get your clothes?" His muddy fingers touch the sheet she's holding up to her collarbone. "Because I like what you're wearing."

"You do?" She is relieved to hear the flirtation in his voice.

"Uh-huh." He leans in to kiss her, and right away, the taste is familiar and warm – not just his mouth, but his smell and skin. When she pulls back from the kiss, still holding tight to the sheet, she blinks several times. The sunlight is bright around them; she can see him so clearly. *Can he see her clearly too?*

"Doesn't the world look beautiful after the rain?" He takes in the hillsides with an almost proprietary pride.

"It is... beautiful."

"Yeah." He pivots toward the hill's crests. "Do you like being outside?"

"Outside? Sure, I like the outside."

"Spending time outdoors is really important to me."

"Oh," she says, unsure what to make of this announcement. "I... love being outdoors."

He looks at her, with a smile that is almost a laugh: "That's really good to know."

She tries to think what to say next but nothing comes to mind.

Grabbing her sheet between his fingers, he comes closer. "You know, the only trouble with this nice outfit of yours is that you won't be able to wear it to the library."

Her head dips to catch his words. "Did you say the library?"

"Yeah, I've been thinking, and we should probably bike to the El Cerrito library this morning."

"What?" This is the worst idea she's ever heard of. "Why?

"Well," he keeps his voice level, "we have to find out what those files on the dot drive say. Otherwise, we remain in the dark about what's happening to us."

"*What's happening to us...*" She repeats the phrase in her head, and yesterday's fears cramp her head, like brainfreeze from a milkshake. "We can't go to the library." Everything here on these hills is nice, so nice. They can't leave. *No, no, no.* "I don't care about the dot drive."

"I planned a way for us to stay real safe." He wipes his muddy fingers on his shorts: "You can take Tia's bike, and I'll ride my own. We'll wear oxygen masks and hats, and since the ride from here is mostly downhill, I bet we'll be going fast enough so that no surveillance will—"

"No. We're not doing this."

"But we have to find out what's on David's dot drive."

"No, we don't. You said we were safe here!"

"For a night, not forever." His voice lowers, and she can tell that he is striving to offset her alarm with his calm. "Relly and Sara are determined to get what they want, and that's the dot drive in the toothbrush. If we ever want our lives to go back to normal, we have to learn what the files on the dot drive say. Otherwise, we'll stay powerless in this situation."

Powerless. She turns away, looking up the hill. Relly's men said that if Matteo were caught, Relly would arrest him as a terrorist. There's no way that Matteo can go to the library. Her chest tightens like a rope knot is tied around her lungs. "What about the Deddlers? Couldn't we use one of their Keeper ports?"

"The Deddlers? That place is booby-trapped with alarms and surveillance."

"I'm not saying *break in*. Can't we knock on their door?" She has to squint into the sunlight to watch his face.

"They're not there; no one is. And the Deddlers wouldn't keep their Keeper ports there anyway. They have six houses; I can't remember the last time they came back to this one. They're richy-rich types."

"You don't like them?"

"Nah, they're takers. You know the type. They paid Tia crap wages, and when she retired, she asked if she could live in what was then a crappy old shed on their property." He rubs at the dirt on the back of his hand. "The Deddlers made her buy the place from them. That piece-of-shit structure used to be where the Deddlers stored their lawn mowers and gardening equipment, and it would have meant nothing for them to give Tia the place. Instead, they took her whole life savings and acted like they were being generous about it."

"But Tia's place is so nice now," she rests her hand on the artichoke tattoo on his bicep. "With the solar panels and the kitchen and the tub, it's cozy."

"That's all stuff we brought in. Rachel's family paid for the materials, and Rach and I came out here every weekend for a year and built everything up." He glances up the hill toward the house. "It was fun to transform the place. I framed the walls and installed the solar panels and Rachel sewed curtains and put countertops in the kitchen."

"That's… great, that you and Rachel did that." Jess takes her hand from Matteo's arm. A hawk screeches, and she looks overhead like she's interested in watching the bird glide through the air. Did Matteo imagine that she was Rachel when they were together last night? He could have. The house and hills and garden – these are all places he came with Rachel. Maybe he wishes she was Rachel right now. "I'm going to get dressed," she says, pulling the sheet tightly around her as she turns toward the hilltop.

Matteo follows her up the hill. "You know, if we get to the library when it opens, we can be in and out fast. I doubt De Sel is combing the surveillance feeds of the El Cerrito library, so there shouldn't be any problems. We can print the information from the dot drive; then, fast, bike back here."

"No." The word comes out sharp, and she doesn't even turn to say it. Matteo cannot go to the library. If Relly catches him, she will arrest him as a terrorist. Maybe she will hurt him, torture him. No, he cannot go. She has to go alone. Her stride picks up speed; the mud that had seemed miraculous a few minutes ago is now annoying for how it sticks to the soles of her feet.

"You can't say 'No.'"

Her sheet catches on a nail on Tia's porch, and she has to turn to un-snag it. "I can. I did. You have to stay here. I'll go by myself." She pulls the screen door back and walks into the dark, cool house, straight toward Tia's bedroom.

Matteo catches the door before it hits the door jam, following her. "I know you like to call the shots, but you can't *keep* me from going."

She turns back to him. "Didn't you hear what those men said about Relly declaring you a terroris—"

"I heard."

"Then, it should be obvious that you can't leave here." She walks into Tia's room.

Matteo follows close behind. "There's no way you're going by yourself."

"There's a way." She pulls open Tia's closet to see what clothes she can borrow. Only a dozen or so items hang there. Tia probably took most of her clothes to the retirement home.

"Either I go or we go," Matteo stands behind her, "but I won't let you go by yourself."

Jess pushes through the few options hanging in the closet; the shirts and skirts are tiny but there's an old blue t-shirt that might work. She loosens the sheet from her chest and rearranges it so that it knots at her waist.

"Did you hear me?" Matteo's voice comes from behind.

"No, I didn't," she says and tugs the blue t-shirt over her bare torso. "You're being unreasonable so I'm not listening."

"*I'm* being unreasonable? Give me a break, Rach."

Her head whips back.

"Shit, sorry." His hand runs through his mass of black hair. "I don't know why I said that. I know you're not Rachel—"

"Doesn't matter." She turns back toward the closet. There's a sting behind her eyes, and she's blinking fast to keep the tears from falling. It us not merely that Matteo called her the wrong name. All of yesterday's horrible confusions are now rushing toward her like a tsunami wave. No options, no safety; having to act brave when that's not at all how she feels. Last night, with the Scotch and the bath and sex, she had crammed the day's horrors away, as though stuffed into a drawer that she pushed tightly closed. Now, the drawer has been yanked open, and like Pandora's Box, the messy horrors spill out as awful as before. *He called her Rachel.* She yanks a black skirt off its hanger; this is what she will wear.

"Jess," Matteo steps closer. "If it's not obvious to you, the reason I don't want you to go to the library by yourself is..."

She lets the sheet fall to the ground in order to step into the skirt.

"—because I don't want something to happen to you." He pauses. "Nice butt, by the way."

She does not say anything, just further shimmies the skirt's narrow elastic up to her waist.

He comes closer, touching her back. "I'd be worried about you; that's why I have to come too."

"I won't let you." She bends to gather the sheet off the floor, but then: stops. A deep line stands out on the back of the closet wall; it looks like a cut in the wood paneling. She peeks upward; the cut comes straight from the floor and stops a foot below the ceiling. She reaches her hand toward the back of the closet. The paneling is beveled at the joists. Yet, she is sure what she is feeling with her finger is not a bevel but a long, deep slice straight through the wood.

"What are you doing?" Matteo asks from behind her.

She pushes all the hangers back to the far corner of the closet, and there it is, as clear as day: a door.

Matteo comes beside her to see what she is examining. "Whoa."

In the center of the door where she'd expect to see a knob is an old-fashioned padlock. Jess puts her head closer to the lock and examines it closely. There's lettering on it. All caps: P.O.P.

POP?

That's weird, she has a sensation she's heard the word "pop" recently, in some unexpected context. She reflects, searching her memories, and then it comes: "Oh god."

MATTEO

Even though Matteo has not picked a round-shackled padlock since his first week of training with Beck, this lock is not hard to crack. He finds bobby pins in Tia's bathroom and after five minutes of poking around, the shackle falls loose. He swings the thin wood-paneled door back on its hinge, and what he sees makes him stumble backward: "Shit."

Shallow, narrow shelves line the interior closet from floor to ceiling. Packed tightly on these shelves are guns. Semi-automatic rifles. Glock handguns. Laser pistols. Six-shot revolvers. Sub-machine guns. Explosive grenades. Tear gas grenades. And boxes and boxes of ammo. There is no uniformity in the make or model. Some look brand-new; others are ancient.

Matteo is scared to touch them, but he examines them closely enough to recognize that there is not one tranq gun among this stash. Every single one of these guns is illegal to have in a home. That's no small offense. Carrying an illegal firearm can put anyone in prison for a year. At all of California's highway borders, there are short tunnels with inductive scanning systems that check the cars for weapons, and drones frequently use radar scans to go street by street looking for the guns that, after the State Capitol massacre, were prohibited. With the tree cover that surrounds Tia's house, he guesses this spot was a perfect hiding place.

Jess stands beside him, scanning the shelves. "I guess Tia had something to hide after all."

Honestly, he would be less surprised to find stacks of cash or bags of cocaine. "I don't understand. She's the kind of woman who shoos bees from her house rather than kill them."

Jess is inside the closet, examining the shelves. "All the guns have 'POP' written on them." She turns to Matteo. "POP must be the name of the group."

"The group? What group?"

Her eyebrows rise: "The one the De Sel guys said you were a part of."

He studies the way she is standing, her hip jutted, with that tiny black skirt and the blue t-shirt barely covering her stomach. "Wait, are you thinking...? You think I knew about this?"

"You built the house, Matteo." Her tone drops like a hammer.

"Yes, but..." He runs his hand through his hair; this does look bad. "I promise you, there was no door in this closet when I built this house. None. I would have made the shelves deeper." He smiles.

Jess' face does not shift from stone-set. "You have to tell me the truth."

He thinks *fastfastfastfast.* He could tell Jess everything. Draw her the picture: He works for Beck; Beck told Matteo to take Jess to Tia's house – *Wait, is Beck in on this? Oh, crap, probably.* Jess' expression reminds him of a whip waiting to crack. This explanation is long and convoluted, and her suspicion: it would increase, not decrease. No, he must take a different route.

He steps tight into her space and puts his hands on her hips, looking straight into her eyes. "I'm not with POP. I swear I'm not." This is the truth, he reminds himself; he's not lying. "I had never even heard about POP until yesterday. When Relly was about to take you in, there were two men—"

Jess continues, "They yelled, 'Pop.'"

"Yeah, and I thought that was weird. I noticed it because Relly was about to haul you away and then she stopped, like there was a cause-and-effect with the men shouting the word."

Jess is searching Matteo's face. His expressions, his tone, his phrasing: he knows she's scrutinizing all of it. "But that's my whole exposure to POP. And, you know, we don't even know if it's the name of that terrorist group. Tia's not... she's not a terrorist." He is saying this, but he is not certain he believes it. He looks around the small bedroom, the tall shelves filled with guns facing him. He can't stand anymore; he sits on Tia's bed.

"Did Tia ever talk to you about guns?"

"No, never. Like I said, she's a peaceful person. But..."

Jess stands over him: "But?"

"She is – how should I say this? She's no friend to the wealthy. She really gets riled that some in this country have so much and others nothing. And she'll talk a blue streak about how capitalism makes greed sound noble when it's nothing more than selfishness pure and simple." Matteo thinks about how Tia used the phrase "rich bastardo" all the time: "Meh, he's a rich bastardo." The label was one she gave the Deddlers, Berkeley hills people, San Francisco people, Hollywood people, Silicon Valley people – really, anyone who was wealthy and selfish.

A lot of people.

"Has she ever talked about a group that she meets with?"

"Not once. And you have to understand: Tia's a good person."

"Salt of the earth?"

"What?"

"Never mind." She sits beside him on the bed.

He wonders if this POP piece could clarify any of yesterday's confusion. If Relly did not apprehend Jess because of that man yelling 'Pop,' then POP must scare her. Okay, that information stacks well enough. Moving on... If Beck knows about Tia's house, then is Beck part of POP? Possibly. And if David hired Beck, then does David know about POP too? No idea. The speculations drift too far. He retraces to determine the little he truly knows: POP is a word that scares Relly, and POP is a word that is written on these guns. He stands up: "Let's get out of here."

"You don't think we're safe here anymore?"

"Definitely not."

He walks out of Tia's bedroom toward the front door, kicking at the pillows and sheets on the living room floor as he goes. "Try to find us food," he bellows back to Jess. He wishes Tia believed in nutrition pods; he does not think there is any food left. "I'm getting the bikes." The screen door whacks behind him as he storms onto the porch.

His pace is clipped as he heads behind the house where the cellar door sits. Pushing down on the knob, he yanks the heavy door back, plodding down the three steps to the cool space beneath. Tia's bike is in front of him; he could take it and turn back up the stairs. Instead, he punches the bike seat hard, making the bike fall to the ground. There is nothing he can do; no one to call; nowhere to hide. He hates this particular powerless that he knows too well.

This morning, when he woke, he lay on the mattress on the floor for a long time. Jess was still sleeping beside him naked, her arm loosely draped over his side. The sunlight was streaming through the thin golden curtains which Rachel had sewn, and he watched the dust in the air catching the light and the sliver of sunlight moving across Jess' smooth back. Stretching his body into Jess' warmth, he began to consider that maybe yesterday's mess was nothing more than a huge misunderstanding. *Really, how could it be otherwise?*

That was when he hatched the library plan. If they could bike to the El Cerrito branch first thing, download the information from the dot drive, send it to Relly and Sara Claredge, even De Sel, then maybe, *maybe* everyone would leave them alone. After all, he and Jess were just two regular people. They had done nothing bad, and if everyone received what they were looking for, then shouldn't everyone leave him and Jess alone? That was what he had thought this morning.

He yanks Tia's heavy bike from the ground, lifts it to his shoulders and carries it up the three cellar stairs. Outside, the sun's brightness makes the grime and dust on the old bike too apparent. Everything is wrong. He drops the bike at the porch and when he walks into the house again, Jess' head springs up from pouring oatmeal into a Tupperware container.

He gestures to the bedroom: "We should leave after I lock up the... guns." The sentence sounds ridiculous, but he keeps walking.

At Tia's closet shelves, he studies the wall of firearms. He could take one or two, he supposes, though the idea doesn't sit well. He has never shot a gun – not even a tranq. When Beck first hired him, Beck had told him to take a two-day training at a shooting range, but Matteo refused. Rachel had died only a month earlier and then there had been the mess with Hua Chan, and he could not stomach shooting a gun, even if it was just a tranquilizer type. Matteo thought for sure he would lose the job, but to his surprise, Beck allowed him to take a holographic shooting tutorial instead.

Matteo arranges the closet's padlock and is pressing the lock's shackle into the ring when he re-opens the door and takes two of the teargas grenade cans. *Might as well.*

When he walks outside, the light is shockingly bright, as though yesterday's storm scrubbed the dingy skies with window scrapers. With this visibility, drone surveillance will be able to spot them like they are animals escaped from the zoo. He tries not to think about the odds against this trip or consider how they have no place to return to. No, just go. It's not safe here. The place has to be bugged, maybe with video cameras too. Actually, it is a miracle POP people has not already surrounded the house.

Jess is wiping the grime from Tia's bike seat with the hem of her t-shirt. He looks inside the bikes' satchels to see what she packed: some food, a pen-flashlight, a Swiss army knife, and an empty oxygen tank and mask.

"Here," she says and hands him the custodians' hat that has her hair glued inside it. "You should wear it again today."

He nods, and hands her one of the tear gas grenades. "It won't kill anyone – just slow them down."

She slips the small can into her bag without saying anything.

He walks to Tia's front stoop and locks the door, leaving the key in the flowerbox full of wilted succulent plants.

"Do you have the toothbrush?" he asks as he comes back to the bikes.

She nods, her hand over her eyes like a visor: "Do you want to carry it?" The statement has the tone of an apology.

"You keep it," he says.

"Are we going to the library?"

He shrugs. "I don't know where else we'd go. Everything comes down to what's on that dot drive, and the library's the only place to open it." His head nods to Tia's bike, "You shouldn't ride that old thing; take my bike."

"No, I like this one." She comes toward him, her hands coming to his chest: "Matteo…" Her closeness feels good, and he puts his hand on her hip. "You can tell me if you're part of POP. I don't know a lot about what they do, but I grew up poor and I want the poor to have more too. If that's what POP stands for, maybe…" She shrugs, "I just want you to tell me the truth."

Her face is so earnest it hurts. He thinks again about telling her that he works for Beck. He could, and yet… her hip's curve is so nice under his fingertips. Besides, they really need to go. "I'm not part of POP," he says and kisses her freckled lip, wishing this were the only truth he had to tell.

JESS

She bikes down the hill with no braking, trying to keep up with Matteo as he pivots his bike around the hill's turns. The deep decline allows them to fly at an astonishing clip, and as the cypress trees whiz by her, the sharp wind on her face presses her cheeks backward. Even with the speed, colors stream with incredible vibrancy, like the colors themselves are celebrating their liberation from smog and dustiness. Between trees and houses, she can glimpse the Bay. *Wait; there are the bridges!* As she glides downhill, she catches glimpses through the trees: the green ink of the Bay waters, the stark whiteness of the buildings near the Bay, the vast blueness of the sky. When finally there is an extended opening, the whole wide swath of the Bay Area stretches before her. *Breathtaking.* The vista is so clear that she wants to lift her hand from the handlebars to touch it. Just the other day, there had been no view, only a wall of yellow grimy smog. *Was that only yesterday when she was jogging in the hills?* It does not seem possible.

Even with the anxiety roiling her stomach, she cannot help but notice how strong Matteo looks as he coasts his bike downhill, the wind pressing against his t-shirt, his shoulders so broad.

Is he part of POP? She cannot decide what she thinks. His initial interest in her would be explained if he was with POP. Yet, his kindness would not be; he's not at all terrorist-like. What is surprising is how little it matters. She has no Keeper to call from. No place she can run to. No police to ask for help. Matteo is all she has. There is no one else.

Ahead of her, Matteo pulls off the road and tucks into the boughs of a cypress tree. She squeezes the handle brakes of the bike, and the tires squeak to slowness until her bike has stopped beside Matteo's.

"In the next block," he says, his cheeks flushed, "we'll start running into more traffic surveillance cameras." They had already agreed that once they moved into the more highly trafficked areas of El Cerrito they would put distance between themselves, since Relly's drones would be more likely to be looking for them together than separately.

They had also agreed that Matteo would enter the library two minutes ahead of her and spend his time in the library doing web research on De Sel and Sara Claredge. Jess had protested that she should go in first, but Matteo had insisted: "We need all the information we can gather, and nothing will happen to me in two minutes, trust me."

Now, Matteo leans toward Jess' handlebars so that as he points down the hill it is to her vantage point. "Here, I want to show you where the library is." The grids of streets and boxes of houses look map-like from where they stand. "Do you see the elevated BART track over there? The park beside it? The library is that beige-ish building; do you see it?"

"The one just across from those houses? It's kinda small for a library."

"Yeah, I've only been there one time with Tia, but the space doesn't hold much more than digital downloads and a kiddie corner. There's a big open room on the top floor and a smaller room in the basement." He rummages in his satchels for his custodian hat and puts it on.

She smiles: "You look completely different with that hair on." He has a lumberjack quality when he wears the custodian hat.

"Good different?" There's eagerness in his tone.

"Different different," she says, then regrets she did not simply say "yes." She cannot decide how warm she wants to be toward him.

"Are you going to put on your earrings and pink lipstick?" He pushes down his long sleeves so his artichoke tattoo is covered.

"I guess." Maybe they are fooling themselves that different styling will make them unrecognizable on camera. When they were on campus, Relly had no reason to believe they could change clothes or styles; the element of surprise was on their side. Now, Relly has surely reviewed the elevator's surveillance footage and figured out how they left the tunnels. A disguise will no longer be enough to help. It is hard to imagine what will be.

Matteo grabs the oxygen mask from the satchel and puts it over his nose and mouth. "Count to 120 before you start down, and remember everything we said." He is about to push off on his bike, when he turns and lifts the mask off. "If they find me, promise to run, okay?" There is no time to respond before he is zipping down the hill.

She begins to count, trying not to think how pathetic it is that she does not even have a watch: "Nine, ten, eleven…"

Matteo is down the hill, gliding fast on his bike. She plots the route she plans to take, the lefts and rights. Matteo is a speck now, almost at the library. She puts on her rings, earrings and lipstick. She is about to kick off when she tries to spot Matteo one last time. She looks, but he is nowhere. The fear fills her so fast she cannot swallow.

Starting her descent, she tries to keep her head facing downward as Matteo instructed. Once she's biking in the flats, there are more traffic lights and buses; a few coffee shops line the street. She follows the route the way she had set it out, ticking off each block she passes until she is at the library. The structure is a stone facade with big plate glass windows. A few concrete stairs lead up to enormous doors with long metal handles.

Parking her bike in the library's side lot, she grabs her bike satchel beside Matteo's bike and following Matteo's example, she does not bother locking up. Jogging to the front of the building, she pulls the door back, and right away, there is the sound of "Baa, Baa, Black Sheep." A gray-haired woman with a white sock puppet on one hand sings, bringing gusto to the song despite the fact that no children are near. A younger woman puts pillows on the colorful rug that sits in front of a small curtained stage. Apart from this brightly colored area, there is a central checkout desk with a rounded counter where two older women sit. To the left sits a long table with a glass screen driving down its middle. The table holds eight chairs on each side, and in front of each chair is a drive port with a projector facing the long glass screen.

A clock over the librarian's desk says that it is 9:32:36. Matteo and she agreed that he would stay in the library only eight minutes total, she only six; however, without a benefit of a watch, she's not sure how well she is keeping to their plan. She will aim to leave by 9:38.

Walking quickly to the long table, she takes a corner spot. A young Asian woman with purple hair sits at the farthest point and pays her no attention as Jess pulls the toothbrush from her satchel and rolls the one dot drive into the palm of her hand. Placing the dot delicately into the sunken drive holder, she watches it revolve in the case – the process reminds her of a TicTac getting an MRI – and right away, a projection on the glass ahead of her shows the content of the drive.

Only three documents. Doc.IP.11.17.33, Paper 09.13.33 and Paper 09.09.33, and three message files, DM1, DM2, DM3.

That's it? Dot drives can hold up to 200 terabytes; she was expecting a great deal more content than a document, two measly papers and text messages. *And why would David save text messages on a dot drive?* Messages are automatically saved on Keepers, and nobody sends vital content in these short files anyway. She badly wants to open just one of the message files, just to see, but the plan is to open the documents, print them, leave.

Jess glances at the clock – 9:35:47. *Time is passing too quickly.* She highlights the files and sets the command for "print all." Fast, she pulls the drive out of the port, slips it back in the toothbrush head and stands up, ready to get the hell out of there. Scanning the empty room for the 2D printer, she finally locates it behind the librarian's desk, where two women stand chatting.

She hustles to the desk and leans into the counter. "I'd like to have the pages I printed please."

One of the women peers at her over her bifocals: "Honey, that was a lot of pages you printed." The librarian turns to her friend. "Sophie, do you understand why anyone would print paper pages when they could use their Keeper's projector screens?"

On some level, Jess is aware she has passed this judgment on others herself; there is really no excuse for printing on paper these days. However, she is not in the mood right now for an eco-diatribe. "Could I have my pages please?"

"Once you give me $27 you can."

Oh, shit. It hadn't occurred to her that she would have to pay for the pages, which is dumb; of course, libraries charge for this service. Her face must convey her alarm because the librarian looks at her wrist fast. "Hey, you're not even wearing a Keeper. How're you going to pay me without a Keeper?"

"I have cash." That is a lie. Jess opens her bike satchel to go through the motions of looking for bills she knows are not there. The clock overhead says 9:38:32. *Shit. She has to get out of here.* The librarian chatters to her friend in a nasal, high-pitched voice. "Sophie, can you remember the last time we had a cash payment? Do we even *have* cash in the till anymore?" Jess eyes the stack of her documents on the printer desk behind the counter. If she dives over the countertop she thinks she could reach them. *Could she do that? Just grab them and run?*

Outside, there's a screech of tires braking. Jess' head snaps to the windows. Through the plate glass, a state police car jolts to a stop, just at the library's curb. *How could they have found them so fast? NoNoNoNo. This can't be happening.*

The librarians turn toward the windows too. Two police officers bolt from the passenger and driver-side doors of the cars. The librarian is astonished: "Sophie, look at the cops!"

As the librarians stare out the window, fast, Jess hurls her torso over the counter and stretches her arms to snatch the pages from the printer. Outside, the cops are heading fast to the front doors. Her heart hits like a doorknocker. *Go! Fast, to the stairs.*

With her satchel under her arm and the papers held tight in her right fist, she makes her feet scurry down the library's stairs. The librarian's whiney voice calls after her: "Come back and pay! I'm going to tell these cops on you!" Her body is on fire. She can't think; she can only move her feet down the stairs. "Matteo! Matteo!" she yells as she goes. "We have to go!"

Matteo has papers and satchels in hand; he points to a door that is in the back of this low-ceilinged room. "This way!" They run toward it, weaving around the grid of tables and chairs, lugging the cumbersome bike bags with them. "What happened?" Matteo shouts back.

"Cops. Here. For us." There is no one else in this basement space, which is good since anyone watching would assume they're criminals. *Are they?*

The basement space is smaller than upstairs, and they arrive at the door in no time. Matteo pushes it open; Jess braces for an alarm to sound; none does. He bolts outside, sprinting toward the library's side lot. "Come on!" he yells.

But Jess hesitates at the door's threshold.

She can hear the cops' shouts upstairs. They are close. She and Matteo can't outrun them. *They'll shoot at him; tranquilize him; take him away.* Her hand goes in her satchel. The tear-gas grenade is surprisingly cool in her warm and crowded bag. The cops' footsteps clomp down the first stairs. Fast, she pulls the can out, dislodges the safety valve, and yanks hard on the pin. There is a soft pop; it is live. She lobs the can toward the stairs, and it hits against the thinly rugged floors: thud, thud, thud.

"Jess!" The urgency of Matteo's exclamation makes her turn: *"Come on!"*

She starts to run to the side lot, trying to hold the satchel under her arm. When she turns the corner of the library, she sees Matteo standing by the bike rack looking at Tia's bike seat. *Why isn't he getting on the bike? Go!* Instead, he is grabbing at a sheet of paper that is rubber-banded to the top of the bike seat. The paper has their names on it, "Jess and Matteo," like a note passed in school.

"What does it say?" She is by his side now and watching him unfold the sheet of paper. "Who's it from?"

He doesn't answer because there's a sound, like thunder cracking, from the library. She whirls around to look at the library. The teargas grenade must have exploded. *She did that.*

"Leave the bike," Matteo barks.

She turns back to him: "But how will we—?"

"The tires were slashed!" He is running again.

She follows him, trying to keep her bag from jostling back and forth across her chest. "Hurry!" Matteo shouts, heading into the street.

She looks behind as she runs. No one has come from the library yet; the tear gas grenade must be slowing them down. *Maybe they are hurt. Maybe they are trying to evacuate the building.* She thinks of the woman singing with the puppet on her hand.

"You have to go faster," Matteo bellows back.

She is trying, but with the bag under one arm and her printed papers in her other hand, her run wobbles. A biker whirs past them on the street, eyeing them curiously. This is pointless. Where are they going? It's bright daylight. She hears a siren start up. Another biker cycles past. They have nowhere to hide. The cops are coming in cars. They don't even have bikes anymore. She just exploded a POP tear gas grenade. *Is she a terrorist now?*

Ahead of her, Matteo crumples the paper note into a tight ball and clenches his fist around it.

"What did it say?" She cannot imagine how he could have read it; wouldn't he need more time?

He keeps running, his heavy satchel bumping against his side, as his answer whips back: "It says: 'Trust POP.'"

MATTEO

What a stupid fucking message. Even with his fear – pulsing hard, hurting – there is outrage. They slash his tires and want to be friends. *Trust? Fuck them.* Given his fear, he is surprised to be giving time to this indignation. He would expect his thoughts to be erased by the jostling of his body, the adrenaline of his fear. Yet, the bright, bright sunlight keeps the moment sharp. He notices the turquoise color of the passing biker's shirt, the graffiti on the back of the building that says, "Fuck the rich," the overly-bright yellow in the fake forsythia hedges. Jess' heaving breaths beside him. This experience should be absurd and dreamlike, but there is no blur. Every sensation is vivid.

When he was eleven, his parents told him they were getting a divorce at an ice cream shop. It was news he had anticipated for months with the expectation that when the time finally came, there would be a gush of emotions, a virtual symphonic soundtrack that would crash into him like a wave. Instead, the moment played out in real time, like all other moments. He observed how his mother's eyeglasses were dirty, how his father had a swish of vanilla cream on his lower lip. He expected emotion to carry the details away, but no. Each second lasted as long as it always had.

So, it is now. His boots hit the pavement over and over again. He hears his breath, his exertion. Beside him, Jess' face is strained, sweating, her new bangs pasted against her forehead. The papers she has in her hand flap as she runs. These sheets must hold the contents from the dot drive. What do they say? Will he find out? Does Jess still think he's with POP? *Trust me.*

Police car sirens' swirl with a high-pitched whine, then pulse: high, low, high, low. The cars cannot be more than four blocks away, maybe less. Are there two sirens? Three? *Fuck.*

They run past a large park with jungle gyms and swing sets. He notices the people in the park – mothers, nannies, children – they have all stopped their play and conversation. They are standing, gawking at the spectacle that he and Jess make with their panting sprint. The park-goers must know that the sirens are for them.

Matteo shouts behind him: "Follow me." This next block has rows of small stucco craftsman houses, pale pink and powder blue. They dart toward the narrow corridor between two houses, then into the alley behind the yards. More sirens squeal. The cars are coming closer and closer.

Beside him, Jess' breathing is coming out like asthmatic gasps; her face is long with fear. The sirens are so close. He scans his options: *Hide in bushes? Run into a house?* Ahead, where the alley meets the road, a car brakes hard and turns fast into the alley. It is a long block, but the car is speeding straight toward them.

In the middle of the alley, Jess quits running.

He stops too. The sound of his pounding heart fills his head; he gulps for air and grabs Jess' hand in his. Not long ago, he had wanted to die. He reminds himself of that now as the small car hurls itself to a turning stop in front of them.

Matteo hears the shouting words before he sees the man's bearded face. "Get in! We're POP."

JESS

Her palm is slick with sweat but she cannot let go of Matteo's hand. Her legs, perspiration-wet under her short skirt, peel off the vinyl-plastic seats of this tiny backseat as the car screeches first one way, then the next. *So fast, so unbearably fast.* Her face twists, looking out the small backseat windows, trying to determine the proximity of the police cars. The sirens' shrillness whirls.

A flat screen is on the front dashboard and from it, a black, dreadlocked man is shouting directions to the bearded man: "Bruno, take the next left, then onto the lawn, eastbound."

Matteo is looking out the small backseat windows, his head swinging one way, then the next. "There's three now," and she knows he is referring to the number of cop cars pursuing them. *How can this tiny car slip away if three cop cars are coming for it?* It is not possible. They *will* be caught. She cannot swallow; her throat is too thick with fear.

The bearded man, Bruno, drives like a racecar driver. The houses and cars whiz past. It is not merely the speed that is breathtaking; it is the braking and hairpin turning. His car is small, no more than half the width and length of a normal electric car. Jess braces each time they turn, expecting the car to flip.

"Where are you taking us?" Matteo pushes into the front seat.

"Don't talk!" Bruno directs his head to the video screen: "Only Jake talks."

"Matteo..." the man on the video screen speaks, and Jess shivers at how comfortably he says Matteo's name. *Do they know each other?* Maybe Matteo *is* part of POP. "I'm watching your car from video feed that we're capturing from aerial drones. That's how we know where Bruno should go."

"But if they're watching us from the sky too..." Matteo doesn't finish, but Jess understands his question. They have no advantage that the cops do not also have. *There's no hope.*

"We have planned this," Bruno mumbles. He rips the steering wheel to the right. The burnt rubber smell of braking tires fills the car. "We know what we're doing."

"Can you tell us the plan?" Jess asks, trying to keep her body upright, though the car's swerving makes it impossible.

"Bruno will deliver you to a safe spot," Jake on the video screen responds. "We'll retrieve you later. Unfortunately, there's no other way for this plan to work."

The car jumps the curb to ride on a wide sidewalk; Bruno keeps his hand on the horn, pulsing it, and people rush out of his way.

Matteo shouts over the horn, "This is a plan of POP's?"

"Of course," Jake says, irritation in his tone. "Everyone at POP is doing all we can to keep Jess safe. Now that David has betrayed us, she is the key."

"The key?" She leans forward from the backseat: "No, you don't understand; I haven't invented anyth—".

"Quiet!" Jake shouts from the video screen. His eyes squint as he touches his temple; his voice shifts to urgency: "Bruno, next block. Enter Solano Avenue there. Fast! Go, go, go!"

Bruno turns the car onto the next street. It's a short block with only three houses on either side of the street; at the end of the street, there are two large orange barrels in the middle of the road, presumably to prevent cars from using the street as a throughput to the larger commercial street ahead. Bruno guns the engine right toward the orange barrels. Jess clenches her eyes shut. *No! The car won't fit! Stop! Stop!*

But the car must have slipped between the barrels, because when Jess opens her eyes again, they are shooting onto Solano Avenue. Cars swerve to avoid the tiny car's explosion into traffic. Horns blare; pedestrians scream as they jump out of the way. Bruno does not even slow; he drives the car straight along the double-yellow line that divides the two lanes of traffic. His body leans forward onto the steering wheel, and Jess guesses his foot must be pressed all the way down on the pedal. They are going five times faster than the surrounding traffic. Her fear throbs with the car's noisy engine.

146

Bruno shouts: "Jake? Cops on Sacramento? Or, it's a go?"

Jess knows Sacramento refers to a street that's seven blocks ahead, but what's the "go?" The shops and people of Solano Avenue stream past. A traffic light looms ahead of them; it is red and Bruno is not slowing the car. She yelps: "The light! It's red, it's red!"

Bruno punches his horn; they speed into the intersection. The crossing cars screech their brakes. There's the sound of what feels like a hundred horns, and Jess' and Matteo's screams are in the cacophony too, their mouths wide with fear. Bruno rips the wheel one way, and then the next, and their bodies veer with the cars like they're on a roller coaster. When they make it through, Jess heaves forward with relief.

"Listen," Bruno shouts. "In a minute, you'll be getting out."

Out? Jess looks out the window. *Where?* She doesn't like this car, but she does not want to leave it. *No, not out.*

Now it is Jake on the screen talking: "There are precisely 42 seconds to discharge. The tunnel ahead will be your exit point. Currently, we are followed by two raven drones overhead, but they can't proceed into the tunnel, and the cop cars are at least..." he pauses, waiting for the data to enter his head, "eighteen seconds behind you. We have this timed precisely. At a spot approximately 25 feet from the tunnel exit, the car will stop, and you will exit the car. At this spot, you will find a door in the tunnel wall that you must enter. From the time the car pauses, you will have approximately fourteen seconds to enter the tunnel door, or you will be caught. Do you understand?"

"What's behind the door?" Matteo yells to the front seat.

There is no answer. Jess sees the tunnel's dark mouth coming toward them fast.

Matteo leans forward into the seat. "Are the cops with De Sel?" Though the question seems to come out of nowhere, she understands Matteo's motive. This is their chance to get information; there might not be another.

"Those aren't cops," Jake says quickly, a grimace of disdain on his face.

She leans forward: "But they're in cop cars?"

Bruno is the one to respond. "Relly got them cars and uniforms. Those guys are the security detail at the Governor's house. They have no idea what they're doing. That's why they can't drive for shit."

Matteo is fast with the next question: "Why does the Governor care about Jess?"

"Same reason David did," shrugs Bruno.

Not a satisfying answer. Jess pulls herself into the middle spot between the driver and passenger seats. "Is David alive?"

Even as fast as he's driving, Bruno peers at Jess. "The Governor's men have him now." He checks his passenger mirror. "Our sources say he hasn't regained consciousness." He switches lanes. "Which is why we need Jess more than ever. She has to help POP save the world."

What? No, they don't understand! "I don't know anything about desalina—" she shouts, but Jake's voice overpowers hers. "Bruno, go to autopilot." Bruno flips a switch and there's a hitch, like a gearshift, in the engine's hum.

The tunnel is coming toward them fast. Matteo shouts at the screen again: "You've made a mistake: David was lying about what Jess researched—"

There is a horrible noise. It is like no sound Jess has heard before: a high-pitched shriek, then a shattering sound. The windowpane collapses forward in small shards. Red splatters everywhere. Jess stares at her lap. It's like a shaken soda can has exploded onto it – except this is blood mixed with clumps of whiteness, like wet toilet paper. Bruno is slumped forward. Before she is sure of what she has seen, they are in darkness. The car is driving through the tunnel now, its speed suddenly slowing.

"Oh god!" Matteo leans forward, and Bruno's body in twitches and gurgles in the seat ahead of hers.

"No," she gasps. She twists back to see the light at the tunnel's end. She wants to go back, rewind. One second, two seconds, that's all. "No!" *Take those seconds back! Stop this now!* Sounds – horrible sobbing sounds – engulf her body.

All she wants is to go back. *Please, go back.*

MATTEO

His back thuds against the seat; the car is stopped. He had been vibrating; now he is still. The engine had been loud; now, it is quiet. They had blurred forward with such speed; now, they sit in this one spot, grounded. Beside him, Jess wails, her skin red, like a baby in hysterics. Car horns blare. He looks behind him, out the back window. The tunnel is dark, but he can tell the honking cars aren't police cars. Just regular people frustrated that the traffic is blocked.

Wetness is splattered across his cheek and lips; it tastes like meat. He wills the retching in his throat back down. Someone is calling his name. "Matteo!" The voice is far away. He does not want to listen. He does not want to be here. *Why is he here?*

"Matteo!" It is the voice again, louder.

He looks at Bruno, and then wishes he had not. The right corner of his head is lopped off, the brain tissue spilling out like curded cheese. His forehead has a rock the size of his palm cratered into it. One of the raven drones must have projected the rock like a missile. Matteo has heard of this way of jury-rigging drones to give them gun-like capabilities. Rocks can kill as well as bullets if they are fired from a drone.

"Matteo, you have to get out of the car." *Where is this voice coming from?* "Look at me, Matteo! *Look at me!*"

"I'm looking," he whispers, the words coming hard to his lips. Then, he actually looks at the video screen. But it is not Jake there; it is Beck. *Beck?*

"Matteo." There is no surfer tone in Beck's voice now; it is tight and serious. "You have nine seconds to get out of this car. Grab Jess. Move. *Now!*"

Beside him, Jess' head moves back and forth across her chest, like a bobble doll, her words bubbling: "No, no, no, no."

"Everything rides on her! She is the only one who can make the solution work!" Like a lion's roar, Beck shouts: *"Go now!"*

The word jolts Matteo's consciousness, like he has been plugged in. *Yes, go.*

He slaps Jess' thigh; no reaction. He slaps her thigh again – hard this time. "Come!" he shouts. Her eyes glare, like a dog growling. Matteo does not care; they have to go. Fast, he opens the back door, grabs both satchels with one hand and Jess' wrist with the other.

"No," she resists. "Let them catch me, I don't care."

"Six seconds!" Beck is screaming now. "She's the only one. You have to save her."

Matteo steps out of the car, yanking hard on Jess' wrist. This time she comes with him, stepping from the car, into the normal world, where people honk at stalled cars. Matteo slams the car door shut, and like that, the small vehicle drives forward again. Autopilot.

Matteo wants to order this moment, to consider all the elements POP had to put in place to make their getaway happen, but there is no time.

"The door's here," he says, directing Jess two short steps. The door is brown, wooden, and set within the tunnel's stone. Sirens are coming closer; he hopes they are not in the tunnel yet. He opens the door – there is no resistance or creaking – and pushes Jess inside. He follows behind her fast, shutting the door tight. A lock automatically turns.

They are in darkness.

JESS

She grabs at her wrist, for her Keeper's flashlight. There is no Keeper on her wrist. No Caerys. She blinks, expecting light to return. The space stays black, still. Moments ago, there was speed, blood, car exhaust, blaring car horns. Now, they have stepped into a black hole. Her cries hiccup from her chest, echoing against the walls and ceilings that hold the darkness.

"Jess?" Matteo's voice is low. She reaches her hands out to find him. He is there: his chest, his face.

"Is the door—"?

"It's locked," he says. "And the POP car drove away..." his voice drifts, like he is working out the consequences, "so the cops will follow it. They'll think we're still in the... car." His voice catches on the last word. She feels his hand tug at her shirt, and he's pulling her into his chest, holding her tight. His body is shaking too, and his low, guttural sounds reverberate against her t-shirt. Standing together tightly, she has the sensation that they are sinking into quicksand, as though the darkness could swallow them whole.

She moves her hands to Matteo's face and tries to say something to soothe him. "We'll be fine. I can..." The words linger limply in the dark. *What can she do? Nothing.* And in that instant, the dark becomes too heavy, too pressing. She needs light. "Where is my satchel?"

Matteo lurches toward the ground, picking up her bag and pushing it into her chest.

"I put a penlight in here," she sniffles, as her hands fish around in the big bag. When she had slipped the thin flashlight into her bag that morning, her thought had been that if they were to return to Tilden Woods that night, a flashlight would help light their way. Now the notion strikes her as naïve, the idea that they would be allowed to hike away from this horror.

"Here," she hits the button, and a beam spreads into the darkness, making it possible to vaguely make out their surroundings. It is a small room, maybe twelve by twelve feet, with dark, concrete walls;

little is in it. Two columns of orange traffic cones are stacked high in a corner. A large metal sign that says "Road Closed" in reflective letters is propped against the wall. Six long, orange A-frame barricades stand in front of it. "This must be where they store the tunnel's traffic stuff," she says, sniffing back her tears, relieved at the room's ordinary contents.

Holding the narrow light upward, she sees a string that is attached to a single, naked lightbulb.

Matteo tugs on it, and the room turns bright. Matteo's hand jolts to shield his eyes, and Jess guesses that the light itself is not as uncomfortable as being seen. His cheeks are dirty and sweat-streaked; splotches of blood smear his t-shirt, and bits of white gunk stick in his black hair. His jaw is set with a grimness that makes him look older than when she studied him this morning. She brings her fingers to his hair to drag out a piece of something white and yucky. She does not want to think what it is, but the possibilities pulse before she can stop them -- *brain, skin, muscle.*

Matteo nods toward the back of the room. "There's a door back there."

She turns to see another plain wooden door as Matteo is already walking toward it. He puts his hand on the bulbously round doorknob and lets it sit.

Jess walks to where he stands. "Is it locked?"

His hand pivots on the lock ever so slightly. "Yes – just a pin tumbler lock, but it works."

"Good. Then no one can come in here."

He rights himself, facing her. "It's locked from the *outside.* Same with the tunnel door. You don't get it; they've trapped us here."

She rushes to the tunnel door; her hand twists the handle: it does not budge. She staggers backward. This small room, its walls so thick and hard and cold. She tries not to panic. POP will come back soon to retrieve them. This is temporary, only temporary. Her head hurts like it's packed with barbed wire.

Matteo walks the perimeter of the small room, his eyes scanning the corners. He stops where the "Road Closed" sign is tilted against the wall; he pushes it to the ground. A joltingly loud clanking fills the space, echoing in her bones. Matteo doesn't flinch. He runs his hands along the back of the sign, then the front.

"Here we go," he says through clenched teeth. He holds out a small strip that reminds her of a metallic Band-Aid. "It's a listening device," he whispers. "They're listening in on us." He throws the strip on the ground and brings the toe of his work boot down on top of it. Jess can hear the wires breaking.

She leans into his ear: "POP's listening?"

"They're the only people who know we're here." He walks over to the cones, his jaw tight.

"But why?"

He puts his finger to his mouth: "Shhh." He pulls a hazard cone off the stack, examines its inside, then throws it on the ground.

She follows his lead; taking a cone off the second stack and reaching her hand inside, she feels for any of the listening device strips. *Why would POP go to the trouble of saving them if they were only going to leave them here?* She pulls the next cone off of the stack.

Within minutes, they have identified four listening devices hidden within the twenty cones, and Matteo finds another two attached to the A-frame barricades. Jess steps on the three she found, and Matteo crushes the rest of them under his boot, stomping on them, grunting, like breaking these small listening devices is an act of revenge. The traffic cones scatter across the floor, some upright, some tipped over, and the smell of their weighty plastic fills the small space.

Matteo leans into her cheek; he whispers: "In case we didn't find all of them, we should still whisper."

She nods though she doesn't care; let them hear. Maybe then they will realize she knows nothing.

Matteo walks slowly, staring at the walls, spinning toward the center. "My guess is there's a video camera in the overhead lightbulb too. I'm going to turn the light off. That way, even if they're filming us, the light will be poor enough that they won't be able to read our lips."

Before she has a chance to look at the bulb, Matteo tugs on the string. He clicks the flashlight in the same instant, and there is a ricochet of light, dark, shadow. In the dimness, his eyes stand out, beacons of anger. He brings his head close, his lips almost touching hers. For a second, she thinks he will kiss her, but instead he whispers: "What did you learn at the library?"

She turns the word in her head: "The library?" *Is it possible she was at the library an hour ago?* She thinks of the lady behind the information desk with her bifocals and the smells of dried paste.

"Jess, you have to focus. We have to figure out what's next."

What's next? What can possibly be next except for waiting here? She does not want to think or problem-solve; she wants to sit: to never think, to never remember. Matteo grabs her wrist, and his impatience comes through like a charge. She makes herself respond: "At the library, I printed what was on the dot drive."

"Do you have the sheets?"

She kneels on the cold concrete and digs through her satchel. "There wasn't much," she says, holding the pages up to him. Matteo throws a cone aside and kneels beside her on the ground. "I didn't read anything," she continues, "but from the file names, I think there is a document and a couple of research papers."

He grabs the flashlight from her and studies the first page, then the second. He thumbs through the rest quickly. "These are just your scientific journal papers. The one about the solar cell and another one about the wind crank."

What? She grabs the papers back from Matteo's hand and sifts through them, finding that the sheets hold familiar diagrams and equations. "That makes no sense. I didn't even conduct the research for these papers with David. It's work I did at Davis. There's no reason for him to have a copy." She flips through more pages. "Hold on." The last two pages of the stack don't have letters but instead are full of symbols and numerals. "Look at this," she holds the papers so that Matteo can see them too.

He takes the sheets back: "Encrypted. David took the time to encrypt one file, but not the others." He drops the sheets back into her lap.

"I don't get it."

"You may want to fight it, but your research is involved in this desal stuff."

She looks up at Matteo, and it would be foolish to argue. There is no reason for David to have copied these papers unless David is relying on them for his desalination solution. Yet, try as she might, she cannot fathom how her wind crank and solar cell could have anything to do with salt or water.

She hears Matteo sit on the ground next to her. "What I don't understand," he whispers, "is that your research papers were sent for peer review months ago; it's not like they're top secret. Even if they haven't been printed in journals yet, they're easy to find."

She turns to him, replaying his sentences in her head. "How... how did you know when my papers were sent for peer review?"

"Uh," he pauses, "I don't know. I just assumed... I mean... have they been published?"

"No." She examines the way his eyes shift downward. "Both papers come out in journals next month – just like you assumed."

He lifts his head with determination: "What else was on David's dot drive?"

Jess does not answer. *How does Matteo know so much about her papers? There is no way for him to have guessed that insight.*

"You have to tell me what else you found." Matteo says, his voice louder. "Come on, we have to figure this out."

She swallows: "A few text messages."

"Text messages?"

"Uh-huh." She grabs the stack of sheets from the ground. "There were only three, but I printed them too; here."

He flips one sheet, then the other. "You've got to be kidding me," he mumbles, shaking his head. He tosses the sheets and penlight near where Jess sits and walks into the corner's darkness.

What now? She holds the flashlight to the sheets. Her eyes fix on all the coding around the "to" and "from" headings. Messages are not usually formatted with so much programming syntax, and it takes her a moment before she sees that "Jessila Prentiss" is the recipient. "These messages are to *me*?"

The message itself is short:

> Fire, all I can think of is our time in the shower. How we work so well, how it's so good. We make magic.

Whoa. Not what she expected. Jess never took a shower with David; he must be talking to someone else. Quickly, she flips to the next message.

> Fire, our bodies fit perfectly. Don't worry; I am with you completely.

That's effusive language coming from David. If she had seen these messages two days ago, she might have felt upset that David was interested in another woman. Now, there's no pang, no heart hurt. She doesn't even care that David is calling this other woman "Fire." Whatever.

The last message:

> Fire, you have my promise. Don't ever doubt that. I want to be with you, no one else. Together, we can be more than we could ever be alone.

Wow. She holds the penlight to light the spot where Matteo stands by the Road Closed sign. He is kicking the toe of his work boot against the concrete floor, and even in the dim light, she realizes what needs to be clarified: "Those messages aren't to me."

His eyes stay on his boot's toe. "Your name is right there after the 'To'."

True. She studies her name amidst all the other coding. "But I never received these messages. They are to some other woman. David never types his messages to me; he only sends me audio… " She pauses. There's a familiarity to this argument; when was it that she was discussing David's messaging habits?

Oh.

And like that, a rush of connections stampedes toward her. Her hand goes to her mouth.

"What?" Matteo walks toward her: "Did you figure something out?"

She looks up at him. "David sent me a typed message yesterday. It was…" she pauses, swallowing, "a high alert message. He asked me to forgive him."

"Forgive? Wait, back up." Matteo sits down beside her again on the cold concrete. "You never told me you received a message yesterday."

"There were so many things happening yesterday that I forgot it was the message that started it. I was out running when I received this message from David saying that he was begging my forgiveness, that he'd been trying to protect me and that he truly… loved me."

Matteo's face pulls back: "Truly loved you? You went to his house because you received that message?"

"Caerys tried to tell me not to go, but I didn't listen. Caerys is my Keeper," she adds as explanation.

"I know. I mean, I know you went to David's." There is a pause. "Did you go to David's to get back together with him?"

"What? No! You're missing my point. Don't you see? David's message yesterday was typed like the ones here. And he's *never* typed his messages before."

She holds the small flashlight to the pages and reads to herself: 'Our time in the shower.' *Shower = Water. Water = desalination.*

The next message: 'How it works so well.' *What would David care about working well? Only the desalination solution.*

She silently reads the next message: *"Don't worry; I am with you completely."*

Then the next: *"Together, we can be more than we could ever be alone."* The words pulse off the page, the meaning immediately clear.

She grabs Matteo's arm. "These messages aren't about sex or love; they're about the desal deal. Don't you see? David's trying to reassure someone that he's still committed to working with them."

Crouching beside her, Matteo peers at the papers. "You're right," he whispers, then reads aloud: "'Our time in the shower.'" He must have set up the desalination solution in the shower, to test it. Then he says, 'I want to be with you, no one else.' He's trying to signal that he won't betray their deal."

Matteo points to the coding at the top of the first message: "I think these messages were sent as comeback calls. That's what all that weird syntax is at the top."

"As what?"

"It means the messages are sent, then pulled back before they're received. It's a way to send secret messages."

"I don't understand." The concrete is cold on her thighs beneath her tiny skirt. She rearranges herself to sit on her knees, facing Matteo. "If a message is never received, what's the point of sending it?"

He puts his hand on her knee: "The message isn't received by you; someone else receives it. It's kind of confusing, but comeback calls are a workaround for two people who know their Keepers are being watched. The two people communicate by using a third person's Keeper as a way station."

"My Keeper was the way station?"

"Yeah, this message hit your Keeper's mainframe and stayed there only for a millisecond before it was pulled back. David must have known his real recipient had a snooping program on your Keeper too. He writes to you in a way that ostensibly could be a real message, so the person tracking his Keeper isn't too suspicious. But the message is actually coded for the person who pulls it off your Keeper."

"That's so much work."

"Yes, it is."

He stands. "David was working real hard to keep his secrets. He knew his Keeper was being watched; your Keeper was being watched. Everyone was watching everyone. Everyone was deceiving everyone." Matteo's jaw is clenched; his eyes are drilling. There are a million reasons for him to be upset; yet, there is a mysterious quality to his anger.

She stands too. "What I can't understand is why the last message came to me instead of being re-directed."

"Well, David didn't pull it back."

"But why not?"

"Maybe he wanted you to come to his house."

"But he told me to run. He screamed out to me—" she shivers, "while he was being beat up."

"I don't know..." He's running his hand across his forehead. "But I do know that we're being moved around like pieces on a chessboard. First to David's. Then to see Sara Claredge. Tia's house. Now, here."

"But you were the one who suggested Tia's house?"

"Right." He takes a big breath: "All I know is something's not right."

"Well, yeah." That is obvious. She holds the flashlight to scan the four concrete walls: solid, gray, ugly. So cold. "I wish we knew what the last file on the dot drive said. Now, even after all we risked, we're still in the dark." She waves the thin light to the ground. "Literally."

He walks straight to her. "Do you really want to find out?"

She is confused by the question. "Well, of course. Don't you?"

He kneels down to the satchel by her feet and moves things around until he pulls a Swiss army knife from the bag. He pulls the pin insert outward. Without saying anything, he walks to the back wooden door.

"What are you doing?" she calls after him, though she knows. He picked the padlock at Tia's house easily. He did it all by sound. He brought his ear right to the lock and moved the bobby pin inside the small keyhole until the padlock popped open. She can't see what's happening now, but from Matteo's short intakes of breath, she can tell the lock is not budging, until with a big exhale, she knows: it has.

They can escape. A cold sweat breaks on her skin. "Matteo..." She walks to where he stands; the words spill: "This is not a good idea. If we go out again, they'll catch us and hurt you." A flash of Bruno's split head rushes into her thoughts. "We can't leave."

He grabs her hand. "We have to." His short statement drops like a rock. "Jess, if you don't have the solution, they'll hurt you too. Don't you see that?"

She doesn't. "They'll hurt us outside, but here, here is *fine*. POP brought us here; they're trying to help us—"

"No, they're trying to help themselves. Not us. We're not safe here." His face is set with certainty.

"I don't know why you say that. POP could be the good guys in all this. I mean, don't you think Sara Claredge is with POP? She wants to end famine; that's good. And Tia is with POP. You love Tia. And they picked us up before we were arrested and... brought us here." Matteo's not interrupting her, and the more she says, the thinner her voice is becoming. "The note said, 'Trust POP,' and maybe that's what we should—"

"Don't trust them." His hand holds hers tightly. "This whole situation is wrong. Why wasn't someone from POP waiting in this room to help us? Why are they listening in on our conversations? They want something – and it's not to help us. POP is a terrorist group. And when they come to collect us, we'll no longer have a chance to get away from. We'll become part of their group. If we leave now, we can *try* to stay good."

"Good?" All she wants is never to be scared again, never to see more blood, never to have to hurt anyone. Goodness is not a top concern.

Matteo whispers, his lips right in front of hers: "Please do this for me."

She does not understand; he had been so angry; now, he is soft. This morning, she was so worried he was with POP; now she is certain he is not. Her confusion swirls like a compass whose magnetic bearings have gone awry, the dial spinning round and round. "But... where would we *go*?"

He takes a sharp inhale, and even in the darkness, she can tell he has a plan that he is scared to share with her. "I have a friend who's really good with encryption. He lives in a tent town near Jack London Square."

Jack London Square is in Oakland, eight miles away. She cannot imagine how they could possibly travel that far. They have no bike, no money. *Would they walk? Take the BART?* Outside, there are cops, drones, satellite surveillance.

He continues, his voice low and plaintive. "It will be hard, I know. But not impossible." He takes the top of her hand and kisses it. "Please, Jess, trust me. POP is dangerous. I want to keep you safe," he whispers.

The sentence hums in her ears like the lines from a lullaby. Soothing, comforting. It is the phrase, she remembers, that Matteo said to her in the Berkeley tunnels. This observation flits through her mind; she re-winds to it.

Huh. The same exact phrasing as her wish.

Like a circuit board lighting up, connections are made.

Matteo knows the power of that phrase for her.

He heard her conversation with Dr. Monique.

He hacked her Keeper; that's why he knows when she submitted her science papers.

Meeting her at the Juju; that was no coincidence.

These understandings arrive in fast pulses, like a strobe light being flashed in her eyes. *Matteo is not who he says he is. How could she have not seen that before?*

Her knees waver as though she is at sea. She snaps her hand loose from his. *Which side does he work for?* No, she cannot think now; there is only impulse. Stumbling a step back from Matteo, she grabs at the door. The knob fumbles in her sweaty hand; she twists harder. A click. Without saying another word, she yanks the door wide and staggers out.

MATTEO

Blackness surrounds him. No sounds. Jess takes small steps with her arms forward and Matteo follows behind, one hand on her back, as though they're playing a version of Blind Man's Bluff. From the dimensions of the space, they are clearly walking through a long narrow corridor. The ceiling is only inches above his head, and the walls are tight around them. With his satchel on his hip, he barely fits. The floor is dirt, and the walls and ceiling are rock. A mineral smell hovers in the air, and Matteo is reminded of the holes gravediggers prepare for caskets.

He has no Keeper on him to set a timer, but in his head he is ticking down the minutes in which they have to move as far away from the tunnel as possible. Wherever this corridor takes them in Berkeley, they need to move quickly from this spot.

In front of him, Jess sighs, and her exhalation has no anxiety, only sadness.

"We'll be out of here soon;" he wishes he had more to offer in the way of reassurance. His plan could be a disaster. The last time they were in open air, it took only ten minutes before they were found. Yet, the entire time they were in that airless, freezing cold concrete cage, he could not ease the itching in his head, like a mosquito buzzing in his brain, that trusting POP would be a mistake.

Tia could have asked Matteo to be a part of POP. Beck too. Why didn't they ask? Because they knew he would never have agreed. If POP is the group that killed the state assembly people, they are straight-up killers. And even if Matteo agrees with this group's political goals, their methods are disgusting. Beck and Tia had to know that he would think that, and so they tricked him to do their work.

What worries Matteo most about POP is that they appear less interested in the desalination solution than in Jess herself. Beck never asked Matteo to gather specific research from Jess' Keeper nor did he ask Matteo to search Jess' lab for a possible desalination solution. Beck's only directive was to "watch the girl," then "to keep her safe."

What is just as perplexing is that POP has never capitalized on the so-called safety Matteo is providing. At Tia's house, POP must have been monitoring them. Yet, no POP emissaries came to them that night asking him and Jess to join the POP fight. Again at the library, POP was close enough so they were able to leave the message on Matteo's bike seat: "Trust POP." Yet, POP only showed up with their getaway car after he and Jess had been chased for a while.

POP does not want to keep them safe; POP only wants to keep them from getting caught by Relly. *Why?*

POP's angle is elusive, but Matteo is sure there is one. He is also certain that POP has been steering Matteo's actions all along. Matteo took Jess to Tia's house only because of Beck's urging to "get her offline." And Matteo never would have considered the El Cerrito Public Library if he hadn't seen Tia's library card on the kitchen counter. Had he never seen the note that told him to "Trust POP," he would have been far more reluctant to enter Bruno's car. At the time, Matteo thought these decisions were made of his own free will, but now he thinks that with every step, he has brought Jess exactly where POP wants her to be. The guilt sits in his body like a stone.

Jess stops: "Look."

He peers ahead. A block of dimmed light is on the floor, and it wavers in the way that dappled sunlight streams through a window.

"Let me go first," he says, trying to step ahead of her.

"No," she says, holding her arm back like a crossing guard to block his passage. With such sharpness to her voice, he decides against protest.

Moving closer to the hallway's end, he is able to make out a door with a circular window at its top, like the sort you would find on a restaurant kitchen's swing door. Once they reach the door, Jess peers through the window. "We're on an incline, I think, but I can't see anything but branch brambles. Should we walk out?"

That was his plan. Still, he is breaking out in a sweat. Leaving this concealed shelter to step back into the lit world is like entering the gladiator's stadium: they will be hunted. "Let's stay low until we figure out where to go." He pushes the door open and sinks to the ground, kneeling within an outgrowth of California sagebrush that sits in front of the door. As he crouches, the bush's brittle, prickly branches scratch against his arms and calves.

Within seconds, he is able to orient himself. They have landed on the west side of the Solano tunnel, on a hill composed from igneous rock formations. There are several of these huge rock formations in this area of North Berkeley – big, craggy rocks that jut from the ground, sometimes taking the space of a quarter block. He guesses this rock formation is of the same piece from which the tunnel was excavated.

Below the rocky hillside is a school building with a small playground enclosed by a plastic Air-Clear bubble. "Oh, that's good," he says.

"What's good?" Beside him, Jess looks out.

"See the plastic-wrapped playground?" He points to the slides and swing sets enclosed within the clear plastic walls: "That's where we should go." Beck always cursed those Air-Clear bubbles because the glossy plastic of the walls created reflective flares that made it difficult for drone surveillance to see inside. "Are you ready to run to the covered slide inside the plastic walls?"

Jess nods, and before he stands, she bolts outward from behind the bushes and sets off down the rock. Watching her light step and short skirt, his chest tightens. *Don't die too.*

He runs after her. No dedicated video cameras should be set to monitor this hill, but the faster they are inside the plastic bubble, the better. Running down the rock is difficult; there is no set path, and deciding how to move down the craggy hillside takes more time than he would like.

Once they hit the level ground, they sprint until reaching the zippered opening of the Air-Clear plastic. Jess tugs the zipper upward; the shiny clear plastic panel spreads open, and they step inside. Even through his fear, he notices how fresh the bubble's air smells.

He runs to the slide. Climbing the small, narrow steps to the wooden slide's landing, they drop to the floor, panting.

The slide's second level has a floor of wood, though the railings around the square space are rainbow colored – garnet red, turquoise, violet, orange, and green. A royal blue tarp is pitched across the slide's top, and sitting within this blue-tinged shadow, Matteo is sure no satellite or drone surveillance can have an angle on them. He estimates they have 13 minutes to leave this spot.

Beside him, Jess pulls out her silver canteen, takes a long swallow and is about to put her water away again.

"Hey, can I get some of that?" He could swear there's a moment of hesitation before Jess extends the canteen to him. The water is warm and tinny-tasting on his parched tongue.

As he is drinking, Jess' fingers come to his cheek, rubbing at them like his mom used to do after he devoured her spaghetti Bolognese. "Was it blood?" he asks.

She nods, her lips twisting. He tries to catch her eyes, but she avoids looking at him.

She's scared. He understands: he is scared too. He slips the canteen back into her satchel. "My friend, Curran is the one who lives in the tent city. He's an excellent hacker, and he'll know how to decode that file on David's dot drive."

Jess does not respond. On the floor, there is a folded picture drawn with magic marker. Jess picks it up, and as she looks at it, her eyes fill with tears again. Blinking, she puts the drawing face down. Matteo can only see the dot marks where the markers bled through from the other side. He leans forward and picks up the sheet.

"Don't—" she whispers, but he is already looking at the drawing. In bright colors, there are two stick figures holding stick hands. Both figures must be girls because there is a skirt and long hair on one and pigtails and a pink shirt on the other. Over their heads are the words "FRIENDS FOREVER" with a heart taking the place of the "o" in "forever." A disproportionally small rainbow sits beside them, like a pet the girls could take for a walk, and multi-colored hearts are dotted across the sky, like raindrops. Matteo is not precisely sure

166

why this picture would make Jess cry, but then again, it is a minor miracle she is not in constant hysterics, given everything that's happening. Were Rachel here, the entire block would be listening to her "processing the situation." He hands the sheet of paper back to Jess: "It's nice, that drawing."

She folds the sheet in half. "Let's talk about your friend."

"Curran? Okay." She is right; they have to stay focused. "I know it sucks that we have to go so far. Especially since if I had my Keeper, I'd probably be able to figure out the file myself."

"You're a good hacker?"

"Not very. Actually, it's Curran who taught me what I know. I don't have a lot of experience—"

She interrupts: "At the Experimental Farm?"

"Right, not a lot of programming at the farm." He could have sworn there is snideness to her question, but she refuses to move her eyes from the ground. "Anyway, I don't think we should try another library."

"Hell, no."

"I'd say we could break into one of those houses—"

"Break in? Like thieves?"

"Not to steal something, just to see if we could find a Keeper to use. But I'm not sure we'd find any devices to use."

"No one leaves their Keepers behind anymore." Her voice is dour, and she runs her fingers along the hem of Tia's tiny skirt.

He is not sure why her sullenness is surprising him; there is a lot to be gloomy about. Still, he feels like when they were in the dark room, they were united, and now they are not. "So, that leaves us with Curran. He's odd. Actually, I suppose I should tell you, he's got some mental health challenges."

Her eyes peer upward.

"He takes a lot of pharmaceuticals. But he's a good person and smarter than anyone I know. Except for you."

"I'm not so smart." She folds the crayon drawing into an even smaller square. "You know, David's house isn't far from here. From his texts, it sounds like he tried out the desalination solution in the shower. Why don't we go there?"

He swears there is suspicion in her tone. "Well," he makes his tone nicer than hers, "those POP guys, not to mention the cops, they have combed David's house fifty times over looking for the solution. And they haven't found it."

"How do you know that?" she asks, her eyes scrutinizing.

"They're still chasing you." His eyebrows rise, expecting her to smile. She does not. "Plus, if we went to David's house, we'd be caught in a split second."

Jess nods, her head still bowed.

"We have to know where to look. We don't."

"Right." With a deliberate action – as though she is making herself do this, she looks across at him. "Matteo?"

"Yes."

"How did Rachel die?"

His head retracts. "What? Why are you asking—"?

"I'm curious."

"About Rachel?"

"No, you."

"Oh." Something has definitely shifted; her distrust is painted across her face. *Is it just because he wanted to leave the room?*

"Can you tell me?" Jess sets her hands on her folded knees; her whole body waits.

"Ah." There's really not time for this conversation. *They have to be away from here in the next ten minutes.* Yet, Jess' eyes convey enough determination that he decides not to avoid the question. "Rachel died from the swine flu, the one in '36. She'd been doing this internship for her social work degree, spending a lot of time at the Martinez tent city. At first, she thought she just had a regular stomach bug, but I knew it was worse than that. Once she received the diagnosis, she was quarantined at the Missoni conference center downtown, and…" *What else is there to say?* "It sucked."

He sits for a second, thinking he is done with his answer. Then, to his surprise, more words come from his mouth: "I don't know if you remember, but there was this month in the beginning of the outbreak when there weren't enough drugs for everyone." It had been a disaster, something out of a fucking apocalyptic horror movie. The Center for Disease Control's protocol was to keep a stockpile of swine flu antivirals on hand in all the big cities, but the '36 epidemic spread fast – faster than the models had predicted. People panicked. Wealthier Americans found a way to buy the available drugs in case they needed it, but their panic purchases meant the limited supplies dwindled even faster. "Rachel's parents have plenty of money, and they kept trying to buy drugs through the regular insurance channels; there weren't any. But I... I finally found some."

"Where?" Jess interrupts his memories.

"On the black market. They cost a lot – a full year of my income. I didn't care."

"You went into debt to buy them?"

He would not have thought this would be her first question. He looks at her serious face; the freckle above her upper lip is quivering. "Well, yes, I did go into debt. To this man, Hua Chan. He's not a good guy, actually."

"Did Rachel's parents pay you back?"

Again, not the question he was expecting. "Um, no. They were opposed to me buying the drugs. You know, it wasn't like Hua Chan was calling his friends at the antiviral supply store. He was stealing the drugs from people who... were sick. And Rachel's parents, they didn't want to be a part of that." He runs his hand across his chin. "I'd just been so certain that Rachel would get better if she could take the antivirals. Then..." He remembers how he sat that night in the midst of those hundreds of rows of beds, the awful smell of that huge place flooding his nose even through his Hazmat helmet.

"Then?"

"She didn't get better. Obviously." He fiddles with his boots' shoelaces. He should be thinking about the minutes ticking away now – probably only seven left – but instead the emotions that have been lodged tight in his throat are coming up. "I was at her bedside, holding her hand and talking to her about how I wanted to plant flowers for her homecoming, and I noticed…" he swallows. *Why is he telling her this?* This is not something he should share with Jess, not now; they should *go.*

"You noticed?"

"I noticed…" his voice wavers, "that her hand wasn't alive anymore. That it had a different kind of stillness to it. I felt like I was holding an object, not a being. So, I knew she was…" he twists his lips, "gone."

He sits for a moment, thinking back to how Rachel's cheeks were slack and purple-y white. As though she had been frozen in time. At this first realization that Rachel was dead, a sound had come from his chest – like an animal moaning – and because he had his Hazmat helmet on, the noise only bounced back onto him, the sadness encircling him, unreleased into the wider air.

"Does that answer your question?" His words hang under the blue canopy, unclear if they are angry or relieved. When there's no answer, Matteo looks from his shoes. Jess' cheeks are downturned in what he used to identify on Rachel as "active crumple."

"Sort of," she says, wiping her cheeks hurriedly.

He is unsure what to make of this response, but a sound from the street makes him peek out the slide's landing. A small, green car is pulling to the curb at the school entrance. A woman leaves the driver's seat and walks to the sidewalk, opening the car's curbside back door.

"Look at that." Matteo points through the brightly colored railings.

Jess crawls toward his side of the slide and examines the street.

A little boy with his oxygen mask and tubing is shuffling out of the back seat. The woman leans down to arrange a too-big firetruck backpack around his shoulders. She holds his hand as he waddles, duck-like, toward the front door.

"What am I supposed to be looking at? The boy?" Jess whispers.

"No, the car." Matteo turns to Jess. "We're going to steal it."

JESS

She is definitely a felon now. Not only has she tranquilized security guards and thrown tear grenades at cops, she has also stolen a car. Sitting in the passenger seat, she rests her head against the edge of the open window. The wind flaps her new bangs upward like a sail.

Beside her, Matteo drives with one hand on the steering wheel and one hand on her passenger's seat back. Glare hits the window shield from a high sun, and all seven lanes on the 880 are moving fast, with the sounds and fumes of speed pushing onto them.

Even with all that is on her mind, she notices the drivers that pass them. Some sip from coffee cups. Others talk out loud to their Keepers. A guy taps his hands on the steering wheel to the beat of a pop song. Jess knows all the words to this song too.

Last night, she was supposed to have attended her apartment building's rain celebration party, and Dr. Monique had made her promise she would talk with at least three men there. "You have to remember that boys have intimidation for you too," she said. In the session's last five minutes, Dr. Monique made Jess practice her flirtation. "Relax your shoulders," Dr. Monique admonished. "Smile. Ah, there, that is *fantastique*. You are very pretty when you smile."

Now, in the car, Jess winces. Matteo must have heard that conversation with Dr. Monique too.

From the driver's seat, Matteo peers at her: "You okay?"

"Fine." She pivots her body even more toward the window so he can't see her face.

"You flinched like you're in pain."

"No, I'm fine," she says firmly.

Matteo is working for De Sel. That is what she deduced; it was not hard. There were but three options: De Sel, the Governor, POP. Since Matteo had just persuaded her to run from POP, he could not be with POP. Matteo had biked like hell to give the cops the slip, so it was unlikely he is with the Governor either. De Sel was left; so, Matteo must work for De Sel. Jess guesses that he took the job to pay off his debt to that bad guy, Hua Whatever. Sure, yesterday Matteo had called De Sel "De Selfish," but how better to throw her off track?

Her analysis is logically sound; in fact, she hates its soundness. She reviews the last 36 hours in the hopes she will prove her theory wrong. *Is it possible that Matteo just happened to be at the juice bar? That he had wanted to help her because he felt bad for her and liked her? That he took her to Tia's and risked his life for her because....?* Nope, didn't work. All along, Matteo has been doing a job.

At the playground, when Matteo suggested stealing the car, Jess considered confronting him then, telling him that she knew who he was, that she wouldn't follow him anymore. *But what would she have done? Where would she have gone?*

Besides, there was hardly time to think. As soon as the mother and boy entered the school, Matteo sprung up, grabbing her hand: "Let's go!" When Jess had not budged, he had crouched beside her, holding her shoulders. "You have to realize: this car is our lucky break. Now, we can make it to the tent city without anyone tracking us. When we're under the car's roof, we'll be un-seen by drones or satellite, and until the mom calls in the car as stolen and the cops come, we'll be safe. We really couldn't ask for better. Come on."

Now, with her head against the passenger car door, she tries to make her plan. First, since there is no way she can break the encryption on David's file by herself, she will go with Matteo to the tent town to find his friend who can crack the file. Then, whatever the file says, it will surely clarify that she is un-involved in this desalination solution. Right? *It has to.* Then she will escape. She has no idea where she will go. She can't call 911 or walk into a police station. The police killed Bruno. They shot at her too.

In the car next to her, a mom is driving with three children in the backseat. One is in a car seat and the other two boys look to be fighting over a game they are playing on a holographic screen. Jess considers her own mom. *Would she help her?* Jess doubts she could travel all the way to Sacramento, but regardless, no, she realizes: her mom would not hide her. "That's too much to ask," is how her mom responded to Jess' teenage requests for trendy boots or glittery

Keeper bands like the ones her friends wore. There weren't many requests that weren't "too much" for her mom. No, she has to find someone other than her mom to help her.

She has no one.

Tears are threatening to leak from her eyes again; she rubs them. She hears the rhythmic click of the car's turn signal, and realizes Matteo is readying to exit the highway on Fifth Avenue.

"If we didn't have to leave this car," Matteo's speaks with a low steadiness, "I'd say we could head into the mountains or desert or something – just escape." He looks to his left side as he eases the car into the off ramp's lane.

She eyes him: "You'd want that?"

"Wouldn't you?" His eyes turn toward her, and the anticipation on his face confuses her.

"Yes," she says fast, so he will look back to the road.

"It's not fair what's happening," he says. His hair is sticking up on one side and matted down on the other, like a grumpy boy. "All I want is to leave technology and pollution and live somewhere simple. You know, grow my own food, and fix up a small place." He peers at her. "That probably sounds boring to you, doesn't it?"

"No." She works hard to keep her voice from cracking. "It sounds nice."

Quickly, he checks her expression. "But you'd miss your research and friends and... the juice bar, right?"

"No. I wouldn't miss much." She has to make herself remember that Matteo makes remarks like this to throw her off track. When he kissed her body last night that was a trick too. "Actually," she shifts in her seat, "why can't you keep driving?"

Matteo coasts the car to a full stop at the red light and turns to face Jess. "Remember how I said we had fifteen minutes? Well..." he points to the digital clock above the video screen, "we're at minute twelve. Already, that mom has noticed her car is missing and called the police. A squad car is on its way to the school – maybe it's already there; that would be fast, but it's possible. And whenever the cop finishes putting all the car's vehicle identification information into their systems – that takes around five minutes – the DMV will trigger a honing device on this car's computer." He pats the dashboard. "Once that signal is sent, the police drones will come and find it." The stoplight goes green, and Matteo pulls ahead.

She sits upright: "Would we be able to hear the honing device when it's activated?"

"No, it's silent tracking. Just a digital signaling that the police drones receive."

"Don't we need to get out of this car right now?" The words rush out.

"Yes," he nods, "we do." He pulls the car over to the side of this street. Matteo un-clicks his seatbelt and before he steps out, he lifts an umbrella from the passenger side floor mat.

"Here," Matteo fumbles with the umbrella handle; "come under." She thinks he must be kidding because there isn't a cloud in the sky, but the black umbrella shoots outward, opening its circle wide. Then, she understands. Under the umbrella, overhead satellites and drones cannot spot them. She settles beside him under the small canopy, and he puts his hand on her back, leaning toward her. "If anyone asks, we're sun-sensitive," he smiles, and though she does not mean to, she smiles back.

The streets are wide in this part of Oakland. The land is flat with few trees or shrubs, and somehow the light is brighter, more crystalline than it was in Berkeley. Only a few cars pass, then a biker. A few of the houses – especially those painted pale yellow and light pink – have remnants of Victorian detailing – a small diamond-shaped window or a porch railing with beveled balustrades. Those details stand out given that most houses are boxy and plain with broken railings and cracked windows. Even with the rain, dust is still apparent in the cracks and crevices everywhere – cars, houses, sidewalks. Jess doubts this fine, brown silt will ever be removed from the wrinkles of this world. It will last as a permanent stain.

Jess' dad used to live in Oakland right after her parents' divorce, and she would visit him there and occasionally stay overnight at his house. It was such a long time ago now – twenty years. Anyway, she is pretty sure her dad did not live in this part of Oakland. There are few people on the streets here, but the faces she sees are all brown and black.

They pass shops with Asian characters written on the windows. "This used to be the edge of China Town," Matteo says. "My dad used to take me here all the time to get this special soup, congee. I didn't like it, but, man, he devoured it – said it reminded him of Hong Kong."

The neighborhood does not look like China Town now. None of the shops are open, and several have broken windows. A few people meander ahead of them, and a lone biker keeps looping back and forth, zig-zagging across the street.

"Ever been to a tent town?" Matteo asks.

"Never." When Jess was a kid, her mom always complained that if her dad kept missing his child support payments, they would end up in a tent town, but Jess has never visited one. In Sacramento, only a few, large parks had transitioned into tent towns, and there, the populations came in during the summer months and went away with the winter chill. In the Bay Area, however, Jess has noticed that people refer to the tent towns as though they are recognized neighborhoods, like Rockridge TT or People's Park TT.

"Stick close to me and don't touch much. The last thing we want is to figure out this desalination confusion and then have you get sick, right?"

"Right." Jess has walked near some of the Berkeley parks before; she has seen the lines of people waiting to use the spigot and the garbage cans that are packed with dirty diapers and fast food bags. People always say the conditions are like a third world country, but Jess thinks it is worse than that. Blocks away from these packed cages of misery are multi-million dollar homes chock full of conveniences and luxuries.

Jess hears the park two blocks before they reach it. A steady hum of humanity grows, like the sort you would hear as you near a Farmer's Market or an outdoor fair. There are, however, particular punctuations that do not sound friendly. Dogs barking. Music blaring from Keeper amplifiers in discordant competition: mariachi, rock, industrial rap. A baby wails – no, actually, it's at least two babies. Then there are the smells. The stench of urine and excrement get closer with every step. "Wow, that's awful," she says, putting her hand over her nose.

Under the umbrella, Matteo takes her hand from her face and holds it in his own. "It is awful, but don't. No one here wants this."

The words' decency stings: *If he's so damn good, why is he betraying her?*

The sounds and smells grow with each step until she peers out from the umbrella, and there it is: The twelve-foot high chain link fence runs the perimeter of the city block, and behind the fence, people and noise and chaos are tightly pressed within. Standing at the entry, Jess knows that walking a few steps forward, she'll be hard pressed to see back out. Tents are everywhere, crammed in tight to fit the space. Many colors and shapes: black and red; blue, yellow, orange. The assortment would be pretty if the fabrics themselves were not so worn and drab.

"Ready?" Matteo asks.

She nods. His hand tightens around hers as he leads her into the tiny path between the tents. The thought occurs to her that she should pull her hand free.

She does not.

MATTEO

Curran lives in the center of the park. He ha always insisted to Matteo that he likes it best that way. "It's safer in the center: more babies, less thugs." It is true that as they move inward, the street noise quiets and children run into the narrow paths.

A few months have passed since Matteo has seen Curran. This tent town is not exactly a fun place to visit, and the last time Matteo made the trek, Curran failed to ask Matteo about Rachel. Maybe Matteo could have cut Curran some slack; after all, Curran's drugs made him groggy, but Matteo had not felt forgiving just then. His wife was dead; he wanted his oldest friend to care.

Curran had been Matteo's buddy since the first day of fourth grade. Showing up in Ms. Yaskel's class, everyone whispered that Curran had to be Matteo's secret twin. This was a peculiar insistence since Curran was enormously tall and Matteo not. Yet, since Curran was also half-Chinese and half-European, and since he wore his black hair super short as Matteo had then, these similarities were apparently enough.

Given the faulty reasoning behind the assumption that the boys would be similar, it was perhaps surprising that their interests did overlap. They both loved figuring out how stuff worked – not with airplane models or boxed science kits, but with more esoteric explorations. When they were ten, they made a flourmill and ground wheat plants into five different kinds of flour; when they were eleven, they synthesized monosodium glutamate from Curran's bedroom chemistry kit. Curran was always fantastic at programming; he knew more programming languages than anyone Matteo had ever met. For this reason, Matteo had asked Curran to help him with some of his hacking projects at Beck Industries. No one was faster at de-coding encrypted lists or bypassing Keepers' thumb-scan passcodes than Curran, and these "consulting projects" gave Matteo the opportunity to add money to Curran's Keeper account. Though Curran had funds coming in, he had a habit of spending his money on technology and gadgets rather than food. He was incredibly skinny.

Now, under the umbrella, Matteo and Jess file through the narrow passageway between tents. Curran's tent is black and yellow striped, like a bumblebee, and Matteo doesn't see it anywhere. *Maybe Curran moved?* All of his interactions with Curran have been via Keeper recently, and Matteo begins to worry that Curran isn't living here anymore. He is just considering whether they should go back to the entrance when, suddenly, Curran is standing right in front of him.

"Hello," Curran says in that bashful way he has, where he bows his head and warbles his words.

Matteo drops the umbrella and hugs his friend. Curran, at six foot six, is the tallest half-Asian man Matteo has ever met, and now, his lanky body looms over Matteo, enveloping him. When he pulls back, Curran's long skinny finger points toward Jess. "She's not Rachel."

Matteo puts his hand to Jess' shoulder: "You're right; she's Jess."

He probably should have prepped Jess for Curran. The trouble is how difficult it is to describe Curran's peculiarity. Curran's parents had never shared the specific diagnosis Curran received, and Rachel always maintained that Curran never had a pathological condition; "I bet he's been diagnosed with schizoid personality disorder, but if you ask me, his problem is that he's addicted to his screens, pure and simple." As with most of Rachel's opinions, she had a point: Curran isn't "normal," but he doesn't have hallucinations or delusions and he isn't even depressed. Rachel had felt that with each visit, Curran became more awkward, less able to focus on people and more impatient to return to his "watched work." At one point, she threatened to contact Curran's parents to ask them to force Curran off his technology. Matteo would not let her. He knew that for Curran, denying his technology was akin to disabling him. His screens were his vision of the world.

"Where's your bumblebee tent?" Matteo asks, turning to see how he missed it.

"I had to get a taller tent," Curran mumbles. "For my newest screen."

"Oh," Matteo nods. "It's really big?"

A smile fills Curran's face: "Huge."

Curran points ahead to a tall orange tent, and once they enter the gold-hued space, Jess gasps. "You have so many screens."

She is right. There are but a few objects that sit under the tent but the hovering holographic screens. A sleeping bag lies on a thin bed mat in one corner. A lamp is plugged into a liquid metal battery in another corner. Two trunks on wheels, like the heavy kind kids take to summer camp, sit against one wall, and a folding chair is plunked down in the middle of the room. Tens screens of different sizes face the center of the room, hovering around the folding chair in a perfect orbit.

Jess walks from one screen to the next, seeing what's on. A press conference at the United Nations. A product launch at RoundWren. A few sporting events. A thermodynamics course taught by a young professor in front of animated graphics. Aerial coverage of a car accident in North Berkeley. The surveillance satellite feed for the Chinese Park tent town. And on and on. "How do you keep all this stuff from being stolen?"

Curran presses a button on his Keeper, and immediately, the holographic screens evaporate into nothingness. "Everything I own is stored here," he says, touching the wide steel cuff that holds his Keeper in place. "People sometimes threaten to cut my arm off to get my Keeper, but I tell them my Keeper is set to spray a death-inducing poison at my command."

"Is that true?"

"Of course."

Jess's eyes widen, and she takes in the thin orange walls, the nylon over the grass floor. "But if you have all that money to spend on holographic screens..." She doesn't finish the thought, because Curran understands what she's getting at.

"From here," he sits in the folding chair in the middle of the room; "I have the power to see everything in the world I want to see. Every event that is videotaped – and that's just about every event there is –

I can see it." Curran clicks the button on his Keeper, and the screens, all twenty-four of them, return.

Jess scans the screens' content, and Matteo can tell that, in fact, she is appreciating Curran's point. It is not merely that Curran can find movies or entertainment or watch news coverage, which of course is what most people access on their screens. Curran has infiltrated all manner of local networks – companies' intranets, individual's Keeper video files, all manner of governmental meeting, high school sporting event, classroom lecture, or press conference – so that anything of interest happening in the world is something he can view in real time from his folding chair.

With three bodies under the tent's nylon ceiling, the air is stuffy, like a car on a hot day with the windows rolled up, and a smell of feet and talcum powder hangs in the air.

"So, man," Matteo announces, "I hate to ask this, but do you have anything we could eat?"

Curran walks to the larger of the two trunks and opens it. He hands Matteo a package of saltines, two green apples and a water canteen. "I filled the water from the spigot yesterday, so it may be warm." Curran does not eat much that requires cooking, and Matteo bets that what Curran's offering is his day's worth of food. Matteo briefly considers refusing the offer, but he cannot resist cracking into the apple with a big bite. Beside him, Jess slurps down on the water canteen. All afternoon, Matteo assumed his shooting headache was because of adrenaline. It is occurring to him he has not eaten all day.

Curran watches them. "You know, I have a couple nutrition pods I can give you too."

Matteo pushes the apple to one side of his mouth: "You sure, man?"

Curran rummages through his trunk and pulls out two nutrition pods in plastic wrapping, both Kung Pao chicken flavored. Curran hands one pod to Jess, the other to Matteo. Usually, Matteo is ethically opposed to nutrition pods, given all the chemical crap they put in them – a day's worth of calories in six bites, but right now, he rips open the wrapper.

"So, we need to see if you can de-code an encrypted file," he says before he takes a bite.

Curran nods as though he had expected this request: "Where's the file?"

Jess snatches her satchel from the orange ground and rummages inside it. Pulling out the toothbrush, she snaps her open palm forward, the pearl-sized dot drive sitting atop it.

As Curran affixes the drive onto his Keeper, Matteo glances at Jess, but she will not look at him. He hopes the de-coding does not take long. If the police drones are able to track the stolen car to Fifth Avenue, cops would move quickly from the car to sticking their batons into tents, barking questions, and demanding everyone out. He and Jess need to stay focused and leave this tent town fast.

A window opens on the largest holographic screen, and the six icons for the dot drives' files are right there. Matteo leans forward, pointing. "See, we've read these ones, but this one – DOC.IP.11.17.33 – is encrypted."

Curran taps on the holographic screen. "How old is the guy who used this file?"

"Around 55."

"Does he have a connection to UC Berkeley?"

"He's a professor there."

"Thought so. He's using an ancient UNIX code; nobody but Berkeley geezers use that stuff anymore." He giggles, his fingers flying. "This will be a cinch to decode." Pushing a button on his Keeper's cuff, a holographic keyboard appears.

Jess is biting her lip; her face is drained of color.

"Don't worry," Matteo whispers.

She does not respond.

"Okay, here we go," Curran says. "It's a letter. From De Sel."

"De Sel?" Jess springs forward to peer at the screen floating above Curran's Keeper.

Matteo is trying to see the small screen too. "Dude, can you throw that letter up to one of your big screens?"

Curran touches his Keeper, and there is the De Sel logo with its royal blue water droplet on a huge screen hovering at their eye level. Right below David's Berkeley address is the all caps designation:

HAND DELIVERED

FORMAT: DIGITAL DOT DRIVE

Strange. Matteo has heard of papers being delivered by hand but never a dot drive. David must have really wanted to keep this communication offline. Curran hits a few keys, and the letter re-sizes to fit the screen.

Dear Dr. Steubingly,

My legal staff has concluded its due diligence in preparation for our meeting on Friday, November 19, at Ellison Hall, Stanford University. As the enclosed analysis explains, we have determined that Dr. Jessila Prentiss must participate in our licensing arrangement in order for this deal to proceed.

Our legal team reviewed the description and drawings of your desalination solution, an invention that you presented as entirely your own despite its substantial reliance on Dr. Prentiss' prior art. We have read with interest about your discovery that Dr. Prentiss' two inventions can be used "side by side" to produce a novel and non-obvious application that substantially differs from the applications Dr. Prentiss originally envisioned. [I assure you that to honor your request that your drawings not be digitized we have excluded your drawings as attachments here. We have, however, included Dr. Prentiss' diagrams herein, as they are included within the patent applications she filed while at U.C., Davis.]

It is our opinion that since your invention appears to utilize Dr. Prentiss' inventions in close proximity to one another without either alteration or modification, an exclusion of Dr. Prentiss from our licensing agreement would put the De Sel Corporation at risk of allegations of infringement, encroachment, and/or patent violation.

Ideally, De Sel would postpone Friday's meeting until we could work out the terms of a new contract to include Ms. Prentiss. However, State Trooper Colonel Brooklyn Relly visited my office this afternoon to inform me that it is the Governor's express request that Friday's meeting continue as scheduled. We do not want to disappoint the Governor or you, but will require that you and Dr. Prentiss meet two hours earlier to review the terms of the new licensing arrangement.

It is our belief that we can nail down the details in time for everyone to sign the deal as planned on the stage with the Governor. Given your concerns about keeping all communications off of Keepers, I will assume that, unless I receive a messenger-delivered response, we will meet in Room 205 of Stanford University's Ellison Hall at 8 am.

Sincerely,

Rajit Chatterjee
Senior VP, Research and Development
De Sel Corporation

Now that this letter is hovering before him in black and white, the explanation feels too obvious. Of course, David was trying to make a deal with De Sel. Matteo still is confused about how POP fits in, but... He looks at Jess. She is standing beside him, completely still. Her hands are open in front of her like she has dropped a ball in a game of catch.

"The rest of the material is just diagrams," Curran says, "Lots and lots of pages." He scrolls through the typed documents on the screen.

"Jess?" Matteo whispers, but her face stays seeped in concentration. "Don't you think this letter helps us? If De Sel wants to make a deal with you, not just David, maybe we could go to De Sel and explain everything. Maybe De Sel would keep us safe."

Her face twitches, but she stays silent.

"Wow!" Curran is looking at a computer rendered drawing of a turbine blade on the screen. "Those blades, you made these?" His eyes on Jess are full of admiration. "They're see-through!" He brings his face right close to the screen to study the graphic.

Jess glances at the diagram on the screen: "Actually, that's not the diagram for the turbine that was patented; that's the old..." she stops, and her hands shoot to her mouth.

"It's the what?" Matteo asks, darting back and forth between the screen and Jess' startled face: "*What?*"

"Old fan," she mumbles. "It's the old fan. Not old man. It wasn't a typo. David *meant* to say old fan."

"Typo?" He says, looking at the diagram and the few words that identify the different parts. There is nothing about an old man on the diagram. "What are you talking about?"

Her eyes have a spooked quality like a dog that can hear something but not see it. "It's at David's house," she mutters.

"Jess," he takes a step toward her. "What's at David's house? The desalination solution?"

She retracts from him, her head shaking slightly: "No."

"No?"

Quickly, her back straightens; "I'm going to find the port-o-lets."

"The port—? I don't think that's a good idea; they're not very clea—" he stops, his eyes darting at Curran. "I'll come with you."

"No, don't. I need to go alone." She picks up her satchel and without hesitation, dashes out of the tent opening.

Matteo jerks forward to follow, but Curran grabs his arm: "Dude, it's the bathroom. Girls go to the bathroom by themselves."

"Right." If Curran thinks he is being weird, that is a problem. Matteo walks back to the hovering screen, the projected white light standing out in the tent's orange air. The diagram of the wind turbine still sits on the screen, and the turbine's blades look like firefly wings with their delicate transparency. *How amazing that Jess created them.*

Above the drawing, the digital clock blinks to 1:25. Matteo runs his hands through his hair. *Shit, they need to leave.*

He feels the ratcheting upward of his adrenaline like a bike tire being pumped too full. All he wants is to deflate. If this hot and foul-smelling spot would be a place he and Jess could be safe, he would sink to the ground and not get up for days. He would come clean with her about everything. Beck Industries. How long he's been following her. How he thinks Beck is working with POP. And he would happily hear about the old fan, whatever that is. He cannot shake the feeling that if they could simply settle in beside each other and think out loud together, they would be able to figure out what is happening and how to make it better. The digital clock clicks to 1:26. He wishes Jess would come back already.

"So, who is that woman?"

He turns to answer Curran's question. "A... friend."

"How'd you meet her?"

Matteo walks to the tent's opening; maybe Jess got lost in the maze of tents. "It's a long story."

"Those two said you wouldn't tell me."

He turns back to Curran. "Those two? Which two?"

"They wouldn't tell me their names. But before you came, I was about to go out for some water, and this man and woman came up to me and told me to stay put."

"Wait, were they cops? Or... were they wearing regular clothes?"

"Definitely not cops. The guy had dreadlocks, and he was kinda tall. The woman had blue hair, blue lipstick. They told me you would need my help hacking something—"

"It's POP." Matteo spins, looking around the small tent. *Shit.* They are here. They have been watching them all along.

Curran blinks. "Pop, what does that mean? Like pop music?"

"Where are the toilets? Which direction?"

Curran points. "Over there, on Harrison Street."

Matteo runs out of Curran's tent, tripping over children, angling around people on the narrow path between the multi-colored tents. The light is bright, but he cannot see far ahead. "Jess!" he screams. There is no answer; a woman from inside a nearby tent starts to laugh. He runs. Finally, the row of six yellow port-o-lets stands in front of him. The smell is awful; he chokes down a gag. "Jess?" he yells toward one door. No answer. He hits one port-o-let door with his fist, then another. "Jess!" No answer from anywhere. He opens one, then the next –finally, the last one; she is not there.

His legs are weak. *Did POP find her? Did they take her away?* He whirls around, and the sunlight makes big splotches of glare. He squints, trying to right his vision.

"You looking for the white girl in the short skirt?"

His head darts in the direction of the question. Two black girls with hair in beaded braids stare back at him.

"Yes." The air heaves in his throat: "I am."

The taller girl points: "She ran that way."

Matteo looks beyond the chain-link fence, into the wide road. A woman walks with heavy grocery bags burdening her steps; a teenage boy wheelies his bike. No Jess. "Was anyone chasing her?"

"Oh, no – that girl, she was racing herself."

JESS

Her side has a horrible stitch. That stupid nutrition pod, she shouldn't have eaten it. She can feel the Kung Pao taste lining her throat, wanting to retch upward. No, she can't throw up. She has to keep running. *Don't stop.* She has to somehow make it to David's house.

The sun is lowering in the sky, and the streets are growing crowded with adults leaving work and kids biking home from after-school activities. Thankfully, no one is giving her much attention. She keeps scanning the streets, searching for people who might be following her. Many types cause alarm. Big men. Agro people. Security guards. Police. Platinum-haired women. Asian men. *Matteo.*

There's an ache in her chest, and it is not just from running. A hurt is expanding like a black hole, threatening to collapse her from the inside out. *Should she have left Matteo? He's with De Sel, right?* It does not feel right.

Her pace, if it can even be called that, is not fast. She's holding her bike bag like a baby, and her steps keep no rhythm since her feet badly want to linger on the ground. Every few minutes, she stops to catch her breath, and then makes herself start again. The air pollution stings her eyes and throat; the inside of her nose hurts. She cannot believe she has gone so long without an oxygen mask. *Thank goodness for last night's rain.*

There are long shadows across the west-side storefronts and office buildings, and she stays within this darkened space, hoping the dim light will make it hard for satellite surveillance or drones to detect her. She wishes she had some disguise. Shadows are not much protection.

To her left, there's an alley, and mid-way down this narrow aisle, a garbage dumpster pushed against a building; this will be a good place to take a break. Huffing, she scampers to it, and crouches, settling herself in the narrow space between the bin and the building's brick wall. The smell is awful: rotting cheese and dirty diapers. She is thankful enough to be hidden that she tries not to care. Her breathing reverberates against the steel wall of the dumpster, and somehow it is a lonely sound. She wonders if Matteo meant any of the nice things he said, or whether he has always been tricking her.

Weeks ago, when Jess sat down for her first session with Dr. Monique, she knew some of the questions her therapist would ask. Jess had reviewed the website that offered the download for the holographic therapeutic software and she had read the descriptions of what a typical 24-session therapeutic experience offered. Jess knew that in the first session, the patient would be expected to explain why she was coming to therapy and what she hoped to learn from the experience. So, when Dr. Monique asked about her therapeutic goals, Jess had her answer prepared.

"I would like to understand why people leave me," Jess said. "My father left me, my step-dad too. For all practical purposes, same with my mom. I mean, I have friends; I've had relationships. I'm not a loner. But especially after what happened with David, I can't get over this feeling that people don't... want to stay with me." Jess' lip had trembled, even though she knew she was making her confessions to a non-person whose body was semi-transparent and whose answers came from software programming.

Now, as Jess huddles behind the garbage bin, she remembers the way that session ended. Dr. Monique put on her bifocals and explained the procedures in her "workplace" required that she code a general diagnosis for each of the clients she saw. She wanted Jess to know that, for her, the diagnosis would be: Ordinary Loneliness. "So many people feel alone these days," she said slightly shaking her head.

Jess did not find the diagnosis comforting. Her alone-ness did not feel ordinary; it felt awful. And with Matteo, even though their time together had been marked by fear and anxiety, there had been moments when they had... connected. She wanted to be connected. With him. He was a good person – *such a good person* – to connect with.

Behind the garbage bin's shadow, the evening air grows cool and the film of sweat over her body produces a blanket of goosebumps. She makes herself think about her next steps. Her plan at David's is unlikely to work, but she has to try. She has figured out so very much.

When David wrote in yesterday's high-alert message that, "as an old fan, I should have known better," the "old fan" was his code to report that the desalination solution only worked with the first turbine that Jess had designed, the "old" one.

There is only one difference between the older turbine design and the newer one: the first turbine's torque is exceptionally more forceful. With that one piece of information, a key entered a padlock in her brain, and *click*, the lock pulled open. There, like a wrapped gift, was her understanding of how the solution worked. She knew where she would find her prototypes at David's. She knew why no one else had found them. And she understood with lightbulb clarity that everyone had been right. Other than David, she is the only person in the world who could possibly fathom how to make these two prototypes work as a desalination solution.

She readjusts her position so that she is sitting, not squatting, in the narrow space. *Ah, much more comfortable.* Now, her plan is to walk the five more miles to David's, find her prototypes, and make them work.

And then...? Her stomach churns. She still has to figure out her next step. Once she puts together the desal solution, she will have the knowledge and power that everyone already assumes she has. How she'll wield that power is something she will have to determine later.

She is straightening her posture to move from behind the garbage dumpster when... there are voices: a man and a woman, and, oh no, they're coming closer. Actually, *shit,shit,shit,* they are heading straight for the dumpster.

Returning to her crouched position, Jess inches back toward the middle of the garbage dumpster. She doubts imagine this couple can see her, not unless they walk right to where the bin meets the wall and peer down the narrow space. Still, her head is so full of heartbeat she can hardly hear the couple's conversation.

The guy has a deep voice with strong California accenting – lots of lazy aahs and "dude." And from the way the woman's deep voice draws long on her vowels, Jess guesses she's black. Their conversation appears to be about whether they should leave "it" or not.

"It will be fine!" the woman says several times, and, eventually, the guy appears to be convinced, since they walk from the dumpster, out of the alley.

Jess nudges toward the bin's edge. She peers into the alley: all clear. She steps from behind the garbage bin and straightening herself, sees right away what the couple left behind.

A rush of pleasure rises at this uncanny luck—then plummets, as through a trap door. She spins, looking behind her, up, this way, the other. *How? How?* Her breath choking, she walks to what rests against the dumpster.

It is an electric bike. Unlocked.

MATTEO

"You should have taken that left," he mumbles from the passenger seat.

"Really?" Curran's word pitches upward.

Matteo knows Curran's panicked; his friend hasn't driven in years. "It doesn't matter. Just take the next left, right there, at the light." He tries to make his voice soothing, but he doubts his irritation is fully camouflaged.

"Okay, okay: right." Curran veers rightward.

"Dude, left. I said: 'left.'"

"Okay, okay, I got it now. Left."

The left-hand signal clicks rhythmically. It would have been faster to take the highway, but there is no way Curran could have handled the Interstate. And, since Curran's Keeper paid for the CareToShare Car, only his fingerprints are allowed on the steering wheel, an aggravating feature of these rentable cars.

Rush hour is in full effect on these surface streets, and the traffic crawls. Matteo is so used to whizzing through traffic on his bike that he has forgotten how tortured driving can be. At each stoplight, they sit through three or four light rotations, move ahead only a block before they arrive at the next light and wait again. Matteo jiggles his legs and runs his hands through his hair, trying to stay calm. He knows the video cameras in the traffic lights and stop signs are recording his presence.

He does not care anymore.

All the effort they took to hide has not worked; POP has followed every step they have taken. Every time he thought he was eluding POP, he was only following the breadcrumbs of POP's trail.

Why was that lock so easy to pick in the tunnel door? Because POP wanted them to leave. *Why had that mom left her car idling as she walked her son into school?* Because POP wanted them to steal her car. Hell, POP probably planted the scotch bottle and library card at Tia's place. POP has watched his and Jess' every move for the last 24 hours, guiding them from one step to the next. Now, Matteo is on his way to David Steubingly's house and so is POP – and Relly and De Sel for all he knows. Anyone who heard Jess say, "It's at David's house," is coming here to see what she will find.

There is no need to rush. Jess has to be on foot, so there will be at least an hour, probably two, before she gets near.

"You know, if that girl ran from you," Curran's hands are gripping the steering wheel, "it's because she doesn't want you to follow her."

"Thanks, Curran. I appreciate you pointing that out for me." Matteo turns his head toward the passenger window.

"You could just come back to the tent town with me."

Matteo wipes his sweaty palms on his shorts. "Well, maybe I'll do that. Later. After I've warned her."

"Warned her?"

"That she's walking into a trap."

After Matteo realized Jess had fled, he returned to Curran's tent and found his friend sitting on the single folding chair, facing the tent's opening.

"Are you mad at me? I don't want you to be mad at me. I thought you would want me to do what I did."

"Curran, it's fine. Tell me what those people said, that's all."

"Um, well the man said you were coming here to ask me to hack an encrypted letter—"

"Wait, did he say 'document' or 'letter'?"

"Letter."

Weird. How did they know the document was a letter?

"And then the woman said that I shouldn't worry, it would be easy to crack, and they—"

"Stop. She knew it would be easy to crack?"

"Yes."

"You're sure about that?"

"Positive."

Matteo's hands went to his head, trying to steady his brain so that it could hook the lines it kept trying to catch. If POP knew the letter was encrypted and knew the encryption was easy to crack, then POP must have read the letter. Why would POP follow him and Jess to a tent town to watch them read a letter they had already read? It made no sense.

Matteo had started to pace back and forth in the small tent. "Did the man and woman say anything else?"

"No," Curran said meekly. "I was getting worried, and they told me not to worry. They said they were here to help you, not hurt you."

"Yeah, they like to say that. Trust POP." Matteo thought of the scrawled note at the library.

And that was when he got it. When Jess had used the El Cerrito library computers, POP had hacked into their systems. When she had slipped David's dots into the drives, they had copied the contents right then, in real time. So, what he and Jess had learned only now, POP had known all day. That is why in the car Bruno was so vehement that they needed Jess more than ever. POP had already realized that Jess was the true inventor of the solution. *And... and...* Too many ideas are rushing from this point, like a hose turned on full blast. If POP followed them to the tent town, then they had been watching them all along. Why? What were they gaining from watching them?

"Curran, do you have a pen?" Matteo grabbed his satchel and searched the dark, deep pockets to see if he might have one himself.

"Did you say 'pen'?"

"Yes, a pen."

His eyes squint in confusion. "Uh, do you want to use my keyboard?"

"I need to—" Matteo grabs a stubby, worn pencil which is in his bag's depths, "I need to write this out." Some confusion can only be clarified by putting it on paper. When he and Rachel would fight, going round and round in circles, Rachel would sometimes announce, "I'm too muddled, I have to make a list about what we're arguing about." Her last list went like this: "If you're angry at me because I'm working at the Martinez tent city, then: 1. I can quit, or 2. You can get over your paternalistic need to babysit me, or 3. We can agree I'll be very careful, and you'll stop nagging me." Even in that instance, the list had put an end to their argument.

In Curran's tent, Matteo grabbed the sheets that Jess had printed at the library and turned the top sheet over to its blank side. On the top center, he wrote: "Why didn't POP talk with Jess now?" He was stymied by the question, because it would seem to be in POP's best interest to approach Jess as a way to promote her alliance with them. He wrote the number 1, but he could not think of any explanation. He chewed on the pencil nub. *Why?* Then, like a break in a game of pool when the balls sink their pockets, Matteo understood. He looked up from his blank sheet: "We have to get a car."

Now, as they make their way through the winding, residential Berkeley hills, Matteo directs Curran where to turn right, then left. Two blocks from David's house, he points to a corner where a drooping, almost leafless flowering pear tree stands. "You should let me out there."

The sky is eggplant colored now, with yellow-green smog sticking to the horizon. The morning's rain-freshness is gone, and the familiar tangy chemical stink hangs in the air's chill. Streetlights flicker on overhead as Curran pulls the car to the curb. Matteo opens the car's tiny door and steps out.

"Matteo?" Usually, Curran's voice has a flat, almost robotic tonality, but there is a tremble to his voice now.

Matteo sticks his head back into the car. "What, buddy?"

"Do you think you could die?

Yes. "No, dude, I'll be fine. Listen, go back and watch me on the screens, and if anything happens..."

"Uh-huh?"

Matteo tries to think whom Curran should contact if something bad happens to him. His parents, sure. They are far away, but Curran should get in touch. Is there anyone else? No, not really. Even now, when there are more pressing worries, this realization scrapes against his heart. "Never mind, buddy. I'll see you soon." He closes the car door, and walks ahead, not looking back.

As he nears David's, he evaluates which spot would be best to look out for Jess. He is not worried about hiding anymore. Even in the dark, Matteo assumes all parties know he is there. POP, De Sel, the cops – between the three groups, he guesses at least thirty people must be watching David's house. And every inch of this block – particularly the interior of David's house – must have a video camera targeted to it.

He stands against a lamppost at the side of David's driveway. He is not worried he will be hurt or tranquilized. Or, at least not now. Once he confronts Jess, then he will definitely be in danger. But, if he understands the situation correctly, all the people watching this block are waiting to learn how Jess puts together her two inventions to make one desalination solution. At this point, his presence is beside the point. He waves to all the folks he can't see. *Bastards.*

David's is a brown-shingled Cape-style house that sits perched on the elevated side of a slope with winding steps that lead to the front door. Except for a lone porch light, the windows are dark and the brown wood shingles blend into the night's growing deepness. Matteo has biked by this house a couple dozen times over the last few weeks. It is a fucking gloomy house.

He walks up the driveway so he can peer into the backyard and check the back patio entrance. Jess won't arrive for another couple hours, but it cannot hurt to make sure he has a visual on all entry points. He scans the small yard that is lined with enormous redwoods; they look like giants in the dark. Amidst these majestic, dying trees, the shadows themselves are ready to pounce. No Jess.

He is shuffling back down the driveway slope when he swears he sees a flicker of light inside the house. On, then off. He stops and studies the house's back half, where the bedrooms and bathrooms are. Nothing. Maybe he imagined it. He is about to walk back to the lamppost when: there it is again. A small luminance – not from a bulb or the bright fullness of a Keeper light.

It is a small flashlight. A... penlight.

How did Jess get here so damn fast?

Without thinking, he charges toward the front door, skipping the steps two by two. He pulls open the door: "Jess! Jess! Don't put the solution together! Don't! Don't!"

JESS

Jess twists the bathtub knob fast to turn the water off. She thinks she heard a man shouting. Sitting in the dark on the bathtub's rim, she listens. There are footsteps; they are coming fast.

She grabs the tranq gun that sits on the sink's counter. *Oh, god.* The steps are determined. Hurried. She clips the penlight back off, tossing it into the sink, so she can use both of her trembling hands to hold the tranq gun. Pointing toward the bathroom doorway, she waits. Her heart punches the insides of her chest.

The footsteps enter David's bedroom, stop, then slowly move toward the bathroom. A man comes to the threshold. From his silhouette, his smell, and his breathing, she knows it's Matteo. Her grip on the gun loosens; her chest sags.

"Are you holding a tranq at me?" he asks in the darkness.

"Uh-huh." Now that her eyes have adjusted, there is just enough dusked light peeking through the closed window shades that she can see the puzzlement play out in Matteo's posture. She reminds herself that even if he is upset with her, she should not care; even if he is familiar, she should not trust him.

"I know you're with De Sel," she says, trying to take the shakiness out of her voice. "Don't say you're not."

"De Sel?" He steps toward her: "That's insane."

"Stop." She points the gun more tightly. "I'm serious."

"Jess, I've been risking my life to keep you safe, and you're—"

"Don't sweet talk me."

"Sweet talk?" He pauses, chuckles: "There's no sweet talk. Can you put the tranq down?"

"You heard my therapy session."

His head cocks: "Well, yes, I did hear your therapy session." He waits. "I'm going to turn the light on."

"No, they'll see—"

The lights on either side of the medicine cabinet stutter on. Matteo is facing her, his eyes blinking, his thick, black hair standing straight up.

"Why'd you do that? I don't want them to see anything in here."

"Jess, this is your chance." His arms gesture to the gray-tiled walls. "Tell all the jerks watching and listening that that you have no idea where David put your two prototypes." He pivots his face toward the corner above the showerhead; his voice rises: "She can't find them either. And actually, she knows nothing about desalination. Can you leave her the fuck alone now?"

She studies him, a smile escaping. He doesn't realize the desalination solution is sitting in the bathtub right underneath the shower curtain she pulled down to cover it.

She has just spent the last hour huddled underneath the maroon nylon sheet, using her small flashlight to light up the process of putting the two prototypes together to create one solution. It works. Beautifully.

In fact, everything over the last hour proceeded with surprising ease. As soon as she saw the electric bike waiting for her beside the dumpster, it was obvious: She was being followed. She did not know by whom, but it was easy to surmise that whoever these people were, they also wanted her to travel quickly to David's. Certainly, there were reasons to be suspicious of these people's assistance. The man and woman who left the bike had to have known she was cowering behind the dumpster. *Why wouldn't they have talked with her or offered her a ride?* Yet, however these questions were answered, there remained only two options: take the bike or leave it. She took it.

With the electric motor turned on, she flew to David's house, breezing past the miserable car traffic and hordes of zombie pedestrians. When she neared David's house, she knew her every move was being watched. She did not care. Her ignorance about the desalination solution had not offered much protection. She was ready to see how much power her knowledge would provide. She propped the electric bike against a redwood in David's back yard and walked from the dead shrubs to the glass patio doors. The doors were, of course, unlocked. As she crossed this threshold, she remembered how it was only yesterday that the De Sel man had tackled her right at this patio entrance. *How could that have only been yesterday?* She pulled the doors wide and walked in, determination in her stride.

She headed straight to the kitchen, opened the refrigerator and saw two plastic-lidded containers with the manufacturer's label "Polly's Perfect Pink Lemonade." *Perfect, indeed.* It was exactly as she had hoped. She opened the freezer and found the ice tray too.

If Relly, POP, Sara Claredge, or De Sel had any idea that her prototypes were housed in liquid and ice, Jess is certain that David's refrigerator would have been ransacked long ago. *But who would have guessed?* Honestly, it was only a fluke that she had decided to store them that way.

When Jess had to pack up her lab at UC Davis, she requested funding for the special "white glove" delivery service that transported delicate scientific instruments and materials, but she did not receive anything but a small personal moving expense. Rather than fund the several thousand dollars for her lab shipment out of her personal funds, she decided to pack and ship her prototypes herself. She knew the voluminous packaging that her raw aerogel and graphene sheets arrived in, but given her budget, she decided the best way to protect her pieces' delicate parts from being chipped or fractured was to ship them submerged in water. As it turned out, Polly's Perfect Pink Lemonade sold a three-gallon mason jar-type container that included a spigot at the bottom. The big label across this clear plastic container said, "perfect for parties and lemonade stands," and it was also perfect for the transport of Jess' prototypes. She placed her aerogel blades in one container and her aerogel crank in another. Given the aerogel's transparency, the prototypes were impossible to see within the pale pink liquid. With her solar cells, she placed the small graphene grids in plastic ice cube trays, filled the tray with water, froze it, then packed the tray in dry ice for the shipment. When she arrived at her Berkeley lab, she had no need for her prototypes, so she took the lazy approach and simply moved everything to her lab's refrigerator and freezer. She had not thought about them in months. Obviously, David had.

In David's kitchen, she grabbed a tub of Morton's salt from the cupboard and carried all her prototypes back through the dim hallway, across David's bedroom and into the back bathroom. She studied the tiny room's ceilings and corners; there were no obvious video cameras anywhere, but she knew they were probably there. A small, high window was on the wall over the toilet and she pulled the blinds down to this window's sill. Remembering how Matteo had said video capture was confounded by darkness, she flipped the lights off, and immediately, the room's darkness became far blacker than the shadowy dusk outside. She pulled the maroon shower curtain from its hooks and draped this enormous plastic covering over herself and the Polly's Lemonade dispenser as she set herself down in the bathtub. She took two things from her satchel – the penlight and the tranq gun – and set to work.

Putting the solution together was a breeze. Knowing that the desalination invention relied on the "old fan's" stronger torque, there was a natural call and response. *Why would a stronger force be necessary for a desalination solution?* Well, because a stronger torque could push salt water more forcefully. Against where would the salt water be pushed? Where else, but against the solar cell, whose graphene structure resulted in a nano-level honeycomb design whose very contact could force the extraction of the salt from the water. Matteo had been right: connection was enough. *Ta-da*, the desalination solution worked.

"Could you please put the tranq down?" Matteo now asks again.

"First you have to tell me why you hacked my Keeper."

"Let's have this conversation without the gun."

"I'd rather keep it," she says, though she knows her voice conveys no such conviction.

"Okay, I'm sitting down; don't shoot me." He sets himself on the low tub landing, slowly straightening his legs in front of him. He looks up at her: "I hacked your Keeper because I'm an observationalist with this company called Beck Industries, and for the last three weeks, my assignment has been to follow you."

She lowers the gun. "An *observationalist*?" The word is strange in her mouth. "You said you worked with the Temescal Experimental Farm."

"I used to work there, before Rachel died. But with my debt for her antivirals, I needed to make more money to pay Hua Chen back."

"Oh." She flips the information in her head like a pancake. *That's not so bad.* Actually, of the possible explanations she has configured for Matteo, this is way better than any she considered. She plunks the gun down on the sink counter, and the lightbulbs flicker in the sconces that bookend the medicine cabinet. She sits beside Matteo on the tub's rim: "You lied a lot."

"I did," he shrugs, "but I wasn't trying to hurt you. I was helping you."

"Who does Beck Industries work for?"

"I'm not sure, maybe POP. But I'm not with POP. I'm not with anyone. Definitely not De Sel." He puts his hand on her knee: "Why would you think that?"

Now the suspicion seems foolish, though moments ago, these worries had pinched at her heart so hard that she can still feel the bruise. "Well, I realized you had hacked my Keeper."

"Did I give it away when I said your journal papers hadn't been published?"

"There was that. But you also kept quoting what I'd said to my therapist about wanting someone who would keep me safe."

"Kept quoting? I said it yesterday, in the Berkeley tunnels."

"And this morning."

"This morning?" He studies his knees, rubbing the dirt from them, thinking. "This morning, whatever I said, it came from me." His eyes go back to hers.

"Oh?"

"It feels good to care about something again."

"Something?" The word comes out as a whisper.

He brings his face to hers: "You. I care about you."

He kisses her, and his sweaty skin and warm mouth already taste familiar and comforting. She puts her arms around his neck, wanting to wrap herself around him and be wrapped within him. As she takes this small nudge forward toward his body, her balance on the bathtub's narrow rim wavers, and her right arm flings out, lifting the shower curtain off the prototypes.

"Oh, crap," she says and rushes to lay the curtain back over the miniature turbine crank and solar cell grids.

Matteo looks at the bathtub. "Wait," he murmurs. "Was that...? His eyebrows lift like they might fly off his face.

In turn, she raises her eyebrows back.

"No way," he whispers. He stops, as though frozen for a moment, then, loudly he proclaims to the walls. "Too bad David screwed up again. He's such a jerk to have lied. There's nothing here. Nothing works. He tricked everyone."

"Maybe we should tell them I know how to use the solution," she whispers to Matteo. "It would give us power."

"They don't want you to have power; they don't want you to have anything." There's the sound of footsteps on the driveway. "We should get out of here." Matteo grabs her hand.

Jess resists. The solution – the magical desalination machine – sits in the bathtub. Jess nods at it, then back to Matteo, her question telegraphing. He slightly shakes his head in response: *Leave it.* Tugging her hand forward, he guides her out of the bathroom into David's bedroom, then down the narrow, dark hallway.

Outside, the footsteps charge closer. Men's voices are shouting commands; Jess can't make out words, though their intensity is alarming. They are coming for her and Matteo. *Oh, god.* She makes her voice very loud: "I wish I could have figured how the pieces fit together, but they simply don't work."

"That's better," he says, as they rush into the living room. He stops short. From the dining room, Keeper lights strobe across the walls and floors. There are silhouettes outside – so many shadows – rushing from the backyard to the kitchen's patio doors. Matteo steps backward toward the bedroom hallway. "This could be bad."

"Will they hurt us?"

He does not respond.

The patio door opens, and the feet run toward her.

"I'm surrendering!" she screams. In the dark, their flashlights come forward fast and she cannot make out the people who hold the light. Faceless shapes, big, with weapons drawn.

"Don't hurt us! Please! Don't—" There's a popping sound, like the crack of a bat, and she hears Matteo yelp.

She turns: "No!" Matteo is on the ground, his face in spasms, his leg twitching like it's been electrified. She throws herself on the ground beside him. "Matteo, no, no, no." She touches his cheek, trying to calm the twitches. "Please, this can't be happening."

That is when she feels the shot to her back thigh. Then her shoulder. The pain pierces, as though she is being branded with a hot poker. Panic clenches her body; she cannot breathe. Everything is black.

DAY THREE
Friday, November 19, 2038

MATTEO

A scratching sound. It won't stop. The sound of digging. Yes, he is digging in his garden at Tia's. Hundreds of tiny seeds sit in his palm, like beluga lentils, small and black. Somehow, he knows he is planting potatoes, though usually potato seeds are bigger and browner than what is in his palm. No matter. He drops the black, flat seeds into the dusty holes, one after the other.

A woman steps down the hill toward the garden. The setting sun behind her floods her outline in orange-gold sunlight, and since her silhouette carries a languorous roll in her hips, he knows: it is Rachel. He wants to call to her, but he cannot because his digging must not be interrupted. Rachel steps closer, and her lips hover over his ear like a caress: "I wish I could be with you." He keeps his hands chipping away at the dusty, brown earth, and when he finally glances upward, squinting at the sun, the woman is not Rachel anymore; it is Jess, and she is crying enormous tears.

"Cry into the holes I'm digging," he says. "The dirt needs water."

Jess shakes her head: "My tears are salty; your potatoes will die. Like me. I will die too."

Matteo forces his eyes open, his breath blustering outward like he has come up from a dive. Darkness is around him; yet, even without being able to see anything, he knows he is nowhere he has ever been before. The mattress under him is thin with a cold metal frame below it, like the cots at sleepaway camp. A musty, moldy smell is in the air's background, with a laundry detergent fragrance in the foreground. The scratching sound is not only from his dream; there is a mouse clawing behind the wall. He is in a basement. "Jess?" he whisper-shouts. "Are you here too? Jess?"

He sits up, and his head pierces like a trumpet is being blown into his ear. Gently, he runs his hand through his hair: no cuts, no blood. He scans his body; there is one tranquilizer puncture wound on his left thigh and another on his back, both swollen outward like pitchers' mounds. His bones ache, and he knows that however he

204

was transported from David Steubingly's hallway to wherever he is now, it was not with care.

He hopes Jess is here with him, maybe sleeping still. "Jess," he whispers again. Stumbling, he makes his way around the room trying to touch as much as he can. As he walks, the powder pink smell of detergent tickles his nose. He half-expects to bump into a washing machine, but there are only cardboard boxes stacked high. No other bed, no other person. No Jess.

Oh, god. This disaster is his fault. He never should have turned on David Steubingly's bathroom light. He had never even contemplated that Jess could have figured out the desalination solution so quickly. *How the hell did she do it? Who figures out a vexing scientific quandary in ten minutes?* It's not like other smart people had not tried. He had been so hopeful too. If he and Jess could show they did not know how to make the desalination solution, the chase would have ended. They could have walked out of David Steubingly's house and moved on with their lives. From darkness into light. From fear to calm.

Nope, that hope had not panned out.

He jiggles the door slightly in the doorjamb. The door weighs nothing; it's probably made of cheap, compression board, and since there is no catch of a bolt in the jam, Matteo realizes the door is not even locked. He rests his hand on the knob but cannot bring himself to twist it fully open. Whatever is on the other side may be worse than this room.

Probably POP or De Sel captured him. If he were with Relly's gang, he would be in a jail cell, and though this room is not nice, it's no prison. He thinks back to the men who shot at him. Engulfed in the flashlight's orb, they were hulking and huge. He hates to consider what will happen when they come to wake him. He folds his arms across his chest, placing his hands in his armpits, trying to slow his body shakes.

From outside the room, there are nearing voices, then footsteps. A light pops on in the room outside, and a narrow band of luminescence spreads across the floor where Matteo stands. People are arguing, and from the several voices' echo, he can tell the room outside must be large and the group small, maybe five to seven people. Several voices speak at once. Squeaks of metal against concrete sound like people pulling out chairs to sit at a table. He cannot make out the full sentences, but the voices' timbre is low and testy: "I told you to…" "Don't tell me what I should have done when you…" "You're the one that let Relly…"

A woman speaks loudly in a voice that suggests she is starting a meeting. Matteo can only make out her tone, which is congratulatory, but not the words. He lies on the ground beside the door. Pressing his stomach against the cool concrete floor, he wedges his face so that his eyes peer out through the two-inch gap between the door and floor. A group sits around a metal table in the middle of a large room, around thirty feet from him. Matteo can see their feet and knees but no matter how much he squints and tries to press his eye against the floor, the angle does not allow for a view of more than a foot above ground level. Since this sight isn't satisfying, he pushes his ear close to the space under the door. Suddenly, he can hear the conversation almost like he is in the room.

The woman is speaking again, her voice tight: "Maybe it was messy, but we got what we needed."

A man speaks: "You should have let us fight for the girl. Relly's guys, they weren't so fierce. We could have taken them." Matteo shifts so he can peer through the crack. The way the man said "the girl" is just like Beck. Though Matteo can only see the man from the waist down, he wears the same kind of khaki shorts and snap-titanium sandals that Beck wears; it has to be Beck.

The woman responds: "If we'd fought for her, we would have lost our focus on capturing the solution. The solution is really all we need."

"Relly's guys didn't think so." This is a different man's voice. "Relly's people didn't give a shit about the solution— or Matteo. They grabbed Jess off the ground, left that house in seconds. They thought Jess was what they needed."

"They thought wrong." It is the woman speaking again. Matteo thinks she must be Sara Claredge. She is wearing heeled pumps that are like the ones Sara Claredge was wearing in David's office, and though Matteo never heard Sara speak, this woman sounds exactly as he imagines she would. "Now that we have the solution, we can reverse-engineer the mechanics. We have the power to create a desalination solution that works better than De Sel's. We win. Everyone else loses."

"Hold on," it's Beck again. "You're giving us a victory speech here, but you keep changing your strategy, so I'm having trouble following you. You used to say that our strategy was to make an investment deal with David Steubingly. Then it was about keeping the girl safe so that – I thought – we would make the deal with her. Now, it's about... what? "

"Beck, the strategy was *always* to own the solution." There is a squeak of her chair pushing backward, her feet against the floor. "Ever since I saw that black box turn that horrible, brine-y ocean water into fresh, drinkable water, all I've ever wanted was to know how to make the solution. Now we know. Now we have the power."

"But what about David? You made a deal with David?"

"Did I? I have twenty-two individuals who are ready to invest in a desalination solution. They don't care if it's David's invention or Jessila's invention – or *mine*." Her heels clack against the floor. "David Steubingly thought he was so clever, but I have outsmarted him. He told me he invented the solution by himself. A lie. He told me he wanted to work to invent a solution that would take the power away from De Sel. A lie. I don't want to rely on liars. Not David. Not Jessila. Now that I have the solution, I – we – win."

A young woman's voice pipes up: "Um, excuse me, Sara, I'm still not understanding. You say we win, but how? If both David and Jess are now with Relly, won't they be at tomorrow's ceremony with the Governor? And if they sign the patent applications to De Sel, doesn't that mean that De Sel owns the *patents*?

Beck chimes in: "Yeah, where's the win, Sara?"

"Well, Beck, this is where it does become complex. De Sel *could* own the patents by mid-morning; but they don't own them now. From all reports, David is still unconscious. And that Jessila girl was hit by multiple darts. She won't wake for *hours*."

"Okay," Beck says, annoyed with the patronizing tone that Sara is using. "We *know* Jess is drugged. What we're trying to say is that when the girl wakes and sits at the ceremony, she will sign over ownership of the patent to De Sel."

"Right. *If* Jessila makes it to the Governor's signing ceremony, she would sign ownership to De Sel. But Jessila will *not* make it there."

"Wait, are you saying—" Beck stops and there's a sound like he's catching his breath. "I don't understand. I pleaded so many times over the last forty-eight hours to let us capture her. We could have picked her up easily at David's house. And at Tia's, it would have been a piece of cake. Now – *now!* – you want to capture her. When it couldn't be harder. I don't get—"

"Not capture her. Come on, Beck. You know I'm not talking about capture." There's another silence that builds like a balloon being blown too tight. "This morning, we have to eliminate both David Steubingly and Jessila Prentiss."

A low guttural groan escapes Matteo. The room outside is also filled with murmurs and gasp. Beck must not be the only one who is shocked by Sara Claredge's strategy.

"That's awful," the young woman murmurs.

"That's revolution," Sara Claredge snaps back.

The metal chair legs scrape against the concrete floor. Matteo peeks again through the gap: Beck is standing, his voice incredulous: "We've been protecting that girl for the last month. We've had Matteo following her, and the car escape route – we rehearsed that so many times. And Bruno, he died for *her*. Now, you want to *kill* her?"

"Beck, you sound so hurt. Did you think I wanted to be Jessila's best bosom friend?"

"Well, I didn't think you wanted to be her murderer. You sure seemed like you cared for her a few days ago."

"Never her. Only the solution. In fact, when she refused to give me the patent application in David's office, I realized then that I never wanted to ask her for it again. These last two days, I've had us follow her so she could show us what she knew. The goal was to gather her knowledge so we would have no need for her. And, thankfully, now that we have the working prototype, she is indeed superfluous. So is David. They die; the solution is ours. Such pure logic gives us a beautifully pure win."

There is a long silence that is eventually broken by an unfamiliar voice. "You think because it's logical to kill her, we should?"

"I won't apologize for being logical. Logic has always been POP's special strength. We have always been willing to recognize that some means do justify the ends. The situation this morning is no different. Now that we have the prototype, we have to grab the power. "

"Power? I thought this was about fresh water," Beck mutters.

"Everything's about power, Beck. And in the next four hours, we either gain it or lose it. If David Steubingly and Jessila Prentiss die, we gain the power to grow food and keep people from dying of hunger. If they don't die, the world continues to sink into a hellhole of starvation and drought. Quite simply, we face a choice between sentimentality or world salvation."

A long silence is eventually interrupted by a small voice: "What you are planning is wrong." This calm and even voice is from a Latina woman. She sounds old. Matteo peers through the crack. There is no angle on the face of this woman, but there are her orthopedic shoes and the thin, wrinkly ankles that are above them. It is Tia.

"I joined POP to be part of a righteous movement, not to forsake my principles when they become inconvenient. We should not kill anyone. Not even David Steubingly." Matteo is glad to hear Tia's familiar voice speak up.

"And what will your principles gain us?" Sara Claredge's voice is intense. "If we allow Jessila to live, how many other people will die? De Sel may license the patent, but they won't use it to make water more plentiful. That company loves water scarcity; it makes more money in droughts. You've seen what is happening in Ethiopia.

Widespread famine, thousands of children dying, and what is De Sel doing? *Restricting* their desalination of salt water into fresh water. Scarcity drives water prices higher, and in Ethiopia, while so many were dying, De Sel's profit margins climbed from 27% to 33%. Don't you see? De Sel will not use any desalination invention to end famine or increase food production. De Sel only cares about money."

Matteo hates listening to this woman's analysis because she is not wrong. De Sel is a sick company.

"Now, if POP wins, it's a different story." Sara Claredge's heels click on the basement floor again. "We have funders ready to build wind-powered desalination plants all around the state. My investors are powerful people, and it would be political suicide for the Governor to ignore our investment and effort. If we have the solution ready to manufacture, he will have no choice but to deliver the oceanic pipelines to our plants." Her voice swells like she's making a speech to a crowd of a hundred, not the seven people who are in the room. "We will make fresh water cheap again. The agricultural industry will thrive. Food prices will drop and with more fresh water, there will be greater sanitation, better health." Her voice takes on even greater momentum. "And once we've made fresh water work here, we can build these same wind-powered plants in famine-ravaged places all around the world. Our invention will save tens of millions, maybe hundreds of millions of people. And it's not just lives saved; we'll reduce electrical consumption, carbon emissions and famine-related tensions all around the world. This is what we can do; this is POP's potential. We can literally save the world."

She pauses, and even though Matteo can't see her face, he knows she is utilizing this pause to make eye contact, to gather buy-in.

"I have given this same speech to dozens of investors over the last three months, and not one of them has turned down the opportunity to get in on the ground floor of this venture. Do you know why? Sure, they anticipate an enormous return on their investment. But they also want to be part of a revolution that saves our state and our world."

Matteo lies on the hard concrete ground, his hands tightening into fists.

"And, sadly, there are but two obstacles to our revolution." Click, clack go her shoes. "David Steubingly. Jessila Prentiss. In order for millions more to live, these two must be sacrificed."

Matteo shudders. He wants to get up, to roar, to punch... but he lies there stiff on the floor, his ear pressed against the door gap.

The professional-sounding man speaks up: "Could we try to capture her instead of kill her?"

"Capturing would mean more death." This is Beck's voice, and he sounds as though he's already considered the option. "I hate to say this, but if we... *kill* her," the word comes out like a foreign one, "that work can be done from afar with a drone or a sharp shooter as she enters the Hall. Even if the girl makes it all the way to Ellison Hall, we can still have someone accidentally bump into her with a poison pin. In all those situations, her death would be hard to trace back to POP. But if we attempt a rescue, we'll be caught. Relly won't let her go without a fight, and we'd risk losing more people. After what happened with Bruno, I want to be careful."

There is a long silence.

"They're planning to kill her too." Matteo recognizes the voice as the man who has spoken before. "I was the one tracking David these last couple months, and before David realized his Keeper was hacked, I listened in on the conversations he had with Brooklyn Relly. It was the two of them that came up with the idea to give Jess the tunnel code. And that's because Relly wanted a place where, if the need arose, she could kill Jess out of sight." He pauses, then continues in a softer voice: "No matter what *we* do, Jess is not long for this life."

A different kind of silence – somehow sadder – fills the space.

"Yes," Sara says, "her death is inevitable." The sighs and shifts in the seats are the only response. She lowers her voice. "If only Jessila could have joined with POP and worked with us to make the world a better place, that would have been wonderful. But sadly," her words curdle into a hush, "that option is not possible."

No one responds.

"Since I have everyone's assent," her voice seesaws upward, "I'd like to move toward developing our plans for proceeding. Beck, you mentioned drones, but I believe we will have less risk of detection with the poison pill since I'm worried the surveillance cameras can catch a..."

Matteo sits up, and with his ear away from the gap, the words are only sounds, no meaning. His own thoughts are just as amorphous – only feeling, no logic. His breathing staggers in short, sharp huffs. He is scared, and not just by what he heard, but by the impulse that is trilling through his body. He stands, and his torso wavers, like it is disconnected from his hips.

What he is thinking is half-cooked. *He could die.* He grasps in the dark for the doorknob. His palm sits there for a second; a shiver runs through him. *Should he think this through? No.* He swings the door wide back. Stumbling, he steps into the room's white light.

Sara's back is to Matteo, and she is so busy discussing Ellison Hall's layout that she must not hear the door's creak. Matteo walks forward with stiff, even paces. Tia looks up. Then a black, tattooed man. A blue-haired Asian woman. A younger, bearded man. A dreadlocked, white woman. Beck. Sara's sentence falters as she becomes aware that they are staring at something behind her. As she turns, her curly mop of hair jiggles atop her head.

"Sara Claredge." Matteo wants to make his voice loud, but his words are hoarse and quivering instead. He steadies himself, planting his hiking boots tight on the floor as Sara's astonished expression turns to face him.

"Don't kill Jess Prentiss," he says. "I'll retrieve her for POP myself."

JESS

She has the feeling that someone is biting into her shoulder. And her leg too. She moves her hand to touch her upper arm, and the action stirs her drowsy brain like a spoon in porridge. *Matteo.* At first, it's a grasp at a thought, then a grab. *Matteo, oh god, Matteo.* Her eyes fly open.

She is in a large room. A bedroom. Queen-sized bed. Pale blue duvet cover tucked tight around her chest. *Don't panic.* She is wearing a white nightgown which is embroidered with colorful flowers. All the dust, dirt, sweat, caked blood: gone. Her skin smells like citrus. *Someone has cleaned her and dressed her; who?*

The walls are covered with broadly striped wallpaper with alternating shades of blue, white and gray. Thick double-hung blue curtains with tassels are pulled back to reveal a set of French doors that look as though they lead to a balcony. It's dark outside, though some light is building in the lower sky. A lamp on a nearby table gives off a low glow. Jess tries to sit up, but the blankets are cinched across her body tight, holding her in place.

A woman's voice outside the room is calling: "Don't worry, Jess." The voice carries as though in song. "I'm coming... coming." The door clicks and opens at such an even rate that it must be electronically controlled.

In the room's dim light, a woman flows toward her. She has short, platinum hair and three gemstones on each cheekbone; her blue nightgown has a lingerie top and a flowing, satiny full-length skirt, like an old-time Hollywood starlet. The woman bends down toward her, a smell of roses wafting off her tan skin as she settles on the duvet cover. "You must be so confused," she croons. "I've been waiting up all night to see if you would wake. Luis keeps telling me to come to bed, but I can't sleep. I've been too worried about you."

Jess lifts her hand to make room for the flow of the nightgown which billows upward like a sail as the woman sits down. Her motherly concern does not jibe with who Jess knows this woman to be. "Relly?" she asks, knowing her confusion sounds childlike.

Relly takes Jess' hand in her own and smiles: "You can call me Brooklyn. I'm here to take care of you, to keep you safe."

Keep her safe? The words, which are meant to be reassuring, instead wake all her worries, like an alarm clock is buzzing. *How did Relly know from the other room that Jess had woken? Are they being recorded?* "Where's Matteo?" Her eyes dart to the door that Relly entered, which is now closed tight again. "Is he okay?"

"Yes, of course. I'm afraid those awful POP thugs roughed him up a bit, and we had to take him to the hospital—"

"Hospital? How badly is he hurt?" The image of Matteo on the ground rushes to her, his eyes bugged, his face twitching. "I have to see him—" she tries to move her legs. The pain is shocking; she falls backward.

"Now, now, there's no rush." Relly smoothes the comforter back around Jess, keeping the blanket tight. "He's fine, and if everything goes as we'd like at the announcement, he'll stay fine."

The announcement? Her brain hurts like it has been origami-folded into convoluted creases. "What do you mean '*if* it goes as we'd like'? Matteo *has* to stay fine."

Relly puts her finger to her lips: "Shhh, there's no need for this tone. His safety rests in your hands, so you need not worry. And for your own healing, please, please: No more outbursts."

Oh god, oh god. Her hands rush to her face, so Relly won't see her lip quivering. "Why is his safety in my hands? What do you want from me?"

"Oh, honey," Relly answers, putting her hand atop Jess' lap, "it's not so bad as all that. What you have to do is what you'll want to do. Signing a few documents, that's all. You are about to become very, very wealthy. Matteo will be proud of you, I'm sure."

Something is not right. With effort, she pushes herself upward to sitting. "I don't understand; what are you trying to get from me?"

"Jess, all we've ever wanted was for you to join us in this business venture."

She evaluates Relly's saccharine smile, then scans the room to see if there is a way out. The door to the bedroom is closed tight. The floor-to-ceiling window is plate glass, no openings. The striped wallpaper pulses. "Where am I?"

"At the Governor's house." Relly responds, her voice light and buoyant, as though their conversation is nothing but friendly. "You might think that means we're in Sacramento, but no, we're actually in the house that Luis keeps in the Los Altos hills. See," Relly stands up and walks to the French doors, pulling the curtains further back. The sky has lightened considerably in a short time. "Isn't this view beautiful? I love it in here when the sun starts to rise over the hills. Don't you?"

Jess could give a shit about the stupid view, but nonetheless she leans forward, squinting to make out the setting amid the early-morning dimness. The room must be on a second or even third story, because the courtyard and pool are far below them. In the distant hills, the sun is peaking over brown rounded peaks, the yellow-gray light clinging to the hills outline like a glow. She brings her eyes to Relly's: "When can I see Matteo?"

"Well, dear, as soon as you sign the papers." Relly stands and smiles, and Jess is reminded of the game show models that showcased products on the programs her grandmother watched during the day.

"Do you work for De Sel?" Jess asks.

"Oh, goodness, no. I tried to tell you the other day: I work for California." Relly straightens the pillows around Jess to make them more orderly. "My job is law enforcement, nice and simple. Luis Ramos is my fiancé, so that makes me a tad different than the usual cop." She stops fidgeting with the pillows. "Though not that much." Relly's close-lipped smile stretches wide across her face. It's an assertive smile, and despite Relly's floaty nightgown and her henpecking arrangement of the pillows, Jess can smell the determination behind her perfume.

"You shot at me. When we were in the basement, you told your men to hurt me."

Though Jess' statement is an accusation, Relly responds calmly, tilting her head as though to reflect on the memory itself. "True, but only because I was trying to protect you. Tranquilizing you was the easiest way to keep you safe."

"You wanted to hurt Matteo too." Jess tries to sit up even more, but with the sheets so tight, she only heightens herself by an inch. "You were going to issue a warrant for him and say he was a terrorist."

Relly's face creases with confusion; she shakes her head. "That's only because I thought Matteo was with POP. Now, of course, I realize Matteo wasn't aware of how he was being puppet-stringed, but the truth is he messed everything up when he made you run from us."

"That's because he was trying—"

"I know, I know. He was trying to take care of you. Please, don't start going on again over Matteo. It's been horribly difficult for David to watch you gushing over him."

"David? He's been watching me? I thought he hadn't regained consciousness."

"Yesterday, David came out of his stupor, thank god, and he watched the video feed that came out of his house last night. It was very upsetting for him, as you can imagine."

Jess takes a second to process this information. "Did you ever figure out why those De Sel men beat David up?"

"Oh, honey," Relly says, "those men weren't with De Sel. Those were POP thugs who beat David to a pulp."

"But the men who beat up David were wearing De Sel jackets?"

"Which should have been your first tip they weren't with De Sel." She touches Jess' hand. "Don't you see? POP are the bad guys. David worked so hard to make the right deal for your desalination solution, and then Sara Claredge came along and ruined everything. She's an unbelievably selfish and conniving woman, a real power-hungry bitch, if you don't mind me using the word."

"Sara Claredge cares about feeding people."

216

"Jess, please, the woman plays like she's an earth goddess, but all she cares about is power. Sure, she calls her new enterprise an *environmental empire*, but don't be fooled. She plays hardball. She ordered her thugs to beat David until he told them where the desalination solution was – which, thank god, he never did. The woman is a terrorist, and she is willing to kill anyone in her way." Relly sighs big, then smiles: "How about I order you some eggs and toast?" She pats the comforter: "And a pot of coffee?"

"Okay."

"With cream?" Relly stands.

"Sure."

"I'll order juice too. Apple-carrot's your favorite, right?"

"Uh-huh."

Jess watches Relly whisperspeak the order to her Keeper. Her lips move slightly; her forehead wrinkles crease and un-crease. There could be comfort in watching this interaction, in being back in the world where Keepers take care of needs, the views are beautiful, the sheets smooth – that is, if Matteo could be safe too. "Relly, you said that in order to see Matteo, I have to sign papers. What *exactly* do the papers say?"

A flutter of confusion washes Relly's face. She sits beside Jess again, and the bed covers stretch even more tightly across Jess' lap. "Well, the first papers would be ones to sign with David, before we leave for Stanford. It's about structuring the shares of the limited liability corporation you're creating with him. Then, we go to Ellison Hall; that's where the announcement will take place. There, you'll sign the licensing agreement with De Sel." Relly pats her hand with excitement: "That's the contract that will make you rich!" The top-most gemstone catches a glint of the rising sunrays and her face's shape contorts as the light glints across her face.

Jess tries to lean forward, but the tightness of the covers makes it hard. "Is De Sel buying the solution?"

"Of course." Relly's eyebrows rise. "I thought that would be obvious."

"Yes, very obvious." De Selfish. There's the rub. If she signs the papers, Matteo is safe, but De Sel wins. "Will De Sel use my solution?"

"You mean, like actually change their water plants?" Relly runs her finger over her thumb's shiny blue nail polish.

"Right. Will they make their plants wind-powered so that fresh water will be cheap again? And food can grow and be more affordable?"

Relly's face grimaces: "Oh, goodness, listen to you." Her hands fall to her lap. "What does it matter what De Sel does with your solution? You'll still be paid." Relly pulls the covers back: "Here, let's have you sit at the table so you'll be ready to eat when your breakfast arrives."

With effort, Jess swings her feet to the floor, ignoring the stab of pain that cuts into her thigh, pretending the room is not undulating with these small movements.

Matteo would understand why her solution should be used. He would care about the poor and the hungry, not only the stupid money. She hopes that he is okay, that they have not hurt him. The recognition comes in a rush: He is all she cares about.

A robe lies across the foot of the bed, and Relly picks it up, holding it open for her. "Twenty Nepalese women worked a week to embroider all these beautiful flowers on the nightgown and robe. Isn't it to-die-for?"

As Jess' arms sink into the robe's smooth sleeves, she doesn't say what she is thinking – that it is disgusting to ask twenty people to work on a single nightgown. "I prefer sleeping naked," she mumbles as she ties the belt around her waist.

"Yes, you do."

At the sound of this voice, Jess' head cranes toward the door.

A man stands in the doorway, carrying a tray holding a coffee pot and dishes. His face is streaked with black and purple bruises; one eye is swollen shut and his lower lip bulges with a cut. It is David.

MATTEO

"This road goes to the back of his house," Beck mumbles and takes one hand from the steering wheel to rub the sleep from his eyes. He turns the pick-up truck onto a narrow dirt road that is tucked within the bramble of dead shrubs and yellowed grasses.

Matteo sits up straighter. They must be close. A honey-colored light peeks through rounded, clay hills, creating a view that would register as pretty if every muscle in his body were not tensed with dread. The car jostles hard over each hole it hits, and the reverberations fly into Matteo's leg as though stones were being thrown straight to his puncture wounds. He swallows; if they are this close to Governor Ramos' house, he needs to break the silence he has kept through this hour-long drive from Berkeley.

"That rock that killed Bruno..." his voice is creaky; "it is because the drone set the velocity of the strike too high, and if we set a tranq dart's velocity to break a window, then—"

"Don't worry, our drone cuts the window before discharging the dart. You know, Relly's technology is for shit." Beck glances across at him, then back at the road: "The drone I'll be using this morning is state of the art."

"Oh, great." Matteo wonders if Beck sees the twisted irony: POP led the State Capital massacre so that firearms would be outlawed; yet, POP continues to use them. The hypocrisy is stunning, but Matteo won't waste the breath to comment on that now.

"Listen," Beck says, both hands gripping the steering wheel tight. "I know you're mad at me, and dude, I get it. But you have to understand: no one expected this situation to play out like this."

"Right," Matteo mutters, hoping that if he agrees, Beck will shut up.

Beck steers the car to the shoulder and brakes to a stop. "Listen, you can stay pissed, but all of us at POP, we're just trying to do the right thing."

"You're boy scouts, I get it." Matteo keeps his head facing his passenger side window, knowing if watches Beck's eager sanctimony now, he will want to smack him.

Beck continues: "When Sara said she had this deal, we thought it was amazing. Creating fresh, clean water – what could be wrong with that, right? We started tracking David just as a precaution. Then, like three weeks ago, Jaden – that's the observationalist who was tracking David – realized there was nothing on David's Keeper about water or salt or actually any recent research of any kind. Nada. Sara started to wonder if this desal solution was something David had actually invented himself. She didn't want to be securing investors for an invention that wasn't even David's own. So, Sara confronted David and told him that she was ready to pull out of the deal unless he came clean with how he built his solution. That's when everything went crazy. As soon as David left this meeting with Sara, he bought a disposable Keeper from a convenience store and called Brooklyn Relly. Jaden could only hack into part of the conversation, but he heard David talking about the girl in a strange way, saying stuff like 'if they find out, they'll make the deal with her.' From what we pieced together, David had started a romantic relationship with the girl solely so she would fall asleep next to him. Then, he used her thumbprint to gain access to the secure regions of her Keeper and look at all her research notes and diagrams. That's an old man's version of Keeper hacking for you, right?" Beck chuckles. "Anyway, now he was telling Relly that he had all the research information he needed, and the girl was only liability, not asset. He said that it was time to 'bring her into the tunnel.'"

Despite himself, Matteo is rapt. He turns to look at Beck.

Beck nods, looking pleased to finally have Matteo facing him. "So that's when everything about our strategy shifted. We realized: hey, the girl is the key. Quite the fucking shock, actually. Sara sat down with some of us higher-ups at POP and came up with a gameplan. First, we hacked into Berkeley's tunnel code and disconnected David and Relly's thumbprint from gaining access. Second, we got you to track the girl – see, we really did want to keep her safe. And then the third big part of the plan was to step up our observations of David. We had to figure out what game he was playing and who he was playing it with. Over three weeks, we had so many people following him and listening in on his communications, it was crazy. He knew it too. He was trying hard to evade us. A few days ago, he received a hand-delivered package at his campus offices, and with a bit of sleuthing, we realized it was De Sel who had sent the package. De Sel! That's when Sara realized that David had been playing her all along. He didn't give a shit about saving the world; he actually *wanted* to work with corporate America. Sara went bezerk. That woman is willing to do anything to keep this deal from falling apart."

Matteo turns back toward the passenger side window. Yes, Sara is willing to kill Jess.

Please god, he cannot lose Jess too.

Beck touches Matteo's shoulder. "Dude, don't you see? I've always been trying to do the right thing. I never meant to put the girl – or you – in a bad way; you've got to believe that."

Beck pushes a button on the dash to turn the idling engine off. With the stillness, Matteo can feel Beck's eager eyes waiting for him to face him.

"So, this is it?" Matteo's head nods toward the outside.

No governor's mansion is anywhere in sight. The pick-up truck is parked next to a long hedge of tall rusty-brown evergreens that make an impenetrable wall. Matteo studies the poor trees – a brand of coniferous called Green Giant. They never stood a chance in this climate; their brown brittle needles are nothing but a fire risk now.

"Yeah," Beck points into the trees, "behind this hedge is a sloped backyard with a pool at the basin. And the main house, it's just beyond the pool." Beck touches his shoulder. "Don't worry, dude, it's going to be *fine*."

Matteo wants to grab Beck's jaw, grip his face tight, scream into it: *No, dude, it's not fine!*

They both know that this plan – Plan A – is unlikely to work. And Sara Claredge made them agree that if Beck was willing to try Plan A, he also had to be willing to carry out Plan B. Beck has a bottle with a poison pin in his pocket for that possibility. So, yeah: "*Fuck you, man. Nothing's fine.*" is what Matteo would like to shout back.

Instead, he shakes Beck's hand off of his shoulder and says, "Let's get out the drone."

JESS

David used to have such charisma that, even with his relatively modest frame, he commanded a room. Now, with the way his seersucker pajamas peek out from beneath his thick royal blue robe and how he takes small, pained steps, he resembles an invalid. "Where should I put this?"

"Why not on the table here?" Relly gestures toward a round, polished table which sits before the enormous glass balcony doors.

When David sets down the tray, he opens his arms wide as though to take in the sight of Jess. "Oh, Fire, it's so good to see you. I've been worried sick about you."

"It's true," Relly says, "he has been agonizing."

David's arms stretch even wider, and Relly gives Jess a small nod, of the sort a mother gives when she wants to encourage her child to respond. Jess cannot decide what to do. She is relieved that David is alive; she did not want him dead, of course. Yet, her mouth tastes of bitterness. She takes staggered steps away from David's opened arms toward the breakfast tray. She pulls out the tables' chair and settles into it. "I know you tricked me, David," she says.

Relly gasps. David tut-tuts: "Oh, Fire, I'm pained to hear you would think that."

Jess ignores him. She lifts the bell-shaped cloche from the plate to reveal a steaming omelet with crispy potatoes. The smell wafts upward – cheese, scallions, parsley. Jess has to swallow; she is salivating so much. A bud vase, heavy silverware and a red thermal coffee pot are arranged on the tray. "So fancy," Jess mumbles, as she unrolls the fork from the cloth napkin.

"Luis' chef is particular about his presentation," Relly explains, as she seats herself on the bed next to the table. "You know, Jess, with all the money you're about to have, you could hire a chef too. Once you sign the papers, the sky's the limit for what you can buy. You're such a lucky woman."

Jess has never had a desire to slap anyone before. In her world of quiet labs and libraries, assaulting another person would have been outrageous. Yet, after days of running and fear, the blood that pours to her fingertips is coarser. Her hands itch, and an image breezes across her brain of how her palm would smack satisfyingly strong against Relly's gemstoned cheek. Jess chews, swallows, and takes another bite.

Though she aims to keep her eyes on her plate, she is uncomfortably aware of David's admiring stare, a gaze that somehow conveys that he finds Jess' eating to be itself an accomplishment for which he should take credit.

"I know you're upset," he says, "but these two days haven't been great for me either. I found out last night how much Matteo was tricking you, *seducing* you. When I saw on the video feed how he kissed you in my very own bathroom, I almost retched."

Relly rises from her position on the bed and her nightgown's long skirt cascades outward with the sudden movement. "I think that's my exit note," and she smiles, as though she has said something witty. The door automatically opens as Relly approaches; then, once her nightgown's material has fully escaped the exit, slowly shuts again.

The tension that settles over the room is thick, as though the air itself holds expectation. Jess sets her fork down and begins what has to be said: "I know you stole my inventions. I know you tried to sell them as your own; I know you're the reason I was chased and shot at and—"

"Fire, that's not the truth—"

Jess does not stop: "And now I know you're using Matteo as some sick ultimatum to make me sign your stupid deal—"

"Jess, Jess, give me a chance." His voice is mild, almost patronizing. He points to his face. "Look at what they did to me." Around his left, closed-up eye, the blackness of the bruise is like someone spilled ink on his face; his nose is doubled in size; his cheek's skin looks like someone has run sandpaper over it. His voice shifts to a whisper: "I endured this for you."

"For me?" she scoffs. "Oh, please, don't lie more!"

"You truly don't understand the situation, do you?" His words are firm. "I made a beautiful deal for you." He folds his hands in his lap. "The way I put it to Relly is that I have made you *a gift*."

"*A gift*? They're *my* inventions!" She wishes there was some way to escape this conversation. The door to the bedroom is closed tight and seems to only open from outside controls; the windows are plate glass, no latch to loosen.

"Now, now, Fire." He picks up the red coffee thermos from the breakfast tray. "It's true that I found your inventions in your lab's refrigerator, yes." He pulls a coffee cup from the tray. "But I'm sure you will concede: I saw what you did not. The graphene fabrication on your solar cell is so beautiful. And that turbine – it's unbelievable how powerful it is. But I alone realized what they could become." He pours the coffee, adds the cream and sits back in his chair, facing Jess. "By now you know how the solution is constructed, yes?"

"Yes, I know."

"So, you see that the two pieces of your brilliant work became far, far more brilliant when I put them together. One plus one is greater than two. That's true about your inventions – and it is true about us."

David's brand of smooth is something that has always stood out about him. He has a way of spinning a subject toward its most optimistic angle, and, in fact, she has always liked that he could persuade her that her glass was not only half full, but filled with the most delicious drink imaginable. His eyebrows arch: "I've made a wonderful business deal for you."

"I don't care about business."

"Precisely." His hands clasp together. "That is why it was imperative that I look out for your best interests. Because I care about you."

She keeps reminding herself to disbelieve every word David says. *Don't listen. Look away.* Studying the scene outside the enormous window, she notices that the Governor's lawn is not the bright green of artificial turf but instead the varying pale and dark greens of real, watered grass. How strange that the Governor uses a sprinkler system when he is the one who signed the legislation outlawing their use. A fence runs the length of the patio, and just beyond it, Jess notices two men standing near bushes. They are wearing oxygen masks, like all gardeners must, and carrying something tight to their chest, though it is hard to tell what it could be. Leaf blowers? There aren't many leaves to blow.

"Fire... look at me," he pauses, waits.

Sighing, she turns to him.

"I've been around the block a few times. I know how science intersects with business, and scientists always get a raw deal." He extends his arm across the table, trying to make sure she stays facing him. "If I hadn't masterminded a way to make a better deal, you would have sold your inventions for a song."

She finds it strange that he is working so hard to mollify a fear she never had. She shakes her head: "You don't know what the solution would have sold for."

"Don't I?" his voice becomes invigorated. "De Sel is a monopoly; there is no market incentive for them to buy innovations. Quite the opposite. De Sel's bid would have been laughably low unless the company had some reason to worry another company would buy the invention. What I had to do was create the impression there was a competitive bid. Don't you see?"

What interests Jess now is not David's economics lesson but watching how animated he is becoming. His tone is eager, almost plaintive. He sounds – maybe for the first time – like he is telling the truth.

"Of course," David continues, "I couldn't snap my fingers and, like that, come up with another enterprise that would buy a desalination solution. No other Fortune 500 energy company wants to touch De Sel's market space. And even if I could find investors brave enough to go head-to-head with De Sel, they would never amass a bid for the patent until they'd done due diligence. That process would take forever. Remember, all I was looking for was a bid, not a buy." His words are quickening, his eyes animating with zeal.

226

"What I needed," he continues, "was a way to bring together a group of rich, dreamy people who cared about making water more available. Folks who thought they knew business but didn't." He holds up his coffee mug, as though to toast himself. "Sara Claredge was the answer. No one knows more wealthy Agro types than she does. With all her capital campaigns for third world causes, she is constantly mingling with rich Hollywood types, liberal start-up founders – just the saps I wanted."

He's very proud of himself, clearly. Jess dabs the napkin to her lips, lays it on her plate. Despite her intentions of remaining contemptuous of his deceptions, questions are circling her thoughts like bothersome moths. She leans back in her chair: "That's why you told Sara about the solution?"

David smiles at her interest. "Well, I *showed* Sara the solution but told her almost nothing. The reason my plan worked is that no one had any idea how I made the desalination solution work. Everyone saw a black box where salt water went in the top and fresh water came out the side. But I never let anyone look in the box, and no one ever saw what was inside As you know, the prototype models are quite small, and thanks to the aerogel, very light. The box I built around the two prototypes was slatted with wood, with open air between the slats – like a picket fence. I wrapped the box with highly opaque black fabric, and no one could see inside. This design allowed enough ventilation to the system that the turbine could turn quite quickly, around 15 rotations per second, which pressed the water hard against the graphene sieve. Of course, no one knew that was what was going on inside. Most of the investors assumed our solution involved a chemical process, say, an additive that broke the salt molecules from the water molecules. No one really knew how I'd done it. Not a single, solitary, other person on earth." He smiles, and the bruise's colors crumple along his smile lines.

He is so proud of his cunning that she nods to keep him talking.

"And once those Agro loonies saw the box, it was like they'd seen Jesus turning water into wine. Everyone wanted in. Did they care about market valuations, scalability assessments, infrastructure evaluations, patent reviews?" He shakes his head with a smirk: "Nope. All these rational people were willing to act nutso because it was for water. You know their one big demand? Make sure the patent sale agreement was signed in front of the Governor. I'll give credit to the crazies for at least recognizing that without state support for water pipelines and municipality agreements, their desal solution would go nowhere. That's why Sara became positively obsessed that the Governor's support had to be documented. She promised her investors that we would sign the patent in front of Ramos so she could portray her business deal as this huge political rebuke to De Sel." He chuckles as though this idea is ludicrous.

"But Sara said it was you who set up that meeting with the Governor?"

"Yes, that's right. Sara had no way of knowing this, but Luis and me, we're old buddies. We met in graduate school and became friends because we both liked playing chess. No one knows how to work both sides of a deal better than Luis. So, when I explained the situation to him, Luis called Sara personally. He told her how proud he was to support a new enterprise that would benefit the state and explained how he'd make sure his press team invited a lot of outlets to cover the event – and this is where he got brilliant. He told Sara he was worried that if he informed the press that the event would be about a new water desalination method, it would raise De Sel's hackles. So, instead, he said, 'Let's tell the press I'm coming to tour your Third World Institute, and then we'll make the announcement about the desalination patent together.' Well, she couldn't have been more thrilled. Publicity for her institute, the Governor's support; she thought it was divine.

"Of course, the Governor hadn't given her a thing. The press still knew nothing about the Governor's support for her desalination effort. All along the plan was to sign the patent with De Sel at that meeting, but Sara never knew that. She gave us everything we wanted, and we didn't have to give her a thing."

"You say that like it's an admirable feat?"

"Well, isn't it? Look at what I did: Sara told her investors that the Governor of California was supportive of our new desalination venture, and they, in turn, became willing to invest hundreds of millions of dollars to license our invention – even though the patent hadn't even been filed! Thanks to those investors, I was able to go back to De Sel and show them about this investment plan for our patent license." His face beaming, he brings his palms together like he's praying. "And you know what De Sel did? They put together a much, much higher price to license the patent." David's palms open; he can barely contain his pride. "To win at the game of capitalism, you have to know the rules – and there aren't any."

Jess tries to keep disdain from showing on her face. "If you are planning to license the patent to De Sel, then why are you still signing the application at Sara's institute?"

"Why the hell not? The Governor's schedule was already arranged, and isn't it as good a place as any to make the deal?"

"You enjoy stabbing Sara in the back?"

"Look at what she did to me." He points to his face. "Do you really fault me that I want to make my message loud and clear: I won; she didn't."

"What about the Governor? Does he win too?"

"Of course," David nods as though it's a trivial question. "Luis gets a cut of the licensing fees going forward. He rubbed my back, so I rub his." David smoothes his hands on his pajama pant: "You see, Fire, that's the way business works."

Jess can tell that David feels he's instructing her. Does he see the hypocrisy of extolling the virtues of reciprocity to a woman whose invention he stole? Apparently not. It's remarkable, actually. She peers out the window to avoid meeting David's gaze. The sun is higher now above the hills, its orb cloaked in smog. The clouds' yellow-grayness reminds her of over-boiled eggs. Those same gardeners are still standing amongst the distant hedgerow – funny, she could swear they are pointing at the house.

With awkward bracing, David stands from his chair and walks – painful small steps – to her chair. She notices that he is holding a small digital tablet in his hand and assumes this tablet must hold the contract David wants her to sign. Squatting, David uses his free hand to grab hers.

His face stays beseeching as he kneels beside her: "Fire, you have to understand. I did this all for you."

"Oh, please." She yanks her hand from his.

"I'm not lying. I adore you. I have from the moment I laid eyes on you."

"David, you broke up with me three weeks ago."

"Fire, that was only to keep you safe." David swallows. "Three weeks ago, Sara showed up in my office and demanded that I show her my research—""

"Which was *my* research."

"And she started to threaten me with her POP... *thuggery*."

Jess squints: "You didn't know Sara was with POP until *then*?"

"Of course not! You think I'd let myself be involved with terrorists?" His head jerks back. "Those people are *nuts*. I want nothing – *nothing* – to do with them." His fingers curl into fists. "When she told me she 'had connections to POP,' I was such a dolt, I wasn't even sure what POP stood for. Then, she explained. The massacre, the guns, the bombs. Well, I was a wreck." He leans toward her, his eyes soft: "I realized I'd put you in danger. That's why I had to end our relationship."

Jess tries to find the cause and effect: "Um, why did that make me safer?"

"Oh, Fire," David wipes his hands on his royal blue robe. "I was trying to shield you from POP's violence. Of course, my plan was to get back together as soon as I made this deal for us."

"For *you*."

"Fire, please, I wrote to you two days ago declaring my undying love."

"That message was only to pass along information about the solution. Don't lie, *old fan*."

He looks down at the tablet he holds, and she can see his mental gears downshifting. "My love," he stands and holds the tablet outstretched toward her: "Do you know how much money I've made for you? You won't believe it. Try to guess how much." He shakes the tablet to make her look at it.

She keeps her eyes down. If she looks at the number, this will be harder. She likes money. Those people who say they do not, well, they have never been poor. There were countless nights when drifting to sleep her last waking thought was, "*If only I had more money.*" Even now, she is aware that money affords a certain brand of respect you cannot precisely replicate without it. *No, she won't look at that number.*

David whispers again, "I'm giving you the best of everything."

"And nothing that's good." She pushes herself to stand. "David, I'm not stupid. I know you're only playing at this luvvy stuff so I'll sign your agreement. The truth is: you don't care for me, and I don't care for you."

David's jaw flexes; his eyes narrow. "If you want to see Matteo again, you need to sign."

"No," she slings back her response, "if you want me to sign, you need to bring me Matteo." As she straightens her weakened body upward, she notices that something is flying toward the window.

It's like a bird, but not a bird. With a body the size of a shoebox, the wingspan is much wider. The speed is fast, its trajectory straight. She points: "Oh god!"

David turns fast. "A drone."

He is right. She has seen hundreds of drones in her life, but never one coming straight at her. The drone's speed quits right at the window, hovering close to the plate glass. A circular blade pops outward. "No!" he screams. "It's cutting the window!" David takes quick, short steps toward the door. "Let me out!" he screams, fists banging on the door.

It is too late. The blade pops a one-inch diameter circle from the windowpane as though it's a wine opener pulling out a cork. One second more, a dart shoots forward through the window's hole. Jess watches the dart fly, clearly with a honing device, straight for David.

She screams, but her loudness makes no difference; the dart hits David's back. "David!" His leg and face twitch as he staggers to the ground.

From the hallway, there are footsteps, fast and pounding. Relly's voice is loud, coming nearer: "Get down, get down!" Jess tries to cower near the bed; her arms hold her head, such feeble protection.

The dart splits into her left hip, the pain searing like she has been lashed with a whip. Stumbling to the ground, it is the colors that fade first. Relly stands over her, her voice loud but dimming, like a volume knob turning to zero. Jess' legs go numb, then her hands, and finally there's the sensation, now familiar, of falling into blackness.

MATTEO

His backpack jostles against his side as he runs, making it difficult to push the binoculars into it. As he twists his torso forward, pain drives down the back of his legs.

Ahead of him, Beck hollers, "Hurry! They'll have dogs running in seconds."

Trying to move his legs faster, Matteo's balance teeters. Making it to the hedge, he pushes through the brown, spiky evergreen needles to get back to the road. Beck is already opening the pick-up truck's driver door. As he approaches the car door, Matteo notices that the truck is painted with a logo for "Sal & Son's Landscaping and Gardening," and mowers and blowers are sitting high in the carriage. The drone is back there too, like a bird come home to roost. Matteo puts his hand on the passenger side handle, but his hands are shaking so violently he can't push the button to open the door.

Minutes before, Matteo had watched from binoculars while Beck stood beside him, controlling the drone from a panel. The sun bounced off the big second-floor window, but Matteo could still see that Jess was standing there, wearing a white flowing, gown-like thing. She was facing David directly, maybe yelling at him. Upon seeing the drone, she cowered, and even through the binoculars, Matteo saw how her body shrunk with fear. When she was hit, her fall wasn't the polite collapse to the ground they show in the movies. Her body wavered in pain, and she hit the ground hard. He could have sworn she was dying.

"You didn't shoot a bullet, right?" Matteo asks, as he sidles into the passenger seat.

Beck presses the engine button on. "Of course not, just tranqs." The side of his t-shirt where he held the drone remote control panel to his chest is dark with sweat. He hits the accelerator; the truck slides forward.

"Did you use a different kind of dart for David than for Jess?"

"Yes," Beck nods, "very different darts."

"She won't die?" Matteo wishes he could keep himself from seeking reassurance from Beck. He does not want to need anything from this man.

"No, man, no." Beck's hand goes to Matteo's shoulder. "She's sleeping. That's all. We'll go get her now. Don't worry."

Matteo runs his hands over his face; he doesn't want Beck to see how full his eyes are.

"Man, I keep telling you," Beck revs the engine faster, "you can count on me."

Matteo leans against the passenger-side window, trying to steady himself. The truck speeds ahead onto unpaved roads, dust kicking upward and clouding their ability to see forward.

After a few minutes, Beck holds out his wrist for Matteo to see. "Look, Sara just hit my Keeper with some specs on Ellison Hall." A projection screen pops outward. "It's not a big venue for a Governor's visit. I guess she wasn't kidding when she said the event was meant to be low-key." Reluctantly, Matteo examines the 3-D model that's hovering above him.

"See," Beck continues, "room 205 is just an amphitheater-style classroom – maybe two hundred seats. Sara's sources said state troopers are supposed to do a security sweep of the whole building at 8:30 am, and that should give us plenty of time to have you set up inside before then."

"Right." The mention of the time reminds Matteo that yesterday he had woken with his body pressed against Jess. She had been whole then, no puncture wounds and no drugs adulterating her blood.

"Apparently," Beck cuts into his thoughts, "they're putting metal detectors at all the entrances to the lecture hall – which is both good and bad for us. No one will have a tranq or bulleted gun to use against us, good. But we can't carry one in either, bad." Ahead are surface streets, and Beck slows the car to prepare for the turn.

"You'll have your poison pin," Matteo whispers. "Metal detectors won't catch that."

"True." Beck turns onto the surface street, and the ride instantly becomes smoother. "Don't worry, dude, we'll get her out before that becomes an issue. You worry so much!"

Death by poison pin is a pretty awful way to die. Matteo knows about "pins," thanks to a drug gang he had observed a year ago. These hustlers were not the brightest, and they had messaged back and forth about how if they "pinned" the guy, no one would ever be able to figure out what killed him. *Unless someone reads your Keeper messages, idiot.*

When Matteo was observing this gang, pins had only arrived on the scene as a potential weapon to replace guns for "hits." Matteo had seen right away that pins would be huge. They look like thumbtacks, though the pointy part is a small syringe filled with concentrated poison. Depending upon which poison is used, death can be instantaneous or take hours. Since most of the pins' poisons remain difficult to trace, the resulting deaths appear to be of natural causes – heart attack, stroke, etc.

"So, uh, what's the poison in the pin you have for Jess?" Another knot ties in Matteo's stomach just saying these words.

"I'm guessing Tetrodotoxin, TTX. With TTX, the death goes fast – pretty fast, at least."

Matteo's jaw clenches.

"Anyway, let's talk about how we're going to get her, before there's any need for a pin." An entry ramp to the 101 is ahead, and Beck veers his car to the right to enter. "Those bags you put in the trunk, they've got clothes in them."

"Clothes?"

"Yeah, disguises and shit. There are some beard and mustache pieces, a pair of eyeglasses. A Stanford security guard outfit. Dress outfits with press passes, you know, if we choose to go that route. And I'm pretty sure Jaden packed EMT clothes too."

"EMT?"

"Those ambulance guys. You know, that's probably the best plan. Think of how dizzy you were a couple hours ago. That's how bad the girl will feel, probably worse."

Matteo thinks of insisting that Beck call Jess by her name, but then decides it is not worth the words.

"You know, I wonder if we could get a stretcher." Beck's fingers drum the wheel: "Let me check on that." His eyes narrow, his cheeks twitch, and he begins whisperspeaking with his Keeper. The car's speed slows as Beck silently converses, and one after another, cars pass them.

Matteo examines all the passengers who are heading to work in the rush hour. A self-driving car with four Latino guys whizzes past; they're laughing; dressed in matching maroon shirts. A driverless bus pushes ahead with blurry-eyed, slack faces staring out; the despair radiates from the windows. A car slides past with a white woman, in gemstones and pink hair, sipping from her travel mug and talking to her young son in the backseat. Each car is roughly three tons of steel, burns gallons of gas and emits carbon dioxide, all to move people, usually no more than two, weighing rarely more than 400 pounds, across these lanes of blacktop. If the cars could somehow become invisible, the passengers would sit separated by mere feet. So many people gathered in one space, together, but not at all together. *How do people come together?*

Matteo's eyes glance again across the various lanes of traffic and humanity, and to his surprise, an idea comes with this sweeping regard.

Huh.

Matteo readjusts in his seat, thinking, thinking. It is strange that after days of puzzling over the same confusions, this new idea would arrive, so clear and complete – as though an envelope had been slipped into his brain's mail slot. Here it is, a new approach staring back at him – so different to the ones he has mulled before.

"Dude, we've got an ambulance!" Beck slaps at Matteo's leg, and Matteo's trance-like ponderings are broken. "I swear, we're going to pull this off. I just know it." Beck grins as he shifts lanes to exit the highway.

Matteo pivots in his seat to listen as Beck details his plan. Matteo will take the backpack into Ellison Hall and change into the EMT disguise – "better put a beard or mustache on too." Then, Matteo will do the "necessary reconnaissance" to learn where they are keeping "the girl." Once the ambulance arrives – "half an hour later, tops" – Beck will message Matteo, and together, they will "barge" in like they are responding to an emergency call. They will "strap the girl to the gurney" and head out.

Matteo watches Beck's face more than he listens to his words. *Could Beck possibly believe he's describing a good strategy?* POP's political aspirations are not dumb. In fact, Matteo agrees with most of them. Beck is a smart guy too; he knows how to use technology and surveillance better than most anyone Matteo knows. Still, as Matteo listens now, what is striking is the plan's naiveté. There is no getaway beyond the building and no contingencies beyond the morning. Matteo wipes his sweaty palms on his shorts: "If we get Jess out, what then?"

Beck exhales: "Well." He takes his hand off the steering wheel to push his hair from his forehead. "I guess Jess signs the patent to POP, and that's that."

That's that? "Don't you think De Sel and the Governor will come after her?"

"Nah, probably not."

Of course they will. Why wouldn't they? It's preposterous to think the Governor would allow a terrorist-linked group of investors to become the source of California's fresh water. *How does POP delude itself so?*

They are driving into the Stanford campus. The layer of dust that constantly coat Berkeley, Oakland and San Francisco is absent in Palo Alto. Even with his stack of worries, Matteo wonders: *How do they keep the streets so clean here?* Power washes are against the law, but he cannot think of any other way these streets would stay free of the brown muck which coats California everywhere else. He pushes the button to let the car window down; even the air is sweeter.

The white Stanford buildings have terra-cotta roofs and are set neatly back from the road with meridians of plastic turf. Stanford didn't let its fields go "naturally" as Berkeley did, and the bright green openness of the synthetic fields shines in the clear sun. They drive down a palm tree-lined street, and Beck turns onto a narrower service street that winds to the building's back entrances. "See, over there," Beck points to a large loading dock: "That's Ellison Hall." The car slows to a stop.

Matteo opens his passenger-side door and Beck meets him back at the car's open trunk. "You know, I had a feeling you'd like that girl. She's smart like you. And nice in that 'aw, shucks' way you have."

He's not sure what point Beck is trying to make. Being "nice" is working out so great for him and Jess right now. Rummaging through the various backpacks, Matteo stuffs the pieces of clothing he wants into his backpack.

Beck continues, "I bet Sara would love it if you and Jess were to join POP."

"You guys bomb people."

Beck takes a step back, his face wide with shock. "No, dude, not me. I mean, some of our guys do that kind of thing. But the East Bay POP has never hurt anyone."

"Except Jess. Doesn't she count?"

"Dude, I'm trying hard to keep her safe. You have to realize, Sara is a visionary, and she wants to, like, start a revolution. But, usually, POP is nothing more than a bunch of Agros trying to draw attention to inequality. You know who my biggest client is at Beck Industries? The Berkeley PD. The cops make most of their drug busts because of our observationalists. And you could never tell anyone this, but a lot of those Berkeley cops are part of POP. People Over Power, man. Nothing scary or violent. Just a way of fighting against the injustice of rampant capitalism."

"And killing people to steal business patents." Matteo slings the backpack over his shoulder. "Put that in your sales pitch."

"Dude, we're gonna get her out."

Matteo does not respond; he takes a cap from the EMT outfit and pulls the brim low over his brow.

"Did you take the mustache and beard stuff too?"

"Yeah." Matteo does not bother to explain that the brown, shaggy beards Jaden packed would look ridiculous on his half-Asian face. He starts to walk toward the loading dock.

"Wait, you left the Keeper!"

Matteo walks back to grab the black disposable Keeper from Beck's outstretched hand. "I forgot," he mutters.

"Dude," Beck pats his shoulder, "I need a way to contact you when I come with the ambulance."

"Right." Matteo again walks toward the loading dock.

"Half an hour!" Beck calls after him.

"Got it," Matteo shouts back without turning. He punches a big green button that sits beside the loading dock door, and the slats on the door groan upward. When the door has lifted three feet off the ground, Matteo crouches to slip underneath.

The space inside is cool and dark, and to his tremendous relief, no one is there. A green button sits on the inside wall too; Matteo presses it, and the slats of the door halt their upward swing, then slap back toward the ground, stomping out the sunlight. The squared space is concrete and dingy, with walls of empty shelving, a digital clock that reads 8:12 and a large dumpster that smells of cardboard and salad dressing. *Perfect.*

Matteo grabs the lanyard with the press pass from the backpack and slips it over his neck. Then he flings the backpack over the tall garbage bin's walls. He chucks the disposable Keeper inside the bin too. Apprehension hits his stomach like a sucker punch. *Maybe this is a mistake; maybe the POP plan is better than his. Maybe his plan is too simple; Jess will die.* Panic pulls on him like a magnetic force locking his feet to the ground.

He makes himself move away. He heads down the dark corridor, first with a shuffle, then faster, until he's running as fast as he can.

JESS

Her head snaps forward, waking her. She is in dimness, being dragged toward light. A strange man is pulling her, grabbing at her thighs to bring her nearer to him. *Where is she?* She wills her eyes wider.

The back seat of a car. The man is dragging her toward the door, now lifting her out. He has a shaved head and a black gemstone in each cheekbone. He is a big man, though he still sways backward to cradle her tall body in front of him. His steps are short and bracing, and the impact of his feet hitting the ground reverberates into her hip with wincing pain. Abruptly, he bends forward at the waist; she worries he is ready to drop her, and her arms tighten around his neck. She yelps when he releases her, the shock of her butt bumping hard against a surface. A wheelchair.

She tries to sit upright in this rigid, metal chair, but she can't arrange her body out of its slump or keep her head from drooping. Dried blood is smeared across her white robe. *Those poor women who worked on the embroidery; their work has been ruined.*

A woman's voice behind them is commanding. "The entrance over there, fast." Though Jess can't look up, she knows it is Relly speaking. The wheelchair flies over the sidewalk – the man must be running – and each bump over the sidewalk's seams jolts into her hip.

Jess' eyes want so badly to close. *Keep them open.* A big building is ahead, a university building. *Is it Ellison Hall? Will Matteo be there?* She wants to see – to figure out what is coming next – but the wheelchair's rolling rhythm is lulling, and before she can stop it, sleep lures her back into its hold.

MATTEO

The first task is easily accomplished. He finds two empty glass bottles in a back room recycling bin, fills them both in the men's room sink. They are not much, he knows, but they will make it through a metal detector and fit in his shorts pockets.

The second task, making it to the room, is harder. Room 205 is on the second floor, and since Ellison Hall is a new building, surveillance cameras are everywhere. The halls are wide, windows big, with lots of light colored wood paneling everywhere. He will be spotted easily if he is not careful. Ducking into the men's room, he waits until a flurry of activity indicates a passing period. Emerging, he keeps his head down, the EMT cap's brim covering his face, and leans forward onto the pads of his feet to make his gait appear different than usual. Immersing himself in a large group of backpacked students, he treks up the stairs, holding papers he pulled from a bulletin board and flipping through these sheets as though their contents mesmerize him. He makes it to the second floor certain no video shot has been taken of his face.

There are no signs of heightened security, which is strange. He remembers the time he and Rachel went to hear former Governor Lara Liu speak at Berkeley. There, they sat in a basketball stadium with thousands of students, and state troopers were everywhere. This morning, Matteo has not seen a single sign on a bulletin board about the Governor's visit; no state troopers are in sight; and the students are not talking about a Governor's visit either.

The second floor has an open sitting area and wide hallways with blocks of varying linoleum colors. He asks a ponytailed Asian student where room 205 is. "Right across from the Institute. Down the hall, near the windows."

At the end of the hall, he plants himself in front of the floor-to-ceiling windows, the sun pouring from behind, encasing him in shadow. He would bet a million dollars the turning surveillance camera he is eyeing – the only one in this section of hallway – does not scan the area in front of this window. The installers had to know that if they used a rotational scope that included this sun-drenched space, the camera would have to constantly adjust its aperture to focus correctly; they would not do it.

Room 205 sits across from an office with glass doors, the Institute for Third World Environmental Policy. This is Sara Claredge's organization, though Sara will not be coming to her office today. Matteo assumes she does not want to be around if Plan B is activated.

Already, members of the press are gathering in the hallway, outside the locked double doors to Room 205. A black man with a teased-out Afro and thick-framed glasses. A curvy Latina woman. A white, skinny guy in bad pants. An acned, Stanford-sweatshirted guy in a man bun. Each of them is looking at their Keeper screens; there is no chitchat or camaraderie. Matteo doubts any of these members of the "press" are from traditional news organizations; they look more like freelancers or bloggers.

"Are they doing a security sweep in there?" Matteo asks, his voice puncturing the silence.

The black man looks at Matteo. "Are you talking to us?" he asks with a degree of surprise.

"Yeah." Matteo gives a big smile. He has not been a smile-y sort of guy for a long time, but his plan will only work if he is friendly. He has to convince this group to fill water bottles too.

"I think they're almost done." The Stanford guy steps forward to offer this information to Matteo, a perfunctory politeness. "They should open the doors in a few minutes." He puts his wrist back in front of his face again, studying his Keeper.

The time has come for the third task.

"It's crazy, isn't it?" Matteo says in a voice that suggests he is continuing a conversation rather than starting one. "How the Governor is screwing over the people of California?"

There are some raised eyebrows, a few embarrassed side-glances: *Who is this guy?*

Matteo sees it; he understands, but he persists: "It's like Ramos doesn't even care about the drought."

242

"Drought?" It's the black guy in heavy glasses who is talking. "Man, what are you talking about? This meeting is about the Governor visiting the Institute, talking about the third world. Nothing about the drought."

Not going well. Matteo's about to try again when something from the yard below catches his eye. A bald-headed man in a state trooper uniform is pushing a woman in a wheelchair. The woman's head is slumped forward; there is blood on her white gown.

Jess.

Beside her: Relly. Dressed in red, her platinum hair shining in the sunlight.

Even from two flights up, Matteo can tell Relly is muttering to her Keeper and grimacing because her heels keep sinking in the turf.

He brings his head to the glass, wishing it were easier to study Jess' face amidst all the movement. She is bloodied; she is unconscious. Then again, they would not be pushing her here in a wheelchair if they did not expect her to sign papers shortly.

Matteo springs toward the group, a new sense of urgency in his words. "You guys," he taps the black man's shoulder and smiles widely at the curvy woman. "You have to see this." He points out the window.

The crowd eyes each other, clearly skeptical of Matteo's enthusiasm.

"No, really, I have to show you. That woman in the wheelchair, do you see her? She's trying to save California from the drought. And I know this will sound crazy, but today, at this meeting with the Governor, some people will try to kill her."

JESS

Relly is lifting Jess' arm high up in the air. "Stop," Jess wants to say, and to her surprise the word does not stay in her head but comes out into the air.

"Oh good, you're awake!" Relly chirps, as she places Jess' hand down again. "Just trying to get you dressed. A bit..." she lifts Jess' right arm forward, "*tricky.*"

Jess sits in the wheelchair, and Relly faces the seat straight on, slipping the straps of a bra onto Jess' shoulders. "Here, lean toward my body," Relly says, and Jess can tell that she is expected to lean her forehead into Relly's chest. She cannot. "Oh, goodness, no need for such modesty. We're both women here." Relly grabs Jess under her armpits and pulls her into her bosom, wrapping her arms around Jess' back.

Jess braces for the pain, but to her surprise, her body does not sear with distress. "How long was I asleep?" she whispers.

"Not long." Relly clasps the bra hook into place, then leans Jess against the wheelchair's back. "But you're feeling better, aren't you?" Her eyebrows arch and her lips curl like there's a tease to the question.

Jess nods. The pain seems to have lifted from her body like mist from the earth at daybreak. In fact, her whole body seems to be levitating, her head floating.

From the wheelchair, she peeks around Relly's torso to see a windowless room, quite small, the only door closed tight. The air is stale, and strips of overhead light fixtures create shadowy buildup in the corners. A white smartboard is affixed to the front wall and a long seminar table with chairs runs down the center of the space, though Relly appears to have pushed many chairs aside to make space for Jess' wheelchair and clothing bags.

Jess notes these things, but the observations feel as though they are being made through glasses with the wrong prescription; the edges seem soft and fuzzy, and the lighting flutters. She looks at Relly. "What did you do to me?"

"Oh, I gave you some help." Relly's head tips in the direction of a chair to their left. On its seat is a syringe and two empty injectable vials.

Jess leans from the wheelchair to grab the empty vials. The words are blurry, but she can see they are long with many syllables. Levoamphetamine. Oxycodone hydrochloride. "Aren't these serious drugs?"

"Please. When you have pain, you take painkillers." Relly crosses the classroom and pulls a dress out of a garment bag. "If you think they're good now, wait a half-hour."

"But..." It is hard for Jess to form sentences; the words seem to drift in front of her like dandelion seeds in a breeze. She wants to ask if Relly checked for counter-indications before injecting her with two drugs at the same time, but the question is too long.

"Stand up." Relly lifts one hand upward as though she is a ballet instructor. In her other hand, she holds out a dress. Even in her loopy state, Jess notes the richness of the dress' material: sky blue saturated evenly over satin smoothness. She's never worn anything so girly before.

Jess pushes upward from the arms of the wheelchair, and though her balance wavers, she catches herself. Her near-naked body is covered in a shocking constellation of bruises. The puncture wound on the calf of her right leg is mounded and purple and a similar swollen mound sits on her left thigh. Her left shoulder shows mottles of blues, blacks and greys. An enormous bandage is taped over her hipbone, and the blood has so fully seeped through that only the edges closest to the tape are white anymore. Jess brings her fingers to touch the tape.

"Don't!" Relly slaps at her hand. "Those drone shots always create such awful puncture wounds," she mutters, with a tsk-tsk sound. "You know, with tranq guns, they've perfected how to parachute the darts properly, so the needle injects but doesn't fully submerge.

But..." her nose wrinkles in disgust, "not so much for the drone darts."

Jess stares at her: "You killed Bruno with a drone."

"Bruno?" Her face exaggerates her confusion: "Who is Bruno?"

Jess swallows. "He was the man driving the POP car." The words are hard to pull from her throat: "Near the Berkeley tunnel."

"That was *not* supposed to happen. The rock was supposed to shatter the windshield, not blast through it." Relly holds the dress open at her feet. "Here, step into it."

With concentration, Jess steps one foot and then the next into the dress.

"Of course, if POP had stopped then everything would have been peachy. That death is on their conscience, not mine." Relly raises the dress up: "Here, arms in the sleeves."

Jess nods and aims her hands into the blue satin sleeves. "Were you the one David was messaging? About love and showers?"

Relly freezes, then locks with Jess' eyes: "Oh, but you are clever." With a sharp tug, Relly zips up the dress from the back. "Yes, David was messaging me. I think he purposefully made the messages risqué because he knew Luis would read them too. Those men are always flaunting their peacock feathers!" Relly makes a pleased face as she examines how the dress looks on Jess. "You don't look half bad."

"What was the point of sending the messages anyway?"

"Well," Relly picks a shoebox out of a duffel bag, "David knew his Keeper was hacked, so he couldn't contact me or Luis the regular way." Relly takes a pair of satin heels out of tissue. "So those messages were our way to check that everything was still on track. David told me he sent the last message when he saw the POP thugs marching through his backyard. That 'come to me' message was like a clanking alarm bell." She places one pump down on the ground by Jess' feet, then the other. "Here, step forward."

"What about the 'old fan'?" Jess steps into one shoe. "Did you understand what he meant by that?"

"Ah, the old fan. I'd assumed it was a typo until David told me otherwise last night. He said he wrote it to leave some clue about how the whole gizmo worked. You know, in case those POP thugs had offed him."

Offed him? Gizmo? The words swirl and twirl in Jess' drug-addled head wanting to alight into fantastical images. She has to keep grounding herself in the present. "When do I see Matteo?" Standing in the blue pumps, Jess towers three inches above Relly's head.

Relly's face sours, and she shoves the tissue paper back in the shoebox, pushing the box top back down. "With Matteo, I'm afraid he hasn't been released from the hospital."

Jess' skin prickles with goosebumps; she steps toward Relly. "You said he would be here. Why isn't he here?"

Relly rolls her eyes: "Oh, stop with your panic. The hospital wants him to rest more."

Relly walks to her purse, rummages through it, finally retrieving a small lipstick. "Set your head to me." The lipstick is a bright, bubblegum pink, and Relly shapes her mouth in a wide O, asking Jess to mimic the position.

"No." Jess swats the lipstick down to the ground. "I have to see Matteo."

Relly stares at where the lipstick sits on the floor. "What the hell are you—"

"I won't sign the papers until I see Matteo."

"Oh, please." Relly leans down to pick up the fallen lipstick, then swings back upward. "I need to make something clear: you don't call the shots, Jessila. You do what *I* say, and I'm saying: Sign the papers." She takes a deep breath in: "Now, let's keep moving forward. We were originally scheduled to do a photo call in the Institute's lobby – some snaps of you shaking hands with the Governor and De Sel's corporate representatives. But there's no way David can handle that situation now. I don't know if you care, but David is not well."

"No?"

"No." Relly's eyes drift to the ground, her face suddenly slack with sadness. Only two days ago, when Jess watched David being punched, worry for him had consumed her too. But now in this drowsy classroom with bruises spilled on her body and her brain cloudy with narcotics, she cannot find that same concern. All she wants is to see Matteo. His name repeats in her head like a prayer. *Please be okay.*

Relly's eyes re-focus on Jess. "We'll head straight to room 205 where the Governor will make a brief presentation and then you'll sign the papers on stage. Ready?" Relly does not wait for Jess to answer; she yanks the door open wide. "Let's go."

A man and woman stand directly in front of them, as though their ears had been pressed to the door. Jess wobbles, almost stumbling, as she tries to take in their faces.

"Hello, Brooklyn," the man says.

The word seems to have an echo. The man is Indian – jet black hair, skin the color of tea and when he speaks, his o's are round like hula hoops. Rajit Chatterjee?

Relly holds her hands out like she's stopping traffic. "Raj, I made it clear that we would see you upstairs."

"Why, Brooklyn, I thought we'd share the elevator up." He leans forward to Jess, his head bowed. "You must be Jessila Prentiss." His right hand goes forward: "Such an honor to finally meet you."

Jess worries if she shakes his hand she will lose her balance so her arm stays stiffly by her side. Besides, Rajit's voice has an unctuous quality that, even in her blurred state, she wants to analyze.

The woman leans toward Jess too, almost whispering. "Jessila, we've been trying to meet you for ages."

It is hard for Jess to fully focus her eyes. The woman before her is Asian, in her mid-30s, with a geometrically severe bob and a single red gemstone at the top of each cheekbone.

"You see," the woman continues, "we want to see if you would be open to participating in the licensing agreement with De Sel all on your ow—"

"De Sel?" Jess whispers.

Relly tugs hard on Jess' arm. "No. We aren't having this conversation. There are papers to sign."

Relly yanks her forward toward the elevator, only ten feet away. Jess tries not to fall; her feet stumble and sweat breaks out across her back. The drugs make the sounds swirl.

"If I may," Raj hurries to catch up with them. "It is, in fact, about the papers that we've been hoping to talk with Jessila."

Relly punches the elevator button: "No!"

"What do you want to say about the papers?" Jess says to Raj, and her words sound to her as though they are spoken under water.

Relly puts her arm around Jess' shoulder to usher her into the open elevator. Raj and the Asian woman step into the small elevator too. The doors clamp shut. *Such a small space. So stuffy.* The elevator lurches upward. *Oh, god.* Jess' stomach flips.

Raj leans toward her. "De Sel is interested in proceeding with this licensing agreement with you as an *individual*. A single party, not a team."

"You can't have this conversation." Relly grabs at Jess' arm to turn her away from Raj. "The Governor does not want—"

"A single party?" Jess mutters. In her head, she has to work hard to make these words have meaning. Heat washes over her torso, she's sweating everywhere.

The jet-black haired woman pushes against Relly to get closer to Jess. "De Sel wants to work *only with you*. After all, it is your patent-pending inventions that are being utilized in the desalination solution. Not Professor Steubingly's."

Jess has to replay the words to understand the meaning. *They don't want to work with David?* She had never considered the possibility that David would not be a part of the deal. He was, after all, the person to discover the solution. The elevator lurches to its place on the second floor, jostling Jess forward. The doors split open.

"We're here, everyone off," Relly's voice calls like she is announcing a stop on a train ride. Hooking her hand around Jess' waist, she ushers her forward.

With a single step, Raj inserts himself between the two women, cornering Jess and pushing Relly toward the elevator door. "Jessila, you're a brilliant young woman. We're puzzled as to why you would grant Professor Steubingly such a claim to what you've made. Your inventions were made at Davis, well before you were in his Berkeley research group. He doesn't have a right to your work. You see that, right?"

"Jess, please don't listen to this man." Relly is pulling Jess away but Rajit follows closely.

His ideas are slippery, like wet soap. Rajit brings his face closer to hers. His nose is big; his cheeks slightly pockmarked, and it is clear he's holding his face to make his expression sympathetic. She is trying to understand what confuses her – *wait, there it is.* "What do you gain?" Jess asks in one breath.

"All he cares about is money." Relly snaps from behind Rajit's back.

Rajit turns back. "That's rich, coming from you." He faces Jess again. "Have you read the agreement?"

She shakes her head. She does not care about the agreement. The idea that people are quibbling about a deal is infuriating. Matteo is hurt, Bruno is dead, and for days, they have been running and scared. So very scared. *She doesn't care about money.*

Rajit continues: "You see, Jess, Professor Steubingly is requesting a salaried position within De Sel and millions of dollars of funding for his lab at Berkeley. Yet, he's also taking 95% of the very large licensing fee, which leaves you with a very small piece of the pie. And, Jessila..." Rajit smiles too sweetly, "isn't the pie all your recipe?"

"That's enough." Relly pushes between Rajit and the Asian woman: "Come with me." She clenches Jess' right arm and yanks her down the hall. The pain in her shoulder is like a nail is being driven into it; she wobbles not to trip.

The black-haired woman skitters to block Relly, but Rajit holds up his hand: "Let her go." More loudly, he calls after Jess, "You don't have to sign the agreement today. Just pretend to sign when we're on stage now, and we'll work out a better deal for you later. Remember: don't sign!"

Jess thinks of yelling a response, but the words do not form in time.

Relly's heels clack on the floor as she rushes forward. Jess struggles to stay upright on her satin pumps, and the hallway swings before her like she is on a carousel. A swirl of shapes and ideas whirl fast. She tries to catch them. Rajit wants to make the deal only with her. That means Jess does not need David. Or Relly. Or the Governor. The power is all hers.

She jerks her hand free from Relly's arm and plants her feet. "I'm not coming with you."

Relly retraces the one step and brings her nose close to Jess' face. "Yes, you are," she whispers through gritted teeth.

"No, I'm not."

Relly's eyes flare, and she brings her Keeper to her mouth. "Get me Klay," she says into her wrist screen. Relly flicks her head upward toward Jess: "Watch what your stupidity will get you." To her Keeper, she sneers: "Klay, listen, get the pistol – not the tranq pistol, the real bulleted pistol – and hold it straight at Matteo Wu's heart. When I tell you, pull the trigger."

MATTEO

Jess emerges from the left side of the stage, and the first thing Matteo notices is how pretty she looks. The blue dress clings to her mild curves, and her bobbed hair frames her face. He would never have guessed she had been unconscious less than an hour ago. Her walk is slow, and it is only as she settles into her seat at the long table and folds her hands in front of her, that he sees that her eyes are full and her lip quivers. He lurches forward in his chair, though of course he cannot go to her now. Not yet.

The stage sits sunken in the front of the room with stadium-like seating rising above it. The front-most part of the stage juts into the seating, and at the back of the stage is a dark black curtain.

From this tall curtain, Governor Luis Ramos now emerges. He ambles forward, and though his smile is swaggering, the crowd's applause is only polite, no more. The Governor stops, lifting his arms outward: "Come on, Stanford, you can do better than this!"

The clapping intensifies; some laugh; there are a few whoops. The Governor himself chuckles as he sits in the center of the table waiting for the rest of the participants to join him on stage.

At the long narrow table that sits center stage, five chairs sit evenly behind five placards. The Governor sits in the center spot, and Jess is to his left sitting behind the placard that bears her name. Now an Indian man settles behind a placard that identifies him as Rajit Chatterjee, Senior Vice President of Research and Development, De Sel Corporation, and a gemstoned Asian woman strides onto stage and sits at the placard that identifies her as Lila Ming, the Assistant General Counsel at De Sel Corporation. The four members of the panel sit, but the seat behind the fifth placard – the one for David Steubingly – remains unfilled. Lila purses her lips. The Governor cranes his neck to look at stage left.

The clapping dissipates. Silence, then whispering.

Throughout, Jess sits, unmoving, her hands folded on the table in front of her.

Matteo puts the water bottles between his legs to wipe his sweaty hands on his shirt. He is in the tenth row from the stage, seated with eighteen members of the "media." All of his new acquaintances are watching the stage as intently as he is.

In the hallway upstairs, when Matteo told his story to the press group, a few of the men and women instantly believed him. Yet, another guy called him a "conspiratorial nutcase" and two middle-aged women barraged Matteo with questions: *How did he know POP was the terrorist group? Why was this Jess woman so special? Could this desalination solution, like, actually make water affordable again?*

Matteo answered as many questions as he could, but when two troopers opened the doors to Room 205 and asked the members of the press to take their seats, Matteo worried that he had not convinced the group to follow his plan. Only as everyone was picking up their bags and readying to walk inside 205 did the black guy with the thick glasses announce: "Listen, guys, it can't hurt to fill some water bottles, right? Worse case: we have a drink nearby if we're thirsty." Matteo had wanted to hug him.

The press people are a motley crew. They are exactly nine men and nine women; and some of the people are young, a few are parent-like, and others are senior citizens who appear to freelance for the fun of it. A few are Traditionalist types, though most are Agros. The races of the group span the spectrum: black, brown, white and all the shades in between. Their styles include mall wear, surfer wear, student wear, sweat suits, and there is even one guy in a suit and tie. Matteo doubts there is a unifying quality to these people except the press pass they wear around their necks and the stern, tight expression now on their faces. They are waiting to see if Matteo is right. If he is, they will have the story of the year.

In the seats ahead, two guys have already started video recording from their Keepers. "I'm streaming, dude," says the man with the bun in the Stanford sweatshirt. On his left, two older white men shake their filled water glass bottles as though to show they are itching to begin. Matteo is not a praying man, but a phrase keeps repeating in his head: *Please, please, let this work.*

Finally, from left of stage, Brooklyn Relly pushes a wheelchair toward the table, the sound of her heels echoing across the stage. A bald-headed trooper – the same one that Matteo saw pushing Jess' wheelchair outside – rushes ahead of Relly to remove the chair that sits at the table, and David's wheelchair is pushed into the spot next to Jess.

David looks terrible. His neck seems to have lost muscle capability, and his head tilts to the side. His eyes are barely open, and his non-bruised skin is the color of gravel.

Rajit Chatterjee leans forward across the front of the table, trying to find an angle on David's face. "Is he okay?" Rajit asks the Governor, but Ramos is focused solidly forward, his energy intent on jocularity.

"Hello, Spartans!" the Governor roars, as though he is ready to start a pep rally. Ramos is not a big man, nor particularly handsome. He has a receding hairline and a paunch; yet, his eyes are big and electrified, his cheeks ruddy. He stands and opens his arms wide, like the Rio De Janeiro statue of Jesus.

As though a call has been issued to "get to your marks," Matteo's heart pounds so hard his seat is vibrating.

Ramos begins: "Usually, when I'm on stage, I have to wait through a long introduction before I ever get to the mic." The audience chuckles. "Today, however, Professor Sara Claredge was unable to make it, and she asked me to emcee." He claps his hands together: "I couldn't be more thrilled." Pleased laughter comes from the crowd..

"Many of you came this morning expecting to join me for a tour of the Institute for Third World Environmental Policy. But I am here today to do something a little different than take a tour. As Governor of this great state, one of my biggest pleasures is facilitating the relationship between scientific innovation and business commercialization. Today, I ask you to join me in witnessing a fantastic partnership between two innovative scientists and the De Sel Corporation. As you will soon see, this partnership will help California overcome its water shortage. What is especially cool about this licensing agreement is that its benefits will be felt globally, especially in the drought-ravaged nations of the third world. For this reason, I asked the parties to this exciting agreement to join me here this morning, at the Institute for Third World Environmental Policy, so that we could all have the privilege to witness the inauguration of a licensing agreement between the De Sel Corporation" he gestures to Rajit and Lila, "and the scientists Jessila Prentiss and David Steubingly."

The Governor turns back to the crowd. "Folks," his voice booms big, "let me tell you what this deal does. We're about to make water *cheaper, more abundant,* and *less energy-intensive* to filter. This desalination agreement will be a win for business" – he raises his hand upward with his index finger pointing, "a win for government" – he holds up his second finger, "a win for the environment – and I'm not done yet," his cadence rises as his third finger goes up, "*and...* a win for the people!" He holds up his fourth finger, his smile goes wide. "It's..." the Governor winks, then whispers into the mic: "a *grand slam!*" As the audience claps and hoots, Ramos bring his mouth right to the microphone: "We're talking a home run with runners on base!"

Several of the people in Matteo's aisle lean forward so they can telegraphically send their doubts to Matteo. The Governor isn't sounding duplicitous. His speech doesn't sound anti-populist or anti-environment. Matteo can tell: his press friends are questioning if he told them the truth.

Matteo opens his eyes wider, trying to telegraph what should be obvious: The Governor is *lying.* Corruptors talk sweet and deal dirty; their black is white, their up down. Yet, Matteo can see that his new friends in the press corps don't share his cynicism. He knows what he needs to do.

Matteo stands. "Excuse me," he shouts. His throat is full like he swallowed a lemon, his knees shaking. "Excuse me," he shouts louder. There are murmurs and movement and people turn to face him. "I think you're lying!" his voice cracks like a whip.

The Governor's face falls; he squints toward where Matteo is sitting, the glare of the stage lights must be making it hard for the Governor to identify him.

Jess leans forward, squinting too: "Matteo?"

He makes his voice as loud and strong as he can: "De Sel doesn't care about people or the environment – only profits!" He keeps his face toward the stage, but he can hear the crowd whispering, and their impression of him does not sound positive. He better talk fast. "De Sel has never once lowered its prices on water. The company limits water production to keep prices high. They won't give us cheap, fresh water."

Jess bolts upright: "Matteo! You're safe!"

The Governor makes a motion to the back of the room. "Security?" As Jess moves away from the table, the Governor pulls on her dress to yank her back to her seat. "Security! Security!" He is shouting now: "I need guards now!"

The crowd mutters and shuffles, trying to get a better angle on Matteo. Then a woman beside Matteo points at the stage: "He's standing!"

"Look!" comes from the crowd.

Even the guards who are nearing Matteo's center seat turn to look at the stage. It's David. He is pulling himself to his feet. "Don't!" he yells in a voice that croaks. He lifts his finger as though to scold Matteo. "Don't ruin my deal." His words slur; his head wobbles loose on his neck. "I will win..." his finger wavers. Now, he looks as though he is pointing at Jess: "And you will die." A gasp bursts from the crowd, and the noise makes David look into the seats, his face indicating surprise that his actions have an audience. His head shakes like a wobble toy. He staggers on his feet and collapses.

Gasps and shouting explode from the audience.

Rajit stands and rushes toward the wheelchair, putting two fingers toward his wrist to feel for David's pulse.

Relly jogs from backstage. "Is there a doctor in the audience?" she shouts into the audience, almost hysterical.

The audience rustles and some stand, whispering and looking.

"I'm coming!" a voice calls out.

Matteo turns, and sees Beck. Dressed in his Emergency Medical Team uniform, he jogs forward from the back of the room. In the rush of fear pumping through his blood, Matteo still catches the farce: Beck will administer aid to the very man he poisoned only hours before.

The thought is only a flicker, a millisecond, because a security guard grabs at his jacket, and Matteo yanks his arm from his clutch. Trying to move away, he stumbles down the narrow path, knocking knees, reaching the aisle. Another security guard comes toward him from the back of the room. He only has seconds for his plan. "Jess!" he yells. "Jess!"

A security guard grabs at his shoulder pulling him backward. Matteo is ready to fight back. He takes the filled glass water bottle he holds in his free hand and with all his effort, swings his arm forward, cracking the water bottle against the man's neck. He has never hit anyone before, and the sensation of the filled glass bottle landing hard on this man's neck is sickening. The man falls back on his butt, and Matteo resists an urge to pull him up. Instead, he rushes to the stage's edge.

"Jess! Jess! Curran is watching!"

A guard tackles Matteo from behind, clubbing the back of his head as he drags his shoulder down. *Fuck, that hurts.* Matteo wavers, trying to stay upright.

Relly is wiping foam from David's mouth, and the Governor is rushing to David's side. Amidst the brawling bodies, the cacophony of noise and confusion, Jess' eyes meet Matteo's, and she staggers forward to reach him.

"No! Stay there!" he shouts, though his face winces when a guard puts a tight grip on his wrist. "Curran is watching!" The guard twists his wrist up into his back. *Ouch.* "Curran has the dot drive. And he can hear what you tell him. Do you see what you could do?"

Jess' face scrunches into puzzlement: "What? What could I do?"

He has to make her understand. "The solution, it's yours—" the guard twists his arm so tightly that he has to bend downward. "You could give…" He staggers forward; the trooper is pushing him down.

Before he hits the ground, he sees her face light up like sunshine.

JESS

She grabs the microphone from the table: "I give my invention away. Curran, if you can hear me, upload my papers and the patent applications; make them so everyone can see them. Put them online. I give my inventions away, to the world. They are everyone's. Open source. Everything I made belongs to everyone. There is no ownership."

She finishes her statement and stands still like a statue.

Around her, people are screaming and men wrestling – utter chaos. And yet. She feels as though she is standing within a bubble. The students push and bump into each other as they rush toward the aisles of the room, but...

She swears there is a beam of glowing light that runs from one person to another, like a dot-to-dot picture. *Are her eyes making tricks?* She thinks of star constellations, how the stars always appear to be randomly dispersed, no picture at all, until someone points the way to draw the lines and then, ta-da: a vision. She closes her eyes; *she must be imagining this.*

Emotions push against her ribs, and a tightness clenches her throat in a sob. She opens her eyes again. It is chaos, connection, unity, complexity. It is nature and she is in it.

Everyone is in it.

MATTEO

The panic is full-blown now. Screams, bodies moving, people running for the door. Rajit Chatterjee is giving David CPR; Relly is screaming: "Oh god, he's dying."

Matteo has managed to get off the ground, but the same guard who yanked him down is now taking jabs at him. Matteo dives to avoid the punches. In the center, Jess stands at the stage's table, looking into the light.

Matteo could not hear all of what she said into the microphone, but he thinks he heard Curran's name, and "give" and "world." The moment must be recorded now.

A second security guard has joined their fray, and he lands a punch to Matteo's shoulder. Matteo pivots, and as he does, he sees Beck take a step away from David's wheelchair. Beck's fingers go to his temples; his lips muttering like he is arguing. He pulls something from his shirt's side pocket.

Matteo absorbs another blow to his back; his arm is grabbed as he staggers. Whatever Beck's holding, it is small. His face's features warp into a horrific scrunch – a repulsion and sadness that is mixed with crazed determination, and he pivots from David and steps toward Jess.

No, no, no, no.

Matteo tries to jerk forward out of the trooper's reach, to stop what is about to happen. "Jess!" he screams, "Jess, look out!"

But she does not hear him. Her posture stands undaunted, almost as though she is in a trance.

The crowd is not watching the stage anymore; they are busy spilling into the aisles, rushing to get to the exits. Around him, voices and bodies moving; noise and mayhem.

Matteo watches as Beck grabs Jess' arm, and she turns fast. "Don't!" she screams, but Beck does not stop, though something about the angle at which his fingers are pinched together and moving toward her makes his intent obvious. She ducks and screams a blood-curdling scream.

Matteo shouts as loud as he can: "He's the one trying to kill her! Throw the bottles! Throw the bottles!"

The security guard punches Matteo between the shoulder blades; then there is another blow to his neck. He stumbles forward. Then: a kick to his side. Matteo tries to see what is happening to Jess, and as he cranes his neck, the thoughts fly: *There are too many people on this stage who want to hurt them. Jess can't beat Beck. She will die.*

This is when the first glass lands on stage. Like a bomb exploding, the glass splits on impact, water splashing high, then crashing to the ground in wide puddles. Another bottle lands, with the cackle of glass splitting, water bursting.

The remaining audience erupts in shrill screams, like a high-pitched chord of terror. A whooshing stampede, like swallows in flight, heads toward the door.

Another bottle hits. The Governor, hands covering his head, jogs backstage flanked by a security guard on one side and a trooper on another.

Relly screams, "We have to get David out of here!"

Another bottle hits. Then another. The press corps is following the plan.

The floor under Matteo's body slickens with water, and as the guard tries to resume punching him, another glass bottle lobs into the guards' back, and Matteo slides enough away so he can push himself semi-upright.

Staggering forward, Jess and Beck are just ahead, with Beck rising from a fall. Beck's forehead is bleeding; Jess is trying to kick him down, but her legs have no momentum. Matteo rushes at Beck, knocking him onto the slippery ground. With a roll, Beck lands atop him, pummeling Matteo's chest, smacking his face.

Shards of glass catch in Matteo's back; with each punch, they lodge deeper.

Jess screams: "Get off him!" She's saying it again and again, and though Matteo's eyes blink shut, he thinks she is pelting Beck with a water bottle over and over again.

When there is a moment of stillness, he allows his eyes to open. Jess reels backward, standing over an unconscious Beck, her face fierce, her body heaving, and her dress wet and bloody.

Wetness and glass are everywhere. There are sounds of weeping and shock.

To his left, Relly and the man from De Sel are shuffling to wheel David offstage; Relly is barking orders. Matteo cannot make out the words.

No more bottles crash. Maybe the mess is over.

He pushes himself up from the ground in a contorted push-up, wincing at the glass that presses into his palm – when he sees Relly's bald-headed trooper. The broad-backed man is walking across the stage, a deliberate march, coming straight toward Matteo. The trooper's hand is pulling something from his holster.

Is that a real gun?

Before he can move, Jess' scream peels outward with her body: "No!"

JESS

The word springs from her mouth, so loud. Without meaning to will her body's movement, she is like a bird: beautiful and soaring. The colors rush her face.

That cop cannot hurt Matteo. No, she has to save him. To love him. All that matters is that she keep him safe.

MATTEO

Even as the micro-moment is unfolding, Matteo worries for how it will end. In the split second when Jess is airborne, he sees her eyes ablaze in determination.

Her body lands hard onto his, gutting his breath. The shot reverberates. For a moment, he is not sure whose body is hit. He gulps in air, surveying his arms, legs, and torso.

"Jess?" he asks, her cheek so close to his. "Jess?" When he touches the warmness that is spilling onto his legs, the liquid is too thick and warm to be water.

JESS

Her mother dips a wide, wood-handled paintbrush into a gallon can of paint, and the brush emerges dripping with its bright yellow pigment. Her mother skims the brush against the paint can's rim then brings the brush forward to the bike, which suddenly appears, standing on its kickstand perch in the middle of the bare living room floor. The bike is Jess' bike, the one she received from Zeke when she was seven. *Why is her mother painting it yellow?*

"Stop," Jess yells just as the paintbrush is about to touch the bike's frame. Her mother stops, holding the paintbrush aloft, the canary color dripping to the living room's hardwood.

Somehow Jess knows the matte, yellow paint is meant for walls. The bike's existing paintjob is from the manufacturer, with glittery, incandescent pink, yellow, and purple colors that swirl as though pumped from a toothpaste tube. "If you paint the bike, it will be ruined," Jess tries to explain.

"The bike is ruined already," her mother says through set teeth. "Zeke gave you that bike as a trick, to buy your love."

It is curious to hear her mother offer this explanation since it was always Jess' father, not her mother, who made that accusation previously.

"No, Mom," Jess says. "Zeke was giving me a true gift. He was genuinely generous."

Her mother starts to cry. "Are you sure?"

"Yes. I am very sure."

Jess opens her eyes.

There is a dimmed, brownish gray light here. Her eyes push wider open. A cabinet that holds a machine flickers dots of lights. Some numbers flash. A bed with rails. Hospital? Yes; her right arm has tubes inside it; a pulse clamp hugs her pointer finger. There are smells of piquancy and bleach.

Matteo sits beside her in a chair, though she cannot see his face since his forehead rests on the bed's edge. Small cuts mark his neck, some with X's of thin white tape over them. *Did he need stitches? Did she?* Her body's under a blanket, and again, the blanket presses tight across her sides, though this time she feels no impulse to free herself. Stillness is fine.

Matteo's shoulders shudder; his hands grasp hers even tighter. This situation must remind him of how he sat beside Rachel's bed. He must be worried that his sadness will repeat. She has to tell him. Her hand twitches in his.

"You're awake." His head lifts, his eyes bloodshot, his nose red. He wipes his cheek and leans closer to her face, whispering. "Everyone is talking about you – about what you did. The nurses said videos of the conference are on the web. And the FBI, they're outside your door. You're safe now."

He directs his head to the doorway, but she cannot lift her head to look; it would hurt too much. She only wants to say one thing to Matteo before sleep pulls her away again.

Her lids must be fluttering because Matteo's lips are trembling again. "Jess," his throat is choked; "I have to tell you... It's only been a few days, but..." His nose is stuffy. "You... saved me." He brings his head down to their clasped hands; his body is shaking. "You *saved* me."

She wants to say so many things in return. About the connections she saw and how right it felt to give her solution away. How *he* taught her that goodness. But her tongue is thick in her mouth, so she picks only the words most important for him to know: "Don't worry, I won't die."

A YEAR LATER
Tuesday, November 21, 2037

MATTEO

The potatoes are damn deep in the ground. He digs further using a small shovel until, finally, he reaches the gently rounded spheres. He tugs on them with his fingers and pulls them up, placing them in a big, blue ceramic bowl. These are the first potatoes he's planted at Tia's; they have turned out well. Purple, red and yellow skins, smooth and small. He thinks they can eat them with their Thanksgiving meal.

The dream is what made him plant the seeds – the one where Rachel and Jess came to him as he tossed seeds on Tia's hillside. The float-y colors and backlit images of that short story stayed with him, rolling like a marble in his head, first in the evenings when he had sat at Jess' side in the hospital and later as he lay beside her for weeks at Tia's house.

When they first returned from the hospital, he and Jess stayed in bed for days, their naked bodies intertwined under the sheets, waking only for sex, food and sunsets. Watching the evening's velvet pink and orange colors lavishly splayed across the hilltops, they would hold each other's hands, silently taking in how their lives had melded together in every respect.

Throughout this hushed winter-y time, the potato dream played at the back of his waking and resting hours, never disappearing. In March, he took heirloom potato seeds from the Temescal Experimental Farm – he was working there again – and planted them in Tia's hillside steppes. He had no expectation the potatoes would take. There was chard, basil, onions, kale and peppers that he had planted too, and he was just as pessimistic about their chances. The dirt on the hill was chalky brown and powder dry, and watering the garden was no longer an option.

Since what people referred to as the "November storm," there had not been another real rain, and across the East Bay, municipalities were imposing stricter rations on water usage, installing cut-offs to residential pipes once the household's daily allotment had been reached. Each able-bodied adult was allowed 30 gallons a day, so that in a 24-hour period a person could wash some clothes or dishes (rarely both), take a 3-minute shower and make a meal (always saving the pasta water). Certainly, there was not water enough to keep an acre's worth of vegetables alive.

On a late-April Friday morning, as Matteo and Jess were biking tandem down the El Cerrito hills on their way to work, Matteo called behind to Jess' bike. "I'm going to pull the garden up this weekend. I might as well salvage the seeds," he shouted, his words whizzing behind him in the air.

"No, don't," Jess shouted forward. "Not yet."

That evening, as the sun was sinking lower over Tia's hillside, Jess drove up in an electric pick-up truck. Xu was in the passenger seat, and something enormous was under blankets in the pick-up bed.

"You can't look until it's set up," Jess said, with a mischievous glint in her eye as she pushed him inside their home. After two hours, when the clouds were still pink-y gray in the darkening sky, Jess trudged back into the house and grabbed Matteo's hand. "Now you can come see."

He doubted he would be able to make out anything in the dark, but since he had already guessed at what he was to be shown, he did not quibble over that point. He allowed Jess to lead him ahead. She liked to lead.

"Here it is," she said, and she flicked on her new Keeper's flashlight and tilted the illumination forward. It was, of course, her desalination solution. There were three clear wind turbine blades that came together like a pinwheel; these blades were three feet in diameter and they sat over top of a table that had two levels to it, like a billiard table. On one side of the table was an enormous funnel and at the other was a spout. With a slight declining angle to the table, perhaps five percent, the water flowed downward. On the bottom level of the table, Matteo saw the press and what he assumed were the graphene sheets. "Do you want to see how it works?" Jess asked, her voice eager.

He and Xu lifted a thirty-gallon barrel of smelly ocean water. They poured it into the funnel, and Jess released the turbine constraints.

"It's not a very windy night," Matteo said, in case the turbines did not turn fast enough to create the necessary torque.

"It won't matter," Xu said. "You'll see. It works like magic."

And it did. A year's worth of planning and effort had finally paid off. Here was the tabletop desalination design that was the first project of Jess' new water Institute, the idea for which had been birthed quickly in the strange, swirling days after the Stanford Ceremony.

The first week in the hospital, Matteo did not leave Jess' bedside and had no access to a Keeper. Nonetheless, there was a sense – from the way the nurses approached them, in their repeated questions about whether they were sure they did not want a screen brought to their room – that made him wonder how the video of the Stanford Ceremony had been received.

Four days after Jess had been admitted, the nurses on duty came to give Jess a sponge bath and comb her hair. "You're about to have visitors," they said.

Twenty minutes later, Governor Luis Ramos and Rajit Chatterjee arrived, with a camera crew behind them.

Jess sat upright in her hospital bed, Matteo by her side, as the Governor smiled, chuckled and guffawed enough to make up for his and Jess' stunned silence. The Governor presented "Jessila" with an executive order to build an Institute for Fresh Water at the UC Berkeley campus, and before Jess or Matteo could pose a question, Rajit Chatterjee stepped forward and smiling broadly for the cameras presented Jess with a cardboard recreation of a $100 million dollar check. "De Sel is deeply committed to fabricating the best desalination solutions. De Sel wants to make water as affordable and available as possible," he said, smiling broadly to the cameras.

It was political gamesmanship: Ramos and Chatterjee left hurriedly with the camera crew.

In the quiet after their blustery departure, Matteo accepted the nurse's offer of a temporary Keeper and spent some time reconstructing the world's response to the video. Apparently, the fourteen-minute segment of the Stanford ceremony had been spliced and diced, messaged and forwarded, viewed online and in news' programs by hundreds of millions of people. The most violent segments were the ones viewed most frequently: Governor Ramos yanking a fragile Jess away from the microphone. A man dressed as an EMT physically wrestling Jess down to the ground. The California State trooper walking deliberately to shoot point blank at Matteo. The violence captured provided instant credibility to the idea that more was at stake than a small, esoteric licensing agreement. The accusations that Matteo posed before the melee were taken quite seriously. The public demanded to know: *Was there now a cheaper way to make fresh water?* Since Jessila Prentiss had given away her desalination solution to the people and since the video clearly showed her throwing herself in front of a bullet to save Matteo, the public was inclined to believe their side of the story.

When Matteo left the hospital for the first time, a crowd of press approached him with their Keepers posed outward to record his responses. "Do you consider yourself a hero?" was the loudest question thrown from the huddle.

"Not at all," he answered firmly, shuffling forward to the waiting car.

"What about Jessila Prentiss? Do you consider her a hero?"

He grinned: "Of course. She's the one saving us from the drought." He slipped into the car's back seat and closed the door.

In the hospital, Jess stayed in bed for days. She found it hard to walk or even sit without pain. Many decisions needed to be made, and she relied on Matteo to help her sort through them. "Are you sure you don't want to choose on your own?" he kept asking.

She grabbed his hand; "I'm very sure." So, without much discussion, they began to plan Jess' future with the unspoken understanding that it would be a future they shared.

Should Jess accept this opportunity to run a Water Institute? Yes, they agreed, no reason not to try. *Should she accept the De Sel money?* No, absolutely not. Their conversations were fluid and easy, finding that without much discussion, they held the same position. Together, they brainstormed over a name for the Institute, finally deciding on

The Institute for the People's Own Water, whose acronym, IPOW, seemed to capture the struggle that had led to its creation.

The night before Jess was released from the hospital, Matteo told her that David Steubingly had died. "When?" Jess asked, the freckle on her lip quite still.

"The night of the ceremony."

"Almost a week ago?"

Matteo nodded.

"You didn't tell me?"

He moved up further toward the head of the bed. "I had to get you better first." He noticed her eyes were welling with tears. "He was pretty awful to you."

"He was greedy." She wiped her cheeks with her palms. "Greed makes people awful."

As Jess waited to be wheeled out of her room the next day, another wheelchair entered her room; Tia was in it. The attendant pushing Tia had bulging biceps, and this man's obvious strength only made Tia's frailty more pronounced. Her skin was grayer and drabber than when Matteo had seen her in the POP laundry room; her breathing came in gasps, hollowing out her chest. She seemed to prepare for her sentences, and when she spoke her words were evenly spaced in thickly accented cadences.

The first thing she announced was that she had a lot to say, so, *por favor*, don't interrupt until she was done.

"The money that Sara collected through her investors," she said, "will now be donated to Jess' water institute. Don't argue. Sara will not be involved; she is out of POP now. This money has no strings. Trust me." She paused for breath, then began again: "You must live in my house. I will never live there again, and it would give me pleasure if you would. Don't argue; again, it is best." Then, Tia paused and looked at Jess. "I pray you are better soon. You are brave and good for mi Matteo. I will never forgive myself..." her voice faltered, "for not fighting harder to save your life." She touched Matteo's hand with her paper-thin palm and looked up into his eyes. "This is from Beck," and she gave him an envelope stuffed thick. "Don't read it now. A ride is waiting for me in the lobby; please take me downstairs so I can go."

As he wheeled her down the long hall, he could not help but ask more questions. "Is Beck in jail?"

"Oh, goodness no. He was out on bail very quickly. He will never be convicted. He has too many friends in the right places."

"But the video shows him trying to kill Jess?"

"Does it? Beck told the police the video shows he was trying to *save* Jess. He said safety was his first priority because he knew she was *extraordinario*."

"That's bullshit."

"That's life." She touched his cheek. "Read his letter. He explains a lot. It is easy to make the wrong choice."

As Matteo helped her into the car, Tia said, "Please do live in my house; you would give me my last happiness."

Matteo did not go directly back to Jess' room, but instead went to the hospital's courtyard and read Beck's seventeen-page, hand-scrawled letter. Beck begged for forgiveness on every page. "There was such confusion in that moment, and I thought I had no choice but to follow Sara's orders. She kept barking at me through my Keeper, saying I would let the whole world down if I didn't do what she demanded, and repeating that we could still win if I used the poison pin. 'Don't be weak,' she said; 'Are you too scared to be strong?' Everything was happening fast, and... I made a mistake. Dude, you've got to believe me: I'm so glad Jess did not die."

Well, at least Beck finally used Jess' name. "Listen, I paid Hua Chen for you," Beck continued. "Paying your debt was one thing I could do to show you how sorry I am, and I was glad to do it."

Matteo read the note through twice. Of course, it is easy to say the right things, harder to do them. Matteo thought about ripping the sheets into tiny pieces and throwing them in the courtyard's garbage can, but in the end, he could not. He slipped the thick envelope into his jean's back pocket before going back to Jess' hospital room.

When they left the hospital a week later, they went straight to Tia's house. Shortly after, Matteo rented an electric pick-up truck and moved his and Jess' stuff into the hillside house. The little space bulged at the seams with their odd collection of boxes, bags and clothes strewn on hangers. There was almost no place to sit, and Tia's bed wasn't what either of them wanted.

"Would you mind if I changed the curtains?" Jess asked tentatively.

When he kissed her with his response, they began their plans for renovation. They would make a bedroom big enough for both of them. A real kitchen. A study where guests could sleep. Over the months, they worked together on the designs and eventually started the building project together, the bedroom being the first project.

At first, he worked on the house only a few hours a day while Jess worked at her old lab offices. Once her body grew stronger, the IPOW offices were opened in a larger space at the Lawrence Berkeley labs. She and Matteo agreed that the Institute's first goal should be to fabricate desalination solutions for neighborhood use. IPOW created a marketing campaign urging communities to pool their resources to purchase the wind-turbine desalination solutions as neighborhood collectives. Until the underground piping infrastructure was built, the Institute encouraged those with electric trucks to collect ocean water, which of course was abundant, and transport it to cities and suburbs where it could be purchased. The hope was that neighborhoods would purchase the billiard-sized table solutions to create fresh water for lawns and gardens, car cleaning, and household cleaning.

Once this smaller model of the desalination solution was perfected, the Institute would then focus on raising the money to build the massive machinery required at centralized desalination plants. Initial calculations showed these wind-turbine-powered desalination plants would cost a tiny fraction compared to the reverse osmosis De Sel plants, and the energy required to keep the solution running was almost entirely wind-powered. There was enough excitement around the idea that Matteo didn't doubt wind-powered desal plants would ultimately be built in California and beyond.

The potatoes are now stacked high in the bowl. He wipes his dusty hands against his shorts and makes his way up the hill carefully balancing the bowl.

For all his love of growing vegetables, he is a piss poor cook. At first, he and Jess struggled to feed themselves because Jess was also a disaster in the kitchen, and take-out was not an option this high in the hills. Lately, however, she has been trying to bake. For her mother's visit for Thanksgiving, she made two apple pies, and this morning when they were in the oven, man, they smelled good. Cinnamon-y and lightly sweet.

As Matteo plods up the rough hillside, he sees Jess' truck making its way up the hill.

A smile washes across his face.

JESS

She is glad the ride is almost over. Her mother has fired constant questions all the way from the Oakland airport. "I saw on the Institute website that you said David Steubingly co-invented the solution with you. Why'd you do that, dear?"

"Because he *did*."

"But it's your patents."

"Which I would have never thought to put together as he did."

"Hmm." Silence. "You also said it was Matteo's idea to give the solution away? Darling, you can tell me: Is he jealous of how much attention you're receiving?"

"No, mom; he's the reason I'm getting the attention. It was his idea. He was the one who understood the connection."

"The connection?" She laughs. "What does *that* mean?"

Jess would never try to explain the experience she had in Room 205 to her mother, or for that matter to anyone. Even when she broached the subject with Matteo, the phrase she used – *I saw our connections* – well, it came out hackneyed and sentimental. Embarrassed, she had explained her experience was probably just a reaction to the drugs.

She knows it was far more.

Now, Jess slows the truck to a stop and cuts the engine.

"Wait, we're here?"

"Uh-huh," Jess answers, exiting the truck.

"But where's the house?" Her mother scampers out of the truck, her head weaving around her.

Jess points ahead.

Her mother takes a few steps following Jess' finger. "*That's* your house?"

"Uh-huh."

"Does it have indoor plumbing?"

Jess laughs: "Yes, Mom." She walks into the lovely stillness of the space. The quiet and openness of the hills seems to expand her from within, like a deep inhale. Tonight, the smog levels are low, and the twilight colors are crisp enough in the big sky that she wants to grab them and hold them in her hand.

Behind the house, Matteo's mop of black hair is bobbing up the hillside. "Come on, Mom, there's Matteo." She is aware of the excitement in her own voice, as though she is a girl with a prize.

Her mom takes tentative steps forward as though to gird against the earth's unevenness.

But Jess, she runs to him.

ACKNOWLEDGEMENTS

I would like to thank many people for their huge help in giving this book life. My agent, Faye Bender, thank you for your insights, kindness, and hard work. To my first readers, Carol and Demetrios Moschandreas, Neal Grossman, Karen Kraut, Justin Grossman, Sophia Grossman, and Lara Grossman: you made my book better for your love, your feedback, and for your caring enthusiasm. And most especially to my husband, Jeff Grossman, who not only read the book several times, provided invaluable scientific knowledge and clarifications, but who, most importantly, is my model of salt-of-the-earth goodness. Thank you for all the happiness you bestow on my life.

Made in the USA
Columbia, SC
21 December 2019